THE
NIGHT
STALKER

Also by Robert Brydza:

The DCI Erika Foster crime thriller series
The Girl in the Ice
The Night Stalker

The Coco Pinchard romantic comedy series
The Not So Secret Emails of Coco Pinchard
Coco Pinchard's Big Fat Tipsy Wedding
Coco Pinchard, the Consequences of Love and Sex
A Very Coco Christmas
Coco Pinchard's Must-Have Toy Story

Standalone Romantic Comedy Novels
Miss Wrong and Mr Right
Lost In Crazytown

THE
NIGHT
STALKER

ROBERT BRYNDZA
A DETECTIVE ERIKA FOSTER NOVEL

bookouture

Published by Bookouture

An imprint of StoryFire Ltd.
23 Sussex Road, Ickenham, UB10 8PN
United Kingdom

www.bookouture.com

ISBN: 978-1-78681-006-9
eBook ISBN: 978-1-78681-005-2

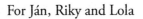

For Ján, Riky and Lola

Good things of day begin to droop and drowse,
While night's black agents to their preys do rouse.

William Shakespeare, *Macbeth*

CHAPTER 1

It was a sweltering summer night in late June. The black-clad figure ran lightly, streaking through the darkness, feet barely making a sound on the narrow dirt path, ducking and twisting gracefully to avoid contact with the dense surrounding trees and bushes. It was as if a shadow were sweeping silently over the leaves.

The night sky was just a thin strip between the trees high above; the light pollution from the city cast the undergrowth in dusky shades. The small, shadow-like figure reached a gap in the undergrowth on the right, and stopped abruptly: poised, breathless, heart racing.

A strobe of blue-white lit up the surroundings as the 7.39 p.m. train to London Bridge switched from diesel, extending its metal arms to the electrified lines above. The shadow ducked down as empty glowing carriages rumbled past. There were two more flashes and the train was gone, plunging the narrow strip of undergrowth back into darkness.

The shadow moved off again at speed, gliding soundlessly as the path curved slightly away from the tracks. The trees began to thin out to the left, exposing a row of terraced houses. Snapshots of back gardens slid past: neat dark strips with patio furniture, tool sheds, a swing set – all still in the thick night air.

And then the house came into view. It was a Victorian terrace, like the others in the long row – three storeys of pale brick

— but its owner had added a large glass extension at the back, which jutted out from the ground floor. The small shadow knew everything about the owner. Knew the layout of the house. Knew the owner's schedule. And most importantly, knew that tonight he would be alone.

The shadow came to a stop at the end of the garden. A large tree grew against the wire fence that backed on to the dirt track. In one place the trunk had grown around the metal, the folds of wood biting down on the rusting post like a large lipless mouth. A heavy halo of leaves burst upwards in all directions, obscuring the view of the train tracks from the house. A few nights previously, the shadow had taken this same route and had neatly clipped the edges of the wire fence, loosely tacking it back in place. The fence now pulled away easily and the shadow crouched down and crawled through the gap. The grass felt dry and the soil below was cracked from weeks of no rain. The shadow came up to its feet under the tree and in a fast, fluid motion crossed the lawn in a swoop of black.

An air-conditioning unit was attached to the rear wall of the house. It whirred loudly, masking the faint crunch of feet on the gravel that lined the narrow path between the glass extension and the house next door. The shadow reached a low sash window and ducked down underneath the wide sill. Light shone out, casting a square of yellow on the brickwork of the neighbouring house. Pulling up the hood of the running suit, the shadow slowly inched upwards and looked over the wide windowsill.

The man inside was in his mid-forties, tall and well-built, dressed in tan trousers and a white shirt rolled up at the sleeves. He moved around the large open-plan kitchen, took a wine glass from one of the cupboards, and poured himself a glass of red. He took a long gulp and topped up his glass. A ready meal lay on the counter, and he picked it up, slipped off its cardboard sleeve and pricked at the plastic lid with the corkscrew.

Hatred rose in the shadow. It was intoxicating to see the man inside, knowing what was about to unfold.

The man in the kitchen programmed the microwave and placed the meal inside. There was a beep and the digital countdown began.

Six minutes.

The man took another gulp of his wine and then left the kitchen. Moments later, a light came on in the bathroom window directly above where the shadow crouched. The window swung open a few inches, and there was a squeak as the shower was turned on.

Heart hammering, the shadow outside the window worked fast: unzipping a money belt, pulling out a small flat screwdriver and easing it into the crack where the window met the sill. With a small amount of pressure, it popped open. The sash window moved up smoothly and the shadow slid in through the gap. This was it. All the planning, the years of angst and pain…

Four minutes.

The figure stepped down into the kitchen and moved swiftly, pulling out a small plastic syringe and squirting its clear liquid into the glass of red wine, swirling the wine around before gently placing the glass back on the black granite counter.

The shadow stood for a moment, listening, enjoying the cool waves from the air conditioning. The black granite countertop sparkled under the lights.

Three minutes.

The shadow moved quickly through the kitchen, passing the wooden bannister at the base of the stairs, and slipped into a pool of darkness behind the living room door. A moment later, the man came down the stairs, wearing just a towel. The microwave gave three loud beeps to say it was finished. As the man padded past barefoot, the smell of clean skin wafted through the air. The shadow heard a clink as the man pulled cutlery from the drawer, and a scrape of a stool on the wooden floor as he sat down to eat.

The shadow exhaled deeply, emerged from the shadows and quietly climbed the stairs.

To watch.

To wait.

To exact long-awaited retribution.

CHAPTER 2

FOUR DAYS LATER

The night air was close and humid on the quiet South London street. Moths fizzed and bumped in the orange arc of light cast by a streetlamp illuminating a row of terraced houses. Estelle Munro shuffled along the pavement, arthritis slowing her progress. When she drew close to the light, she stepped down from the pavement and onto the road. The effort to step down off the kerb made her groan, but her fear of moths outweighed the pain in her arthritic knees.

Estelle eased her way through a gap between two parked cars and gave the streetlight a wide berth, feeling the heat from the day's sun radiating off the tarmac. The heatwave was in its second week, pressing down on the residents of London and the south-east of England, and along with thousands of other old people Estelle's heart was protesting. The siren of a far-off ambulance blared, seeming to echo her thoughts. She was relieved to see that the next two streetlights were broken, and slowly, painfully, she edged between two parked cars and rejoined the pavement.

She had offered to feed her son Gregory's cat whilst he was away. She didn't like cats. She'd only offered so she could have a good nose around the house, and see how her son was coping since his wife, Penny, had left him, taking Estelle's five-year-old grandson, Peter, with her.

Estelle was out of breath and pouring with sweat when she reached the gate of Gregory's smart terraced house. In her opinion, it was the smartest house in the whole street. She pulled a large hanky out from under her bra strap and wiped the sweat off her face.

Light from the orange streetlight rippled across the glass front door as Estelle fished out her key. When she opened the door, she was hit by a wall of stifling heat and she stepped reluctantly inside, onto letters strewn over the mat. She flicked the light switch by the door, but the hallway remained in darkness.

'Bloody hell, not again,' she muttered, pulling the door closed behind her. As she felt around to pick up the post, she realised this was the third time the power had tripped whilst Gregory had been away. The lights in the fish tank had done it once before, and another time Penny had left the bathroom light on and the bulb had blown.

Estelle fished her mobile phone from her handbag and, with an awkward fumble of gnarled fingers, unlocked the screen. It cast a dim halo of light a few feet in front, illuminating the pale carpet and narrow walls, and she jumped as she saw her ghostly reflection in the large mirror on the left-hand side. The half-light gave the lilies on her sleeveless blouse an inky, poisonous quality. She focused the light of her phone down onto the carpet and shuffled towards the living room door, feeling around on the inside wall for the switch, to check it wasn't just the hall bulb that had gone. She flicked the switch on and off, but nothing happened.

Then the screen of her phone timed out and she was plunged into total darkness. Just the sound of her laboured breathing filled the silence. She panicked, fumbling to unlock the phone.

At first her arthritic fingers wouldn't move fast enough, but finally she managed it and the light came back on, casting the front room in a circle of dim blue.

It was stifling inside: the heat pressed down on her, closing off her ears. It was as if she were underwater. Dust particles twirled in the air; a cloud of tiny flies floated silently above a large arty china plate filled with brown wooden balls on the coffee table.

'It's just a power cut!' she snapped, her voice resonating sharply off the iron fireplace. She was annoyed that she'd panicked. It was just the circuit breaker, nothing more. To prove there was nothing to be scared of, she would first have a drink of cold water, and then she would get the electricity back on. She turned, shuffling purposefully off towards the kitchen, her arm outstretched with the phone.

The glass kitchen seemed cavernous in the phone's half-light, extending out into the garden. Estelle felt vulnerable and exposed. There was a distant whoosh and a click-clack as a train passed on the track beyond the bottom of the garden. Estelle went to a cupboard and pulled down a glass tumbler. Sweat stung, as it dripped into her eyes; she wiped her face with her bare arm. She moved to the sink and filled her glass, wincing as she drank the lukewarm water.

The light went out on the phone again, and a crash from upstairs broke the silence. Estelle dropped the tumbler. It shattered, glass spraying out on the wood floor. Her heart pulsed and pounded, and as she listened in the darkness there was another scuffling sound from above. She grabbed a rolling pin from a pot of utensils on the counter and went to the bottom of the stairs.

'Who's there? I've got pepper spray and I'm dialling 999!' she shouted up into the darkness.

There was silence. The heat was oppressive. Thoughts of snooping around her son's house were gone. All Estelle wanted to do was to go home and watch the Wimbledon highlights in her cosy, brightly lit house.

Something darted out of the shadows and came straight at her from the stairs above. Estelle stepped back in shock, almost dropping the phone. Then she saw it was the cat. It stopped and began to rub at her legs.

'Bloody hell, you gave me a fright!' she said, relieved, her pounding heart slowing. A foul smell floated down from the landing above. 'Just what I need. Have you done something nasty up there? You've got a litter tray, and a cat flap.'

The cat looked up at Estelle nonchalantly. For once, she was glad of its presence. 'Come on, I'll feed you.'

She was comforted as the cat followed her to the cupboard under the stairs; she let it rub against her legs as she found the electricity box. When she opened the little plastic flap she saw that the power had been turned off at the mains. *Strange.* She flicked it on and the hall filled with light. There was a distant beep as the air conditioning whirred to life.

She came back into the kitchen and turned on the lights. The room and her reflection bounced back at her from the huge windows. The cat jumped onto the counter and watched her quizzically as she swept up the broken tumbler. Once she had dealt with the glass, Estelle opened a sachet of cat food, squeezed it into a saucer and placed it on the stone kitchen floor. The air-conditioning was working fast. She stood for a moment and let the cool air wash over her, watching as the cat daintily licked and nibbled at the square of jellied food with its small pink tongue.

The bad smell was intensifying, rushing into the kitchen as the air-conditioning sucked air through the house. There was a clinking as the cat licked the last of the empty saucer, then darted to the glass wall and vanished through a cat flap.

'Eat and run. Leave me to clear it up,' said Estelle. She grabbed a cloth and an old newspaper and moved to the stairs, climbing slowly, her knees complaining. The heat and the smell got worse the higher she climbed. She reached the top and moved along the brightly lit landing. Methodically, she checked the empty bathroom, the spare room, under the desk in the small office. There was no sign of a present from the cat.

The smell was overpowering when she reached the door to the master bedroom. It caught in her throat and she gagged. *Of all vile smells, cat mess is the worst,* she thought.

When she entered the bedroom, she flicked on the light. Flies buzzed and whined in the air. The dark blue duvet was thrown back on the double bed, and a naked man lay flat on his back with a plastic bag tied tight over his head, his arms tied to the headboard. His eyes were open, bulging out grotesquely against the plastic. It took her a moment to realise who it was.

It was Gregory.

Her son.

Then Estelle did something she hadn't done in years.

She screamed.

CHAPTER 3

It was the least enjoyable dinner party DCI Erika Foster had attended in a long while. There was an awkward silence as her host, Isaac Strong, opened the dishwasher and began to load plates and cutlery, interrupted only by the low whirr of a plug-in electric fan in the corner. It barely made a dent in the heat, instead just pushing waves of warm air across the kitchen.

'Thank you, the lasagne was delicious,' she said, as Isaac reached over to take her plate.

'I used half-fat cream for the Béchamel sauce,' he replied. 'Could you tell?'

'No.'

Isaac went back to the dishwasher and Erika cast her eye around the kitchen. It was elegant, with a French-rustic theme: hand-painted white cabinets, work surfaces of pale wood, and a heavy Butler sink in white ceramic. Erika wondered if, as a forensic pathologist, Isaac had deliberately steered clear of stainless steel. Her eyes came to rest on Isaac's ex-boyfriend, Stephen Linley, who sat across from her at the large kitchen table, watching her suspiciously with pursed lips. He was younger than Erika and Isaac: she guessed thirty-five. He was a strapping Adonis of a man with a beautiful face, but its expression had sly flashes that she didn't like. She forced herself to defuse his attitude with a smile, then took a sip of wine and willed herself to say something. The silence was beginning to stretch uncomfortably.

This didn't usually happen when she had dinner with Isaac. Over the past year they'd shared several meals in his cosy French kitchen. They'd laughed, divulged a few secrets, and Erika had felt a strong friendship blossom. She'd been able to open up to Isaac, more than she had to anyone else, about the death of her husband, Mark, less than two years previously. And, in turn, Isaac had talked of losing the love of his life, Stephen.

Although, whereas Mark had died tragically in the line of duty during a police raid, Stephen had broken Isaac's heart, leaving him for another man.

This was why it had been such a surprise to Erika to see Stephen when she'd arrived earlier that evening. In fact, not so much a surprise –

it had felt more like an ambush.

Even though she had lived in the UK for more than twenty-five years, Erika had found herself wishing this dinner were happening back in her native Slovakia. In Slovakia, people were direct.

What's going on? You could have warned me! Why didn't you tell me your idiot ex-boyfriend would be here? Are you insane to let him back into your life after what he did to you?

She'd wanted to shout when she'd come through to the kitchen, and had seen Stephen sitting languidly in shorts and a T-shirt. But she'd felt awkward, and polite British convention dictated that they all gloss over it, and pretend things were normal.

'Would anyone like coffee?' asked Isaac, closing the dishwasher and turning to face them. He was a tall, handsome man, with a head of thick dark hair swept back from a high forehead. His large brown eyes were framed by thinly shaped eyebrows, which could be arched or drawn together to communicate all manner of wry emotions. Tonight, however, he just looked embarrassed.

Stephen swirled the white wine in his glass and looked between Erika and Isaac. 'Coffee *already*? It's barely eight o'clock, Isaac, and it's bloody hot. Open more wine.'

'No, coffee would be great, thank you,' said Erika.

'If you must have coffee, at least use the machine,' said Stephen. He added, territorially, 'Did he tell you? I bought him the Nespresso. Cost a fortune. From my last book advance.'

Erika smiled blandly and took a roasted almond from a dish in the centre of the table. As she chewed, it seemed to crackle through the silence. During the awkward meal, Stephen had done most of the talking, telling them in great detail about the new crime novel he was writing. He'd also taken it upon himself to tell them all about forensic profiling, which Erika had thought was a bit rich, considering that Isaac was one of the leading forensic pathologists in the country, and that Erika herself, as a detective chief inspector with the London Metropolitan Police, had successfully solved a string of murder cases in the real world.

Isaac started to make coffee and switched on the radio. 'Like a Prayer' by Madonna cut through the silence.

'Turn it up! I love a bit of Madge,' said Stephen.

'Let's have something a bit more mellow,' said Isaac, scrolling through the radio stations until the sweet mournful strings of a violin replaced Madonna's squeaky voice.

'*Allegedly*, he's a gay man,' said Stephen, rolling his eyes.

'I just think something more mellow would suit right now, Stevie,' said Isaac.

'Christ. We're not eighty! Let's have some fun. What do you want to do, Erika? What do you do for fun?'

Stephen, to Erika's eyes, was a host of contradictions. He dressed very straight, like an American Ivy League athlete, but his movements had a camp lightness to them. He crossed his legs now and pursed his lips, waiting for her answer.

'I think… I'm going to go and have a cigarette,' she said, reaching for her bag.

'The door's unlocked upstairs,' said Isaac, looking at her with apologetic eyes. She pulled her face into a smile and left the kitchen.

Isaac lived in a townhouse in Blackheath, near Greenwich. The spare bedroom upstairs had a small balcony. Erika opened the glass door, went outside and lit up a cigarette. She exhaled smoke into the dark sky, feeling the intensity of the evening heat. The summer night was clear, but the stars were faint against the haze of light pollution floating up from the city stretching out in front of her. She followed the path of the laser from the Greenwich Observatory, craning her head to where it vanished amongst the stars high above. She took another deep drag on her cigarette and heard the crickets singing in the dark back garden below, mixed in with the hum of traffic from the busy road behind.

Was she being too harsh in her assessment of Isaac allowing Stephen back into his life? Was it just that she was jealous that her single friend was no longer single? No – she wanted the best for Isaac, and Stephen Linley was a toxic individual. She reflected, sadly, that there might not be room in Isaac's life for both herself and Stephen.

She thought of the small, sparsely furnished flat she struggled to call home, and of the lonely nights she spent in bed staring into the darkness. Erika and Mark had shared their lives in more ways than just as man and wife. They had been colleagues, joining the Greater Manchester Police in their early twenties. Erika had been a rising star in the force and was rapidly promoted to detective chief inspector, senior in rank to Mark. Mark had loved her all the more for it.

Then, almost two years previously, Erika had led the disastrous drug raid that had resulted in the death of Mark and four of their colleagues. Afterwards, the grief and burden of guilt had at times seemed too great to bear, and she had struggled to find her place in the world without her husband. A fresh start in London had been tough, but her work in the Homicide and Serious Crime Command within the Metropolitan Police was the one thing she had been able to pour her energy into. But where she had once been a rising star in the force, now she was tainted, and her career progression had ground to a halt. She was direct, driven and a brilliant officer who didn't suffer fools – but she had no time for the politics of the force, and she had clashed repeatedly with her superiors, making some powerful enemies.

Erika lit another cigarette, and she was just deciding she would make an excuse to leave quickly when the glass door opened behind her. Isaac poked his head round and came onto the balcony.

'I could use one of those,' he said, closing the door and moving over to where she stood by the iron railing. She smiled and offered him the packet. He teased one out with a large, elegant hand and leaned over as she lit it for him.

'Sorry, I really screwed up tonight,' he said, straightening up and exhaling smoke.

'It's your life,' said Erika. 'But you could have given me a heads-up.'

'It all happened so quickly. He showed up this morning on the doorstep and all day we've been talking and… I won't spell it out. It was too late to cancel, not that I wanted to cancel.'

Erika could see the angst playing over his face. 'Isaac, you don't need to explain yourself to me. Although, if I were you, I'd pick lust as your explanation. You were overcome by lust. It's much more forgivable.'

'I know he's a complicated individual, but he's different when we're alone together. He's vulnerable. Do you think if I approached it in the right way, if I set proper boundaries, it could work this time?'

'Possibly… And at least he can't kill you off again,' said Erika wryly.

Stephen had based a forensic pathologist in one of his novels on Isaac, only to kill the character off in a rather graphic gay bashing.

'I'm serious. What do you think I should do?' asked Isaac, his eyes filled with angst.

Erika sighed and took his hand in hers. 'You don't want to hear what I think. I like being friends with you.'

'I value your opinion, Erika. Please, tell me what I should do…'

There was a creak as the glass door opened. Stephen emerged barefoot, carrying a full tumbler of whisky and ice. 'Tell him what he should do? About what?' he asked tartly.

The awkward silence was broken by a message alert tone chiming from the depths of Erika's bag. She pulled out her phone and read the message, frowning.

'Everything okay?' asked Isaac.

'The body of a white male has been discovered in a house in Laurel Road, Honor Oak Park. Looks suspicious,' said Erika, adding, 'Shit, I haven't got my car. I took a cab here.'

'You'll need to assign a forensic pathologist. I could take you in my car?' said Isaac.

'I thought you had the night off?' Stephen demanded, indignantly.

'I'm always on duty, Stevie,' replied Isaac, looking eager to leave.

'Okay, then, let's go,' said Erika, and couldn't resist adding to Stephen, 'looks like coffee from your machine will have to wait.'

CHAPTER 4

Erika and Isaac arrived at Laurel Road half an hour later, their awkward dinner party rapidly forgotten. Police tape closed off the road in both directions and support vehicles added to the cordon: a police van, four squad cars and an ambulance. The vehicles' blue lights pulsed across the long row of terraced houses. In several of the front windows and doorways, neighbours stood gawking at the scene.

Detective Inspector Moss, one of Erika's most trusted colleagues, walked over to meet their car as it pulled into a space a hundred yards down from the police cordon. She was a short, solid woman and was sweating profusely in the heat, despite her knee-length skirt and thin blouse. Her red hair was pulled back from her face, which was awash with freckles – a small group of them clustered under her eye, forming what looked like a tear. However, in contrast to this, she was upbeat, and gave Erika and Isaac a wry grin as they got out of the car.

'Evening, boss, Dr Strong.'

'Evening, Moss,' said Isaac.

'Evening. Who are all these people?' Erika asked, as they approached the police tape, where a group of tired-looking men and women stood staring at the scene.

'Commuters from Central London, arriving home to find their street is a crime scene,' said Moss.

'But I live just there,' one man was saying, pointing with his briefcase to a house two doors down. His face was flushed and weary, his thinning hair plastered to his head. When Moss,

Erika and Isaac drew level with him at the police tape, he looked to them, hoping they had come to give different news.

'I'm DCI Foster, the senior investigating officer, and this is Dr Strong, our forensic pathologist,' said Erika flashing her ID at the uniformed officer. 'Get in contact with the council, organise these people beds for the night.'

'Very good, ma'am,' said the uniformed officer, signing them all in. They ducked under the police tape before they could get involved with the commuters protesting at the thought of a night on camp beds.

The front door of 14 Laurel Road was wide open, and lights blazed from the hallway, which was busy with CSIs wearing dark blue overalls and face masks. Erika, Isaac and Moss were handed overalls, and they suited up on a patch of shingle in the tiny front garden.

'The body's upstairs, front bedroom,' said Moss. 'Victim's mother came over to feed the cat. Thought he was away on holiday in the south of France but, as you'll see, he never made it to the airport.'

'Where is the mother now?' asked Erika, stepping into the thin overalls.

'She was overcome by the shock and heat. Uniform just went with her to University Hospital, Lewisham. We'll need to get a statement when she's recovered,' said Moss, zipping up her own suit.

'Just give me a few minutes to examine the scene,' said Isaac, as he pulled up the hood of his own suit. Erika nodded, and he went off into the house.

The heat, volume of people and bright lights all helped to tip the temperature in the upstairs bedroom to over forty degrees centigrade. Isaac, with his team of three assistants and the crime scene photographer, worked in an efficient, respectful silence.

The victim lay naked on his back in the double bed. He had a tall, athletic frame. His arms were pulled up and outwards and tied to the headboard with thin twine, which was biting into the flesh of his wrists. His legs were splayed, feet apart. A clear plastic bag was moulded to his head, the features distorted underneath.

Erika always found naked corpses much more difficult to deal with. Death was undignified enough, without being exposed in this way. She resisted the urge to place the sheet over his lower body.

'The victim is Dr Gregory Munro, forty-six years old,' said Moss, as they stood around the bed. His brown eyes were wide open and surprisingly clear beneath the plastic, but his tongue was beginning to swell and poke through his teeth.

'Doctor of what?' asked Erika.

'He's the local GP. Owns and manages the Hilltop Medical Practice on Crofton Park Road,' replied Moss. Erika looked over at Isaac, who was standing on the opposite side of the bed, examining the body.

'Can you give me a cause of death?' asked Erika. 'I'm assuming asphyxiation, but…'

Isaac released the victim's head, the chin coming to rest on the bare chest. 'The evidence points to asphyxiation, but I'll need to determine that the bag wasn't placed over his head postmortem.'

'A sex game gone wrong? Autoasphyxiation?' asked Moss.

'Hypothetically, yes. But we can't rule out foul play.'

'Time of death?' asked Erika, hopefully. She was now sweating profusely under her crime scene overalls.

'Don't push it,' said Isaac. 'I won't be able to give you a time of death until I've had a closer look and opened him up. Extreme heat or cold slows putrefaction: in the case of the heat in this room, it's drying out the body. You can see the flesh has started to discolour.' He pointed to where the skin was blooming in shades of green around the abdomen. 'This could indicate he has been here for a few days, but, as I say, I'll need to perform the post-mortem.'

Erika cast her eye around the room. A long wardrobe of heavy wood lined the wall next to the door, and in the nook of the bay window there was a matching dresser with a mirror. To the left of the window was a tall set of drawers. Every surface was clear: there were no books or ornaments, or any of the general detritus that accumulates in a bedroom. It was very neat. Almost *too* neat.

'Was he married?' asked Erika.

'Yes. The wife is no longer on the scene. They've been separated for a few months,' said Moss.

'It's very tidy, for a newly single man,' said Erika. 'Unless the attacker cleaned up,' she added.

'What? Had a vacuum round before he scarpered?' asked Moss. 'I wish he'd pay me a visit. You should see my place.'

Despite the heat, Erika saw a couple of the crime scene officers working around the body hide their smiles.

'Moss, not the right time.'

'Sorry, boss.'

'I think the arms were tied post-mortem,' said Isaac, gently indicating the wrist area with his latex-gloved finger. The skin around the armpits was stretched in white lines against the shades of waxy skin underneath. 'There's very little abrasion on the wrists.'

'So he was already in bed when the attack happened?' asked Erika.

'Possibly,' replied Isaac.

'There's no discarded clothes. He could have undressed normally for bed and tidied them away,' said Moss.

'So someone could have been hiding under the bed or in the wardrobe, or could have come through the window?' asked Erika, blinking as sweat ran down her forehead into her eyes.

'That's for you to find out,' said Isaac.

'Yes, it is. Lucky me,' replied Erika.

Erika and Moss came downstairs to the open-plan living area, where a team of crime scene technicians was working on the rest of the house. One of the technicians approached them. Erika hadn't met him before. He was in his early thirties, with a handsome face and a high Nordic forehead. Sweat glistened through his blond hair. When he reached Erika, he looked up, realising how tall she was at just over six foot.

'DCI Foster? I'm Nils Åkerman, crime scene manager,' he said. He had a slight Swedish accent under his perfect English.

'You're new?' asked Moss.

'To London? Yes. To murder and mayhem, no.' Nils had a pleasant, handsome face and, like many people who dealt with death and horror on a daily basis, seemed respectfully detached, with a dark sense of humour.

'Good to meet you,' said Erika. Their latex gloves crackled as they shook hands.

'What do you know already?' he asked.

'Take us through it from the top,' said Erika.

'Okay. So the mother shows up around seven-thirty to feed the cat. Lets herself in with a key. The power had been switched off at the mains when she arrived. And it looks as though it had been off for a few days. The contents of the fridge and freezer were decaying.'

Erika looked over to the large stainless steel fridge-freezer, where a couple of brightly coloured child's finger paintings were attached with magnets.

'The Internet and phone connections had also been cut off,' added Nils.

'Cut off from not paying the bill?' asked Erika.

'No, the Internet cable itself was cut,' said Nils, moving to the kitchen counter and holding up a plastic evidence bag containing two pieces of cable. One was connected to a small modem. He held up another bag. 'This is the victim's mobile phone. The SIM card and battery are missing.'

'Where was it found?' asked Erika.

'On the bedside table. It was still plugged in and connected to the charger.'

'There's no other phone in the house?'

'Just the landline downstairs.'

'So, whoever did this took the SIM and battery out of the phone after it had been put on the bedside table to charge?' said Moss.

Nils nodded. 'It's a possibility.'

'Hang on, hang on,' said Erika. 'Was there anything else on the bedside table? The bedroom looks very bare.'

'Apart from the phone, there was nothing else,' said Nils. 'We did, however, find these in the bedside table drawer.' He held up another evidence bag containing four gay porn magazines: copies of *Black Inches*, *Ebony* and *Latino Males*.

'He was gay?' asked Erika.

'And married,' added Moss.

'How old was he again?'

'Forty-six,' replied Moss. 'He was separated from his wife. But these magazines are old. Look, they're issues dated 2001. Why would he keep them here?'

'So they were hidden, and he was secretly gay?' asked Erika.

'Maybe they'd been stashed away for years. Maybe he liberated them from the attic when his marriage broke down,' said Nils.

'That's too many maybe's for my liking,' said Erika.

'We found the packaging for an individual microwave lasagna on the kitchen island. It was on a plate, and beside it was an empty wine glass and a half-full bottle of red wine. We're about to send them off to the lab,' said Nils. 'You should also see this.'

He took them through the large kitchen, past a big sagging sofa covered in felt-tip pen marks and a large tea stain. An overflowing box of toys sat between the edge of the sofa and the glass back wall looking out over the garden. The glass had been retracted, allowing the three of them to step out onto wooden decking. Erika savoured the drop in temperature. Floodlights had been put up in the back garden, which Erika could see extended down to a murky thicket of trees, where several figures in overalls were crouched down, examining the grass.

They doubled back down a narrow gravel passage along the outside glass wall and came to a sash window, which was level with the sink in the kitchen. A drain below was giving off an evil, vomit-like smell.

'We've dusted the window, the gutter pipes, the window of the house next door,' Nils said. 'Nothing. We did find this, though.' He turned their attention to the base of the white-painted sash window. 'See here, in the wood?' His latex-gloved finger hovered over a small square impression in the gloss paint, no more than half a centimetre wide. 'The window was forced up using a blunt flat instrument, perhaps a screwdriver.'

'This window was closed when you arrived on the scene?' asked Erika.

'Yes.'

'Good work,' she said, looking back at the tiny impression in the paint. 'Were there any footprints you could get from the gravel here?'

'A mixture of vague impressions, could be a small pair of feet, but nothing we can make a cast from. Now, if we can come back inside,' said Nils. They followed him back round the house, through the glass doors, into the kitchen to the other side of the sash window.

'Can you see here, there should be sash stops,' said Nils, indicating two small square holes on either side of the sash window frame.

'What's a sash stop?' asked Moss.

'Two small plastic hooks, which work on springs poking out of the inside of the upper second sash frame. They are there to stop the bottom frame of the window from being forced upwards. They've been removed.'

'Could Gregory Munro have removed them?' asked Erika.

'Not if he was worried about being burgled, which I think he was. The house has a top-of-the-range security system. Motion sensor lights in the back garden. When the power was cut, it should have triggered the alarm. That's what they are designed to do – but nothing.'

'So, whoever did this removed the sash stops from this window and knew the combination of the security alarm?' asked Erika.

'Yes, it's a theory,' said Nils. 'There's one more thing.' He took them back out through the glass doors. When they reached the bottom of the garden, they ducked down to look under the tree and found the wire fence had been propped open.

'The garden backs on to the train tracks and the Honor Oak nature reserve,' said Nils. 'I think this was the access point. Fence was clipped with wire cutters.'

'Shit,' said Moss. 'Who the hell do you think did this?'

'We need to find out more about this Dr Gregory Munro,' said Erika, staring up at the house. 'That's where we'll find our answers.'

CHAPTER 5

It was an old desktop PC on a large creaky metal stand with wheels, tucked in under the stairs of a modest house. The chat room home screen popped up. It was basic, no fancy graphics. The mainstream chat rooms were moderated, but this one occupied the backwaters of the Internet where the pond scum could thrive.

There was a beep on the screen and the name of a user called DUKE flashed up and started to type.

DUKE: Any1 up?

The hands moved fast across the keyboard, eager to talk.

NIGHT OWL: I'm always up, Duke.

DUKE: Night Owl, where you been?

NIGHT OWL: Busy. I've gone three days straight without sleep. Almost my record.

DUKE: My record is four. The crazy, trippy hallucinations were almost worth it. Naked girls. So real ***bites knuckle***

NIGHT OWL: Ha! I wish my hallucinations were so friendly. I can't stand to have the lights on, they cause me pain… But then the shadows seem to come alive. Blank eyeless faces watch me from the corner of my eyes. And I see him.

DUKE: You having a tough time of it?

NIGHT OWL: I'm used to it… You know.

DUKE: Yeah. I do.

DUKE: So? Did you do it?

NIGHT OWL: Yes.

DUKE: Seriously?

NIGHT OWL: Yes.

DUKE: You used the suicide bag?

NIGHT OWL: Yes.

DUKE: How long did it take?

NIGHT OWL: Almost four minutes. He fought against it, despite the drugs.

There was a pause. A bubble popped up, saying 'DUKE typing…' Then the screen fell silent for a moment.

NIGHT OWL: U still there?

DUKE: Yeah. I never thought you'd do it.

NIGHT OWL: Did you think I was bullshitter, like most of the people online?

DUKE: No.

NIGHT OWL: You don't think I'm strong enough?

DUKE: NO!

NIGHT OWL: Good, because I'm serious. I've had too many years of people underestimating me. Thinking I'm weak. Walking all over me. Abusing me. I am NOT WEAK. I have POWER. Mental and physical POWER, and I've unlocked it.

DUKE: I don't doubt you.

NIGHT OWL: Don't you dare.

DUKE: I'm sorry. I never doubt you. Ever.

DUKE: How did it feel?

NIGHT OWL: Like God.

DUKE: We don't believe in God.
NIGHT OWL: What if I am HIM?

A few minutes passed with nothing, and then DUKE wrote:

DUKE: So what happens now?
NIGHT OWL: This is just the beginning. The Doctor was just the first on my list. I have the next one in my sights.

CHAPTER 6

Erika pulled into the car park of Lewisham Row police station just before eight the next morning. Work at the crime scene had gone on until the early hours, and she'd only had time for a couple of hours' sleep and a shower before coming into work. The hot air was thick with exhaust fumes as she stepped out of her car, and lorries crunched gears as they crawled past on the ring road. There was a distant whirr and clank from the cranes working on the high-rise buildings that were dotted around in various stages of development – the squat concrete building of the station was dwarfed in comparison. Erika locked her car and made her way across the car park to the main entrance, grumpy from lack of sleep, already sweating and in need of a cold drink.

It was cooler inside the reception area, but the warmth, mingling with a nasty cocktail of vomit and disinfectant, wasn't improving the atmosphere. Sergeant Woolf sat hunched over his desk, filling out a form. His stomach hung over his trousers, and his round jowly face was red and glistening with sweat. A tall, thin lad in a grubby tracksuit stood waiting nearby, eyeing his belongings nestled in a plastic tub on the desk: a brand new iPhone and two packets of cigarettes still sealed in plastic. The lad's gaunt, hungry face didn't match the expensive belongings he was waiting for, and Erika had a feeling it wouldn't be long before he was back.

'Morning. Any joy on getting them to serve iced coffee down in the canteen?' Erika asked.

'Nope,' said Woolf, rubbing at his face with a hairy forearm. 'They seem to have no problem dishing up the food stone-cold; I don't see why they can't do it with the coffee.'

Erika grinned. The thin lad rolled his eyes. 'Yeah, 'ave a chat, cos I've got nowhere to be. I just want my iPhone back. It's mine.'

'This was seized at the scene of a crime four months ago, you can wait another ten minutes,' said Woolf, giving him a hard stare. He put down the pen and buzzed Erika through a door into the main part of the police station. 'Marsh is already here, said he wants to see you as soon as you're in.'

'Right,' said Erika. She went through the door and the buzzing stopped as it closed behind her. She passed empty offices in the stuffy, fluorescent-lit corridor. It was still early in the day, but lots of officers had taken holiday and the atmosphere seemed to have clicked down a gear.

She took the lift up to her boss's office on the top floor. She knocked and, when she heard a muffled reply, entered. Detective Chief Superintendent Marsh stood with his back to her in front of the window, looking out over the concrete sprawl of cranes and traffic. He was tall and broad, and his close-cropped hair was a spray of salt and pepper. When he turned, Erika saw that his lips were locked around a bright green straw, which led down to a large Starbucks iced coffee. He was handsome, if exhausted. He raised his eyebrows and swallowed.

'Morning, Sir,' she said.

'Morning, Erika. Here, thought you could use one too.' Marsh went to his messy desk and picked up another iced coffee, which he handed to her with a paper wrapped straw. The cup left a large wet ring on the printout of the preliminary report on Gregory Munro's murder, which Erika had emailed through in the early hours of the morning.

CHAPTER 7

The incident room at Lewisham Row was a large, airless communal office. Harsh strip lighting cast the police officers inside in an unflinching glare. Glass partitions on either side faced onto corridors, and running along one side of the glass partition was a bank of printers and photocopiers. Erika stood at one of the printers, feeling a familiar tingling mix of anticipation, horror and excitement as she read the preliminary findings that had been sent through from the post-mortem on Gregory Munro. The pages emerged one by one, the paper warm to the touch.

Her team was already hard at work, many of the officers having come from the crime scene after just a few hours' sleep. Sergeant Crane – the blond-haired, perpetually active engine of the incident room – moved between the desks, preparing for the briefing with a pile of printouts. Moss was manning the ringing phones with Detective Constable Singh, a small, pretty officer with a sharp mind. A new member of the team, Detective Constable Warren, was pinning up the case evidence gathered so far on the vast whiteboards covering the back wall. He was an enthusiastic, good-looking young lad.

Detective Inspector Peterson entered and regarded the busy incident room. He was a tall, handsome black officer with a crop of short dreadlocks. Along with Moss, he had become one of Erika's most trusted colleagues. His cool, smart sophistication provided a good balance for Moss's down-to-earth crudeness.

'Good holiday, Peterson?' asked Erika, looking up from the report.

'Yeah. Barbados. Peace, quiet, sandy beaches… This looks the opposite,' he replied wistfully, but Erika's attention was already back in her report. Peterson sat at his desk and looked around at the stark shabbiness of the incident room.

Moss put her hand over the phone. 'You sure you've been away? You don't look like you've caught much of a tan…'

'Ha, ha. I had a bowl of porridge for breakfast this morning with more colour than you,' Peterson grinned.

'It's good to have you back,' she winked, before going back to her call.

'Okay, good morning everyone,' said Erika, moving to the front of the room. She pulled out a series of crime scene photos and began to stick them to the whiteboard.

'Victim is forty-six-year-old Gregory Munro. Local GP.' The incident room fell silent as they absorbed the photos. 'I know some of you were at the scene last night, but, for the benefit of those who weren't, I'll take you through what happened.'

The officers remained silent as Erika recapped the previous evening's events. 'Forensics have just got back with the toxicology and preliminary findings from the post-mortem. There was a small amount of alcohol in the victim's blood, but a very high level of Flunitrazepam: 98 micrograms per litre. Flunitrazepam being the generic name for Rohypnol, or Roofies.'

'Everyone's favourite date rape drug,' said Peterson, dryly.

'Yes. Residue of the drug was found in a wine glass at the scene, in the kitchen,' replied Erika.

'His drink must have been spiked. Unless he wanted to kill himself? As a doctor, he'd have known such a high dosage could kill him,' said Moss.

'Yes, but it didn't kill him. He died from asphyxiation. You can see the clear plastic bag tied tight over his head with a length of thin white cord.' Erika pointed to a photo of Gregory

Munro staring blankly through the plastic. 'His hands had been tied post-mortem. Gay porn magazines were also found in his bedside drawer. So, the magazines, the asphyxiation with a bag, coupled with the date rape drug means we'll need to rule out any sexual element. There were no signs that he had been raped, no swabs of hair or bodily fluids found other than his own…' Erika paused and regarded the officers staring back at her. 'So, I want us to work on the assumption that someone broke into the house, and Gregory Munro was drugged, then asphyxiated. I also believe that this wasn't random. Nothing was taken, no money or valuables. The phone lines and power were cut, which indicates a level of planning involved, and whoever did this needed to have disabled the security system *before* they cut the power.

'Now, I want the usual drill: a door-to-door on Laurel Road and the surrounding streets. Uniform has already made progress with this, but I want everyone who lives on that street, or who was in the area, interviewed. Pull all records on Gregory Munro: bank, phone, emails, social media, friends and family. He was separated from his wife so I presume he'd contacted a solicitor: find out. Find out if he was on any gay dating sites. Also, get the hard drive of his phone, check for any gay dating apps. He might have hired a rent boy. He's also the local GP; find out everything you can about his work – did he have problems with colleagues or patients?'

Erika went to the whiteboard and indicated photos taken of the garden.

'The killer accessed the house through the fence, which backs onto the train tracks and a small nature reserve. Pull any CCTV that you can find on and around the train tracks, plus stuff from the nearest train stations and surrounding streets. Crane, you'll co-ordinate things here in the incident room.'

'Yes, boss,' said Crane.

'I think Gregory Munro knew the person who did this, and unlocking his personal life will help us unlock the whereabouts of the killer. Okay, let's get to work. We'll reconvene here at six to share our findings.'

The officers in the incident room sprang into life.

'Is there any news on Gregory Munro's mother?' asked Erika, moving over to where Moss and Peterson were sitting.

'She's still in hospital in Lewisham. She's made a good recovery, but they're waiting for a doctor to discharge her,' said Moss.

'Okay. Let's pay her a visit – you too, Peterson.'

'You don't think she's a suspect?' asked Moss.

'No, but mothers are often a hive of information,' said Erika.

'I know what you mean. Mine has her nose in everybody's business,' said Peterson, getting up and grabbing his jacket.

'Then let's hope Estelle Munro is the same,' said Erika.

CHAPTER 8

University Hospital Lewisham was a sprawling mix of buildings in old brick and futuristic glass, with a new wing of blue and yellow plastic. The car park was busy, and a steady stream of ambulances was pulling up at the Accident and Emergency department. Erika, Moss and Peterson parked the car and made their way on foot to the main entrance, a large glass and steel box opposite A&E. As they approached, they saw an elderly lady parked outside in a wheelchair, shouting at a nurse crouching down beside her.

'It's disgusting!' she was saying, stabbing at the nurse with a gnarled finger topped with red nail varnish. 'You keep me waiting, and when you finally discharge me I'm sat here for over an hour in the heat! I don't have my handbag, or my phone, and you're doing nothing!'

Several people coming out of the main entrance took notice of this, but a group of nurses on their way in didn't bat an eyelid.

'That's her – Estelle Munro, Gregory Munro's mother,' said Moss. As they drew level, the nurse noticed them and stood up. She was in her late forties, with a kind but tired face. Erika, Moss and Peterson introduced themselves, holding up their ID.

'Is everything all right here?' asked Erika. Estelle squinted up at them from the wheelchair. She looked to be in her mid-sixties and she seemed to be an elegant dresser, but after a night in hospital her pale slacks and floral blouse were crumpled, most of her make-up had sweated off and her short auburn hair was sticking up in tufts. On her lap was a plastic bag containing a pair of black patent leather court shoes.

'No! Everything is not all right *here*...' started Estelle.

The nurse put her hands on her broad hips, interrupting: 'Estelle was offered a lift home by the police officers who came to take her statement this morning, but she declined.'

'Of course I declined! I'm not pulling up outside my house in a police car! I would like to be taken home in a taxi... I know how this works. I am entitled to a taxi. You people just want to cut corners...'

In Erika's experience, grief and shock affected people in different ways. Some crumpled in a heap of tears, some went numb and couldn't speak, and others became angry. She could see Estelle Munro was in the latter category.

'I've been kept prisoner all night in that God-awful hell-hole called A&E. I just had a funny turn, that's all. But, no – I had to queue up, and the drunks and drug addicts were seen first!' Estelle turned her attention to Erika, Moss and Peterson. 'Then your lot asked me endless questions. You'd think I was the criminal! What are the three of you doing here, anyway? My boy is lying dead... He was murdered!'

At this point, Estelle broke down. She clutched the armrests of the wheelchair and gritted her teeth. 'Stop crowding me, all of you!' she shouted.

'We've got an unmarked car. We can take you home right now, Mrs Munro,' said Peterson kindly, crouching down and offering her a tissue from a small pack in his pocket.

She looked up at him with tears in her eyes. 'You can?'

Peterson nodded.

'Then please, take me home. I just want to be at home, on my own,' she said, taking a tissue and holding it to her face.

Thank you, mouthed the nurse.

Peterson took the brake off the wheelchair and started to push Estelle towards the car park.

'She was admitted in a bad way, extremely dehydrated and in severe shock,' said the nurse to Moss and Erika. 'She didn't want to call anyone. I don't know if there is a neighbour, or a daughter perhaps? She needs to remain calm and get some rest when she's home.'

'Peterson will work his magic, he's always a hit with the old dears,' said Moss, as they watched him manoeuvre the wheelchair down the kerb and across the car park. The nurse smiled and went back through the main entrance.

'Shit, I've got the car keys, come on!' said Erika. They hurried across to catch up with Peterson.

'Oh, this heat…' said Estelle, despairingly, when they were all inside the baking hot car. 'It's been going on for days!' She was in the front beside Erika, and Moss and Peterson were seated in the back.

Erika leant across and helped Estelle with her seatbelt, then started the engine. 'The air conditioning will kick in any moment now.'

'How long have you been parked here?' asked Estelle, when Erika showed her ID to the man working at the barrier. He waved them through.

'Fifteen minutes,' said Erika.

'If you weren't police, you'd have to pay one pound fifty. Even if you don't use the full hour. I kept asking Gregory if he could do anything about patients having to pay. He said he would write to our Member of Parliament. He's met her, you know, several times – at official luncheons…' Estelle's voice trailed off and she searched around in her lap for the tissue, and dabbed at her eyes.

'Would you like some water, Estelle?' asked Moss, who had bought some bottles from the vending machine at Lewisham Row.

'Yes, please. And it's Mrs Munro, if you don't mind.'

'Of course, Mrs Munro,' said Moss, and she passed a small bottle of water dripping with condensation through the gap in the seats. Estelle managed to get the lid off and took a long drink. They drove through Ladywell, past the large park next to the hospital, where a group of young lads were playing football in the hot morning sunshine.

'Thank goodness, that's much better,' said Estelle, sitting back as the cold air conditioning began to wash over them.

'Could I please ask you a few questions?' said Erika.

'Can't it wait?'

'We'll need you to make an official statement later, but as I said, I'd like to ask you a few questions… Please, Mrs Munro, this is important.'

'Go on, then.'

'Gregory was due to be going on holiday?'

'Yes, to France. He was going to make a speech for a conference of the BMA, the British Medical Association.'

'He didn't call to say he had arrived.'

'Obviously not.'

'Was that unusual?'

'No. We weren't in each other's pockets. I knew he would phone me at some point during his trip.'

'Gregory was separated from his wife?'

'Yes, *Penny*,' said Estelle, her lip curling nastily as she said the name.

'Can I ask why?'

'*Can you ask why*… You're asking, aren't you? Penny instigated it. She filed for divorce. If anyone was going to file for divorce, it should have been Gregory,' said Estelle, shaking her head.

'Why?'

'She made his life a misery. And after all he did for her. He gave her a quality of life. Until they got married, Penny was still living with her awful mother, aged thirty-five. She had very few prospects. She was just a receptionist at Gregory's surgery. No sooner had they started going out, she fell pregnant. She forced his hand and he had to marry her.'

'Why did he have to marry her?' asked Moss.

'I know it's the fashion these days to bring bastards into the world, but my grandson was not going to be a bastard!'

'So you pushed them to marry?' asked Moss.

Estelle turned to her. 'No. It was Gregory. He did the honourable thing.'

'Had he been married before?' asked Erika.

'Of course not.'

'Penny and Gregory were married for four years. So he would have been forty-two when they got married?' asked Moss.

'Yes,' said Estelle.

'Did he have many girlfriends in the years leading up to his marriage?' asked Peterson.

'A few. No one I could have called serious. He was very driven, you see, with medical school and then the practice. There were some nice girls along the way. He could have had his pick, then he goes for that grasping receptionist…'

'You didn't like her?' asked Peterson.

'What do you think?' said Estelle, eyeing him in the driver's mirror. 'She didn't love him, she just wanted his money. I told him that at the beginning, but he wouldn't listen. Then, one by one, things happened and I was proved right.'

'What happened?' asked Erika.

'The ink was barely dry on the wedding certificate and she was pushing for Gregory to put things in her name. He has – had – several rental properties. He was self-made, you know, worked hard for it all. One of the properties was in my name, to give me a bit of security, and she wanted it changed to hers! Of course, he refused. She got her brother involved…' Estelle shook her head in revulsion. 'I tell you, the phrase "dragged up" is perfect for that family – Penny, her brother Gary. He's a vile skinhead, always in trouble with the police. Yet Penny is devoted to him. I'm surprised you don't know him. Gary Wilmslow.'

Erika exchanged a glance with Moss and Peterson.

Estelle went on: 'Things came to a head last year when Gary threatened Gregory.'

'How did he threaten him?' asked Erika.

'It was all about choosing a school for Peter. Gregory wanted him to board, which would have meant sending him away. Penny resorted to getting Gary round to intimidate Gregory, but Gregory stood up to him, and not many people stand up to Gary Wilmslow. Gregory gave him a good thrashing,' said Estelle, proudly.

'And then what happened?'

'Then the rot set in. Gregory didn't want anything to do with Gary, but Penny wouldn't cut him out of her life. And Gary didn't take kindly to losing a fight. Word got around, I'm sure. Penny and Gary had everything to gain if Gregory was no longer around. She'll now inherit. I tell you, you'll save yourself a lot of taxpayers' money if you arrest her brother. Gary Wilmslow. He's capable of murder, I'm sure of it. Only last week he was at it again, threatening Gregory. Barged into his office, in the surgery, no less – full of patients.'

'Why did he threaten him?'

'I never found out. I just heard about it from the practice manager. I was going to ask Gregory when he returned from holiday, but…' Estelle began to sob again. She looked up as the Forest Hill Tavern pub came into view on the corner. 'It's just on the left, here, and my house is on the end,' she said.

Erika came to a halt at a smart end-of-terrace house. She wished the drive had been longer.

'Would you like us to come in with you?' asked Erika.

'No, I wouldn't. I just need some time and space, thank you. I've been through a great deal, as I'm sure you will appreciate… If I were you, I'd go straight over and arrest her brother. It's Gary, I'm telling you.' Estelle waggled a crooked finger. She undid her seatbelt with difficulty and removed the court shoes from the plastic bag.

'Mrs Munro, we will need to send some officers over for you to make a formal statement, and we need someone to come and identify your son's body,' said Erika, softly.

'I saw him once, like that… I don't want to do it again. Ask *her*, ask Penny,' Estelle said.

'Of course,' said Erika.

Peterson got out of the car and round to the passenger side. He took Estelle's shoes and placed them on her feet, then helped her out of the car to her front door.

'Looks like this is getting interesting,' said Moss quietly to Erika. 'Money, property, families at war: never bodes well.'

They watched Peterson help Estelle up the steps. She opened her front door and vanished inside.

'No, it doesn't,' agreed Erika. 'I want to talk to Penny. And I want to talk to this Gary Wilmslow.'

CHAPTER 9

Penny Munro's house was in Shirley, an area of south-east London just a few miles from where they'd dropped Estelle. It was a modern ex-council house, with dun-coloured pebbledashed walls and lattice work on the new PVC windows. The front garden was neat, with a strip of immaculately lush green lawn, despite the lack of rain. A small pond was covered in netting, beneath which an explosion of lily pads was in bloom. A large plastic heron, frozen with one leg drawn up, was surrounded by a collection of huge, rosy-faced gnomes.

When they rang the bell, an electronic version of 'Land of Hope and Glory' chimed out. Moss raised an eyebrow at Erika and Peterson. There was a long pause, enough for a whole verse to play, and then the bell fell silent. The handle waggled, and the door opened slowly – just a few inches. A tiny, dark-haired boy peered round at them with bashful brown eyes. Erika could see so much of Gregory Munro in his little face – the eyes and high, proud forehead – it was quite eerie. A television blared out from behind a closed door in the hall.

'Hello, are you Peter?' asked Erika. The boy nodded. 'Hello, Peter. Is your mummy here?'

'Yes. She's crying upstairs,' he said.

'Oh, I'm sorry about that. Could you ask her if we can speak to her, please?'

His eyes travelled over Erika, Moss, and finally, Peterson. He nodded, then threw back his head and yelled, 'Mummy, there's people at the door!'

There was a clink and the sound of a toilet flushing, and then a young woman with red swollen eyes came down the stairs. She was thin and attractive, with shoulder-length, strawberry-blonde hair and a small pointed nose.

'Penny Munro?' asked Erika. The woman nodded. 'Hello. I'm DCI Foster. This is DI Peterson and DI Moss. We're very sorry about your hus—'

Penny began to shake her head frantically, 'No. He doesn't know... I haven't...' she whispered, pointing at the little boy, who was grinning as Peterson stuck out his tongue and crossed his large brown eyes.

'Could we have a word, on your own, please?' said Erika.

'I've already spoken to some officers.'

'Mrs Munro, it's very important.'

Penny blew her nose and nodded, shouting, 'Mum! Muuum! Jesus, she's got that telly up again...' She opened the door in the hallway and the sound from the television intensified. The theme tune for *This Morning* blared out, rattling the thin frame of a mirror on the wall by the door. A few moments later, a large, elderly woman with a cloud of greasy grey hair and almost comically thick-framed glasses appeared at the living room door. She wore an androgynous green jumper and trousers, the legs of which were too short. They flapped above her swollen ankles, which poured over the edges of a pair of tartan slippers. The woman peered myopically through her murky glasses.

'WHAT DO THEY WANT NOW?' she bellowed, looking annoyed.

'NOTHING, JUST TAKE PETER,' shouted Penny.

The old woman gave the police officers a suspicious look and nodded. 'COME ON, PETEY,' she said, her voice high and reedy. Peter took her pudgy hand and sloped off into the living room, looking back at them for a moment. The sound of the blaring television dropped when the door closed.

'Mum's deaf, and in a world of her own,' said Penny. The sound of a car backfiring on the street outside made her jump and begin to tremble. She craned her head round them and looked up and down the street as an old red Fiat roared past, driven by a young man in shades and no T-shirt.

'What is it, Mrs Munro?' asked Erika.

'Nothing… It's nothing,' she said, unconvincingly. 'Come through to the kitchen.'

CHAPTER 10

They sat in a tiny sweltering kitchen cluttered with ornaments and frilly tea towels. The window overlooked a back garden even more infested with gnomes than the front. Erika found their manic rosy faces creepy and wondered if they were super-sized so Penny's mother could see who was who.

'Last time I spoke to him – Gregory – was three days ago,' said Penny. She remained standing, leaning against the sink with a look of disbelief on her face. She lit up a cigarette, grabbing an overflowing ashtray from the windowsill.

'What did you talk about?' asked Erika.

'Not much. He was going off to France, for some conference.'

'The British Medical Association?' asked Moss.

'He's one of their senior members.'

'And was it odd you hadn't heard from him, that he'd arrived safely?' asked Erika.

'We were getting a divorce. We only phoned each other when we had to... I rang him to check he was still going, and that I could keep Peter. We've got... We *had* an agreement that he would stay with his dad on Saturday nights.'

'What else did he say?'

'Not much.'

'Is there anyone you can think of who would do this to your husband?'

Penny stared out at the garden and flicked her cigarette ash into the sink.

'No… There were people he'd fallen out with, but everyone has that. I can't think of anyone who hated him enough to break in and… suffocate him.' She began to cry. Moss took a box of tissues off the kitchen table and offered her one.

'Thanks,' Penny said.

'The house had a security system. When was it put in?' asked Erika.

'A couple of years ago, after the extension was completed.'

'Did you always use it?'

'Yes. Gregory always set it when we went away. He used to put it on at night too, but when Peter started walking there were a few times when he came down in the dark for a drink and set it off, so we stopped… But we added extra locks on the windows and doors.'

'Can you remember the name of the security company?'

'No. Greg arranged it all. How did… whoever did it… break in?'

'That's what we are trying to find out,' said Erika. 'May I ask why you and Gregory separated?'

'He'd grown to hate everything about me: the way I dressed, the way I talked, the way I was with people. He said I was too flirty with men in shops, he thought my friends weren't good enough. He tried to cut me off from my mother, but his mother was always welcome, always there. And he didn't get on with my brother, Gary…'

'Was he ever violent?'

'Gary wasn't violent,' Penny said, quickly.

'I was talking about Gregory,' corrected Erika.

A look passed between Peterson and Moss, and Penny noticed it too. 'Sorry, I'm confused. No. Gregory wasn't violent. He could be intimidating, yes, but he never hit me… I'm not stupid.

The relationship wasn't always bad. When he met me, he thought I was a breath of fresh air: exciting, a bit mouthy and funny.'

Erika looked at Penny and saw how men found her attractive; she was pretty and down to earth.

Penny went on: 'But men just want flings with those kind of girls. When we got married, he expected me to change. I was his wife, his representative, that's what he said. I was representing him in society! But I wasn't going to be that kind of wife. I think he only realised that afterwards…'

'What about Gregory's mother?'

'How long have you got? Their relationship makes *Oedipus Rex* look like a sitcom. She's hated me since the word go. She found him, didn't she?'

Erika nodded.

Penny's face clouded over. 'She didn't phone me. I had to find out from some copper knocking on the door. That says a lot about her, doesn't it?'

'It wasn't her responsibility to inform you. She was taken to hospital with shock,' said Moss.

'She mentioned that there was an incident between Gregory and your brother, Gary?' asked Peterson.

At the mention of Gary, Penny stiffened. 'It was just a row, family stuff,' she said, hastily.

'She said it was a physical fight.'

'Yeah, well, boys will be boys,' said Penny.

'But they were grown men. Your brother has been in trouble with the police before,' added Peterson.

Penny's eyes darted between the three officers. She stubbed out her cigarette in an ashtray with a heap of old dog ends. 'My brother's on probation for attacking a bloke in New Cross,' she said, exhaling cigarette smoke up to the ceiling. 'He's a bouncer in a club. The bloke was off his head on drugs, so it was self-defence. But Gary – he went too far. You leave him out of this. I know my brother isn't a saint, but there is no way he had anything to do with this, you hear me?'

'Is that what made you jump earlier, at the front door? Did you think it was Gary?' asked Erika.

'Look, why the hell are you here?' Penny folded her arms across her chest and narrowed her eyes. 'I've already had coppers at the door telling me and asking questions. Shouldn't you be out there trying to catch this bloke?'

'We never said it was a bloke,' said Moss.

'Don't get smart. You know most killers are men,' said Penny.

Erika shot Moss a look: she could see that Penny was closing down on them. 'Okay, okay, Mrs Munro. I'm sorry. We're not investigating your brother. We have to ask these questions, to build up a picture and help us catch who did this.'

Penny lit another cigarette. 'You want one?' she asked. Moss and Peterson shook their heads, but Erika took one from the packet. Penny lit it for her.

'Gregory wanted to send Peter to boarding school,' Penny said. 'To send him away, a little boy! I put my foot down and said no. The weekend before Peter was due to start at the local primary school, I found out Gregory had cancelled Peter's registration, and had gone ahead and accepted the place at the boarding school!'

'When was this?'

'Easter. I phoned Gregory, but he told me Peter would be going that Monday, and I wasn't to stand in the way of him getting a decent education. It was as good as abduction! So Gary went round to get Peter. He kicked the door in, but he didn't… He wasn't violent, okay? Estelle was there. She went after Gary with a glass ashtray, and then it all kicked off. Bet she left that part out, didn't she?'

'So you'd say your relationship with Estelle isn't good?'

Penny laughed bitterly. 'She's a bitch. She creates fantasies to excuse her son's behaviour. When we got together, she hated me on sight... She ruined everything: our engagement party, the wedding. Gregory's father died when he was small; Gregory was an only child and it made them depend on each other, him and his mum. What do you call it? *Co-dependent.* I thought at the beginning of our marriage that I might win him over, or at least become the person who was the closest to him, but she made sure I was always second in line. Sounds bloody pathetic, don't it? I hear myself telling you all about it and I sound pathetic.'

Erika looked at Moss and Peterson, realising that there was one more question she had to ask.

'Mrs Munro, I am sorry to have to ask this, but did you know of your husband having any relationships with men?'

'What do you mean? Friends? He didn't have many friends.'

'I mean, sexual relationships with men.'

Penny looked between them. The clock ticked in the background. The kitchen door suddenly flew open and crashed into the fridge behind. A small, compact man with a bald head strode in. He wore jeans, a T-shirt and a pair of black lace-up boots. Sweat glistened off his head, and patches bloomed under his armpits and dotted his chest. He carried with him a dank, sweaty smell of aggression. His face was a mixture of confusion and fury.

'Sexual relationships with men? What the fuck is this?' he demanded.

'Are you Gary Wilmslow?' asked Erika.

'Yeah. Who are you?'

'Sir, I'm DCI Foster. This is DI Moss and DI Peterson,' said Erika. They rose and held up their ID badges.

'What the fuck is this, Penny?'

'They're just asking me questions about Greg – routine questions, okay?' Penny said wearily, as if placating her brother was a regular chore.

'And you're asking if he was a poofter?' said Gary. 'Is that the best you lot can do? Greg might have been a tosser…'

'Gary!'

'But he weren't a poof. You hear?' said Gary, holding up a finger and prodding the air for emphasis.

'Sir, may we ask you to wait outside whilst we finish?' started Peterson.

'Don't call me "sir". You don't mean it!' Gary said. He opened the fridge and stuck his head inside, muttering, *'Darkie bastard.'*

'What did you just say?' asked Peterson. Erika could see he was breathing fast.

Gary stood up, holding a can of lager, and shut the fridge door. 'I didn't say nothing.'

'I heard you,' said Erika.

'So did I,' said Moss. 'You called my colleague a "darkie bastard".'

'No, I didn't. Even if I did, this is my house, and I can *say* what I like. And if you don't like what you hear, you can fuck off… Come back with a warrant.'

'Mr Wilmslow, these are routine questions for a murder enquiry…' started Erika.

'You lot are fucking useless. It's easier for three of you to sit here hassling us when we've had a death in the family than go out there and look for whoever did this.'

'May I remind you that racially abusing an officer is a criminal offence,' said Peterson, moving close to Gary and staring him in the eyes.

'So is murder, but I'd be within my rights to defend myself if you're gonna get aggressive, on my property.'

'GARY!' shouted Penny. 'Leave it. Go and see if Mum and Peter are okay… Go on, now!'

Gary raised the can and opened it, spattering lager over Peterson's face. There was a tense moment, then Gary took a slurp of his beer and left, slamming the door behind him.

'I'm sorry. I'm really sorry… He don't like the police,' said Penny. She pulled some paper towel off a roll and handed it to Peterson with a trembling hand.

'Are you okay to continue? We're almost finished,' said Erika, as Peterson wiped his face. Penny nodded. 'We don't ask these questions lightly. We found some gay pornographic magazines in your husband's bedside drawer.'

'You did?'

'Yes. We need to know why they were there. They were probably nothing, and he was just curious. But I have to ask you if you know whether Gregory was bisexual, or acting on any impulses to seek out or meet men? It will help us with our enquiry. If your husband was living a secret life and meeting up with men, or inviting men…'

'All right, yes, I get it!' snapped Penny. 'I bloody get it!' She lit up another cigarette and exhaled, chucking the lighter down on the draining board with a clank. She looked like she didn't know how to process this information. There was a long pause. 'I dunno… Once… On one of the rare occasions we got drunk together, Gregory talked about wanting to try a threesome. We were on holiday in Greece, we were having a good time… I thought that he meant with him and another girl, but he wanted… He wanted another guy to join in.'

'Did this surprise you?' asked Erika.

'Course it bloody surprised me! He was always so conventional, missionary position and all that.'

'What happened?'

'Nothing happened. He bottled it, said he was joking, to see what my reaction would be.' Penny crossed her arms over her chest.

'What *was* your reaction when he told you?'

'I dunno. It was a gorgeous island, we were having a great time. There were some well hot Greek blokes. I figured it could have been fun, something crazy and fun. We never had fun.'

'And did it disturb you that he'd suggested it?'

'No. I loved him – at the time I loved him – and he was so strait-laced, it felt nice that he'd shared something with me...' She broke down and began to cry.

'So, do you think your husband could have been gay?'

'No, I don't,' Penny said, lifting her head and regarding Erika with a grim stare. 'Now, is that all?'

'Yes, thank you. We'd like to send an officer over later to collect you, so that you can come and identify your husband's body,' said Erika.

Penny nodded, tears in her eyes. She stared out at the hopelessly jolly back garden. 'If you do find out anything more, about Greg, about him being gay... I don't want to know. Understood?'

Erika nodded. 'Yes, understood.'

When they reached the car out by the pavement, it was baking hot, so they left the doors open for a moment to cool it down. Erika rooted inside her handbag, pulled out her phone, and dialled Lewisham Row.

'Hi Crane, it's DCI Foster. Can you run a name for me, please? Gary Wilmslow, 14 Hereford Street, Shirley. Everything we've got. He's the brother of Penny Munro, the victim's wife. Also can you arrange a formal interview with Estelle Munro, and sort out family liaison officers for both her and Penny?'

They were just getting back into the car when Gary emerged from the front door, holding Peter's hand.

'Mr Wilmslow,' said Erika, doubling back to the front gate, 'can you tell me where you were on Thursday night between 6 p.m. and 1 a.m.?'

Gary went to a garden hose coiled over around a tap under the living room window, and began to unravel it. He handed the hose to the little boy.

'I was here, watching *Game of Thrones* with Penny and Mum,' he said.

'And that was all night?'

'Yeah, all night. We've got the fucking box set.'

Peter took the hose and braced himself, pointing it at the grass. He looked up and grinned a gap-toothed smile. Gary turned on the tap as Peter directed the spray over the grass.

'And they can verify this?'

'Yeah,' he said, with an icy stare. 'They can *verify* that.'

'Thank you.'

Erika came back to the car, and she, Moss and Peterson got in. She fired up the engine and the air conditioning.

'You know, we could arrest him right here and now. There's a hosepipe ban,' said Peterson.

'Yeah, but he's got the kid using the hose,' said Moss.

'He's one of those slippery bastards, isn't he?' said Peterson, ruefully.

'Yeah,' agreed Erika. They watched him smoking a cigarette as Peter watered the grass. He looked up and stared at them.

'Let's leave him for a bit,' said Erika. 'See what he does. He's a possible suspect, but we need much more.'

CHAPTER 11

It was late afternoon on the geriatric ward at the Queen Anne Hospital in London. Nurse Simone Matthews sat in one of the few single rooms leading off the ward. Beside her, in a hospital bed, lay an elderly lady called Mary. Her thin sleeping form barely made an impression underneath the blue blanket that was neatly tucked around her. Her face was gaunt and jaundiced, and through her slack mouth her breathing was ragged.

It wouldn't be long now.

The Queen Anne Hospital was housed in a decaying redbrick building, and the geriatric ward could be a dark and challenging place. Watching people unravel both mentally and physically took its toll on the senses. Two nights previously, Simone had been tasked with bathing an old man, who up until then had been a model patient. Without warning, he had punched her in the face. She'd been sent for an X-ray, but luckily her jaw hadn't been fractured. Sister had told her to take a couple of days off, to rest and get over the shock, but Simone had been stoic, insisting on coming back for her next shift.

Work was everything to Simone, and she wanted to be with Mary, to sit with her until the end. The two women had never spoken. Mary had been on the ward for ten days, and had been drifting in and out of consciousness. Her organs failing, her body slowly shutting down. No family or friends had visited, but Simone had built up a picture of her from the personal effects stowed in the small locker by the bed.

Mary had collapsed at a supermarket, and had been admitted wearing a threadbare dress and old gardening shoes. She carried with her a small black handbag. There wasn't much inside, just a tin of peppermints and a bus pass, but in a zip-up pocket in the lining Simone had found a small, creased black-and-white photo.

It had been taken in a park on a sunny day. Underneath a tree, a beautiful young woman sat on a tartan blanket, a long skirt bunched around her legs. Her waist was trim and the swell of her bosom under her crisp white blouse showed an enviable hour-glass figure. Even though the photo was black and white, Simone guessed Mary had been a redhead – it was something about the way the sun shone on her long curly hair. Beside Mary was a dark-haired man. He was good-looking, with a hint of danger and excitement about him. He squinted into the sun, with one of his arms slung around Mary's small waist, gripping her protectively. On the back was written: With my dearest George, Bromley, summer 1961.

There was one other picture of Mary, from the ID photo on her bus pass. It had been taken three years previously. Mary stared fearfully into the camera against a stark white background, a rabbit caught in the headlights: limp grey hair, her face creased and lined.

What happened to Mary between 1961 and 2013? thought Simone. *And where was George?* As far as she could tell, they hadn't lived happily ever after. From the medical records, she could see that Mary had never married. She had no children or dependents.

From the bed, Mary spluttered. Her sunken mouth slowly opened and closed and her breathing caught for a moment, before settling back into its ragged rhythm.

'It's okay, Mary, I'm here,' said Simone, reaching out and taking her hand. Mary's arm was thin, the skin loose and covered with dark stain-like bruises, from repeated attempts to find a vein to connect the IV line.

Simone checked the small silver watch pinned to the front of her uniform and saw her shift was coming to an end. She took a hairbrush from the locker beside the bed and began to brush Mary's hair, first away from her high forehead, then supporting her head so she could reach the rest in long strokes. As the brush moved, the thin silver strands glowed in the sunlight coming through the small window.

As she brushed, Simone wished that Mary could have been her mother, wished she would open her eyes and tell her that she loved her. She'd loved George, Simone could see that in the photo, and she was sure Mary could love her too. A different kind of love, of course. The love a mother has for her daughter.

Simone's mother's face flashed across her mind, causing her hands to tremble so badly that she dropped the hairbrush.

'ONE OF THE WORST CASES OF CHILD NEGLECT EVER SEEN!' the newspaper headlines had screamed. Ten-year-old Simone had been found by a neighbour after her mother had gone away on holiday, leaving Simone chained to the bathroom radiator. The neighbour, and the journalist she'd contacted, thought they'd saved Simone's life, but life in the children's home had been worse. When her mother had finally returned from holiday, she'd shown up at the home unannounced and the police had been called. Simone's mother ran before they could arrest her. Later that night she'd jumped off Tower Bridge and drowned in the freezing Thames. Simone liked to think her mother had killed herself out of guilt, but she couldn't be sure.

Simone picked up the hairbrush and forced her shaking hands to relax. 'There, you look lovely, Mary,' she said, stepping back to admire her work. Mary's thin hair was neat, the silver strands now fanned out on the crisp white pillow. Simone put the hairbrush back in the locker.

'Now I'm going to read to you,' said Simone, reaching behind the plastic chair and rummaging in her bag for the local newspaper.

She started with the horoscopes – she knew from the medical notes Mary was a Leo – and then she read out her own. Simone was a Libra. She then turned to the front page and read out the story about the doctor from South London who had been found strangled in his bed. When she'd finished, Simone put the newspaper down on her lap.

'Mary, I've never been able to understand men. I never know what my husband, Stan, is thinking… Stan, it's short for Stanley. He's like a closed book. It makes me feel lonely. I'm glad I've got you… You understand me, don't you?'

Mary carried on sleeping. She was far away, back in the sunny park, sitting on the blanket with George, the man who had broken her heart.

CHAPTER 12

Erika, Moss and Peterson arrived back at Lewisham Row station just before 6 p.m., and they regrouped in the incident room.

'So, Gregory Munro seems to elude us,' said Erika, addressing her officers in front of the whiteboards. 'His mother thinks he's a saint; his wife paints him as sexually confused, and tightly wound. We visited his medical practice and ran into two of his patients, who have vastly different opinions of his bedside manner... I also spent half an hour on the phone with his practice manager who, after hearing her boss was dead, went off to Brighton for the day for some bar-hopping in the sun. She's worked for him for fifteen years, and she had no knowledge of his impending divorce, or that his wife left him three months ago.'

'He compartmentalises his life, then?' said Crane.

'That's one way of putting it,' said Erika. 'We've requested details of any feedback or complaints made against him by patients. The practice manager wasn't too keen, but I mentioned a warrant and she changed her tune. She should have it sent over by tomorrow morning at the latest.'

Erika turned and regarded a new addition to the whiteboard. A mugshot of Gary Wilmslow. In the photo he had a little more hair on his head, and stared into the camera with a glowering face and bags under his eyes.

'So, the closest we've got to a suspect so far is the victim's brother-in-law, Gary Wilmslow. There's a motive: he hated

Gregory and they'd had several run-ins. And his sister will inherit Gregory's considerable estate. As a family, Gary, Penny and
their mother seem as thick as thieves, if you excuse the pun.
What have we got on Gary?'

The atmosphere in the incident room changed as Detective
Chief Superintendent Marsh entered. Officers sat up straight-
er and looked more alert. Marsh perched on the long table of
printers and indicated to Erika that she should keep going.

Crane stood up. 'Okay, Gary Wilmslow, aged thirty-seven.
Born in Shirley, South London. Currently works sixteen hours
part-time as a bouncer at a nightclub in Peckham… Just enough
hours for him to still claim benefits. He's a charming individual,
with a record as thick as a Miss Universe contestant,' he said,
dryly. He put his biro between his teeth and rooted around on
his desk, locating a large file, which he opened. 'Wilmslow was
tried as a juvenile in 1993, for an attack on an old man at a
bus stop on Neasden High Street. The old man was in a coma
for three days but recovered to give evidence. Gary spent three
years in Feltham Young Offender Institution for that one. Then
in 1999 he was tried and found guilty of GBH and ABH, spent
eighteen months inside. Did another two years from 2004 to
2006 for dealing drugs.' Crane was flicking through pages in the
thick file. 'He got another eighteen months in 2006 for attacking a man in a snooker hall in Sydenham with a pool cue. He
was charged with rape in 2008, but the charges were dropped
due to insufficient evidence. He was then tried for manslaughter
last year.'

'That was whilst he was working as a bouncer?' asked Erika.

'Yeah, he works at the H20 nightclub in Peckham, or *Haitch
Twenty*, as it's known – and hated – by uniform division at the
weekends. Gary Wilmslow's barrister argued that he was acting
in self-defence, and he was given a two-year sentence. He got

out after one year and is currently on licence… What's interesting is that his barrister was paid for by none other than Gregory Munro.'

Erika went back to the whiteboard and looked at Gary's photo. The officers leaned back in chairs and there was a silence as they chewed it over.

'Okay. So Gary Wilmslow's a scumbag. He's got a record as long as a crocodile's arse, but did he do this?' asked Erika, tapping the crime scene photos of Gregory Munro lying dead on his bed, arms bound to the headboard, his head misshapen through the plastic bag.

'Gary Wilmslow's also given us an alibi,' said Crane.

'He's taking the piss with that alibi: they all stayed in watching TV!' said Peterson, barely disguising his hatred.

'Okay, but remember he's out on licence and Penny is very protective. Please let's not jump to conclusions,' said Erika.

'Boss! Look at his record, he's more than capable. I say we bring him in.'

'I hear you, Peterson, but this murder was planned very carefully and executed with real skill, leaving virtually no forensic evidence. Gary Wilmslow is an angry little thug.' Erika took the file from Crane and flicked through. 'All of these crimes were spur of the moment – violent, impetuous outbursts of anger.'

'The motive of inheriting Gregory's money is very strong,' said Peterson. 'Three London properties, a medical practice. Have we looked into life insurance? Gregory Munro would most probably have damn good coverage. And then there was the personal hatred towards him. The means of entry could have been *staged*,' said Peterson.

'Okay, I hear you,' said Erika. 'But we need more evidence if we are going to bring him in.'

DC Warren stood up.

'Yes. What have you got?' asked Erika.

'Boss. We've had more stuff back from the lab. Four fibres have been lifted from the fence wire at the bottom of the garden; they are all from a piece of black clothing, a cotton Lycra mix. There's been no luck with lifting any bodily fluids, though.'

'What about behind the house? The railway line?'

'Um, there's a nature reserve,' Warren stuttered, unnerved by Marsh's silent presence watching from the back of the incident room. 'It's small, but it was created seven years ago by some local residents. It runs a quarter of a mile along the train tracks in the London-bound direction and then stops at Honor Oak Road before the train station... I've already requested CCTV from South West Trains on the night of the murder.'

'How far does the nature reserve go in the other direction?' asked Erika.

'A hundred yards past Gregory Munro's house, and it's a dead end. I've requested CCTV from the surrounding streets, although regular surveillance has been withdrawn from several of the cameras in the area.'

'Let me guess, austerity cuts?' asked Erika.

DC Warren again stuttered his response. 'Umm, I'm not sure of the exact reason...'

'I can't comprehend how the idiots in government think that getting rid of CCTV cameras is somehow helping to save money...' started Erika.

Marsh interrupted. 'DCI Foster, this is something that's happening all over London. There just aren't the resources to man the thousands of CCTV cameras across the capital.'

'Yes, and these same CCTV cameras were down eighteen months ago when we were trying to track down a killer. It would have saved thousands of hours of police time and resources if we'd had access to the images on just one camera...'

'I hear you, but this isn't the forum,' said Marsh. 'Now, I think you should continue.'

There was an awkward pause. Officers looked at the floor. Then Erika went on, 'Okay. Pull all the CCTV you can. See if there were any suspicious-looking characters hanging around. Anything: height, weight... If he arrived by train, bike, bus, car...'

'Yes, boss,' said DC Warren.

'How are we doing with the door-to-door, and pulling the bank and phone records of the victim?' asked Erika.

DC Singh stood up. 'Lots of people on Laurel Road are away on holiday, and plenty more were out on the night of the murder. With this weather, people have been going to parks and pubs after work, staying out late. Also, Gregory Munro's neighbours on either side are on holiday until the weekend.'

'So you're saying no one saw anything?' snapped Erika, impatiently.

'Erm, no...'

'Bloody hell. What else?'

'Gregory Munro had an annual salary of £200,000. This is partly due to him running one of the largest and most profitable GP surgeries in the south of England. No debt, apart from an eighty grand mortgage on the main residence in Laurel Road. He also owns a house in New Cross Gate, which he rents out to students, and the house in Shirley, where Penny Munro now lives. Phone records are fairly straightforward, nothing unusual. He did phone his wife three days before he was due to go away, as she stated. And all his records check out. He was flying to Nice to attend a conference with the BMA.'

'Was he a member of any gay sites or apps?'

'He did download the Grindr app a month ago. It was found on his phone, but he didn't complete the profile.'

'What about a solicitor? Who's dealing with the divorce?'

'I've left him several messages today. But he hasn't got back yet.'

'Okay, keep on him.'

'Yes, boss,' said Singh, sitting back down, looking despondent.

The officers watched Erika as she paced up and down in front of the whiteboards.

'It's Gary Wilmslow, boss. I think we should bite the bullet. Bring the scumbag in,' said Peterson.

'No. It's not enough right now that's he's a scumbag.'

'Boss!'

'No, Peterson. If and when we bring him in, I want to be sure and I want evidence to back it up, okay?'

Peterson sat back, shaking his head.

'You can shake your head all you want. Don't let your personal feelings cloud your judgement. When the time is right, if it's right, then we'll get him. Okay?'

Peterson nodded.

'Good. Now, has anyone else got anything for me?'

There was silence. Erika checked her watch.

'Okay… Let's refocus this on Gary Wilmslow, with an open mind. Someone check out his employer, and do some digging. Work your contacts.'

The incident room burst into chatter and Marsh came over. 'Erika, have you got time for a chat when you're done?'

'Yeah, I think we'll be a few more hours, sir.'

'No worries, give me a shout when you're done and we can grab a coffee,' said Marsh, moving off to the door.

'You want to buy me *two* coffees in one day?' muttered Erika suspiciously to herself. 'What's that all about?'.

CHAPTER 13

To Erika's surprise, Marsh took her to a frozen yoghurt bar down the road from Lewisham Row station. It had just opened a few days before and it was busy.

'I promised Marcie I would try this place out,' said Marsh, as they joined the queue in the garish neon pink-and-yellow interior.

'Is this to cheer me up? Or are you demonstrating that police budgets aren't all about austerity?' asked Erika.

'My office is at the top of the building. I needed to cool off,' he said. They reached a young girl in front of a humming yoghurt dispenser and Marsh ordered them each a large. They were handed a paper cup of yoghurt each and moved along to a self-service bar with an array of small dishes containing sweets, fruit and chocolate. Erika watched Marsh as he seriously contemplated the selection and then opted for Gummi Bears. She suppressed a grin, and chose fresh fruit.

'So, how are you settling in to your new flat?' asked Marsh once they had found a spot amongst the busy chatter, perched on high stools by a large picture window. Traffic crawled past as the heat shimmered off the melting tarmac. Across the street commuters poured out of the train station.

'I've been there for six months. It's quiet, which I like,' replied Erika, spooning the cold yoghurt into her mouth.

'You're not thinking of buying in London?' asked Marsh.

'I don't know. I'm starting to feel settled here, and in the job, but prices are crazy. Even a shit-hole round here costs a few hundred grand.'

'You're throwing your money away renting, and prices are only going to keep rising, Erika. If you're going to do it, do it soon. You've got your old place up in Manchester, chuck out your tenants and sell it. Get yourself on the property ladder down here.'

'Are you doling out real estate advice too now, sir?' grinned Erika.

Marsh didn't laugh. He shovelled in another spoonful of yoghurt. The multi-coloured Gummi Bears in the cup glistened in the sunlight.

'I want you to steer clear of Gary Wilmslow,' he said, abruptly changing the subject.

Erika was surprised. 'You were there in the incident room, sir. I'm not going to go after him until I have enough evidence.'

'I'm telling you not to go after him. At all. He is off-limits.' Marsh tilted his head down and looked at her over the top of his sunglasses.

'Can I ask why, sir?'

'No. As your senior officer, I'm telling you.'

'You know this kind of thing doesn't work with me. Keep me in the dark and I'll find the light switch.'

Marsh took another big spoon of yoghurt and rolled it around his mouth for a moment before swallowing. He took off his shades and placed them on the table.

'Jesus Christ. Okay. Have you heard of Operation Hemslow?'

'No.'

'Operation Hemslow is focusing on known funders and distributors of child pornography. Gary Wilmslow is heavily involved in a paedophile porn ring, and we're talking on a big scale: digital distribution through websites, and to a lesser extent the manufacture of DVDs. We've had our eye on him for the past eight months, but he's a slippery bastard. He's been under round-the-clock surveillance for the past five weeks.'

'And you need him out in the world, doing his business, so you can catch him doing his business?'

'Exactly.'

'But Peter, the nephew! He's living under the same roof!'

'It's okay. We're pretty sure Wilmslow isn't involved in the procuring of kids directly for the videos.'

'You're *pretty sure?*'

'We're confident.'

'Jesus,' said Erika, pushing her yoghurt away.

'I'm trusting you here, Erika. I'm giving you my confidence.'

'Okay, okay. But can't we get Peter out of there, and Penny too?'

'You know how seriously we take the safeguarding risks in these cases, but we don't have enough concrete evidence yet to give us grounds to take Peter into care. As I said, we've got Gary under round-the-clock surveillance. We'll know if he takes the kid.'

'So, because he is under surveillance, you know Gary Wilmslow didn't kill Gregory Munro?'

'Yeah. His alibi checks out. He was home all night.'

'And you're sure that Gregory Munro's murder is nothing to do with Gary Wilmslow, or Operation Hemslow?'

'Absolutely. We didn't even have Gregory Munro on our radar. Now, I expect you to find a way to lead your team in a different direction. If it were my case, I would go down the gay bashing route. Offload it onto one of the Murder Investigation Teams who specialise in sexually motivated murders.'

'I don't know that Gregory Munro's murder *was* sexually motivated. Right now all we've got is circumstantial evidence.'

'But it's circumstantial evidence there for the taking, Erika. Of course, it's your call, but you could do yourself a favour and offload it.'

'Haven't they got enough to deal with, sir?'

'Haven't we all?' he said, scraping the last of his yoghurt from the pot.

'This puts me back to square one,' said Erika, sitting in gloomy silence for a moment. She watched people stream past the glass window, happy in the summer sun.

'There's also a superintendent vacancy coming up,' said Marsh, swallowing.

Erika turned to him. 'I hope, if you haven't already done so, sir, that you'll be putting me forward. I've been a DCI rank long enough now and I deserve—'

'Hang on, hang on, you don't know where it is,' said Marsh.

'I don't care where it is.'

'You just said you were starting to feel settled!'

'I am, but I feel I've been overlooked lately. There was a superintendent post last year, it came and went, and you didn't...'

'I didn't think you were ready.'

'And what gives you the right to make that decision, Paul?' snapped Erika.

Marsh's eyebrows popped up above his sunglasses. 'Erika, you had only just returned to service after sustaining injuries resulting in major surgery, not to mention the trauma of...'

'I'd also successfully apprehended a killer of four and I handed the Met, on a plate, the leader of a gang of Romanians trafficking Eastern European women to England to work as prostitutes!'

'Erika, no one has your back more than me, but you need to learn to be tactical. To progress in the force you not only need to be a great copper, you need a bit of political nous. It wouldn't hurt to work on your relationship with Assistant Commissioner Oakley.'

'My track record should be enough, and I haven't got the time or inclination to go on some arse-kissing offensive with top brass.'

'It's not about going on an arse-kissing offensive. You just have to be more… user-friendly.'

'So, where is it, the superintendent position?'

'Here in the Met, based in New Scotland Yard, working in the Specialist Casework Investigation Team.'

'You'll put me forward, yes?' insisted Erika.

'Yeah.'

Erika gave him a look.

'I mean it, I will put you forward,' repeated Marsh.

'Thank you. So, even more of a reason for me to steer clear of Gary Wilmslow?'

'Yes,' Marsh said, tapping his spoon in the empty pot. 'Although, for selfish reasons I'd hate to lose you.'

'I'm sure you'll get over it,' said Erika with a wry grin.

Marsh's phone rang, deep in one of his pockets, and he wiped his mouth and pulled it out. When he answered, it quickly became apparent that it was his wife, Marcie.

'Shit,' he said, when he came off the phone. 'I didn't see the time. Tonight is date night. Marcie's mum has got the kids.'

'Sure, say hi to Marcie. I've got to be somewhere too,' Erika lied.

'Let's touch base tomorrow,' Marsh said. He left, and Erika watched as he came out onto the pavement and hailed a passing taxi. He got in and was already engrossed in his phone as the taxi pulled away.

Everywhere Erika looked people were enjoying the sunshine, walking in pairs, friends or couples. She took a big spoonful of yoghurt and sat back for a moment. She wondered if Marsh had played her, or if the promise of a promotion had been genuine. She thought of the Gregory Munro case, and how she was back to square one.

'Shit!' she said, loudly.

A couple of young girls sitting next to her in the window looked at each other and, picking up their frozen yoghurt, moved tables.

CHAPTER 14

NIGHT OWL: Hey, Duke.

DUKE: Jeez. You've been quiet. I've been worried.

NIGHT OWL: Worried?

DUKE: Yeah. I hadn't heard anything from u. I thought you'd been . . .

NIGHT OWL: Been what?

DUKE: You know. I don't want to type it.

NIGHT OWL: Arrested?

DUKE: Shit! Be careful.

NIGHT OWL: We're encrypted. It's cool.

DUKE: You never know who's watching.

NIGHT OWL: You're paranoid.

DUKE: I can think of worse things to be.

NIGHT OWL: What does that mean?

DUKE: Nothing. It means that I'm careful. Like you should be.

NIGHT OWL: I've been watching the papers, the news. They know nothing.

DUKE: Let's hope it stays that way.

NIGHT OWL: I need another one.

DUKE: Already?

NIGHT OWL: Yes. Time is moving fast. I'm watching the next one on my list. I want to do it soon.

DUKE: You sure?

NIGHT OWL: Positive. Can I trust you to organise things?

There was a pause. A bubble popped up, saying 'DUKE typing…' Then it vanished.

NIGHT OWL: U still there?
DUKE: Yeah. I'll do it.
NIGHT OWL: Good. I'll be waiting. This one won't know what's hit him.

CHAPTER 15

Darkness was falling as Erika stepped out of the shower. She wrapped herself in a towel and padded barefoot through to the bedroom, flicking on the light. She'd rented a small ground-floor flat in what was an old manor house in Forest Hill. It was tucked back from the main road on a leafy street. She'd been in the flat for six months, but it was still bare, as if she'd just moved in. The bedroom was clean but spartan.

Erika went to a chest of drawers and looked at her reflection in the gilt-framed mirror propped on top. The face staring back at her didn't exactly inspire confidence. Her short blonde hair stuck up in tufts and was shot through with grey. As a younger woman, she had never worried about her looks. She'd been blessed with an attractive Slavic face: high cheekbones, smooth skin and almond-shaped green eyes. But those same eyes were beginning to crease at the corners, her forehead bore too many lines and her face was beginning to sag.

She looked at a framed photo sitting by the mirror. A handsome, dark-haired man grinned back at her – her late husband Mark. His death was something she felt she would never get over, and this, coupled with the guilt that she was responsible for it, put a skewer through her heart many times each day. What she hadn't expected was how she would feel about ageing. It was as if they were moving even further apart in her mind. The image of him was frozen in her memories, in pictures. As the years passed, she would morph into an old lady, yet Mark would always be young and good-looking.

A few days ago, when she was driving to work, she'd heard the song 'Forever Young' by Alphaville on the radio. She'd had to pull the car over to try and gain control of her emotions.

Erika ran her fingers over the frame for a moment, tracing the outline of Mark's strong jaw, his nose and his warm brown eyes. She picked the picture up, feeling the weight of the frame in her hand. Opening the top drawer, she stared at her neatly folded underwear, and, lifting the first pile of garments, she went to tuck the framed photo underneath. She hesitated, and pulled her hand back. Closing the drawer, she placed the frame back on the polished wood surface.

In a couple of weeks it would be two years since Mark's death. A tear formed in her eye and then fell onto the wood with a soft pat. She wasn't ready to let him go. She dreaded the day she would be.

Erika wiped her face with the back of her hand and walked through to the living room. It was like the bedroom: neat and functional. A sofa and coffee table both faced a small television. A bookshelf lined the wall to the left of the patio windows and provided a dumping ground for takeaway leaflets, telephone directories and a paperback of *Fifty Shades of Grey* left by the previous tenant. Copies of the case files on Gary Wilmslow and Gregory Munro were open on the sofa, and the screen of Erika's laptop glowed on the coffee table. The more she read about Gary Wilmslow, the more frustrated she felt. Peterson was right: Gary had a strong motive to kill Gregory Munro, and now she'd been told not to go near him.

Erika grabbed her cigarettes and opened the patio door. The moon shone on the small communal garden outside: a neat square of grass, with the silhouette of an apple tree at the bottom. The neighbours were busy professionals like her and kept themselves to themselves. She pulled a cigarette from the pack and craned her head upwards, to see if any lights were on in the windows above. The brickwork stretched up four storeys and radiated heat back onto her face. As she lit her cigarette, she hesitated, noticing the large white box strapped to the building with HOMESTEAD SECURITY stamped on it in red letters.

Something sparked in the back of Erika's mind. She hurried back indoors. Clamping her cigarette between her teeth, she grabbed the file on Gregory Munro and started to flick through, passing witness statements, photos. The phone rang and she answered, clamping it under her chin so she could continue looking through the file.

'Hello Erika, it's me,' said Isaac.

'Yeah?' said Erika, her mind more on the case file than the phone call. 'Have you got more on the Gregory Munro murder?'

'No. This isn't a work call. I just wanted to apologise for the other night…I should have told you that Stephen would be there at dinner. I know I'd invited you, and you thought…'

'Isaac, what you do with your life is up to you,' said Erika, her mind only half on the conversation as she rifled through pictures of the rooms in Gregory Munro's house. Close-ups of the kitchen, the ready meal on the work surface… She *knew* she'd seen something in a photo, but she couldn't put her finger on it.

'Yes, but I'd like to make it up to you,' said Isaac. 'Would you like to come over for dinner on Thursday?'

Erika turned the page and stopped, staring at the photo.

'Are you still there?' asked Isaac.

'Yes… And yes, dinner would be great. I have to go,' she said, and before Isaac had the chance to reply, she hung up. Then she hurried to her bedroom and started to get dressed.

CHAPTER 16

Isaac had been talking to Erika on the phone beside his bed. When she'd gone, he sat back and stared at the receiver for a moment.

'She just, sort of, hung up on me. Well, maybe she didn't hang up, but she ended the call abruptly,' he said.

Stephen lay beside him, working on his laptop. 'I told you. She's a cold fish,' he replied as he typed.

Isaac watched the words for a moment as they streaked across the glowing screen. 'That's not fair, Stevie. She's damaged. She's still grieving for her husband, and on top of that she carries the guilt of his death around with her. She doesn't exactly work in the kind of environment that encourages you to show your feelings.'

'How predictable. What a cliché. The damaged female DCI, too busy for anyone but her work,' said Stephen, still typing.

'That's very harsh, Stevie.'

'*Life* is harsh.'

'What about the books you write? Your DCI Bartholomew character is damaged.'

Stephen looked up from his laptop.

'Yes, but DCI Bartholomew is far from a cliché. He's far more multi-layered than whatshername…'

'Erika.'

'He's an anti-hero. I've been praised for his originality, his flawed genius. I was nominated for a bloody Dagger Award!'

'Okay, I wasn't criticising, Stevie.'

'Well, don't lump my work in with your tragic copper friend.'

There was an awkward silence. Isaac began to collect up the empty chocolate bar wrappers which had pooled around Stephen on the duvet.

'I'd like you to get to know her,' Isaac said. 'She's not like that outside work. I'd like it if you could be friends. You heard me invite her for dinner.'

'Isaac, I've got a deadline. When that's passed, sure, I suppose I could have coffee with her,' said Stephen, still typing. 'She wasn't exactly nice to me when she came over. She should be the one making the effort, not me.'

Isaac nodded and regarded Stephen's beautiful face and naked torso. His skin was so smooth and perfect. It shimmered in the soft glow cast by the laptop. Deep down, Isaac knew that he was obsessed with Stephen, and that obsessions were destructive and dangerous, but he couldn't bear not to be with him. He couldn't bear to wake up and have the side of the bed next to him empty.

Stephen's brow furrowed as he typed.

'What are you doing, Stevie?'

'Just a bit of research. I'm in an Internet chat room, discussing suicide methods.' He looked up at Isaac. 'It's research for the new book, in case you get worried.'

'People go online and discuss suicide methods?' asked Isaac, crumpling the chocolate bar wrappers into a ball and peering over at the screen.

'Yeah. There are chat rooms for every kind of quirk and fetish – not that suicide is necessarily a fetish. These people are all seriously discussing the best methods to end it all – the most successful ways you can do it, without being disturbed. Listen to this...'

'I don't want to hear,' said Isaac. 'I've seen too many suicide cases: overdoses, hangings, slashed wrists, gruesome poisoning. The worst are the people who jump. Last week, I had to try and work out what was what on a teenage girl who had leapt off the Hammersmith flyover. She hit the pavement with such force that her jawbone was forced up into her brain.'

'Jesus,' said Stephen, looking up at him again. 'Can I use that?'

'What?'

'That's really good. I could use that in my book.'

'No!' Isaac felt stung.

Stephen went back to his typing. 'Oh, and don't look at my Google search history. It's full of questions like, *how long does it take the skin to putrefy when a dead body is buried in a lead-lined coffin?*'

'I could tell you that.'

'You just said you don't want to talk about work!'

'I can help you. I didn't say I wouldn't help you. I just don't want to talk about it *right now.*'

Stephen sighed and put his laptop on the bedside table. 'I'm going for a fag.' He picked up the packet of cigarettes and got up off the bed, moving over to the balcony doors.

'If you're going to go outside, put some clothes on,' said Isaac, eyeing the pair of small black briefs Stephen was wearing.

'Why? It's late. It's dark.'

'Because…This is Blackheath. My neighbours are respectable.' This wasn't exactly true. A handsome young man had moved in next door, who Isaac suspected was gay. He was terrified that the neighbour and Stephen might meet. After all, Stephen had left him once before.

'On the outside they might be respectable. Who knows what goes on behind closed doors?' teased Stephen.

'Please…' said Isaac leaning over to embrace him. Stephen rolled his eyes and ducked away, pulling on a T-shirt. He put a cigarette in his mouth and moved to the door. Isaac watched him as he went out onto the balcony: his tall athletic frame, the cigarette dangling from his pouty lips, how his underwear clung to his muscular buttocks.

In his work life, Isaac was peerless: a brilliant forensic pathologist with a distinguished career. He was in control of every aspect of his profession and he deferred to no one. In his private life, however, he was clueless. Stephen Linley turned his world upside down. Stephen was in control of their relationship and he was in control of Isaac's emotions. Isaac found that this both thrilled and unnerved him.

He reached over, grabbed Stephen's laptop. He saw the chat room text appearing in chunks and moving up the screen. He minimised the window, and it was replaced by the text of the new novel Stephen was writing. Stephen's novels were dark and violent. Isaac found reading them unpleasant, but he was drawn to them, and was ashamed to admit that he got a thrill from the dark violence, and from the way that Stephen could inhabit the minds of sadistic, brutal serial killers.

He was about to start reading when he realised he'd promised he wouldn't read anything until it was finished. He replaced Stephen's laptop and went out on the balcony, like an eager dog missing its owner.

CHAPTER 17

Laurel Road was quiet and still when Erika inserted the key in the lock of Gregory Munro's house and pulled the crime scene seal away from the door. She turned the key and gave the door a shove, separating the remains of the sticky seal. She stepped into the hallway. There was an urgent beeping noise, and she saw, glowing in the darkness, the panel for the alarm system.

'Shit,' she muttered. She hadn't anticipated that after forensics had completed their work the house would be left alarmed. She stared at the screen, knowing she had only a few seconds before uniformed officers would be summoned, followed by the distraction of paperwork, where she would have to justify her presence. She keyed in the combination 4291 and the alarm deactivated. It was the fail-safe number often used to reset the alarms at crime scenes. It might not be the most secure way of doing things, but it saved a fortune in call-out fees.

It was stiflingly hot, and the rancid meaty smell of Gregory Munro's dead body still hung faintly in the darkness. Erika flicked on a switch and the hallway lit up, the light petering out as the stairs rose into darkness. She wondered how the house would feel to someone who didn't know it was a crime scene. To her, it still seemed to reverberate with violence.

She moved past the stairs and through to the kitchen, turning on the lights. She found what she had seen in the photo: a corkboard beside the fridge. Pinned to it were several takeaway menus, a handwritten shopping list, and a flyer for a security company: GUARDHOUSE ALARMS.

Erika unpinned the leaflet from the corkboard. The design looked professional, but it was printed on ordinary inkjet printer paper. The background was black with 'GuardHouse Alarms' written on it in red. The 'H' of 'House' morphed upwards into an image of a ferocious German shepherd. Underneath this was a phone number and email address. Erika turned the flyer over. Written in blue biro near the bottom was: MIKE, 21ST JUNE 6.30PM.

Erika pulled out her mobile and dialled the number. There was silence, and then a high-pitched tone and an automated voice told her the number was no longer in service. Erika went to the large glass sliding door at the back of the house and, after fiddling with the handle, it yielded with a whoosh. She stepped out onto the terrace. On the back wall of the house above the glass was a white security alarm box with HOMESTEAD SECURITY stamped on it in red letters, the same as the box on the wall of her flat.

She came back inside and called Crane. When he answered, she could hear the sound of a television blaring in the background.

'Sorry to call so late. It's DCI Foster. Can you talk?' she asked.

'Hang on,' he said. There was a rustle and then the noise of the television receded.

'Sorry. Is this a bad time, Crane?'

'No, it's okay. You just saved me from *The Real Housewives of Beverly Hills*. Karen, my girlfriend, is mad on it, but I have aggro all day at work. I don't enjoy watching crazy housewife aggro when I get home. Anyway, what can I do you for, boss?'

'Gregory Munro. I've read through his phone records. It says he made a call to a security firm – GuardHouse Alarms Limited – on the 19th of June.'

'Hang on, I'll just wake up my laptop. Yes, GuardHouse Alarms. It was one of the numbers I chased up this morning.'

'And what?'

'I left a message on their answerphone, then a guy called me back to confirm that someone called Mike had made a home visit. He'd checked and all the alarm systems and security lights were sound and working.'

'What did the guy sound like?'

'I don't know, normal. Whatever that is these days. He did have a twang to his voice, a sort of posh know-it-all type. Why?'

'I've just called the number and it doesn't exist. It's been disconnected,' said Erika.

'What?' There was a pause and she heard Crane's keyboard tapping. Then a tinny ping.

'I just sent an email to the address on the flyer and it bounced back. Mail delivery subsystem error, could not be delivered,' said Crane.

Erika stepped back out into the dark garden and stared up into the gloom to the HOMESTEAD SECURITY box fixed to the wall.

'Jesus, boss. You think this was the killer?'

'Yeah. This leaflet must have been hand-delivered, and presumably Gregory Munro contacted the number and organised for this Mike to come over…'

'Mike was invited in and got to case the joint, gaining access to the layout, the alarm systems, security lights, everything,' finished Crane.

'And it's likely you spoke to Mike today. He called you back on the GuardHouse Alarms phone number.'

'Shit. What do you want me to do, boss?'

'We need a trace on that phone and the email address, asap.'

'I can bet you it's a pre-paid, but I can have a crack at tracking it.'

'We'll need to re-interview the residents on Laurel Road and get details of all delivery people who've been seen here, in particular if they saw this Mike arriving on the 21st June.'

'Okay, boss. I can run some stuff through the computer now. I'll keep you posted.'

'Thanks,' said Erika. There was a click on the line as Crane hung up. She walked to the back fence, the dry grass crisp under her feet. It was still and silent. There was a faint sound of a car in the distance, and the hum of crickets. She jumped as a train blared out of the silence, clattering past on the track at the bottom of the garden.

She moved closer to the fence and crouched down under the tree, examining where the fence had been neatly clipped. Pulling the wire to one side, Erika crawled through the gap. She came up through some long, dry grass onto a path. She stood for a moment in the warmth of the evening, letting her eyes adjust to the darkness. She crossed the narrow dirt path, moved through a gap in the tall trees and came out onto the railway line. She could see where the track stretched away into the distance. She came back to the path and pulled out her phone, activating her torch app and training the light left and right. The path was illuminated for a few feet and then vanished amongst trees and darkness. Erika crouched down under the tree at the end of the garden and looked at the house. It seemed to stare back at her: the two dark upstairs windows were like eyes.

'Did you watch from here?' Erika said softly to herself. 'How long were you here? How much did you see? You're not going to get away with this. I'm coming for you.'

CHAPTER 18

It was barely mid-morning, but already the sun was beating down relentlessly. The front lawns along a row of red-brick terraced houses were burnt in varying shades of yellow. The rush hour was over, and apart from a plane scratching its way across the clear blue sky the road was quiet.

Simone had stopped at the supermarket on her way back from her night shift at the hospital, and now she was walking along the pavement weighed down by several carrier bags. The plastic was digging almost unbearably into her palms, and she was pouring with sweat under her thick jacket. The scar tissue across her stomach was sore and inflamed from the sweat and from her uniform rubbing. She reached the crumbling terraced house at the end of the row and pushed against the gate. It caught on the concrete path, and she threw her weight angrily against it, once, twice, before it yielded unexpectedly and she lurched through, almost losing her balance.

She hurried to the front door, muttering curses, before dropping the bags on the front step with a clunk. She held up her hands, criss-crossed with deep red grooves. A neighbour emerged from the house next door. She was an elderly lady wearing a smart dress. As she locked her front door, she eyed Simone, searching in her coat pockets for her keys. The neighbour's eyes flicked to the crumbling fence between their gardens, and over Simone's burnt front lawn, which was littered with an old washing machine, empty paint cans and a heap of rotting brambles. Her eyes came back to Simone, who was now standing still, facing her.

'Ah, good morning, Mrs Matthews,' said the neighbour. Simone didn't answer; she just stared with large, cold blue eyes. The neighbour found that the gaze made her uneasy. The eyes were dead, without emotion, and set a little too far apart. 'Lovely day…'

Simone glared at the neighbour until she hurried away.

'Nosy bitch,' muttered Simone, before turning and pushing the key into the lock. The hallway was dingy and piled with old newspapers. Simone dragged in the shopping bags and threw her keys on the old, wooden hall table. She turned and closed the front door. It had once been beautiful, that door, with coloured glass in a diamond pattern. On sunny days it would cast a mosaic of soft colours on the pale hall carpet. It was now boarded up, with just a few of the blue diamonds visible at the top, above the piece of wood that was nailed to the door frame.

Simone turned from locking the door and her throat closed in fear. A man stood in the middle of the hall. His mouth hung open and his eyes were clouded over with white. He was naked and water dripped off his pale doughy skin.

She staggered back, feeling the door handle press into her back. She closed her eyes and opened them again. He was still there. Water now poured off him in thin rivulets, over the swell of his huge hairy belly, and the small pale stub of his genitals. The carpet below him was now a darkened circle as the water began to run off him faster. Simone closed her eyes tight, and opened them again. He was coming towards her, staggering along the carpet, his long yellow toenails catching on the carpet. She could smell his breath. Rancid onion mixed with stale booze.

'NO!' she cried, closing her eyes and slamming her fists against her face. 'YOU CAN'T HURT ME, STAN! YOU'RE DEAD!'

She opened her eyes.

The hall was back as it was before: grubby and gloomy, but empty. Another plane scratched its way across the sky, the sound muffled, and she could hear her own laboured breathing.

He'd gone.

For now.

CHAPTER 19

It was on a hot sticky afternoon, a week after the discovery of Gregory Munro's body, that Erika was summoned to attend a progress meeting about the Gregory Munro case at Lewisham Row. The investigation had ground to a halt, and her conviction in her abilities had taken a knock, so she went in feeling less than confident.

The meeting was held in the plush conference room on the top floor, and in attendance were Detective Chief Superintendent Marsh, Colleen Scanlan, the matronly Met Police media liaison officer, Tim Aiken, a young criminal psychologist, and Assistant Commissioner Oakley, who sat imperiously at the head of the long conference table. Oakley never tried to hide his dislike for Erika. He had neat, sly features, and his steel-coloured hair was always immaculately groomed, reminding Erika of a sleek fox. However, the heat had taken away a little of his sleekness today. His usually immaculate hair was soaked in sweat, and he had been forced to remove his Met Police jacket, with its epaulettes sewn with the ornate symbol of his rank, and sit with his sleeves rolled up.

Erika opened the meeting, detailing how the case had progressed so far.

'Boosted by the discovery that our killer engineered a pre-visit to Gregory Munro's house, my officers have been working round the clock examining hundreds of hours of CCTV from the cameras in and around Honor Oak Park train station. The residents of Laurel Road have been re-interviewed, but no one remembers seeing a representative from the fictitious Guard-House Alarms. The company itself doesn't exist. The email address on the leaflet was fake, and the phone number was from an untraceable prepaid phone.'

Looking around the conference table, Erika realised that the meeting was a make or break opportunity to retain the large amount of manpower she'd been assigned. In addition to the pressure she was feeling, the air conditioning had broken, leading to an uncomfortable sticky atmosphere.

She went on, 'I am aggressively pursuing every detail of Gregory Munro's personal life. I believe he knew or had previously met his attacker, and that his private life could unlock the identity of the killer. But with a case of this complexity, I will need more time.'

'The victim's brother-in-law, Gary Wilmslow, is also under investigation for unrelated crimes, which are part of Operation Hemslow,' interrupted Oakley.' I trust that the two investigations will remain separate, and officers on the Munro murder will be kept away from Operation Hemslow?'

'Yes, sir. That's all under control,' said Marsh, giving Erika a look. There was silence as all eyes around the table stared back at her. Marsh changed the subject. 'What about the presence of gay pornography at the murder scene? I understand that Gregory Munro had downloaded a gay dating app on his mobile phone?'

Marsh had already discussed this with Erika. She realised that he was asking the question for Oakley's benefit.

'Yes, sir. There were some gay porn magazines and he'd downloaded the Grindr gay dating app, but he hadn't activated it. There were no contacts or messages,' replied Erika.

'So the victim was potentially engaging in homosexual be-haviours, anonymous meetings with men?' said Oakley.

'There is no evidence, beyond a few dog-eared gay porn magazines, to show Gregory Munro was acting on any homo-sexual impulses,' said Erika.

'Why haven't you considered investigating the gay cruising areas around London? Public lavatories? Parks?' pressed Oakley.

'I have considered them, sir. We know of several areas, but they're not covered by CCTV. My officers are stretched to the limit dealing with the evidence we *do* have, without going off to make general enquiries in the bushes...'

'He was a married man with homosexual desires. I can't see why this hasn't been your main line of enquiry, DCI Foster?'

'As I said, sir, we have several lines of enquiry. I would need more officers, if I was to start...'

'You already have a large team, DCI Foster. Perhaps we should talk about how you are using your resources, before you come cap in hand for more?'

'I can assure you, sir, that every one of my officers is being used to the best of their ability.'

Oakley picked up one of the crime scene photos of Gregory Munro and studied it. 'Violence in the gay community is often linked intrinsically with sexual desire. Don't men like this seek out clandestine encounters? Invite dangerous men into their houses?'

'We obviously know different kinds of gay men, sir,' Erika shot back. There was silence around the table.

'It's the heat; it's getting to us all, sir,' said Marsh, glaring at Erika.

Oakley scowled and took a neatly folded handkerchief from his pocket and pressed it to his face, wiping under his sweaty hairline. The way he gently lifted his fringe made Erika suddenly wonder if he wore a wig. A 'syrup'. The word popped into her head. Syrup… Syrup of figs… wig… She remembered Mark telling her about cockney rhyming slang when she'd first come to England, and how much it had made her laugh.

'Is something funny, DCI Foster?' asked Oakley, as he tucked the handkerchief back into his pocket.

'No, sir,' said Erika getting a hold of herself.

'Good, because alongside the issue of manpower levels the media has seized upon your failure to find a suspect as another reason to give the Met Police a good kicking. First the local, and now the national newspapers.' He indicated the papers in the centre of the conference room table, which bore the headlines: '**SUPER GP KILLED IN BED**' and '**POLICE STILL HUNTING KILLER OF TOP DOC**'. 'You've been rather quiet, Colleen, what can you add to this?'

'I am working…' started Colleen and paused.

She was going to say, 'robustly' thought Erika.

'I'm working very hard to ensure that my press team steers the media in the correct direction. Of course, there is little new evidence to give them,' she added, trying to throw the blame back onto Erika.

'It isn't our job to keep spoon-feeding journalists. I think it was a little premature to release information this early,' said Erika. 'We should have been at least two steps ahead and ready with more information. Now they've gone and done exactly what I thought they'd do and found their own angle, linking this case to the austerity cuts by the government.'

'Yes, where did they get this quote, DCI Foster?' asked Oakley, picking up one of the newspapers. '"Across London, 14,000 CCTV cameras are no longer in use; police don't have the man-hours to effectively keep residents of the capital safe." You've been rather vocal about the lack of CCTV cameras, haven't you?'

'Are you suggesting that I've been briefing the press about this case, sir?'

'No, the Assistant Commissioner is not suggesting that,' interrupted Marsh.

'Now, Paul, I can speak for myself,' snapped Oakley. 'What I'm saying is that it doesn't do to start fear-mongering, DCI Foster. You lead and influence a vast number of officers. Your team has been given a great deal of manpower for this murder investigation. I just don't think it's good for morale if you are constantly harping on about what you haven't got. How many more officers do you believe you require?'

'Sir, I am not being negative, and I don't harp,' said Erika.

'How many?'

'Five. I have prepared a paper for you which details exactly how I will use—'

'A week has passed since the murder of Gregory Munro, and I need to ensure that manpower is being properly deployed,' interrupted Oakley.

'Yes, sir, but—'

'I would strongly advise that you refocus our investigation, DCI Foster, working on the assumption that Gregory Munro invited a man into his house for the purpose of sexual intercourse, and that this man, whomever he was, saw an opportunity and killed him. A crime of passion.'

'A gay bashing?' said Erika.

'I don't like that phrase, DCI Foster.'

'But the press loves it. And the gay community will, no doubt, experience a backlash of negativity if we refocus the investigation with that angle. We also found evidence of forced entry through the kitchen window, and the fence at the rear of the property had been clipped. It doesn't sound like Gregory Munro invited whoever did this into his house. The fake security firm leaflet is our strongest lead. This is summer holiday season. We haven't yet spoken to all of the Laurel Road residents because some are still away on holiday. We're also going through the list of complaints from Gregory Munro's patients. Again, this is taking time.'

'Have any complaints proved to be a worthwhile lead so far?' asked Oakley.

'As of yet, no, but…'

'I'd like to hear from our criminal profiler,' said Oakley, cutting her off yet again. 'Tim?'

Tim Aiken, the criminal psychologist, had remained silent until now. He had a short, shiny mop of hair, designer stubble and, despite his shirt and tie, wore a thick bunch of multicoloured woven bracelets on his wrist. He looked up from where he had been doodling a series of cubes in his notebook. 'I think the man we're looking for is a very controlled individual. He plans every move very carefully. Physically, he's strong. Gregory Munro wasn't a small man and there was little evidence of a struggle.'

'Gregory Munro was drugged; he had a huge dose of flunitrazepam in his body. Flunitrazepam is used as a date rape drug. Whoever broke in made time to drug him, and then waited for the drug to take effect,' added Erika.

'Yes. There is also widespread use of flunitrazepam in the gay community for a sexual high, for enjoyment,' replied Tim.

'I doubt many people who've had it slipped into their drink in a bar enjoyed themselves,' said Erika.

Tim went on, 'The killer could have been very intuitive, using a honeypot method with the security leaflet to lure the victim into calling him. Coupled with the use of a sedative, we shouldn't rule out the possibility of a homosexual element.'

'Gregory Munro wasn't sexually assaulted,' said Erika.

'True, but our killer may have had issues with masculinity, and previous bad experiences with type A, or alpha males. He may want to suppress masculine individuals.'

'Bloody hell. How much is he costing us?' asked Erika when the meeting had ended, a sticky, uncomfortable forty minutes later. She was walking down the stairs from the conference room with Marsh.

'Don't hold much stock in forensic profiling?'

'I think it can be helpful, but so often they're called in and seen as miracle workers. Forensic profilers don't catch criminals, we do.'

'Don't complain. He works for you, remember. He talked Oakley out of cutting your budget.'

'Only by blinding him with science.'

'You don't seem pleased?'

'I'll be pleased when we catch whoever did this,' said Erika. 'Tim didn't really tell us anything we don't know already. Although the whole thing about alpha males is an interesting theory. But how do we put that to good use? It's so broad. We can't put every aggressive dominant male under surveillance. The world is full of them.'

Marsh rolled his eyes. 'You could do yourself a favour by trying to build bridges with Oakley.'

'I didn't pull him up on his homophobic attitude, that's a start. And anyway, what's the point? He's never going to like me, sir. I'm never going to be on his Christmas card list.'

They had reached the landing for Marsh's office. 'Keep me in the loop, okay?' he said, as he made to go through the double doors.

'Before you go, sir, any more news about the superintendent post up for grabs?'

Marsh stopped and turned back to face her.

'I've already said I'll be putting you forward, Erika.'

'Have you informed Oakley that you intend to put me forward?'

'Yes.'

'And what did he say?'

'I can't go into details about the process, you know that. Now, I have to go.' Marsh turned to go back through the doors.

'One more thing, sir. What's happening with Peter Munro living under the same roof as Gary Wilmslow? I'm concerned for his welfare.'

Marsh stopped and turned back.

'For the past week, Peter has only left the house with his mother to go to school. We have several of the rooms inside bugged. As far as we know, he's fine. And Gary Wilmslow is old-school working class. He talks about honour and family and all that. He wouldn't let anyone touch one of his own.'

'You've been watching too much *Eastenders*, sir. Let's hope you're right.'

'I am right,' said Marsh, icily, and disappeared though the double doors to his office.

'I seem to be *so* popular with everyone. All I'm trying to do is my bloody job,' Erika muttered to herself, as she carried on down the flights of stairs.

When she reached the incident room, the ceiling fans were working overtime, but they only seemed to be circulating the heat and the smells of coffee and body odour.

'Boss, I've just heard from uniform division; the neighbours living opposite Gregory Munro's house are back from holiday,' said Peterson, putting down his phone.

Moss was sitting opposite Peterson, her face red from the heat as she came off a call. 'That was Estelle Munro. She says that Gregory Munro's General Medical Council certificate is missing from 14 Laurel Road.'

'When did we hand the house back to the family?' asked Erika.

'Yesterday. I've been through the forensics log, and everything we took away. There is no mention of a GMC certificate.'

'Which means the killer could have taken it. Shit. How could we have missed this?'

CHAPTER 20

When Erika, Moss and Peterson arrived at Laurel Road, it was balmy and quiet. The sun had sunk down far enough so that the houses on Gregory Munro's side were in the shade.

A cluster of men and women in office clothes rounded the end of the road with flushed faces, the men with their sleeves rolled up, carrying their jackets. It was just after five-thirty and Erika realised this was the first wave of commuters returning from work in Central London.

She rang the bell at number 14. Moments later, Estelle Munro opened the door. She was dressed in pale slacks, a smart white blouse covered in a pattern of roses, and a pair of yellow Marigolds.

'Hello, Mrs Munro. We're here about the medical certificate,' said Erika.

'Yes,' was all she said. She stepped back and they filed in. Erika recognised the zesty, lemony smell of cleaning products, which mingled with an overpowering scent of synthetic blossom. It was, however, cool inside the house. The windows were all shut and the air conditioning hummed throughout.

'It was in Gregory's office,' said Estelle, closing the front door and locking it. Erika noticed she'd had the locks changed: a gleaming new Yale and two new bolts.

They followed Estelle up the stairs, moving slowly behind her as she breathed heavily.

'How are things?' asked Erika.

'I'm still cleaning up the mess your lot left,' Estelle snapped.

'We do try to treat the crime scene with as much respect as we can, but a great number of people are involved, all coming into the property at once,' said Moss.

'And all these people, are they any closer to finding who killed my son?'

'We are pursuing several leads,' said Erika.

They reached the top of the stairs. Estelle paused to catch her breath, resting a Marigold-gloved hand on her hip. The heavy curtains covering the hall window had been removed, and it was much brighter on the landing.

'When will my son's body be released, DCI Fosset?' Estelle asked.

'It's DCI Foster…'

'Because I have a funeral to arrange,' Estelle said, teasing off the gloves, finger by finger.

'We'll have to check who our first contact is in the family before passing on any details, I'm afraid,' said Moss.

Estelle's face clouded over even more. 'Gregory was my son. I carried him in my belly for nine months. You will phone *me* first, do you understand? Penny was only married to him for four years. I was his mother for forty-six…' She took a deep breath to compose herself. 'She phoned me up, Penny. Demanding to know when *the body* was being released. "The body"! Not "Gregory" or "Greg" – he hated being called Greg. Penny wants to book the Shirley football club for the wake. A football club! No doubt Gary and his hooligan friends will *get a good deal.*'

'I'm sorry to hear that, Mrs Munro.'

Estelle stepped into the bathroom and ran her hands under the tap. She came back out drying them on a small towel. 'I've had Gary on the phone today, threatening me.'

'Threatening you?' asked Erika.

'Gregory altered his will when he and Penny separated. We've just found out that he left the house to me, and his rental properties in trust to Peter.'

'What about Penny?'

Estelle shot Erika a look. 'What about her? She'll get the four-bedroom house in Shirley. It's worth plenty. Gary was abusive on the phone, he said Penny was owed this house and that I'm to sign it over to her *or else…*'

'Or else what?' asked Erika.

'Oh, use your imagination, DCI Fosset. Or else I'll be dealt with. He'll send the lads round. A car might plough into me on my way home from the shops. I take it you've read Gary's criminal record?'

A look passed between Erika, Moss and Peterson.

Estelle went on, 'I've changed the locks, but I'm still worried.'

'I can assure you that Gary Wilmslow will not cause you any harm,' said Erika.

Estelle's eyes filled with tears and she scrabbled around for a tissue. Peterson was on hand again, and produced a pack from his pocket.

'Thank you,' she said, gratefully.

Erika signalled to Moss and they left Peterson to reassure Estelle. They moved along the corridor to the small bedroom Gregory Munro had used as his home office.

A heavy, dark wood desk was squeezed in against the window, and opposite were a set of shelves with the same dark wood finish. The shelves were filled with a mixture of medical books and paperback novels. Erika noted that Gregory Munro had three of the DCI Bartholomew crime novels written by Stephen Linley.

'Shit!' she said.

'What is it, boss?'

'Nothing…' Erika remembered her conversation with Isaac last week, and that she'd agreed to dinner with him tonight. She looked at her watch and saw it was approaching six.

Estelle shuffled back into the room, followed by Peterson.

'It was here,' Estelle said, pointing to the wall behind the desk where there hung two gold picture frames. One was filled with photos: Gregory and Penny cutting their wedding cake; Penny holding a pair of sunglasses on their cat's unimpressed face; Penny in a hospital bed, clutching what must have been Peter when he was born, with Gary, Estelle and Penny's bespectacled mother standing awkwardly either side. The other frame was empty.

'I asked Penny if she had it, but for once I think she's being truthful when she says no,' said Estelle, pointing to the empty frame. 'If it was the television or the DVD player she'd have had it, but not this.'

Erika went over to the empty frame, pulling on a pair of latex gloves. She lifted it off the wall, finding it was very light and made of plastic.

'Have you touched this at all, Mrs Munro?'

'No, I haven't,' she said.

Erika turned the frame over, but couldn't see anything.

'We should call in a fingerprint technician. It's a long shot, but…'

'Okay, boss,' said Moss. She pulled out her radio and placed a call; a voice came back saying no one was available.

Erika grabbed the radio. 'This is DCI Foster. I need someone today, now, as soon as you can. This is new evidence which we've found at the 14 Laurel Road crime scene, SE23.'

There was a pause and a couple of beeps.

'We've just got a technician finishing up on a burglary over at Telegraph Hill, I'll radio for her to come over as soon as she's finished. Although can you authorise overtime?' replied the tinny voice through the radio.

'Yes. I authorise overtime,' Erika snapped.

'Okay,' came the voice.

Erika replaced the frame on the wall and removed the gloves. 'Okay, so we've got a little wait. Moss, you come with me. Let's talk to this neighbour who's back from holiday. Mrs Munro, would it be okay if DI Peterson waited with you?'

'Yes. Would you like a cup of tea, dear?' asked Estelle.

Peterson nodded.

The neighbours were a couple in their late thirties: a white woman called Marie and a black man called Claude. Their house, opposite number 14, was smart and stylish, and they had an urban coolness about them. The hall was still filled with several brightly coloured suitcases, and they ushered Erika and Moss through to their kitchen. Marie grabbed some glasses and filled them with water and ice from the dispenser in the door of a large stainless steel fridge. She handed Moss and Erika a glass each. Erika took a long drink, savouring the coolness.

'We were shocked to hear about Dr Munro,' said Marie, when they were settled around the kitchen table. 'I know this area isn't the nicest, but murder!' Claude sat next to her and she reached out and grabbed his hand. He squeezed hers reassuringly in return.

'I can understand how harrowing it must be. Although we do stress that, statistically, murder cases are still extremely rare,' added Erika.

'Well, statistically, a bloke being knocked off in his bed a few doors down is one too many!' said Claude, rolling his eyes.

'Of course,' said Erika.

'We need to ask if you've noticed anyone unusual hanging around?' asked Moss. 'Anything, however small… In particular, on the 21st of June between 5 p.m. and 7 p.m.'

'It's not that kind of street, love,' said Marie. 'We're all too busy working and living to peer out of the window at our neighbours.'

'Would you have been in that day, between 5 p.m. and 7 p.m.?' asked Erika.

'That was around four weeks ago…' Marie started.

'Yes, it was a Tuesday,' replied Moss.

'I'd have still been at work. I'm an accountant in the City,' said Marie.

'I finish work earlier, and I work locally for the council,' added Claude. 'If it was a Tuesday, I'd have been at the gym. Fitness First, down the road in Sydenham. They can vouch for me, we have to swipe a card to get in.'

'It's okay. You're not suspects,' said Erika. 'Did you know Gregory Munro well?'

They shook their heads.

'He was always pleasant and polite, though,' added Claude. 'He was our GP, but we never had to go. I think we saw him once, a few years back, when we registered.'

Erika and Moss exchanged a despondent glance.

'There is one thing,' started Claude. He took a sip of his iced water and rolled it around his mouth thoughtfully. Condensation dripped off the glass onto the wooden table.

'Anything at all, however small,' said Moss.

'Oh, yes,' agreed Marie. 'Yes, I've seen them too.'

'Seen who?' asked Erika.

'There seemed to be quite a few handsome young men in and out of Dr Munro's house in the past few weeks,' said Claude.

Erika looked at Moss. 'Can you be more specific?'

'You know, muscly types,' said Marie. 'I thought the first one was some sort of hunky workman that Dr Munro had employed, but then the next day a different young man knocked on the door and went in. He was so good-looking. Sort of high-end good-looking, if you know what I mean.'

'Like a rent boy?'

'Yeah. And they only seemed to stay for an hour or so,' added Claude.

'What time was this?'

'The first two were on weekdays. I can't remember which days. I was coming home from work, so around seven-thirty… Dr Munro sort of hustled the first guy inside when he saw me passing, just said a quick hello. And then an hour or so later, we'd just had our supper and I was in the living room and I saw him leave,' said Marie.

'And the others?' asked Erika.

'There was one on a Saturday morning, I think? Didn't you see him leaving early, Claude?' asked Marie.

'Yeah, the window from our upstairs loo looks down on the street; I was having a pee when I saw this young chap leaving early, around seven on a Saturday morning,' said Claude.

'And didn't you think it was odd?' asked Moss.

'Odd? This is London, and it was before we knew he'd spilt up with his wife… It could have been a friend, a colleague, a medical student, or even a manny – you know, a male nanny,' said Claude.

'Do you think one of these men, you know, killed him?' asked Marie.

'I'm going to be honest with you: we don't know. This is one of several leads.'

It hung in the air for a moment. Marie rubbed at the condensation on her glass. Claude put a protective arm around her.

'Would you be willing to do a police e-fit? If we can get a likeness of these young men it could be very valuable,' said Erika. 'We can get someone over tonight, to do it in the comfort of your home?'

'Yes, of course,' said Claude. 'If it helps you catch whoever did this.'

Moss and Erika came back out into the baking street and moved across to the shady side.

'I call that a result,' said Moss.

'And, with any luck, we could have a photo fit this evening,' agreed Erika. She pulled out her phone and called Peterson for an update.

'Nothing yet, boss,' he said. 'The fingerprint technician still isn't finished over in Telegraph Hill. Estelle Munro has gone out for more milk… I don't have a key to this place, so I can't secure it.'

'Okay, we're on our way,' said Erika. She hung up, tucked her phone back in her bag and looked at her watch. It was gone seven.

'You need to be somewhere?' asked Moss.

'I'm supposed to be going for dinner, with Isaac Strong.'

'I can stay here with Peterson if you want to scoot off. It looks like this is going to be a long boring one. I doubt we'll get any prints off the frame, but I can let you know as soon as, and I'll keep you posted on the photo fit.'

'Don't you want to be getting home, Moss?'

'I'm fine. Celia's taking Jacob to mother-and-baby swimming so I've got the evening, I know you don't get out…' Her voice trailed off.

'You know I don't get out much?'

'I didn't mean it like that, boss,' said Moss, going redder than she already was.

'I know. It's okay.' Erika chewed her lip and squinted at Moss in the sun.

'Honestly, boss, the millisecond we lift a print, I'll call. And the e-fit might take a few hours. What's Isaac cooking?'

'I don't know.'

'By the time you've eaten whatever it is we'll have a some answers.'

'Okay. Thank you, Moss. I owe you one. You phone me the second something happens, however small, okay?'

'I promise, boss,' said Moss. She watched as Erika went back to her car and drove off, and hoped that they would find something to further the investigation.

It looked like DCI Foster needed a breakthrough.

CHAPTER 21

'Next week will be the longest day of the year, and then the nights will begin to draw in,' said Simone. She stood by the small window in Mary's hospital room. It looked down over a cluster of industrial rubbish bins and the incinerator. The brick walls of the surrounding buildings loomed high, closing in on them, but a sliver of the London skyline blazed through a gap in the brickwork. The yellow orb of the sun looked as if it were about to be skewered on the spire of the clock tower above King's Cross station.

Simone came over to the bed, where Mary lay with her eyes closed, the blanket pulled up to her chin. It barely moved with her shallow breathing, and her body seemed to taper away to nothing under the blanket. Simone's shift had ended an hour ago, but she'd decided to stay on. Mary was fading fast. It wouldn't be long now.

She took the black and white photograph of Mary and George out of the locker and propped it up against a water jug.

'There, we're all here together. Me, you and George,' said Simone, reaching through the safety bar to take Mary's hand. 'You look so happy in the photo, Mary. I wish you could tell me about him. He looks quite the lad… I've never had a close girlfriend to talk to. My mother never talked about sex, only to tell me it was filthy. I know she was wrong. It's not filthy.

When coupled with love it must be perfect... Was it perfect with George?'

Simone turned to the photo. George's handsome face squinted at the sun; his strong arm gripped Mary's slim waist.

'Did you enjoy nights out? Did he take you dancing? Did he see you safely home in the dark?'

Simone took out a hairbrush and gently began to brush Mary's hair with soft whooshing strokes.

'The darkness scares me, Mary. It's the time when I feel most alone.'

The whooshing sound of the brush was soothing as it moved through Mary's fine silvery hair. Her skin was pale, almost translucent in places, and a thin blue vein threaded its way across her temple to her hairline. Simone lifted the old lady's head so she could reach the back with the hairbrush.

Whoosh, whoosh, whoosh.

'My marriage isn't happy. Things have never been good, but a few years ago it got worse. So I moved into the spare room...'

Whoosh, whoosh, whoosh.

'It didn't stop him. He comes to me at night. I've tried barricading the door, but he forces his way in...'

Whoosh, whoosh.

'Forces himself inside me.'

Whoosh.

'It hurts. He hurts me...'

Whoosh, whoosh.

'He enjoys hurting me, and he never stops. Never. Stops. Until. He's. Satisfied!'

There was a rhythmic, dull thudding. It took Simone a moment to realise the hairbrush was caught in a tangle. Mary's head was thudding against the metal safety rail of the bed, as Simone tugged furiously at the brush.

Simone let go and stepped back. Blood was roaring in her head, her hands were shaking. Mary lay drunkenly on her side, an eyelid half open where it was pressed against the metal safety rail.

'Oh, Mary!' Simone leaned over and unhooked the brush from the clump of hair at the back of Mary's head. She gently rolled her back to a lying position and tucked the blankets back around her. A bruise was forming under the thin skin of her temple.

'I'm sorry. Oh, Mary, I'm so sorry,' said Simone, running her fingers gently over the bruise. 'Please forgive me…' She adjusted the blankets again. The sun had sunk behind the hospital buildings, and the room was now gloomy and cold. 'I would do anything for you… And to show you how much you mean to me, I want to show you something…'

Simone went to the door and opened it, checking the corridor was clear. Closing the door, she came back round the bed. She bent down and grasped the hem of her nurse's dress. Slowly, she pulled it up, over her thighs, exposing thick dark tights. Her pale fleshy skin shone through the fabric. She kept pulling the material up, over where the waistband of her tights finished, above her knickers, biting into the pale skin of her abdomen. She shifted, pulling the dress higher until the material was bunched above her breasts. An angry swirling mess of pink scar tissue started around what was once her bellybutton and spread out under her ribcage, creasing and mottling the skin. It disappeared under the soft greying material of her bra. Simone moved closer to the old lady and took her hand, pressing it to a swirl of scar tissue, moving the limp hand in a stroking motion

'Do you feel that, Mary? He did this to me. He burned me… Just as much as you need me, I need you.'

Simone stood for a moment, feeling the air cooling her ruined, scarred skin, and Mary's warm hand on her body, then gently she let the hand drop and pulled her dress back down, smoothing out the material. She went to her bag on the floor beside the bed, and retrieved an envelope.

'I almost forgot. I got you a card! Shall I open it?' Simone plunged her finger into the thick envelope and tore it open, pulling out the card. 'Look. It's a watercolour, of a mulberry tree… I figured that the tree you and George are sitting under is a mulberry. Do you want to hear what I've written inside? "To my best friend Mary, get well soon, with love from Nurse Simone Matthews."'

Simone positioned the card on the locker next to the photo and the jug, and flicked on the lamp above the bed. She sat back down and took Mary's hand in hers.

'I know you won't get well. I'm pretty sure of it. But it's the thought that counts, isn't it?' She patted Mary's hand. 'There. We're all cosy again. I'll stay with you here for a bit longer, if that's all right? I don't want to go home. Not until I'm sure he's gone out for the night.'

CHAPTER 22

Isaac answered his front door in shorts and a sleeveless T-shirt. A delicious smell of cooking wafted out.

'Wow, who is this elegant, beautiful woman I see before me?' he said, taking in Erika's long summer dress, her styled hair and dangly silver earrings.

'You make it sound like I'm always dressing like a tramp,' she said.

'Not at all, but you scrub up well,' he grinned. They hugged and she stepped inside, handing him a bottle of white wine dripping with condensation. They came through to the kitchen, and she was pleased to see that she was the only guest for dinner.

'Stephen's writing… He sends his love and apologies. He's on a deadline for his new book,' said Isaac. The wine bottle gave a pleasing pop as he pulled out the cork. 'How about we have the first glass with a ciggie on the balcony?'

They came up to the balcony with their wine, and lit up. The sun was low in the sky, casting long, balmy shadows over the city stretching away from them. 'Oh, this is lovely,' said Erika, taking a sip of wine.

'Before I forget, Stephen asked me to give you something,' said Isaac. He disappeared through the balcony doors and returned with a book. 'It's his latest. Well, the one that's been published the latest…'

'*From My Cold Dead Hands*,' said Erika reading the title. The cover showed a pale woman's hand pushing up the lid of a coffin. In the hand was a letter, dripping with blood.

'It's the fourth DCI Bartholomew novel, but they're all stand-alone, so you don't need to have read the others. He's signed it, too,' said Isaac. He took her wine glass, so she could open the book.

'"From my warm, alive hands, to you Erica, all best, Stephen",' she read. He'd spelled her name with a 'c' instead of a 'k'. She looked up at Isaac and was about to say something when she saw he was desperate for her to take this gift, and for her and Stephen to be friends. 'This is great. I'll be sure to thank him when I see him.' She tucked the book into her bag and took back her wine glass.

'Are we okay?' he asked. 'Last week with the dinner party, I screwed up, and…'

'You've already said sorry three times. It's fine.' She was about to say more when her phone rang.

'Hang on, sorry,' she said, rummaging around in her bag and pulling it out. She saw it was Marsh. 'Sorry, I need to take this.'

'I'll give you some privacy,' said Isaac, slipping back inside through the balcony doors.

'Sir?' she said, answering.

'Who gave bloody Peterson authorisation to arrest Gary Wilmslow!' he shouted.

'What?'

'Peterson arrested Wilmslow an hour ago, pulled him into the bloody nick! Woolf has already processed him and he's in a bloody cell waiting for his brief!'

'Where did he arrest him?' asked Erika, her blood running cold.

'Laurel Road…'

'I was just there a while back.'

'Well, you should have bloody stayed. Apparently Gary Wilmslow barged in to the house, saying he had stuff to collect. He led Peterson to a stash of cigarettes.'

'Cigarettes?'

'Yeah – small fry, black market stuff.'

'Shit.'

'Erika, if he goes down for a few knock-off cigarettes it closes down our direct link to Operation Hemslow…Months of fucking work!'

'Yes, sir. I know.'

'I don't think you do! Why the bloody hell was Peterson arresting him in the first place? You heard Oakley at our meeting. Your investigation is into the murder of Gregory Munro, and Gary Wilmslow is nothing to do with that! I'm on my way back from a conference in Manchester. Now, get down there and control your bloody officers. Bail Wilmslow or, better still, find a way to caution him and let him go!' Marsh hung up.

'Problem?' asked Isaac, coming back onto the balcony with a large china plate beautifully decorated with cheeses and olives. Erika looked at them longingly.

'That was Marsh. Something's kicked off with Peterson. I have to go down to the nick and sort it out.' She took a last sip of wine and handed him back the glass.

'Right now?'

'Yeah, the joys of my job. I'm sorry. I don't know how long it will take. I'll phone you,' she said, and rushed off to her car.

Isaac stayed on the balcony and stared out at the city, thinking that he probably wouldn't hear from her anytime soon, unless there was a dead body.

CHAPTER 23

When Erika arrived at Lewisham Row, the reception area was empty. Woolf was on duty, munching his way through a Chinese takeaway at the front desk.

'You got yourself dolled up for Gary Wilmslow?' he joked, taking in her loose summer dress with the spaghetti straps.

'Where is he?' she snapped.

'Interview room three.'

'Buzz me in.'

Woolf pressed the button to activate the door lock and watched Erika as she swept past into the main part of the station, noticing for the first time that she had curves, and how good her legs looked in a dress.

Erika passed through the heavy steel door separating the cell block from the rest of the station and went into the observation suite, where she found DC Warren and one of the uniformed officers in front of a large bank of video screens. One of the screens showed the sparse interior of interview room three from a high angle, above a table and two chairs. Peterson sat opposite Gary Wilmslow, who had his arms folded and a smug look on his face. Another officer, a young woman whom Erika didn't know, sat on a chair in the corner behind Peterson.

'Who's she?' she asked.

'That's DC Ryan,' said Warren.

'Come on, Gary. Where did you get the cigarettes?' Peterson asked in the interview room. His voice sounded tinny through the speakers in the observation suite.

'They're not mine,' Gary shrugged. The harsh lights made his pale, bald head glisten.

'You knew they were there, Gary.'

'They're not mine.'

'Gregory Munro earned over two hundred thousand a year. And he had income from rental properties on top of that...'

'They're not mine,' he repeated, sounding bored.

'He wouldn't have risked his career for a case of knock-off cigarettes...'

'They're. Not. MINE,' repeated Gary, baring his teeth.

'Is that why you came over to the house? You heard it had been transferred to Estelle Munro's name?'

Gary kept his arms folded and stared ahead.

'Come on, Gary, you're getting sloppy. We heard you from upstairs, threatening Estelle. Is it really your style, threatening old ladies?' said Peterson.

'I wasn't threatening her,' scowled Gary. 'I was protecting her.'

'Protecting her from what?'

Gary laughed and leant forward. 'From you, jungle boy. I know your type. Like horny dogs when it comes to white women. Even saggy old biddies like Estelle.' He sat back and grinned. Peterson looked as if he was going to lose it.

'Where did you get the cigarettes, Gary?' shouted Peterson.

'Dunno what you're talking about,' said Gary.

'You were heard clearly saying that you were there to collect *your* cigarettes. And then we find twenty thousand Spanish Marlboro Lights in the attic. Packed in plastic.'

'I've been lucky enough to have a few Spanish holidays,' said Gary, a maddening smile on his face. 'That's nothing to do with the fags, I'm just making polite conversation.'

Peterson leaned in very close to Gary, so their noses almost touched, and stared at him.

'Get out of my face… Get out of my face…'

Peterson stayed, staring at Gary.

'Get out of my fucking face!' Gary tipped his head back and nutted Peterson.

'Jesus!' shouted Erika. She dashed from the observation suite and ran into Moss in the corridor. 'What the hell are you doing? Why aren't you in there?'

'I'm trying to sort Wilmslow's brief…' started Moss.

Erika pushed past her and yanked open the door to interview room three. Peterson and Wilmslow were on the floor. Wilmslow was on top, punching Peterson in the face. Peterson threw Gary off and slammed him back into the wall. Gary quickly recovered and lunged at Peterson again. DC Ryan saw Erika and moved to help.

'Come on! We need back-up. Get in here, now!' shouted Erika, looking up at the camera. Erika, Moss and Ryan pulled Gary Wilmslow off Peterson and managed to handcuff him. His lip was split and he spat onto the floor. Three more uniformed officers suddenly appeared in the door.

'Woken up, have you? Go on. Put him in a cell,' said Erika.

'Any time, jungle boy,' said Gary, giving Peterson a manic bloody grin as they dragged him out. Peterson slowly got up off the grubby floor. Two of his shirt buttons were ripped and his nose was bleeding.

'What the hell were you doing?' said Erika.

'Boss, he's…'

'Just shut your mouth and clean yourself up. Then we'll talk.'

Peterson wiped his mouth with the back of his hand and left the interview room.

'Boss, he had thousands of cigarettes…' started Moss. Erika put up her hand to silence her.

'I know what happened. What I don't know is why two of my best officers aren't following procedure.'

'I was just chasing up his brief.'

'Outside,' said Erika, noting that the cameras were still recording their conversation.

When they came out into the corridor, Erika continued, 'You know Peterson has a grudge against Wilmslow. He's a scumbag, but he has an alibi for the Gregory Munro murder. Your job is to investigate this murder. Not to start bringing people in for anything that takes your fancy.'

'It didn't take our fancy, it was…'

'Just go home, Moss. I'll sort this out.'

'But…'

'Go home. Now!'

'Yes, boss,' said Moss. She wiped the sweat off her forehead and walked away, leaving Erika alone in the corridor. The harsh fluorescent light beat down on her.

An hour later, Erika found Peterson in the men's locker room in the basement of the station. It stank of floor polish and body odour. Peterson was sitting on a row of benches, resting against the lockers. One of the metal doors opposite was dented, and bloodied tissue was bunched around Peterson's hand.

'He was just asking to be brought in, boss,' said Peterson, looking up and seeing her. 'He barged into the house, knocked Estelle down. He told us to go fuck ourselves.'

'He's scum, Peterson. But if I'd arrested everyone who told me to go fuck myself, the prison system would go into meltdown.'

There were no windows, and the lights were all off apart from the ones above a row of sinks, casting an eerie glow over the room. Erika felt exposed in her thin summer dress, her dangly silver earrings slapping against her cheek. She crossed her arms over her chest.

'So what exactly did you arrest him for, Peterson?'

'He had dodgy cigarettes he was planning to sell!'

'And what proof do we have he was going to sell them?'

'Come on, boss. There were thousands!'

'And if he was intending to sell them, what part of our murder investigation does that come under?' asked Erika.

'Boss, Wilmslow is out on licence,' said Peterson. 'It's got to be worth something. We still don't know if he was responsible for the death of Gregory Munro. This will give us time to look into it more.'

'He's not responsible for the death of Gregory Munro!' snapped Erika.

'We don't know that, boss. His alibi is from his sister and mother, who…'

Erika went to the sink and ran the cold water. She splashed her face, and scooped some up in her hand and took a long drink. She turned off the tap and wiped her mouth with a paper towel.

'Peterson…'

'What?'

'Gary Wilmslow is under investigation for the production and distribution of child pornography. He's potentially a key player in a massive underground paedophile network. He's under covert police surveillance. Because of this, they *know* he didn't kill Gregory Munro. His alibi is sound.'

Peterson looked up at her in shock. 'You're serious?'

'Yes, I'm serious, and I shouldn't be bloody telling you this.'

Peterson slumped forward and put his head in his hands.

'You *cannot* let idiots like Wilmslow get under your skin. You know his type. He knows how to push buttons. He's been doing it from an early age. I thought you were more intelligent than that. Personal vendettas cloud judgement.'

'How close are they to making an arrest?' Peterson croaked, almost fighting back tears.

'I don't know. Marsh informed me a couple of days ago when I wanted to go after Wilmslow. It's called Operation Hemslow. They think there's a factory pressing the DVDs and there's hundreds of hours of... footage being produced and up- loaded to the net.'

The word hung in the air. Peterson leaned back and pressed his palms to his eyes.

'No, no, no, no...' he said. Erika was shocked at how he was taking this. He wasn't trying to shift blame or defend him- self. He pulled his hands away from his eyes. 'What happens now?'

'Ignorance isn't an excuse, and you're bloody stupid... But you didn't know about Wilmslow. You were doing your job, even if you did do it cack-handedly. You're lucky Wilmslow started it in the interview room. I'll tell Marsh I've given you the mother of all bollockings.'

He looked up at her, surprised at her even tone.

'I meant what's going to happen to Operation Hemslow?'

'I don't know.'

'You don't want my badge?' he asked quietly.

'No, Peterson. You don't look like someone who's taken this flippantly.'

'I haven't.'

'Now, go on. Go home. I'll see you here tomorrow, with your head screwed on properly. You'll be given a formal warning. Luckily, it's your first.'

Peterson stood, picked up his jacket and left without saying any more. Erika watched the door after he'd left, concerned. She spent another hour at the police station, sorting things out as Gary Wilmslow was formally cautioned for abusive and racist language towards a police officer.

Erika was having a cigarette out on the front steps when Gary emerged with his solicitor, an expensive-looking man in a grey pinstripe suit. Gary hung back at the top of the stairs. When his solicitor was out of earshot, he said, 'Thanks for getting me off. Talking of getting off, what are you up to? You look fucking tasty.'

Erika turned and looked up at where he was leering down the front of her dress. She climbed the steps and came level with him.

'Attempted rape is as far as you'll get with me, as I'm sure is the case for you with most women,' she said, leaning down towards his face.

The solicitor was halfway across the car park before he realised Gary was missing. He turned back, saying, 'Mr Wilmslow.'

'Bitch,' muttered Gary.

'Takes one to know one,' said Erika, holding his gaze. He turned and went off down the steps to join his brief.

Marsh's car pulled up beside the steps and he got out. He didn't look happy.

'We need to talk. My office. Now!' He stormed past her up the steps.

Erika watched as Gary and his solicitor pulled out of the car park in a black BMW. She had a horrible feeling she'd released something dangerous back into the wild.

CHAPTER 24

'You need to control your bloody officers, Erika. What made you leave them at the scene?' demanded Marsh, pacing up and down his office. She remained standing.

'There wasn't a scene when I left, sir. Peterson and Moss were waiting with Estelle Munro for a fingerprint technician… Wilmslow barged into the house afterwards.'

'Well, I've just had a bollocking from Oakley at SC&O.'

'Specialist Crime and Operations know they have a potential conflict with our case.'

'Yes, and thanks to DI Peterson the two have now clashed.'

'Sir, nothing was mentioned to Wilmslow or his brief about Operation Hemslow. None of my officers know about it. So Peterson was…'

'Bloody stupid. That's what he was.'

'I sent Wilmslow off packing with a caution,' said Erika.

'And you don't think he'll find that suspicious? We've been cracking down hard on black-market cigarettes and evading customs. We busted him with twenty thousand fags, and he nutted a bloody police officer. Isn't he going to be suspicious we sent him on his way with a slap on the wrist?'

'I can't tell you what he's thinking, but he's a career criminal. They spend their whole lives lurching between paranoia and elation.'

'Erika, Wilmslow is the only member of the child-abuse network that we've managed to get close to. Millions have been spent on Operation Hemslow, and if they lose him…'

'They won't lose him, sir.'

'You're heading Operation Hemslow now, are you, Erika?'

'No, sir. Still waiting to hear about the promotion…'

Marsh paced up and down. Erika bit her lip. *Why can't I just shut up sometimes?* she thought.

'What's your progress with the Gregory Munro murder?' Marsh asked, finally.

'I'm waiting to see if we have any prints from a picture frame in the Munro house. It seems his GMC certificate went missing during the break-in. It was only reported when we turned the house back over to Estelle Munro after forensics was done. Also, the neighbours opposite are back from holiday. In the two weeks leading up to the murder, they witnessed a few young guys going into the Munro house. Rent boy types. I should have e-fits tomorrow.'

Marsh paused and looked at her. 'I want you to get this case ready to hand over to one of the Murder Investigation Teams who specialise in sexually motivated murders.'

'What?'

'We've got gay porn at the murder scene, a gay dating app on the victim's phone, now we have neighbours who've seen rent boys going in and out…'

'The identities of the young men aren't confirmed yet,' said Erika, wishing she hadn't said they looked like rent boys. 'If we hand this over, it will get lost amongst a sea of cases. I'm so close…'

'So close to blowing a multimillion-pound covert surveillance?'

'Sir, that's not fair.'

Marsh stopped pacing and sat down at his desk.

'Look, Erika. I'm strongly advising you to let go of this case and hand it over. I will make sure this isn't seen as a failure on your part.'

'Please, sir, just—'

'I'm not debating it any more. Have everything you've got on the Gregory Munro case ready to hand over by tomorrow lunchtime.'

'Yes, sir.' Erika went to say more, but thought the better of it. She hitched her bag over her shoulder and left the office, forcing herself not to slam the door.

When Erika pulled into the car park by her flat, she killed the engine. The thought of going inside made her even more depressed. She wound down the window and lit a cigarette, smoking as she listened to the sound of traffic from the London Road and the hum of crickets in the surrounding bushes.

There was something about this case that was eluding her. Was it Gary Wilmslow? Was it one of the rent boys who'd paid Gregory Munro a visit? Did Gregory have something on Gary, and so he was disposed of? It felt like the answer was just within her grasp. It was something simple, she knew it. It was always a small clue, like a dropped stitch in a blanket. All she needed was to find that clue, grab it, and the whole thing would unravel.

She hated that she was no longer going to be the one to find Gregory Munro's killer. She now had to come back into work tomorrow and tell her team the case was being handed over, just as things were getting interesting.

CHAPTER 25

DUKE: Did it arrive?

NIGHT OWL: Yeah. Just. I missed the post. Had to get it from the collection office… If only they knew what was inside.

DUKE: Was it sealed?

NIGHT OWL: Yeah.

DUKE: You SURE?

NIGHT OWL: It was sealed tight. Had to cut at the padded envelope with a knife.

DUKE: OK

NIGHT OWL: You're jumpy.

DUKE: Yeah. Do you think they open stuff?

NIGHT OWL: Who?

DUKE: Royal Mail.

NIGHT OWL: No. It's illegal. Unless you're a terrorist.

DUKE: OK

NIGHT OWL: Am I a terrorist?

DUKE: Course not.

NIGHT OWL: Exactly. What I do is for the good of society.

DUKE: I know that. And people will be grateful. I'm grateful.

DUKE: But could they have opened it and resealed it?

NIGHT OWL: I'm the one doing this, NOT YOU.

DUKE: Still. It's a risk for me. It's my name on the invoice.

NIGHT OWL: Christ Duke. Don't be a pussy.

DUKE: I'm not a pussy!

NIGHT OWL: Then shut up.

There was a pause. The text hung on the screen for a moment.

NIGHT OWL: U still there?

DUKE: Yeah. Don't take anything for granted. Watch your back.

NIGHT OWL: He's had it coming.

DUKE: He has.

NIGHT OWL: My hatred has intensified into something awe-inspiring.

DUKE: You inspire me.

NIGHT OWL: He will show me awe.

DUKE: You'll tell me, when it's over?

NIGHT OWL: You'll be the first to know.

CHAPTER 26

The streets were deserted as Night Owl rode along Lordship Lane, an affluent area of South London. A row of independent shops slid past, bathed in darkness. All was quiet, save for the ticking of the mountain bike wheels and the distant hum of the city.

It was approaching midnight, but the heat still beat up from the tarmac and Night Owl was sweating under the black running suit. A car would have been quicker, but there were CCTV cameras on every corner, photographing people and number plates. It was just too risky.

The man's address had been easy to find: a search on the Internet. He was well-known and liked to shout about his life on social media. Night Owl grinned with a row of small crooked teeth.

He's overshared one too many times.

With the next victim being a public – and often controversial – figure, Night Owl had been concerned that the house would be heavily alarmed, but a simple visit on a bright hot day the previous week had been enough – a fake cold call with a mocked-up leaflet for BELL SAFE SECURITY. It had been a shock, seeing his face up close. It had been difficult to mask the hatred and remain relaxed and informal.

Night Owl turned off Lordship Lane and came to a halt beside a high wall. The brakes on the mountain bike gave a small squeal, which seemed loud in the quiet street.

The high wall marked the side of a long row of back gardens. The houses stretching away were smart and elegant. Night Owl tucked the mountain bike behind a postbox, which was positioned close to the wall, then used it to scale the wall. Four of the houses in the row had security alarms. A high back wall ran the length of all six gardens, backing onto a bus depot.

The first garden was easy. An old lady lived in the large house and the garden was overgrown; the house windows were dark. Night Owl crossed with a whispering rustle and climbed the low fence into the second garden.

Again, no lights activated, but the owner of this house had built a large extension, jutting out and reducing the garden to a thin strip of grass by the high back wall. The first ground-floor window was dark, but the second was open a few inches and emitted a soft multicoloured glow. It was a large nursery, almost completely bare inside save for a large wooden crib close to the window.

A small toddler with large eyes and a messy fuzz of black hair stood in the crib, its chubby hands gripping the side of the rail. The baby could see into the garden in the soft light emitting from the slowly turning night-light. Night Owl moved to the open window, whispering, 'Hello.'

The toddler shifted a little, grasping the edge of the crib. It was a little girl. She wore a pink all-in-one with a pink knitted matinee jacket. The air was close and heat resonated from the brickwork.

'Are you all hot and bothered?' whispered Night Owl, smiling. The little girl smiled and jiggled on the spot. She pulled at the matinee jacket and gave a little soft wail.

There were still three more gardens to cross, but Night Owl felt for this little innocent girl, slowly grilling in the hot room. The window pulled open easily, and Night Owl hitched a leg up and inside. The little girl looked up with big round eyes, unsure of the person who had climbed into her room.

'It's okay… It's all right,' whispered Night Owl. 'You are innocent. You have yet the chance to wreak havoc on the world.' Moving swiftly, Night Owl lifted the little girl and held her up at arm's length. She giggled. Placing her back down again, Night Owl worked quickly on the tiny buttons on the front of the matinee jacket, grasping it so the little girl wouldn't lose balance, then unhooking each arm until the jacket was off.

'There, is that better?' cooed Night Owl. The little girl allowed herself to be lifted and laid down on the small mattress. The material was white with a pattern of small grey elephants. She reached up with her arms as Night Owl slowly wound the mobile hanging above the crib.

As the soft melody of 'Twinkle Twinkle Little Star' began to play, Night Owl retreated from the little girl's view.

The third garden had a security light mounted on the back wall, so it was a tense job to cross it, far enough away to keep out of its beam.

The fourth garden was running a little wild, with tall grass and overflowing flowerbeds. Night Owl moved past a plastic swing set and an overgrown sandpit and crouched down by the utility room door.

Night Owl pulled the hood up so that only a pair of eyes glowed through, listened at the door, then slowly pulled out a long, thin piece of wire and inserted it into the lock.

CHAPTER 27

When TV presenter Jack Hart emerged from the members-only bar in Charlotte Street, Central London, he paused to enjoy the warm summer night. Despite the late hour, a large group of photographers were waiting on the pavement and their camera flashes burst in a flurry as Jack came towards them down a short flight of stairs.

Jack was lean and handsome, with ice-white blond hair shaved fashionably high with a short back and sides, and styled on top with a smooth quiff. His teeth were as white as his hair, and his sharp suit was tailor-made for his tall frame. He was pleased to see journalists from the BBC, ITV and Sky News waiting for him, along with the usual tabloid crowd – some of whom were ex-colleagues. He didn't show this pleasure on his handsome face, though, instead attempting serious contemplation.

'Do you take responsibility for the death of Megan Fairchild?' shouted a reporter from one of the broadsheets.

'Do you think they'll take your show off the air?' yelled another.

'Come on, Jack. You killed her, didn't you?' purred one of the paparazzi, coming up close, his camera firing off a bright flash.

Jack ignored the questions and pushed through them, climbing into a black cab waiting at the kerb. He slammed the door and it drove off slowly, the cameras keeping pace, lenses bumping against the window and filling the interior of the cab with a strobe of flashes. Once they had rounded the corner of Charlotte Street, the driver was able to speed away.

'The wife loves your show, mate,' said the driver, eyeing him through his rear-view mirror. 'S'all made up, though, innit?'

'It's live, and anything can happen,' said Jack, repeating the catchphrase he used at the start of every show.

'I heard the girl who was on your show, that Megan who killed herself, had loads of mental problems. Bet she'd have done it anyway, mate,' said the driver, again catching his eye in the rear-view mirror.

'It's all right. I was going to give you a good tip anyway,' said Jack. He sat back and closed his eyes, the gentle rocking motion soothing him as the cab trundled through Central London.

'Suit yourself, mate,' muttered the driver.

The Jack Hart Show was broadcast live five mornings a week and had risen in the ratings over the past year – but it still had a way to go to beat its rival, *The Jeremy Kyle Show*.

Jack Hart prided himself that the show was broadcast live. It gave them an edge, and kept them in the press. Five days a week his guests, in the grand tradition of *The Jerry Springer Show*, sought out and fought out their fifteen minutes of fame by airing their dirty laundry on camera, and people loved it.

Jack had started out as a journalist in Fleet Street, and learned his murky trade as an investigative journalist exposing torrid celebrity affairs, dodgy politicians and 'human interest' stories. He often described *The Jack Hart Show* as a tabloid newspaper smeared across the camera lens.

Megan Fairchild had been a case in point. Her baby daddy had been sleeping with her own father, but the researchers on the show had failed to dig up that Megan's father had also sexually abused her throughout her childhood. The day after the controversial show was broadcast, Megan had taken her own life and that of her unborn child by drinking a litre of weedkiller.

Publicly, Jack had been repentant, and he wasn't stone-hearted enough not to be saddened by the deaths. But privately Jack and his producers had courted the press exposure, hoping that the media storm would send their ratings through the roof.

He opened his eyes and pulled out his phone, logging on to check his Twitter feed. He was reassured to see that people were still talking about Megan's death, and there were some more great RIP tweets from D-list celebs. He retweeted them and then logged onto the *Go Fund Me* page that had been set up to raise money in Megan's honour. It had just reached £100,000 in donations. He retweeted this with a message of thanks, and then settled back, humming 'And the Money Kept Rolling In' from his favourite musical, *Evita*.

Forty-five minutes later, the taxi pulled up at Jack's large, handsome house in Dulwich. He thanked the driver, feeling part-relieved, part-disappointed that there weren't more photographers waiting for him outside. He could only count five. *They must have got what they wanted outside the bar, without having to schlep across the river*, he thought. He got out and paid the driver through the passenger window. The photographers started clicking away, their bright flashes bouncing off the black taxi and surrounding houses.

He pushed his way through the small group and opened the gate leading up to his front door, thinking that this bizarre scene in a quiet corner of Dulwich in South London could soon be plastered all over the media across the country.

'Do you have a message for Megan Fairchild's mother?' asked one of the photographers.

Jack stopped at his front door and turned, saying, 'Why didn't you take care of your daughter?' He paused and stared broodingly into the cameras as they flashed away. Then he turned on his heel, unlocked the front door and came inside, closing it on the strobe of flashes.

The security alarm began its warning tone and he punched in the four-digit code. The screen lit up green and the alarm fell silent. Jack took off his thin jacket, took out his wallet and keys and put them on the hall table. He came through to the open-plan living area, which looked out over the dark garden. When he flicked on the lights, the vast empty space stared back at him. He went to the fridge and stopped for a moment to stare at the pictures stuck to the door, which had been painted by his small son and daughter. He opened the door and pulled out a bottle of Bud. It didn't make a fizzing sound; the lid popped off soundlessly, clinking as it skittered across the counter.

He took a sip. It was cold, but a little flat. He went back to the fridge and saw it was the last bottle. He was sure there had been three left… He pondered this for a moment, flicked off the lights and made his way upstairs.

The living area was still for a moment. There were some bumps and bangs from the bathroom above, and then the shower began. Slowly, a small, compact figure in black slid through the utility room door, bathed in shadows. Moving swiftly, it crossed the kitchen and climbed the stairs, feet placed wide on each step to avoid creaking.

The landing was in darkness, and a shaft of light from the bathroom fell across the carpet. Night Owl moved close to the door, just a pair of eyes gleaming through the slit in the hood.

Jack was well-built with a strong, lithe body. Night Owl watched him in the shower as he lathered up, the shampoo foaming white against his wet hair. A stream of soapy water coursed down his muscular back and between his buttocks. As he showered, Jack began to hum lightly, tunelessly.

'You disgust me,' whispered Night Owl. The singing stopped as Jack ducked his head under the water, his wet hair now sleek as a seal.

It was intoxicating to stand and watch, undetected. To think that everyone in the country was talking about this man… this arrogant, selfish, bastard. The water was extinguished with a metallic squeak, and Night Owl ducked swiftly back into the shadows.

Jack came out of the shower, passing his son and daughter's bedrooms. He kept the doors closed on their empty rooms. With the doors closed, he could pass them each night without feeling a twang of regret and longing. He padded through to the elegant master bedroom, his bottle of Bud in one hand, towel in the other, drying his hair. He sat naked on the edge of the bed, dropping the towel on the carpet. The Bud was quickly getting warm and flat, so he chugged back the last of it and placed the empty on the spare bedside table, on the unoccupied side.

He thought of his wife's warm, comfortable body. How she'd often be sitting up, pretending to be reading a book when he came home late. The book was always a prop, an excuse for her to be awake so that she could play out her disappointment.

He went to get up and go downstairs for another drink, but his head was suddenly heavy. So were his limbs, and he felt exhausted. He eased himself into a lying position, shuffling round so his head was on the pillow. He reached for the remote control on the side table and flicked on the TV. Footage of him leaving the club on Charlotte Street an hour earlier was running on Sky with a red *'BREAKING NEWS'* banner across the bottom of the screen: 'OFCOM TO INVESTIGATE JACK HART CON-TROVERSY'.

As he looked around the room, the colour seemed to bloom out of the television news in streaks. Jack lifted his head and the room spun violently. He flopped back on the pillow. He was shivering too, despite the heat. He managed to pull the duvet cover out from underneath him and burrowed under, relishing the warmth.

'Hang on, hang on,' he murmured, vaguely aware of the words moving across the screen. The sound from the television rolled over him; the room spun. He jerked his head, as a smear of black seemed to move beside the bed. A flash by the door and it was gone. From somewhere deep in his mind, Jack re-alised that something wasn't right. Maybe he had some kind of twenty-four-hour flu thing. *Hang on, I should call someone, if I'm being investigated by OFCOM*, he thought.

Night Owl worked quickly, moving downstairs and dead-bolt-ing the front door, and then taking a small, neat pair of seca-teurs and clipping the Internet modem and phone cable next to the landline. The lights on the modem blinked off. Night Owl moved to the thin jacket that Jack had hung up in the hall, pulled out a Blackberry phone from the pocket, swiftly removed the SIM card and dropped the phone on the floor, pressing a heel against it as the screen buckled and cracked.

The final task was flicking off the mains electricity. The se-curity panel beeped, and Night Owl keyed in the PIN, then absorbed the silence. The faint sound of a groan floated down from above. Night Owl placed a hand on the bannister and slowly began to climb back up the stairs.

The room now spun violently for Jack, as he lay in bed. It took him a few moments to realise that the television was now dark and silent, and so was his bedroom. Panic seemed to be just beyond his reach, a fuzzy, far-off emotion. His mind went back to his wife, Marie. He reached out to touch her side of the bed in the darkness and was confused. Where was she?

He felt the mattress move and flatten beside him; someone had climbed into bed. He reached his arm out and felt a warm body.

'Marie?' he croaked into the silence. He groped around and felt flesh under thin clothing. 'Marie? When did you come home?' Despite the drugs in his blood, he remembered she was gone. She'd left him. Moved out with the kids. He stiffened and tried to pull away.

'Shhhhh… Just relax,' said a voice. It wasn't Marie's voice. It was sharp and had a strange high tone to it.

Jack tried to get away, the bed tipping and lurching underneath him. His limbs had no strength or coordination. He grabbed at the landline on his bedside table, knocking it to the floor. He then felt the person climb onto his back, and he was turned over onto his front. His limbs flopped helplessly as he tried to fight, but swift, strong hands fastened his wrists together and then flipped him back over.

Jack tried to shout, but his mouth was slack; his voice came out slurred and weak: 'Whouw harrr ou?'

'Just someone who wants fifteen minutes of fame,' laughed the voice. Jack heard the sound of a zipper and a crackle, and then a plastic bag slowly slid over his head. The hands moved fast, pulling at what felt like a drawstring, and Jack felt it gather and tighten around his neck. He started to breathe faster, and the plastic crackled and closed in around his head, growing tighter against his skin. One eye was clamped shut, but the other was trapped open by the plastic. And then there was no more air to breathe.

Night Owl held on fast to the plastic bag, enjoying the sounds: the rattling gasps and retching. Jack carried on thrashing, his strength increasing with his will to live. Night Owl felt an explosion of pain as Jack's head jerked up and made contact with Night Owl's face. Night Owl increased the pressure, pulling the cord around Jack's neck tighter, and bringing a fist up and slamming it down on the squashed, contorted face underneath.

One of Jack's last thoughts were that the photographers might still be outside, and what a great story this was going to be.

Finally, with a shudder and a weak whimper, Jack was still. Night Owl lay with Jack's body for several minutes, watching, breathing through the euphoria, shaking with excitement.

Then Night Owl rose silently and slipped out of the house like a shadow.

CHAPTER 28

It was early the next morning and, despite the hour, the heat-wave had intensified. It seemed to have permeated the walls of Lewisham Row station. Despite the fans being on full power, the incident room was roasting. Moss was standing in front of the whiteboards, addressing Erika and the team.

'There were no prints found on the picture frame in 14 Laurel Road, but we have had a positive ID on one of the young men seen by Gregory Munro's neighbours opposite,' she said. 'Last night, Marie and Claude Morris were able to give us this e-fit image.'

Erika and the rest of the officers regarded the face which had joined the photos of Gregory Munro and Gary Wilmslow. It was of a young man with dark hair swept back off a high forehead and a lean, handsome face.

Moss went on, 'DC Warren decided to broaden his horizons and spent the best part of the night cruising profiles on rent boy websites…'

There were several wolf whistles, and Warren rolled his eyes and blushed.

'And we now have this…'

Moss pinned up a profile photo from a website called Rent-Boiz. It was remarkably similar to the e-fit image. The handsome young man who stared into the camera had the addition of green eyes and designer stubble. Moss paused and wiped her forehead with her rolled-up sleeve, and nodded over to Warren.

He stood, a little shyly. 'Um, okay. His profile name is Jor-diLevi and on the website it says he's eighteen years old and London-based. He charges £250 an hour, and it seems that he'll do most things if the money is right. Of course, he doesn't give his real name or an address. I got in contact with the website administrator, who said that registration is anonymous, so no joy there, but I'll keep working on it.'

Moss gave him a wink and he sat back down. 'Now, we can all agree that this looks like the same guy.' She indicated the e-fit and JordiLevi's profile picture. 'I think this could be a real breakthrough for us.'

There was a round of applause. Erika got up from where she perched by the printers, her heart heavy.

'This is great work, Moss and Warren, thank you. But I have to let you know that after careful review with Detective Chief Superintendent Marsh and the Assistant Commissioner it has been decided that this is a case for one of the Murder Investigation Teams who specialise in sexually motivated murders,' explained Erika. 'I'd like you all to ready your files and the data gathered so far, and this afternoon the case will be transferred over.'

'Boss, can't you see how huge this is? If we can track down this JordiLevi, he could be our direct link to the Gregory Munro murder. He could have witnessed something!' said Moss.

'We just need time, boss,' added Crane, 'and we wouldn't need much. We're gonna set up a fake punter profile on Rent-Boiz and arrange a meeting with this JordiLevi. He might be able to give us an e-fit of whoever it was who called round at Gregory Munro's house and we'd have our suspect.'

'I'm sorry, this isn't a debate,' said Erika. Moss sat back in her chair, folding her arms in frustration. 'I don't like this any more than you all do. Please have your reports and all data relating to the case ready by noon.'

There were a chorus of protests and Erika left the incident room. She went out in the corridor to the coffee machine, fed in the correct change and pressed the worn and faded 'cappuccino' button, but nothing happened. She thumped her fist against it and thumped it again and again, taking out her frustration on the stupid machine. She didn't hear Moss approach.

'All right, boss? Having a spot of caffeine rage?'

Erika turned and nodded.

'Stand back.'

Erika stepped back and Moss raised a booted foot and kicked the machine under the picture of a steaming coffee cup which adorned the front. There was a beep, then a cup plopped out into the dispenser and began to fill.

'You've got to aim for the saucer,' said Moss.

'Brilliant work, detective,' said Erika. 'Is there no end to your talents?'

'I have to say that it also works with tea, and sometimes if you press the soup button.'

'There's a soup button?'

'Yes, oxtail soup. I wouldn't risk it.'

Erika grinned weakly and took her coffee out of the dispenser.

'Can I ask you something, boss? Do you really think this case is better off with another team?'

Erika blew on her coffee. 'Yes, I do.' She hated not being able to talk to Moss about this. She'd always been loyal and a wise sounding board.

'I hear there's a superintendent promotion up for grabs,' said Moss. 'Nothing to do with you wanting to get rid of a tricky case, is it?'

'I thought you knew me, Moss. That's not my style.'

'Good. So why, then? I know you. You don't give up a case easily. You're very Charlton Heston about it.'

'What?'

'"From my cold, dead hands",' said Moss, in a bad American accent. There was a pause. 'Come on, boss, we're bloody close, after banging our heads against the wall for so long.'

'Moss, I've said all I want to say about this. My decision is final.'

'Okay, okay. You can't talk about it. What if you blink once for yes and twice for no?'

'Moss…' said Erika, shaking her head.

'If you can't tell me what's going on, can I at least tell you what I think is going on?'

'Do I have a choice?'

'I think that we're overwhelmed with cases and Marsh is under pressure to massage his figures. This case is getting more complex and a bit of a hot potato. He's offloading it.'

'Moss…'

'I think that the only way we'll find a motive is when a pattern emerges. For a pattern to emerge, there has to be another body.'

'That figures.'

'And I just know what's going to happen when this case is out of our hands. If there's another body, it will be classed as a gay bashing, and there will be no end of fear-mongering and debate about the gay community. There are ten times more murders committed by straight people. When men rape and kill women, people think they're evil. But when someone gay does the same thing, it's seen as an extension of their sexuality! Of their lifestyle as a whole!'

Erika had been watching Moss quietly as she got increasingly worked up.

'Sorry, boss. It's just… I'm sick of it. We were just getting started on this. If we're overworked, then things are going to be no different in one of the other Murder Investigation teams? And I knew this case was in a good pair of hands with you. I can already see the headlines: "Gay Bashing in Suburbia", "Gay Terror in the London Commuter Belt!"'

'I didn't know this was so personal to you.'

'Not directly… Jacob's school did a whole Father's Day card-making exercise the other week, and his stupid teacher – who also happens to be married to the vicar – couldn't get her head around the fact that he has two mothers. She got him to make a card for his daddy who was "out there somewhere". Celia had to restrain me from going up there and slapping her. '

'Sorry to hear that.'

'Shit happens. I just hoped I'd get to see this case through. And I hoped you would. You don't take shit and you always know when to do the right thing. Well, until…'

Erika saw Moss had caught herself before she said 'until now'. They stood in silence for a moment.

'Do you know where Peterson is today?' asked Erika.

'He called in sick, boss.'

'Did he say what was wrong?'

Moss paused just long enough to show Erika she knew something, then said, 'No, boss, he didn't. I'll make sure everyone has their reports ready for you by noon.'

'Thanks,' said Erika. Realising that they both wanted to say things they couldn't, she watched as Moss made her way back into the incident room.

CHAPTER 29

The rest of the morning passed in a depressing haze of an over-heated incident room, and the dismantling of an investigation that had got under Erika's skin.

What Moss had said kept running through Erika's mind. *From my cold, dead hands...* Here she was, with an incredible lead in the Gregory Munro murder, her team poised to work their arses off, and she was going to give up on the case! Just before one, Erika was still sitting at her desk, staring at the computer screen, when Moss came over.

'Boss...'

'Yeah?'

'Did you send the case files over yet?'

Erika looked up, 'No. Why?'

'We've had a call come in from uniform. White male, found naked and asphyxiated in bed in a house in Dulwich. No signs of forced entry or a struggle. Preliminary ID is that it's Jack Hart.'

'Why do I know that name?'

'He hosts *The Jack Hart Show*, tabloid TV for the unemployed and stay-at-home parents. Celia watches it.'

'And uniform think it's the same guy who killed Gregory Munro?'

'Uniform is waiting for someone from the murder investigation, but it sounds like him. Is this still our case?'

'Yeah. Officially, it's still our investigation. Let's get over there,' said Erika.

CHAPTER 30

Jack Hart's house was in an upmarket area of Dulwich, South London. The road climbed steeply, and then fell sharply away. A police cordon had closed off the road, and beyond it they could see five police cars, an ambulance and two large support vans blocking the street. Erika parked close to where three uniformed officers were manning the police tape cordon. A crowd was growing on the pavement in front, holding cameras and mobile phones aloft.

'Christ, word travels fast,' said Erika, when she and Moss got out of the car. They pushed their way through the crowd, which was made up of a large group of teenagers, a cluster of elderly ladies and a woman clutching a tiny dark-haired baby.

'Is it Jack Hart?' shouted a lad with ginger hair.

'That's Jack Hart's house. I've seen him around,' added a young girl with a pierced lip.

'This is a crime scene, turn off your camera phones,' said Erika.

'It's not illegal to film in public,' said a small, ratty-haired girl with a pink fluffy handbag, and for emphasis she held up her phone to Erika's face. 'Smile: you're on YouTube.'

'What about having some respect? This is a crime scene,' replied Moss, evenly. The elderly ladies remained silent, just watching.

'He was a right bastard, Jack Hart. He good as killed that Megan Fairchild. He exploited people, so why shouldn't I exploit him?' asked a boy with a shaved head. Emboldened by his statement, more of the teenagers started to hold up their mobile phones.

'Get this lot moved further back,' said Erika to one of the officers.

'But this is the police tape cordon,' he replied.

'Then use your common sense: move the cordon further back!' snapped Erika.

Just then, a Sky News van arrived with a large satellite dish perched on the roof and parked on the opposite side of the road.

'If you need extra officers, that's not a problem. Just do it,' said Erika.

'Yes, ma'am,' said the officer.

Erika and Moss signed in, ducked under the tape and made their way over to the house.

Erika and Moss were met by a uniformed officer, who took them inside. The temperature in the hallway was cooler. It was tastefully decorated, with a large gilt mirror on the wall and a cream carpet leading up a set of stairs with dark polished wood bannisters. They followed the officer up the stairs, reaching a long landing where the cream carpet continued. The house was eerily silent. Erika realised it must be well insulated to block out the sounds of chaos from the street outside. The master bedroom was at the end of the landing. Sunlight streamed through the open door and particles of dust twirled lazily in the air.

'Jesus,' said Moss when they rounded the bedroom door. The victim's naked body was splayed out on the mattress. He looked tall, with pale skin that was smooth and almost hairless. He lay on his back with a plastic bag over his head, tied tightly around his neck. His mouth was open and so was one eye, the lid squashed against the plastic. The other eye was badly bruised, so that it had swollen shut. His lips were pulled back, as if he were baring his teeth.

'Who found the body?' asked Erika.

'A producer on his show,' explained the officer. 'She climbed up and smashed the window behind you to get inside.'

They turned and saw a large window, which looked out over the garden. There was a hole in the glass, surrounded by a spider web of cracks. The cream carpet under the frame was littered with broken glass.

'So she's confirmed this is Jack Hart?' asked Erika.

'Yeah,' nodded the officer.

'I thought his show was live every weekday? Today is Friday,' said Moss.

They pondered that for a moment.

'Okay. We need to get forensics in here fast,' said Erika reaching for her phone.

Isaac Strong and the team of CSIs arrived quickly and started work in their blue coveralls. A couple of hours later, Erika and Moss came back to the upstairs bedroom also wearing blue coveralls. A row of steel boxes had been placed around the bed to elevate the officers from contaminating any evidence.

'Okay, Isaac. Do you think this is the same killer as Gregory Munro? There's a plastic bag, he's naked, a single male,' started Erika.

'Let's hold off on that assumption for a moment,' said Isaac, looking up at her and Moss from the other side of the double bed. A crime scene photographer leaned in between them and took a shot of the body. 'He's been dead for less than twenty-four hours. We can still see evidence of rigor mortis in the clenched hands, and the mouth and eyes. The house is east-facing and this room, in particular, benefits from shade throughout the day, so the temperature has facilitated a relatively textbook decay. And he was photographed arriving home late last night, so it's more common sense than science. The plastic bag was tied under the chin…' Isaac indicated where the drawstring had been tied tight and was biting into the skin. 'There may have been a struggle; the left eye is badly bruised from a blow with a blunt object, perhaps a hand or a fist. There was an empty bottle of beer on the bedside table, which we've got going off for toxicology tests. Again, there is little sign of a struggle around the bed and in the room; it was all very neat and tidy. The victim could have been incapacitated… overwhelmed by whoever did this. There is no sign of sexual assault. As I always say, I'll know more when I open him up.'

'What's this, on the sheet?' asked Erika, pointing to a white-grey residue which covered the dark blue bed sheet next to the body. She crouched down and peered under the bed. There were a couple of discarded socks, and a thick layer of dust that had been disturbed.

'Dust,' she said, answering her own question. 'It's been disturbed under the bed and brought up onto the mattress.'

'Jeez, someone was under the bed,' said Moss. The crime scene photographer leaned in to take a close up of the victim's body, firing off bright flashes. Suddenly, a flash of light came from behind them. Erika turned and saw a man crouching on the piece of flat roof outside the bedroom window. He was thin, with his hair shorn into a bright blue mohawk. He pushed his camera lens through the hole in the glass and fired off two more photos.

'Hey!' shouted Erika, pulling down her protective mask. She went to the window, but the man, who was dressed in denim shorts and a black AC/DC T-shirt, ducked down and took another couple of shots between her legs. He moved quickly to the edge of the flat roof and, with a tinkle of broken glass, started to climb down, clinging onto a wisteria growing in thick tangles around a gutter pipe.

'Shit, who is that?' said Erika.

'Looks like paparazzi,' said Moss.

They peered out of the window as the man reached the lawn below. There were no officers in the back garden. Erika looked at Moss and they darted out of the room.

CHAPTER 31

Erika and Moss ran to the main staircase, narrowly avoiding a collision with a crime scene technician holding a delicate tray of bagged-up evidence items. They dashed down the stairs and into the open-plan living area. They moved to the glass floor-to-ceiling window which looked out over the back garden, and Erika tried to get it open. The photographer with the blue mohawk was heading towards the fence on the right side of the garden

'I need these open!' shouted Erika, unable to make out anyone's face as the blue-suited technicians looked up at them, only their curious eyes on display.

'Boss, here!' shouted Moss, emerging back through a door next to a steel American-style fridge. Erika followed. The door led to a utility room filled with a large washer and dryer. A long window looked out over the neatly landscaped garden, but there was no sign of the photographer. Moss tried the handle of a sturdy wooden door.

'It's locked! And there's no bloody key!' she cried. They looked out of the window into the garden and saw that the photographer was already half over the fence. Above the washer and dryer were shelves holding cleaning products. Erika spied a heavy metal key on the bottom shelf. She grabbed it and quickly tried it in the lock. The door opened and they burst out into the garden. Erika sprinted to the right, seized the top of the wooden fence and hauled herself over, closely followed by Moss.

She landed on the burnt grass on the other side and grappled for her radio as she ran across the garden.

'He'll come out on Dunham Road,' shouted Moss from behind.

'We have a suspect coming out of a garden which borders Dunham Road, Dulwich. I need back-up there now.' Erika reached the opposite side of the second garden and pulled herself up and over the wall, landing easily on the other side. She could see the photographer was still ahead, his blue mohawk vanishing over the next fence. *I cannot let this guy get away with photos of the crime scene – they could be uploaded online within minutes*, thought Erika.

She dashed across the next garden, skirting round a plastic swing, and vaulted the fence, landing painfully up to her knees in a pond with a splash.

'Hey, you're trespassing! Those are koi carp!' shouted a young woman in a short summer dress and sunglasses who emerged onto a terrace.

'I'm a police officer!' shouted Erika, sloshing up out of the pond and over to the next fence. She saw she'd gained on the photographer: he'd reached the fence at the edge of the next garden and was hooking his leg over the top.

'Stop that man!' cried Erika, and even though it was a valid thing to say, it sounded ridiculous. She turned and saw Moss flop over the fence behind her and land headfirst into the pond with a large splash. The woman on the terrace was now shouting even louder.

The heat was pounding down, and Erika was exhausted and overheating in all her clothes, with the crime scene overalls on top. Moss emerged from the water with pond weed in her hair.

"I'm okay, boss. GO!' she shouted. Erika carried on, climbing up and over the next fence, feeling splinters push through her overalls and clothes into the back of her legs. She saw that the photographer had come to the edge of the last garden, which was lined with a high wall of pale brick.

'Stop right there!' she shouted.

The photographer looked round at her with a red face, his blue mohawk still jutting up like a fin. He hitched the camera over his shoulder, gave her the finger and jumped, grabbing the top of the wall, and hoisting himself up.

Erika ran across the bare, dusty earth of the last garden, through a group of cracked, lichen-covered birdbaths. The photographer slipped back a little, trying to scale the top of the wall, and Erika managed to grab at one of his legs. He kicked out, catching her in the face, and although he was only wearing trainers, the pain shot through her cheek where he made contact. She grabbed at his leg and managed to get one of his trainers off, but he slithered out of her grasp and away, over the curved top of the wall. She heard a thud and a yell as he landed on the other side.

Erika pulled herself up the wall easily, glad of her height. As she straddled the top of the wall, she saw the pavement was lower on the other side. With only one shoe, the photographer had landed badly on his bare foot. He was fumbling with his camera and trying to stagger away. Erika leapt down. Landing easily on the pavement, she was able to move faster and grab him. He fought her, trying to get away.

'No... ou... on't...' she heaved, breathlessly. Moments later, Moss appeared at the top of the wall, slithered down, landed on the pavement and dashed over. She managed to pin the photographer's hands behind his back and cuff him as Erika kept hold.

'Fucking bitches!' he shouted.

'You need to calm down,' said Erika.

'Why? Are you arresting me?'

'We're detaining you,' said Moss.

'On what grounds?'

'On the grounds that you didn't stop, you fled the scene when all we wanted to do was talk to you. You kicked my colleague in the face,' said Moss.

'It ain't illegal to take photographs!' he said, trying to shake them off.

'That was a crime scene,' said Erika.

'Well, it ain't illegal to photograph a crime scene either!'

'Yes, but I am seizing your camera as evidence. It may contain information helpful to our case,' said Erika, trying to catch her breath. She had never seen Moss so angry. Her hair and overalls were soaking wet and she was sweating. Erika grabbed at the camera, which was still looped over the photographer's shoulder on a strap. She opened the flap at the side and peered inside.

'Where's the memory card?' she demanded.

'Dunno.' The photographer stared at her defiantly with his small beady eyes.

'Where is the memory card? Did you dump it? Because we can have those gardens searched,' said Moss.

He smirked and shrugged. 'You won't find it.'

'What's your name?'

He shrugged.

Erika reached between his cuffed hands, pulling his wallet from his back pocket. She opened it and pulled out his driving licence, reading: 'Mark Rooney, age thirty-nine. Who do you work for?'

'I'm freelance.'

'Why were you taking photos?'

'That's a stupid question. It's *Jack Hart*. I didn't know he was dead, did I?'

'How do we know that you weren't responsible? It hasn't been made public. There has been no formal identification.'

'I told you, I didn't know he would be dead. He was fine last night.'

'You were here last night? Why?' asked Erika.

'He's all over the press since that girl killed herself.'

'What did you photograph last night?'

'Him coming home in a cab, then I got some shots of him in his bedroom.'

'What time was this last night?' asked Moss.

'Dunno. Twelve-thirty, one?'

'And did you stay all night?'

'No.'

'Why not?'

'I got a tip-off. One of the Kardashians is in London, I heard she was staying out late on the lash. Kardashian pictures are worth a lot more than Jack Hart…'

'Okay, we've all had a nice chat. Now I need you to hand over that memory card,' said Erika.

'I told you, I haven't got it!'

'You had it five minutes ago.'

He smirked. 'Oh. I must have forgotten to put it in my camera. It happens. Memory cards are fiddly little things. Actually, now I think of it, yes, it slipped my mind. I forgot to put it in.'

'You know what, I'm sick of this,' said Moss. She let go of the photographer's handcuffed arms, unzipped her overalls and retrieved a latex glove from her trousers. She rolled up the sleeve of the overalls and pulled on the glove. With her free hand, she grabbed Mark's blue mohawk and pulled his head back.

'Hey! What are you doing? Ow!' he cried. Moss shoved two gloved fingers in his mouth and deep to the back of his throat.

He collapsed forward and threw up over the pavement. Erika and Moss managed to jump back a little.

'The things we have to do,' said Moss, as he coughed, gagged and spat. Erika spun him around to face the wall.

'Just as I thought. You swallowed it, you cheeky bastard,' said Moss as she retrieved a small, black, dripping memory card from a pile of puke on the pavement, and gingerly bagged it up in a clear evidence bag. 'Better out than in, as my mother always used to say.'

'You bitch! I'll sue for police brutality,' shouted Mark, slumped against the wall, still coughing.

'Don't be a baby, I used a clean glove,' said Moss, pulling it off and dumping it in a nearby litter bin. A police car rounded the corner with its sirens blaring and came to a stop beside them at the kerb.

'About bloody time,' said Erika, as the same two uniformed officers from the police cordon climbed out of the car.

'Sorry, boss, there's a one-way system we hadn't anticipated,' started one.

'They assaulted me, police brutality!' shouted Mark.

'Take him to the nearest train station and drop him off,' said Erika.

The officers pushed him into the car and they drove off, leaving Moss and Erika still panting and out of breath.

'Good work,' said Erika, taking the evidence bag with the grubby memory card and holding it up to the light.

'Did I go too far? Sticking my fingers down his gullet?' asked Moss.

'I don't know what you're talking about,' said Erika. 'Now come on, let's get back to the house.'

CHAPTER 32

The crowds had built at the top of the road when Erika and Moss returned to the crime scene. They could see that news crews from the BBC and ITN had joined the Sky News van. They were met by the crime scene manager, Nils Åckerman, who gave them fresh blue overalls to change into.

'The phone lines have been severed, just like they were at the Laurel Road crime scene,' he said, as Erika and Moss got changed.

'It's the same killer, it's got to be,' said Moss, as she zipped up the blue overall and pulled up the hood. Erika zipped her suit up, silent for a moment. They handed their soaked and muddy suits over to a technician, who placed them into an evidence bag.

'I need you to see what you can get off this,' said Erika, handing Nils the smaller clear plastic evidence bag containing the memory card. 'It had been swallowed, but not for long.'

'Shouldn't be a problem,' he said, taking the bag. 'But first, I need you to see something.'

They followed him back inside and down the cream carpeted hallway, still busy with CSIs in blue overalls, through the open-plan living area and into the utility room that overlooked the back garden. The door was open. They stepped back out into the sunshine. In the distance, a lawnmower whirred.

'We've checked all of the windows in the house. They are a mixture of UPVC plastic and triple glazing that is very hard to access unless you break them. They are all locked from the inside, apart from the bedroom window, which was smashed by the colleague of Jack Hart when she discovered his body,' said Nils. Erika and Moss followed his gaze, looking up at the broken window at the back of the house. 'There are no prints or any other signs of forced entry.'

'What about the front door?' asked Erika.

'Locked from the inside with a Yale lock and a dead bolt,' replied Nils. 'Which leaves this, the utility room door, which I believe was the point of entry.'

The door was made of stout wood, and painted with deep blue gloss. The handle was of heavy iron, and the sturdy metal key Erika had found on the shelf was in the lock on the inside.

'It was locked. I had to unlock it when we chased after the photographer,' said Erika.

'I'll get to that in a moment,' said Nils. He pushed the door closed. 'If you look very closely here on the outside, there's a tiny strip of wood at the bottom which has an older coat of paint.' They crouched down on the grass outside the door and noted the centimetre of pale green running along the bottom of the door frame.

'A draught-excluding strip had been stuck on with adhesive when the door was green. The draught-excluding strip had recently been removed; we found it behind the washer and the dryer,' said Nils, opening the door and stepping back into the utility room to retrieve a long, thin strip of rubber from the top of the washing machine. He placed it over the green strip at the bottom of the door and then took it away again. 'Can you see where it's been peeled away from the base? It leaves a quarter-inch gap under the door.'

Erika looked at Moss.

'That doesn't explain how he got in, unless he's Flat Stanley,' said Moss.

'I'll show you,' said Nils. He motioned to one of the fingerprint technicians, who came through from the kitchen with a long piece of wire and a sheet of newspaper. He then closed the door and locked it, leaving them outside in the garden. Nils knelt down, unfolded the double sheet of newspaper and slid it through the quarter-inch gap under the door. He then took the wire, slotted it through the keyhole, and gently pushed and twisted the wire. Erika and Moss watched through the window and saw the key shift, pop out of the lock and land with a clink on the newspaper below. Nils then carefully slid the newspaper out from under the door, bringing the key with it, which he inserted into the lock and opened the door.

'*Voilà!*' he grinned, triumphantly.

They stared at him for a moment. A small drain beside the door gurgled.

'You're wasted in forensics. You should have your own magic show,' said Moss.

'It's brilliant, but how do you know this is how he got in?' asked Erika.

'We found a piece of broken wire inside the lock, and a small piece of newspaper had caught on the wood under the door,' said Nils, producing an evidence bag from his pocket with a flourish. It contained a stub of silvery wire and a scrap of torn newspaper.

An image popped into Erika's head. A bathroom filled with steam. Mark, wearing just a towel around his waist, pressing a similar-sized scrap of toilet tissue onto a shaving cut, a spot of blood soaking through.

The whirr of the lawnmower starting up again jerked Erika back to reality.

'Were there any prints on the draught-excluding strip?' Moss was asking. Nils shook his head. 'If the killer got in using this newspaper-under-the-door trick, how did they get out again – lock the door and leave the key on the shelf?'

'They didn't. Just like at Gregory Munro's house, they could have paid a visit previously. Taken the key, had a copy made, and then replaced it,' said Moss.

'It makes sense. It's a bit of a stretch, but it makes sense. Would it hold up in court, though?' replied Erika.

'Yes, coupled with the print we've lifted from the outside of the door, down here in the bottom half,' he said, indicating the glossy blue paintwork.

'You lifted a fingerprint?' asked Erika.

Nils beckoned the fingerprint technician back over. 'It's not a fingerprint…' He showed them a piece of white card with the perfect outline of an ear. 'He put his ear to the door, to listen,' said Nils.

The ear print was small, almost child-like. Despite the sweltering heat in the garden, it gave Erika the shivers.

CHAPTER 33

Erika and Moss had moved to one of the large police support vehicles parked in front of the house. Sitting across from them at
one of the small plastic tables was Danuta McBride, the woman
who had discovered Jack Hart's body. A uniformed officer came
over with three plastic cups of tea and placed them on the table.
They all took a cup and sipped.

Erika calculated that Danuta was in her late forties. She
looked pale and shocked. Her dark hair was long and sleek,
worn with a blunt fringe. She wore a floral print wraparound
dress over her large frame, cinched in at the waist by a thick belt.
She had a large smartphone on a lanyard around her neck, and
on her feet she wore hot pink toe trainers.

'How did you know Jack?' asked Erika.

'Um, I'm the executive producer of his show. And we're partners in HartBride Media. Our company, which makes the show.'

'Have you known him long?'

'Yes, we were at university together. We studied journalism.'
Danuta looked at them with disbelief in her eyes. 'Can I have a
cigarette? I've been asking your colleagues for the past couple of
hours.' She indicated the two young uniformed officers at the door.

'Course. I could use one, too,' said Erika, pulling out her
cigarettes and lighter.

'Sorry, you can't smoke in here – health and safety,' said one
of the uniformed officers, a dark-haired lad.

'Well, you go and breathe outside, and we'll make sure we don't burn the furniture,' said Erika, easing a cigarette into the corner of her mouth and offering the pack to Danuta. She took one gratefully. As Erika lit up for them both, the uniformed officer went to say something else, then thought better of it.

'Can you think of anyone who would want to do this to Jack?' asked Erika, placing the cigarette packet down on the table. The ceiling fans were working hard inside, but it was still hot.

'Take your pick,' Danuta said, exhaling smoke and looking down at the small plastic table.

'You need to be more specific,' said Moss.

'He was a pantomime villain… He was Marmite. Loved by millions and hated by millions in equal measure. He was an investigative journalist for years on *the Sun*, then *the Mirror* and *the Express*, the *News of the World*. He was a bloody good one. Always got the story, whatever it took. And he'd split up with his wife a few months back, after she caught him shagging one of our researchers. So he's made plenty of enemies on the way to the top, but who hasn't? I can't think of anyone who'd do… *that*…' Danuta's eyes filled up with tears for a moment and she wiped them with the back of her hand. 'Since Megan Fairchild committed suicide, he's been getting a lot of hate mail. Well, I say hate male, most of it's from trolls online.'

'How did he feel about Megan's death?'

'What do you think?' Danuta snapped. 'We both felt devastated. The crazy thing is that Megan *wrote to us*. She came down to London for auditions. Twice. We explain to everyone what the show is like. We warn them about the press coverage, potential intrusion, but they still want their fifteen minutes of fame. Although they barely get five minutes, let alone fifteen. Jack used to say he wished Andy Warhol was still around, so he could see what these crazies are prepared to do to get on TV.'

'What time did you come over to Jack's house?'

'Dunno, around eleven. He was supposed to come to a crisis meeting with the producers and the network about the whole Megan business.'

'I thought the show went out live every morning at 9 a.m.? Today is a Friday,' said Erika.

'It's only live Monday to Wednesday. We record another two shows "as live" on a Wednesday, after the live morning show. Saves money on studio time.'

'And you didn't see anyone hanging around?'

'No, I only saw the bedroom and I freaked out, climbed back down into the back garden and called 999.'

'Do you know Jack's wife?'

'Yeah. Claire; she left him a couple of months back. Took the kids.'

'How old are his kids?'

'Nine and seven.'

'I've read in the press she's been diagnosed with cancer?' said Moss.

'She got the diagnosis a month after she left him. He told her to come back, tried to patch it up, but she refused. The press didn't report that bit; they prefer to paint him as the villain, saying that he cheated on her while she was sick. Claire's been staying with her mum by the sea in Whitstable.'

'Have you ever been romantically involved with Jack?' asked Erika.

'We shagged a couple of times when we were students. I'm married now, and Jack was like a brother to me.' Danuta's cigarette had burned right down. Erika pushed a plastic cup into the centre of the table for them to use as an ashtray.

'How did you get in the house? You said you climbed?' asked Moss.

'Yes. I climbed up to the bedroom window at the back.'

'Is that something you'd normally do?'

'No. Well, only once before, when he slept in on a live show day, and to be fair that was the day after he'd done the *Text Santa* twenty-four-hour charity broadcast. He was dead to the world... I mean, he was asleep. I climbed up and banged on the window until he woke up.'

'And today, you broke the window?'

'Yeah.'

'Why? Did you think he was still alive?'

'No... Yes... I don't know. He had a bag over his head. I thought I might be able to save him. There's a small stone ashtray on the roof. Jack used to go out there for a smoke. I used that to break the glass. And then when I got inside, I saw he was past help...'

'Did you think he was trying to kill himself?'

'No.'

'What did you think it was, then?'

'I don't know.'

'Was Jack heterosexual?' asked Moss.

'Course he was bloody heterosexual! And he wasn't a homophobe. We've got gay guys working on the show who he gets on with. Got on with.'

'Was he a big drinker, drug taker?'

Danuta looked out of the small van window over to the house where crime scene officers were filing in and out.

'We're asking this in confidence. It will help our investigation,' said Erika.

'He liked a smoke...'

'Marijuana?'

Danuta nodded. 'And he dropped E once, years ago when we made a documentary at Burning Man – but we all did. He liked to go out on the lash, but I wouldn't say he had a problem with drink, or drugs.'

'Okay.'

'Does he own the house?' asked Moss.

'Yes.'

'Is there anything else you can think of?'

'Be gentle when you tell his wife, okay? She's been through a lot.'

Erika nodded. They watched through the window as a black body bag emerged from the house on a stretcher and was carried over to an ambulance. From far up the street, the crowds had swollen even more. Camera flashes went off like tiny bright pinpricks.

There was a knock on the open door of the van, and Crane popped his head around the door.

'All right, boss, can I have a word?'

'Thank you, Danuta. We'll arrange you a lift home,' said Erika. Danuta nodded weakly. Erika and Moss excused themselves and came out of the van.

'There's a neighbour wants to talk to you. She says someone broke in to her house last night and stole some baby clothes,' said Crane.

'How can she be sure?' asked Erika.

'There were stolen off her baby.'

CHAPTER 34

'And nothing else was taken?' asked Erika, moving towards a pair of windows in the nursery. The room was on the ground floor, looking out over a yellowing lawn with overgrown flower-beds. The sun streamed through, casting two bright squares on a new beige carpet. The walls were freshly painted in white, with a border of marching multicoloured elephants.

'No. Nothing…' said the young woman, who lived two doors along from Jack Hart's house. She looked pale and ex-hausted, and clutched her tiny dark-haired daughter close to her chest. They both had short, thick dark hair and large brown eyes.

Moss moved from the freestanding wooden crib in the cen-tre of the room to a tall wooden set of drawers on the left-hand wall. On top were a changing pad, a large bottle of lotion and a baby monitor.

'Was this monitor on at the time?' asked Moss.

'Yes.'

'Was the baby monitor on all night, Mrs Murphy?' asked Erika.

'Please, call me Cath. Yes. It was on all night. Our bedroom is next door. I check on Samantha often.'

'How often is that?'

'Every three hours. I set my alarm.'

'Do you know what time the piece of clothing went miss-ing?'

'I can't be sure. I didn't notice until this morning.'

'And you heard nothing unusual through the baby monitor? Nothing that, in hindsight, was odd?' asked Moss, moving over and holding out her finger. The little girl grabbed it in her tiny hand and giggled.

'No. Samantha is a very quiet little baby. I didn't put two and two together until I heard the commotion outside. Is it true that Jack Hart was found strangled? Much like that doctor was a couple of weeks back?'

'We can't comment on the case,' said Erika.

'This is my home! I have a right to know!'

'We are treating his death as suspicious. That's all we can say.'

'He was a nice man. Jack Hart. He was one of the only people on the street who always said hello. He stopped to ask about Samantha. Put a congratulations card through the door. Nothing like the man on the television.'

'Has anyone been round in the last couple of weeks, asking door-to-door about security alarms?' asked Moss.

'Not that I know of. I can ask my husband when he gets back.'

'When is he back?'

'Late, tonight. He works in the city.'

'Okay. Was one of these windows open last night? There's no sign of forced entry.'

The woman looked guilty. 'Yes, but I only opened it a little. This area is usually so safe, and we're tucked in here amongst the houses. It was such a hot night. I didn't know what to do. I wanted to keep her warm, but I didn't want her to overheat. You hear all these conflicting things about babies…' She started to cry and clutched the little girl tighter.

'Is Samantha your first?' asked Moss. Her finger was still grasped in the little girl's tiny fist. Cath nodded. 'It's tough being a mum,' Moss said. 'Everyone's doing it, but no one wants to admit how hard it is. And I'm talking as a police officer.'

Cath relaxed a little, and smiled. Erika looked around at the freshly painted nursery, half-listening to Moss and the neighbour talking about children. She pushed her maternal feelings to the back of her mind and went over to the window, peering out at the grass on the other side.

'And you're sure your husband or a nanny hasn't taken the jacket to be washed?'

'We don't have a nanny. I've searched the house, and the laundry. I am the only one who gets up for her during the night, and she's too small to undo all the tiny buttons...' Cath's voice trailed off again; she clutched little Samantha tight. 'Why would someone do that? It's just sick. It's deliberately spreading fear. I'm locking all of the windows. I'm never going to open them again!'

Erika and Moss emerged from the house a few minutes later.

'I want that nursery fingerprinted from top to bottom. And every single garden in this row gone over with a fine-tooth comb,' said Erika. 'Whoever did this is going to have to slip up somewhere soon. He's killed two people.'

'So we're talking serial killer now?' asked Moss.

'I don't know. Why take the baby's clothes, though, and leave the baby unharmed? It doesn't add up. He's also visited the victims' houses beforehand, in broad daylight, and we've got nothing.'

'We've got an ear print,' said Moss.

Erika thought of the ear print again, its black outline on the fingerprint paper. It made her feel cold.

CHAPTER 35

It was late when Erika returned home to her flat. When she unlocked the front door, the heat and darkness were overwhelming. She flicked the switch in the hall, but the light didn't come on. She stood on the threshold in the darkness for a moment, and then the light in the communal hallway, which was on a timer, cut out. She was plunged into darkness.

Jack Hart's face appeared in her mind. His eye trapped open under the plastic. A silent scream.

Erika took several deep breaths, came back out to the front entrance and pressed the timer switch. The lights came back on and began to make a light ticking sound. She came back into the threshold of her flat and pulled out her phone, activating the torch. It cast its bright arc of light over the inside of the flat and she cautiously made her way down the darkened hall and into the bedroom. She scrabbled on the wall and found the light switch, but nothing happened. She swung her arm from left to right, illuminating the corners of the room, crouching down to shine the light under the bed. She opened the wardrobe doors.

Nothing.

More images flooded her mind: Gregory Munro, Jack Hart. Lying naked on their backs, naked bodies exposed, heads misshapen through the tight clear plastic bags.

There was a click as her front door closed.

'Shit,' she said, under her breath. Her heart began to thump against her chest. She could still smell the sickly aroma of the pond water on her sweaty skin. Quickly, she came out of the bedroom and, keeping one eye on the front door, she reached round the bathroom door for the light pull. It did nothing when she yanked it. She rounded the corner of the bathroom door and directed the phone light inside. It was empty: white toilet, bath and sink. She yanked back the white shower curtain. Nothing. The reflection from the phone's light bounced back at her from the mirror, momentarily dazzling her. She tried to shake the painful sensation and the bright spot in her vision as she hurried back out of the bathroom, past the front door and through to the living room.

She tried the light switch but, again, nothing. It was just as she'd left it: messy. A couple of flies buzzed around above the old coffee cups on the kitchen counter. She relaxed a little. The flat was empty. She returned to the front door and put the chain on, and then came back through to the living room. She grabbed the string for the large blinds over the patio window and pulled them up with a whoosh.

A silhouette of a tall man stood in front of the window. Erika screamed and staggered back, falling over the coffee table with a crash of cups.

She dropped her phone, plunging the room back into darkness.

CHAPTER 36

As Erika lay on the floor, the silhouette of the tall figure was still for a moment, then swayed a little, saying, through the glass, 'Boss? You in there? It's me, Peterson.' He cupped his hands against the window and peered inside. 'Boss?'

'What the bloody hell are you doing coming to my flat?' asked Erika, getting up and pulling open the patio door. The light pollution from the surrounding sky bathed Peterson in an orangey glow.

'Sorry, I couldn't find the front door. I didn't know it was on the side of the building.'

'Spoken like a true detective,' said Erika. 'Wait here a second.'

She retrieved her phone from the shadows under the coffee table, turned the light back on and grabbed a chair so she could reach the fuse box high on the wall above the television. She opened it and reset the trip switch. The lights all came on in the flat, apart from the one in the hall above the front door.

She could now see Peterson properly in the open patio doors. He wore blue jeans, an old Adidas T-shirt and he had a couple of days' stubble. He rubbed at his bloodshot eyes.

'Bulb's gone,' Erika said, more in relief than explanation. She stepped down off the chair and smoothed down her hair, realising she must look a little wild. 'Where were you today?' she added, looking Peterson up and down. She could smell stale booze.

'Can I come in for a chat?' he asked.

'It's late.'

'Please, boss.'

'Okay.'

He came into the living room. A light breeze wafted through from outside. 'This is… nice,' he said.

'No, it isn't,' said Erika, moving back over to the kitchen. 'Do you want something to drink?'

'What have you got?'

'You're not having anything with alcohol in it. You smell like you've had enough.'

She quickly scanned through her rather bare cupboards. She had a nice bottle of Glenmorangie, unopened. In the fridge was an old bottle of white wine with a few inches left. Her coffee jar was almost empty.

'It's tap water or… Um Bongo,' she said dryly, finding two small cartons of the tropical juice drink under some mouldy lettuce in the salad drawer.

'The juice, thanks,' Peterson said.

Erika closed the fridge and handed him one of the juice boxes. She grabbed the cigarettes from her bag and the two of them went out onto the little paved square outside the patio door. There were no chairs, so they perched on the low wall bordering the grass.

'I didn't know you could still get Um Bongo,' Peterson said, pulling the plastic off a small straw and pushing it through the little hole of silver foil.

'My sister and her kids came to stay a few months ago,' said Erika, lighting a cigarette.

'I didn't know you had a sister.'

Her cigarette hadn't lit properly and she puffed, trying to get the tip to glow. She exhaled and nodded.

'How many kids has she got?'

'Two. And one more on the way.'

'Boys or girls?'

'A boy, a girl and a baby… She doesn't know the sex.'

'And the boy and girl are young?'

'What time is it? Shit, I wanted to see the late news,' said Erika. She jumped up and went back through the patio doors. Peterson followed and found her searching around on the sofa under cushions.

'It's here,' he said, fishing the remote out from under an open takeaway box on the coffee table. Erika grabbed it and flicked on the TV.

The ITV news showed the revolving Scotland Yard sign, and the tail-end of an interview with Marsh, who looked weary.

'…Our Homicide and Serious Crime unit has made this our top priority,' he was saying. 'We are following up several lines of enquiry.'

The screen then cut to a clip from *The Jack Hart Show.* The camera moved across a rowdy studio audience, who were up on their feet, booing, shouting and whistling. The shot cut to a young girl sitting on the stage with a lad dressed in a tracksuit and baseball cap. A caption underneath read: I ABORTED MY IVF TRIPLETS TO GET A BOOB JOB.

'It's my life – I can do what I want,' the girl said, unrepentant.

The camera then cut to a close-up of Jack Hart, sitting to one side of the young couple, his brow suitably furrowed. He was immaculate and handsome in a blue suit.

'But it's not just your life. What about those unborn children?' he purred.

A voiceover read, 'Jack Hart was a controversial figure, idolised and hated in equal measure, and today he was found dead at his home in Dulwich, South London. Police have released no other information, but they have confirmed they are treating his death as suspicious.'

'Jesus, someone killed him?' said Peterson.

'Where have you been all day?' asked Erika. Peterson was silent. 'He was killed exactly the same way as Gregory Munro – well, we're still waiting for toxicology,'

On the screen, the studio audience was chanting, 'Murderer! Murderer! Murderer!' The young lad in the baseball cap rose to his feet and started to threaten people in the front row.

'How long do you think we have until the press find out his murder is linked to Gregory Munro?' asked Peterson.

'I don't know. Twenty-four hours, but I hope a bit longer.'

'Have you spoken to Marsh?'

'Yeah, I briefed him a couple of hours ago,' said Erika.

The news report was now showing footage from earlier in the day: people crowding around the police cordon outside Jack Hart's house, and then a wobbly long-lens shot of the body bag being stretchered out of the house.

'Isaac Strong is doing the post-mortem tonight. We'll have the results in the early hours.'

The late news ended and the screen cut to the weather. Erika turned the volume down and turned back to Peterson, who was silently watching the TV with the straw clamped in the corner of his mouth, sucking the last of the juice from the box.

'Peterson, you've shown up at my flat, peering through my window. What's going on? Where were you today?'

He swallowed. 'I had to think.'

'You had to think. Okay. And did you have to do it at the taxpayer's expense? That's what weekends are for.'

'Sorry, boss. The whole Gary Wilmslow thing has screwed me up...'

Erika lit up another cigarette. Events with Gary Wilmslow seemed so long ago; so much had happened in the past few days.

Peterson continued, his voice cracking a little with emotion. 'The thought that I'd compromised a massive paedophile investigation… What if it's scared him off? What if they just pack up and disappear, still abusing kids, making those sick movies? It means I'm directly responsible for all those kids, all that hideous abuse.' He put his fingers to his eyes and his bottom lip began to tremble.

'Hey, hey! Peterson…' Erika put an arm around him, rubbing at his shoulders. 'Now, that's enough. You hear me?'

He took deep breaths and wiped his eyes with the heels of his hands.

'Peterson, he's still under surveillance. Their cover isn't broken. I can see if I can find out more tomorrow.' Erika stared at him for a moment. His eyes had glazed over. 'Peterson, what?'

He gulped, and took a deep breath. 'My sister was abused, when we were little. Well, she was little, I was just old enough not to be of… of *interest*.'

'Who was it?'

'It was the bloke who ran our Sunday school, Mr Simmonds. An old white dude. My sister only told us last year. After she tried to kill herself. She took a load of pills. My mum found her just in time.'

'Did they catch him?'

Peterson shook his head. 'No, he's dead now. She was too scared to tell anyone. He told her that if she said anything, he'd kill her. He said he would find a way into her bedroom and slit her throat. For years, she used to wet the bed. I used to take the mickey out of her for that. If only I'd known. When Mr Simmonds died, my parents attended the big memorial service for him at our local church in Peckham. To celebrate his outstanding service to the community.'

'I'm sorry, Peterson.'

'My sister's nearly forty. She's never been able to escape what he did to her. And what can I do?'

'You can come back to work. You can be the best police officer that you can… There's plenty of other bastards out there that you will catch.'

'I'd love to get that bastard Gary Wilmslow,' said Peterson, through gritted teeth. 'If I could have an hour in a room with him…'

'You know that won't happen, don't you? And if you try and make it happen… Well, Peterson, you don't want to go down that road. Believe me.'

'I'm just so fucking angry,' he said, slamming his hand down on the table. Erika didn't flinch. They sat in silence for a moment, listening to the crickets humming down in the darkness by the apple tree. Erika got up, went to the kitchen cupboard and pulled down two glasses and the bottle of Glenmorangie. She poured a generous measure in each one and took them back over. Handing Peterson one, she sat back down beside him.

'It's one of the most unhealthy emotions, anger,' said Erika, putting her glass down and lighting another cigarette. 'The name Jerome Goodman still makes my blood boil. I've spent hours devising elaborate and painful ways I would kill him. My anger is almost limitless.'

'Is he the…'

'He's the man who killed my husband and four of my colleagues. He's the man who destroyed my life. My old life, that is. And he's the man who nearly destroyed me. But he didn't. I won't let him.'

Peterson was silent.

'My point is that bad people are everywhere. The world is filled with good, but it's equally overwhelmed with bad. People who commit horror and evil. You have to concentrate on what you *can* do, what you *can* influence. The ones who you can hunt down. I know it sounds simplistic, but it took a long while to realise that, and it gave me some peace.'

'Where is Jerome Goodman?' asked Peterson.

'He vanished off the face of the earth, after the shoot-out... I don't know if he had inside help, or got lucky. But he hasn't been found. Yet.'

She went on, 'I believe in fate. I know that one day in the future I will see Jerome Goodman again, and I will get him. And he'll be locked away for the rest of his life.' She emphasised the last part with a clenched fist.

'What if you don't?'

'Don't what?'

'Don't get him?'

Erika turned to him. Her eyes were wide and unblinking. 'The only thing that will prevent me from getting him will be death. His, or mine.' She turned away and took a long drink of whisky.

'I'm sorry. I'm sorry this had to happen to you, boss... Erika...'

'I'm sorry about your sister.'

She turned back to him and their eyes locked for a moment. Then Peterson leaned in to kiss her. She put her hand over his mouth.

'Don't.'

He leant back. 'Shit, sorry.'

'No, don't be. Please, don't be,' she said. She got up and went out, returning a few minutes later with a blanket and a pillow.

'You should sleep on the sofa. Don't drive.'

'Boss, I'm really sorry.'

'Peterson, please. You know me. We're fine, okay?' He nodded. 'And thank you for telling me about your sister. I'm so sorry. But you've helped me understand stuff. Now, get some sleep.'

Erika lay awake for a long time, alone in bed and staring up into the darkness. She thought of Mark, and forced herself to picture his face. To keep him alive in her memory. She'd been so close to returning Peterson's kiss, but Mark had pulled her back. Part of her longed for a man in her bed, a warm body to hold her, but right now it was a step too far.

A step further away from her life with Mark.

CHAPTER 37

Erika woke up just before six. The sun was streaming through the windows. When she came through to the living room, Peterson had gone, leaving a Post-it stuck to the fridge.

THANX, BOSS – SORRY IF I WAS A PRAT
+ THANX 4 LETTING ME CRASH ON THE SOFA
CU @ WORK – JAMES (PETERSON)

She was pleased there was no kiss at the bottom, and hoped there wouldn't be tension with him at work. There was enough tension at work without her personal life getting involved.

It was cool and quiet as Erika walked down the long corridor towards the doors of the morgue. She pressed the call button and looked up at the small camera above the door. There was a beep, and the large steel door automatically popped open with a hiss. The cold air inside flowed out with wisps of vapour.

'Morning,' said Isaac, meeting her at the door. He was still wearing his blue scrubs, which were bloody in places.

They came through the large post-mortem room. The floor was tiled in a Victorian geometric diamond-shaped pattern of black and white. The ceiling was high, but there were no windows, and the walls were tiled in white. A row of metal doors lined one side, and in the centre of the room were four stainless steel tables. Three of them gleamed empty under the bright fluorescent lights. On the one closest to the door lay the body of Jack Hart.

One of Isaac's mortuary assistants, a petite young Chinese girl, was closing up the long Y-shaped incision, which began below the belly button. She was halfway done, having reached the chest plate, and was gently stitching the skin together, working her way up towards where the incision separated and splayed across the shoulders. The stitches were neat, but large and prominent.

'As with Gregory Munro, there were high levels of flunitrazepam in his blood,' said Isaac. 'It was ingested in liquid form. This is consistent with the Bud beer bottle we found on his bedside table, which contained a large amount of flunitrazepam residue.'

'So he was drugged?' asked Erika.

'The levels were higher than what we found in Gregory Munro's blood. I can't say if this was accident or design. Unlike Gregory Munro, Jack was younger and in peak physical condition: very little body fat, well-developed muscles.'

'The killer may have thought he needed a higher dose to incapacitate him,' said Erika. They looked across at the mortuary assistant stitching the chest, as she pulled the well-developed pectoral muscles so they met once again.

'So you think the same person did this?'

'I didn't say that. The similarities are striking, but it's your job to make that call.'

'Okay. Cause of death?' asked Erika.

'Asphyxiation from the plastic bag tied over the head.'

'His face looks different to how Gregory Munro's looked. His face is covered in red marks, and his skin has an odd tinge to it.'

'Gregory Munro asphyxiated rapidly; it took only one or two minutes. With Jack Hart, the strength of his lungs would have given him the ability to retain oxygen under stress, so the asphyxial signs and symptoms are severe. These tiny pinpricks of red on his face are petechial haemorrhages. And the bluish tinge is caused by cyanosis, where the skin is discoloured by poor circulation. The internal organs are all dotted with haemorrhages, too.'

'So how long do you think it took for him to die?'

'Four, five... perhaps six minutes. His hands were tied behind his back, but he may have thrashed around violently and resisted, causing the killer to strike him. The bruised left eye is consistent with a blow to the face and there is bruising to the lips and gums, suggesting pressure was applied to the face. You should also see this.' Isaac moved closer to the body. The mortuary assistant stepped back, and Isaac gently opened the mouth.

'Jesus,' said Erika.

'He almost bit through his tongue,' said Isaac. 'It was an extremely long, drawn-out and painful death.'

'Any sign of sexual assault?'

'No.'

Isaac nodded, and the mortuary assistant moved back to continue stitching. The limp form shifted a little as the thread looped through the skin and was drawn tight. Erika thought the open flaps of skin looked more like painted plastic than human flesh.

'There's something else I want to show you, if we go through to my office,' said Isaac.

His office was warm in comparison to the morgue. Sun poured in through a window high on the wall. The room was lined with bookshelves, which were crammed with medical textbooks. An iPod glowed in a Bose sound system. The desk was neatly arranged, and a screensaver of a swirling cube bounced around on the laptop screen.

'The bag that was used to asphyxiate Gregory Munro and Jack Hart was the same type,' said Isaac, taking an evidence bag from the desk. It contained the crumpled plastic bag, which was mottled with dried blood and a milky residue. The white drawstring was also caked in dried blood.

'How do you mean? From the same supermarket?' asked Erika, taking the bag from him.

'No, these bags are manufactured to assist people to commit suicide. They are known as "suicide" bags or "exit" bags. I should have picked up on this with Gregory Munro. It was only when I saw it again with Jack Hart that I realised.'

'So how does this help someone commit suicide? Why not just use an ordinary plastic bag?'

'It's very difficult to simply stick a bag over your head and wait to suffocate. We are primed with the instinct not to let ourselves suffocate. We call it the hypercapnic alarm response. As a person is deprived of oxygen, they tear the bag off in a panic. So someone came up with the idea of this suicide bag. As you can see, the bag is tall – it doesn't fit snugly over the head, there's space above. The idea is that you place the bag over your head, and thread a plastic pipe under the drawstring before drawing it tight around the neck – but not too tight, as you pipe in an inert gas like helium or nitrogen. People have been known to buy the canisters of helium used to blow up balloons. They breathe the gas, which prevents the panic, the sense of suffocation and struggling, during unconsciousness.'

'So the person who did this would have had to have bought this bag?' asked Erika.

'Yes.'

'Where from?'

'They can be bought online, from specialist websites, I believe,' said Isaac.

'So we could potentially get a list of people who've bought one of these bags?' asked Erika.

'That's now up to you,' said Isaac.

When they were finished, Isaac walked with Erika to the entrance of the morgue.

'You should get some sleep. You look beat,' said Erika.

'I will.' Isaac pressed the release button and the metal door opened. 'Umm, I know that next week is the two-year anniversary of Mark's…'

Erika stopped and turned.

'Mark's death,' she said, holding his gaze.

'Yes, Mark's death. If you want to do something, I'm around. If you don't, that's fine too. We could go out, stay in. I just don't want you to spend it on your own.'

She smiled. 'I'm hoping that I'll be solving this case. It will take my mind off it.'

'Sure. Just know I'm here.'

'Thanks. How are things with Stephen?'

Isaac looked guiltily at the floor. 'Good. He's moving in.'

Erika nodded.

'Don't judge me,' he added.

'I'm the last to judge,' she said, holding up her hands. 'I'll see you soon.' She gave him a grin and walked off down the long corridor.

CHAPTER 38

Erika had called her team for an early morning briefing. She stood in front of the whiteboards with the crime scene photos of Gregory Munro and the new addition of Jack Hart. They were just settling down when Peterson arrived.

'Peterson is back, and he's brought decent coffee,' said Moss, seeing him enter with a large tray of coffees.

'Here you go, boss,' said Peterson, offering Erika the large tray of Starbucks cups.

'Where were you yesterday?' she asked, taking a cup.

'I had a dodgy Chinese,' he said, not missing a beat.

'Okay, well, I'm glad you're back,' she said, giving him a smile.

'Thanks, boss,' he said, looking relieved. He moved around the room, handing out coffee to the other officers.

'So, this dodgy Chinese. Where did you meet her?' asked Moss with a wicked grin, leaning up to take a cup from the rapidly emptying tray.

'It was Kung Pao Chicken,' Peterson said.

'You got her name too! She sounds classy: double-barrelled.'

'Piss off, Moss,' he said laughing.

'Okay. Right, let's concentrate,' said Erika. Everyone in the room settled down to listen. 'So here we are again. We now have two murders, two weeks apart. Both victims live within the same fifteen-mile radius. I can confirm both were killed in exactly the same way: drugged and asphyxiated with a plastic bag.'

She paused as a murmur went around the room.

'One was a regular family GP. The other was one of the most well-known faces on British television. So, as I always say, let's go back to the beginning. And there are no stupid questions.'

'They're both male,' said DC Warren.

'Yes, we can see that from the crime scene photos,' said Erika, pointing at the two men lying naked on their beds. 'And?'

'They were subdued with a date rape drug administered to an alcoholic drink inside their property, which aided the suffocation with the plastic bag,' said Singh.

'Yes, and it's the same specific type of bag used in both murders. A "suicide" or "exit" bag. These are available to buy from specialist sites on the Internet. So we need to check out which sites sell them, and get a purchase history, a list of credit card transactions and addresses.'

'They were both of a similar height,' said Moss. 'Gregory Munro was older, and wasn't as fit and healthy as Jack Hart.'

'The killer adjusted the dose for the size of his victims. Jack Hart was given a higher dose than Gregory Munro, so potentially he had studied them from afar,' said Erika.

'They were both stalked, at night,' added Peterson.

'Why do you use the word "stalked"?'

'The killer could have already been inside their houses when they got home… He probably stalked them round the house, watched them. It might not have been the first time,' said Peterson.

'Yeah, it was planned. He staked out the houses beforehand. He mocked up a fake security firm leaflet for Gregory Munro; he knew how he was going to get into Jack Hart's house,' added Moss.

'Maybe he's ex-military? He left virtually no DNA evidence,' said Singh.

'Or he works in a hospital or pharmacy. He was able to get hold of liquid flunitrazepam and a syringe… We found the cap of a syringe under Jack Hart's bed. Although you can get all that stuff off the Internet these days,' said DC Warren.

'That could link him to Gregory Munro,' said Peterson.

'But how does it link him to Jack Hart?' said Erika.

'There's no history of gay relationships or a gay past with Jack?' asked Peterson.

'Not that we know of,' said Erika. 'His wife is going to formally identify the body later today, but obviously we need to tread easy when we question her. Gregory Munro has a son; Jack Hart has two small children. They're both estranged from the mother. Has anyone got anything to say about that?'

There was silence.

'There must be some reason why this guy is targeting these two men!' said Erika, drawing a large black circle on the whiteboard around the photos of the two men.

'But what the bloody hell does a local GP have in common with a tabloid TV presenter?' asked Moss.

'Well, we need to find that out, and fast,' said Erika. 'The link will be to the killer. Whoever this is, *chose* the victims. Watched them in the days leading up to the murders Now, there haven't been any fingerprints recovered from either murder scene, or from Jack Hart's next-door neighbour whose daughter's nursery was broken into, but we did get an ear print from the outside of the back door at Jack Hart's house. Have we had anything back, Crane, from – where is it again?'

'The National Training Centre for Scientific Support to Crime Investigation,' said Crane. 'I've just heard that they're about to run this through their database of over two thousand ear prints. So we could get a call any time.'

'I'm not holding out much hope, but two thousand ears – those odds are better than I thought,' said Erika.

'I've just had the pictures back off the memory card we confiscated from the journalist,' said Moss, looking at her computer.

'Why has it taken so long?' asked Erika.

'The metal contacts were bent; the photographer probably bent them when he yanked the card out of the camera and swallowed it,' she said.

'Okay, let's put them up on the projector,' said Erika. DC Warren grabbed a multimedia projector off a shelf at the back of the incident room, went over to Moss's PC and plugged it in. After a couple of minutes of positioning, they had it trained on the whiteboard.

Erika turned off the lights, plunging the room into darkness, and then an image of a car on a busy street, surrounded by people, appeared on the back wall.

'Okay, boss, I'll just go through these,' said Moss, clicking with her mouse. A series of similar photos flashed by, and then some paparazzi pictures of an unknown celebrity leaving the Ivy restaurant in a car with tinted windows.

'Okay, here we go. These are Jack Hart's house.'

The first picture was of Jack Hart arriving back at his house on the night of his murder. Moss flicked through the images, taken in a rapid-fire, almost like jerky animation. Jack leaving the black cab, walking to his gate, opening it, stopping for a moment to turn and say something. Then Jack moving to his front door, reaching into his pocket and pulling his key out, opening the front door and going inside.

'Okay, so the paps outside got him going indoors,' said Moss. 'The time stamp on this last photo is… 12.57 a.m.'

She flicked through photos, and the perspective changed to the back garden of Jack Hart's house. She stopped at a photo taken at a low angle, looking up to the back bedroom window, where the light was on.

'Jesus. That bloody photographer was in the back garden before Jack Hart was murdered,' said Erika.

The view then jumped forward to pictures taken on the flat roof directly outside the bedroom window. The curtain was open and there was a view of the bed from the side. Then, again like animation, the naked figure of Jack Hart walked in. He held a towel in one hand and a bottle of beer in the other. He moved to the nightstand over by the opposite window at the front of the house, put the bottle down and sat on the edge of the bed.

'Stop! What's that!' cried Erika. 'Go back, two pictures.'

'Shit, look! There, under the bed,' said Peterson.

Jack was sitting on the bed with his naked back to the camera. A clear silhouette of a figure could be made out, crouching under the bed.

'Hang on, I can zoom the image in,' said Moss, rapidly clicking and pushing the mouse across the mouse pad. The picture enlarged and shifted so the whiteboard was filled with the dark grainy image of a figure crouching under the bed. Two hands could just be made out, fingers splayed on the carpet, and the bottom half of the face had been caught in the light, showing the tip of a nose and the mouth.

It was the mouth that disturbed Erika the most. It was grinning widely and the teeth were on show.

'Jesus Christ. He was already inside the house, waiting for him,' said Erika.

Breaking the silence that followed in the incident room, a phone began to ring. Crane snatched it up and began to talk in a low voice.

'Can you make it any bigger, Moss?' asked Erika. The photo zoomed in on the figure under the bed, but the image was too blurred and grainy.

'I'll get it over to the cyber crime guys and see if they can enhance it any more,' said Moss.

'Boss, you're going to want to hear this,' said Crane, excitedly, having just put the phone down.

'Please tell me it's something – some kind of evidence about the man who is doing this?' said Erika.

'It is evidence. But it's not a bloke.'

'What?'

'Nils Åkerman has been working on the small amount of DNA he swabbed from the ear print on the back door of Jack Hart's house, and some samples of skin cells found on the outside of the suicide bag used to kill him. It's a woman.'

'What?'

'It's from a white woman. Nils ran the DNA through the national crime database, and there's no match, no previous convictions – but the DNA is female. It's a woman who's doing this.'

A murmur went round the incident room.

'But what about the fact that we've linked the two murders?' asked Peterson.

'We *have* linked the two murders,' said Erika. 'What? The link is now thrown into doubt because it's a woman?'

'Shit. Whoever she is, she's got a good lead on us. We've been looking for a bloke,' said Moss.

They let that sink in for a moment. Erika went back to the whiteboard and looked at the figure under the bed, the bottom half of the face emerging from the shadows with a row of grinning teeth.

'Okay. So we go back to the beginning. We re-examine every piece of evidence. We revisit interviews with local residents. And bring that bloody photographer back in for questioning. We're looking for a woman. A female serial killer.'

CHAPTER 39

Simone arrived home after a long shift at work and closed the front door, drinking in the silence in the gloomy hallway. Sloughing off her coat, she went to her computer, which was tucked into the nook under the stairs. She booted it up, logged into the chat room and started to type:

NIGHT OWL: Hey, Duke. U there?

A few moments passed, and DUKE began to type.

DUKE: Hey, Night Owl. What's up?
NIGHT OWL: I saw him again. Stan. My husband.
DUKE: Yeah? You okay?
NIGHT OWL: Not really. I knew he wasn't real, but he was there, as real as anything.
DUKE: Did you start the new meds?
NIGHT OWL: Yeah.
DUKE: Which one?
NIGHT OWL: Halcion.
DUKE: What's ur dosage? 0.125 mg?
NIGHT OWL: Yeah.
DUKE: Visual disturbances are a side effect.
NIGHT OWL: Tell me about it!
DUKE: I've been there, done that. They took me up to 0.5 mg and it still did nothing: endless days of no sleep… So what u up 2?

Simone stared at the screen. It blurred slightly and she rubbed at her tired, scratchy eyes. She'd suffered from insomnia for years. It stemmed from when she'd been taken into care, when she'd been afraid to close her eyes after being put to bed at night in the children's home.

Over the following years, twenty and counting, she had learned to cope with the insomnia, to cope with the feeling of numb exhaustion, the feeling that her body was slowly rotting from the inside. She had learned to function as a normal human being.

She craved sleep – it occupied her thoughts constantly – but when it came to *bedtime*, a phrase that seemed like a bad joke whenever she heard it, her body went into a cold panic. Panic at the knowledge that sleep would be out of her grasp, that she would spend endless hours lying in bed watching the red glow of the digital clock, thoughts spinning wildly out of control in her mind.

Fear, Simone knew, was particularly prevalent at night. When everyone else seems to have departed the world, the insomniacs are alone, stranded in the half-light. Simone's insomnia had guided her into an abusive relationship and an unplanned pregnancy. She'd lost the baby soon after her shotgun wedding to Stan. It was ordinary, the doctor had said. Extremely common to lose the baby the first time you become pregnant. But it hadn't felt ordinary. She'd been devastated. She had thought her life was finally coming right, and she'd been so excited to meet and care for the little life growing inside her.

As a newly-wed, Simone had thought that sharing a bed might help her insomnia, but again she found herself staring into the darkness. She would watch Stan as he moved through the stages of sleep: the gentle rise and fall of his broad chest, the twitch of his eyelids as his eyes flitted underneath.

Sometimes, without warning, the rhythm of Stan's laboured breathing would break, and his eyes would open with a hungry, vacant stare. And then, at the time of night when Simone felt most vulnerable, exhausted and unattractive, he would wordlessly climb on top of her and part her legs with the back of his hand – almost dismissively, as if her legs were a tedious obstacle to what he wanted.

When they were first married, she'd endured this. The sex was often rough. It often left her in pain, but she'd thought that it was his desire for her that caused him to lose control. And besides, she'd felt that it was her job as a good wife. It was her job to make the right noises, to put on enjoyment.

And she'd longed to be rewarded again with a baby; to be given another chance to be a mother.

Then, one night when he was pounding into her, he'd bitten her on the breast. It had shocked her. The shock had almost overridden the pain. He'd lifted his head, her blood glistening on his teeth, and just carried on.

He had apologised profusely the next morning. There were tears and promises to never do it again, and for a while the late-night sex had stopped.

Then, slowly, things reverted back. It had coincided with a time where Simone was getting no sleep, not even a few fitful minutes. She was weak and desperate, and she let him do it. As the months, and then the years passed, she lost all fight, which only seemed to fuel her husband's dark desires. She wondered how her life had ended up this way. Hadn't she had dreams? Weren't there things she'd wanted to do with her life: travel, escape, become someone else?

Her saviour would be a baby, she was sure – but a baby never came, and tests finally showed she was unable to conceive, a result of the complications in her first pregnancy. The devastation sharpened the problems in her marriage to an angry spike. Simone was raped repeatedly, and then left awake in the darkness in pain. Every time, Stan would leave her and go back to the land of sleep.

Sometimes, she thought she would be able to cope with the violence and the abuse if only she could sleep. The lack of sleep was more of a torture. It was unknown, malevolent. The chemicals in her brain were conspiring to keep her in the world, when others could leave and disappear into their dreams.

By the time Simone had reached thirty-five, her husband was drinking heavily and they had fallen into debt. Around the same time, they had the Internet put in, and during her sleepless nights Simone discovered a pinprick of light: online chat rooms. At first, she gravitated towards support groups, speaking to other battered and abused wives whose only outlet for their fears was talking through their experiences. But she saw her own situation reflected back in their posts, and from the outside thought them pathetic.

Then she met Duke.

Duke, like her, was an insomniac. He listened to her without judgement. They also talked about normal stuff: TV shows they liked, funny things that had happened to them. They flirted.

Duke described himself as tall and dark (which Simone doubted) but then she described herself as tall and blonde (which was also a lie). They would go off and have private chats, in cosy virtual spaces, and sometimes it would get hot and heavy. He would describe what he wanted to do to her sexually; she responded. He made her feel loved and desired.

She opened up to him about her situation. Told him about her abusive husband, who she never named. She told Duke everything. Her deepest secrets, desires and fantasies. He did the same in return. The only thing they held back from one another was where they lived, and their real names. He was DUKE, and she was NIGHT OWL.

She couldn't remember exactly when their conversations had taken a darker turn. It had happened one night after she'd been raped. She'd started to refer to it as that – *rape* – and not as sex. She'd been complaining that her doctor had prescribed yet another batch of pills which weren't making a dent in her insomnia. And Duke had written:

DUKE: Maybe the pills would work better on yur husband!

She'd stared at the screen for a long time. Then she'd carried on chatting.

It had taken her two more nights to pluck up the courage. She'd cooked Stan spaghetti bolognese, and as the hot tomato sauce had bubbled away on the stove, she'd opened one of the capsules of Zopiclone, the latest sleeping pill she'd been prescribed. She remembered separating the capsule and holding the two halves over the large steaming pan... Then stirring the white powder into the food.

She'd nervously watched Stan eat a large plateful, and then, when he'd finished, go to the sofa with a beer, put his head back. He was out cold in minutes.

Simone's exhilaration that it had worked had quickly been replaced by fear, and the realisation that she had been stupid. She hadn't thought beyond knocking him out. What if he stayed on the sofa all night? What if he woke up in the morning still on the sofa? He would be suspicious.

It had taken a superhuman effort to rouse Stan and get him upstairs, supporting him like a drunk. She was convinced she had blown it, and was sick with fear, watching him all night. Wild thoughts went through her mind: of running away, of taking her own life. And then the sun had come up, and he'd woken. Irritable, unpleasant – but he had gone to work with nothing more than a comment that he must have been tired.

Is it that easy? she'd thought.

A month passed, and the abuse escalated. On one harrowing evening they were watching TV, and for no reason Stan had snapped, telling her how much he hated her, how she had ruined his life. He'd started to beat her, and she'd managed to get away and lock herself in the bathroom.

She'd sat, cowering in the bath, listening to him rant and crash in the kitchen. Then he'd charged the door and burst in with a saucepan. He'd stripped off her clothes and held her down in the bath whilst he poured boiling water over her naked body.

She'd been badly burnt across her chest and abdomen. The burns became so infected, and she was in so much pain, that Stan had no choice but take her to the doctor. She'd seen this as an opportunity to tell someone about the abuse she was suffering. But Dr Gregory Munro had thought this was a symptom of the paranoia and psychosis linked to her insomnia. He thought she was lying! Stan had played the part well, acting like the concerned husband.

Yes, she'd lost grip on reality in the past, she'd hallucinated, and previously told Dr Munro about things she saw and heard, but now, faced with her burns and her tears, Dr Munro didn't believe her. She'd trusted him, but he threw it back in her face. He took Stan's side, almost pitying him for having such a crazy wife, and had her admitted to hospital.

She was discharged after a week, and for a while afterwards the violence had subsided. But she'd still been too afraid to leave him and had become desperate, feeling there was no way out of her situation.

She'd drugged him again, this time placing two of the pills in the beer he drank in bed. Within minutes, he was out cold. She'd even tried to wake him – prodding at him, shaking him

– but nothing. He woke again none the wiser, complaining, as ever, that he felt groggy.

Around this time, Duke stopped sleeping completely. He started to talk about how he wanted to end his life, detailing how he would do it.

DUKE: I'd use a suicide bag.

NIGHT OWL: What's a suicide bag?

DUKE: They also call them exit bags…

NIGHT OWL: ???

DUKE: It's a large plastic bag with a draw cord. You can use them to commit suicide.

NIGHT OWL: Sounds painful.

DUKE: Not if u use it with gas, like helium or nitrogen. Helium is easier. You can buy canisters of helium for kids' birthday parties. Put the bag over your head and start to fill it with gas… It prevents u panicking, you just drift off to sleep. Endless sleep. Bliss.

NIGHT OWL: Is it that easy?

DUKE: Yeah, with one of these suicide bags it is. I've been visiting this online forum, about suicide. Did you know that if the bag is removed, provided there isn't struggle, it's difficult to determine how a person suffocated, or even died?

NIGHT OWL: Please don't do it.

DUKE: Why?

NIGHT OWL: I need you.

DUKE: You do?

NIGHT OWL: Yes… I was reading about Eastern mythology…

DUKE: Yes! Keep talking! I'm finally dropping off to sleep!

NIGHT OWL: Ha ha. I'm serious. I was reading all about Yin and Yang. Two opposites fitting together. What if we were in bed together?

DUKE: I'm listening. Do we get to be naked?
NIGHT OWL: Maybe… But I'm talking about sleeping. What if we could go far away from here, and sleep together in the same bed?
DUKE: Where?
NIGHT OWL: I don't know. Somewhere far away. We would hold each other and just fall asleep.
DUKE: I'd love that. Imagine, waking up refreshed.

It was then that Simone had experienced a revelation. She decided that she didn't want to die. What she wanted was not to be a victim. She talked to Duke more about the suicide bag, then cleared her history from the computer. He ordered one for her, and had it sent to the hospital where she worked.

The suicide bag wasn't for her, of course. It was for Stan. Simone had realised she wouldn't need helium gas: she had an endless supply of sleeping pills.

The last time Stan raped her, it was particularly violent. As if, somehow, he knew it was the last. It steeled her resolve.

The next morning, when Stan was in the shower, Simone decided that she'd do it that night, when he came home from work. She was downstairs making tea, and eyeing the box of pills sitting on top of the microwave, when there was a loud thud from upstairs. She rushed up to find Stan sprawled in a heap in the shower, under the running water. He was white.

She called for an ambulance, almost as a reflex. He was pronounced dead on arrival. He'd had a heart attack at the age of thirty-seven.

Life changed, and Simone had become the grieving widow. And in death, her husband had become the tragic hero. He never paid for what he'd done to her. She should have felt release, but as the weeks passed, she'd only felt anger. A growing knot of anger at the fact that a man had taken so many years from her.

She'd become obsessed. She'd stopped sleeping all together; all power had been taken from her. She liked to pretend Stan was still alive. That way, he couldn't get any sympathy.

Simone realised she had drifted away. The blur of the computer screen came back into focus. Duke had been writing repeatedly, asking where she had gone.

DUKE: Night Owl?
DUKE: U there????
DUKE: ???????
NIGHT OWL: Sorry, Duke, I was daydreaming.
DUKE: So? What happens next? Do I get to finally meet you? Do I get to lie with you in bed? Far far away?
NIGHT OWL: Soon. Very soon. I just have to deal with the next name on my list.

Simone thought of the list. It existed nowhere except in her head. But it was still very real. When she'd killed Dr Gregory Munro – the doctor who had believed Stan over her – she'd drawn a thick black line through his name. She'd done the same, too, with Jack Hart. Hart had been harder to track down. Back when he'd written the piece about her cruel neglectful mother, he'd been an ambitious journalist; her story had been a nice piece of tabloid sensationalism for him. It had helped him on his way up the career ladder... But Simone had ended up in care, all alone, with a new set of horrors to face. Jack Hart had taken her mother from her.

Simone thought about her next victim and smiled to herself. It was going to be the best yet.

CHAPTER 40

Erika arrived at Lewisham Row station at seven-thirty the next morning. She'd been summoned to another strategy meeting. A meeting that had been hastily arranged when she'd reported back to Marsh the previous day that she was still working on the case – and that they now had a female serial killer.

She parked and came out into the morning heat. The cranes whirred around the half-finished high-rise buildings, and the sky was heavy and humid. Low cloud was forming and glinting like steel in the sunshine. Erika locked her car and made for the main entrance. A storm was brewing, both outside and in her work life.

'Morning, boss,' said Woolf when she stepped into reception. He was hunched over the morning's newspaper and had a half-demolished Danish pastry in his left hand. An article about Jack Hart in the *Daily Star* was strewn with flakes of pastry. The headline read: '**SERIAL KILLER SHOCK IN JACK HART MURDER**'.

'Shit,' Erika said, leaning over the desk to peer at the article.

'Look, they've even done a supplement,' Woolf said, pulling out a glossy black magazine with a giant picture of Jack Hart staring into the camera. 'RIP' was written above his head 'You can't touch it without getting your hands dirty,' moaned Woolf, showing where the black ink had left a murky residue on his hand.

'Maybe that's a metaphor,' said Erika, as she swiped her card on the door.

'Do you really think a *woman* killed him?' asked Woolf, his brow furrowing.

'Yes,' Erika said, pulling open the door and moving through into the station.

The air conditioning had been fixed in the conference room, which only added to the chilly atmosphere. Around the long table sat Erika, Chief Superintendent Marsh, Colleen Scanlan, Tim Aiken, the criminal psychologist and Assistant Commissioner Oakley.

Oakley cut straight to the chase. 'DCI Foster, it greatly troubles me that you have reached the conclusion that these murders were committed by a woman.'

'Sir, there are female serial killers,' replied Erika.

'I know that! It's just that the evidence in this case is paper-thin. We have DNA from an ear print on the back door of Jack Hart's house . . .'

'Sir, we also managed to glean skin cells from the bag placed over Jack Hart's head. It took him several minutes to asphyxiate, and we believe he thrashed around, striking the killer in the face.'

Oakley cocked his head to one side and was silent. Erika knew this to be a technique of his, to remain silent. It often caused the person he was questioning to babble, or to blurt something out which Oakley could later use to strengthen his argument. Erika remained silent.

'I'd be keen to hear what Tim can bring to the table,' said Oakley, turning his gaze on the criminal psychologist. Tim looked up from where he was writing on his pad. His hair jutted upwards from his head, and he had several days' stubble.

'The only compelling evidence that this is a woman comes from two sources. The ear print on the back door, and the plastic bag. This could be explained in many ways. The door had recently been repainted, six weeks before the murder: the print could have been left by one of the workers. There was a case a few years back of an ear print being used in a court case for a home invasion which led to the murder of a man and his wife. The ear print was used to prosecute a man who, it later turned out, had been working legitimately at the property as a plumber.'

'And how do you explain the plastic bag?' asked Erika.

'The utility room is where Jack Hart kept his DIY and garden supplies. In the crime scene report, it states that there were two drawers containing bin liners, plastic freezer bags and old newspapers. It's feasible that the same painter-decorator could have opened these drawers and contaminated the plastic bag with her DNA.'

'The murder weapon wasn't just an ordinary plastic bag. It was a suicide bag, or exit bag. A specialist item which has to be ordered online.'

'Yes, and this suicide bag is much like the industrial plastic and zip lock bags used around the home, in DIY. Leaving the physical evidence to one side for a moment, the profile is more aligned to a male murderer. We shouldn't forget that with the first victim, Gregory Munro, there was a homosexual element to the killing... And both victims were found naked in bed. I don't wish to revert to stereotypes, but female serial killers are incredibly rare, and we need more concrete evidence before we abandon the theory that this is a single white male.'

'So you're saying we should ignore forensic evidence and concentrate on statistics?' asked Erika.

'The coverage in the media is extensive,' interrupted Colleen, who had a stack of the day's newspapers in front of her.

'We need to make a statement, and this is what they call silly season in the press. There isn't a lot else going on, besides coverage of this heatwave. A serial killer story is going to run and run.'

'I believe that a woman is responsible for these killings,' said Erika. 'If the ear print on the outside of the back door were the only DNA evidence, then I would propose we were cautious. But the female DNA is on the bag used to kill Jack Hart, and very shortly we will have more details about the supplier of this bag – a website which has agreed to hand over the details of purchasers. We have more of a chance of catching the killer if we make the focus of our enquiries a woman. I am suggesting that we do a reconstruction. I'd like Colleen to contact the BBC *Crimewatch* programme. They are due to broadcast their monthly show in a few days. We can reconstruct Gregory Munro and Jack Hart's last movements in the lead-up to their murders.'

There was silence. Colleen looked between Marsh and Oakley.

'You've been very quiet, Paul,' said Oakley to Marsh.

'I support DCI Foster's position,' said Marsh. 'I feel that this is a unique case, and with the DNA evidence it would be prudent to concentrate on finding this woman. As a caveat, I would suggest to Erika that we also pursue the line of enquiry that this woman could have been working in tandem with a man. We could ask for members of the public to consider that also.'

'But this is almost unprecedented. In all my years of police work, we've never put in place a hunt for a female serial killer,' said Oakley.

'Perhaps you should get out a bit more, sir,' said Erika. Marsh shot her a look.

'Very well, it's your call, Erika. Although I will be monitoring this very closely,' said Oakley.

Erika left the meeting and walked down the stairs to the incident room, buoyed by her victory. She heard the door open on the floor above. Looking up, she saw Marsh, and stopped to let him catch up with her. They met on the landing, where a huge glass window looked out over the vast sprawl of Greater London. Dark clouds were forming on the horizon.

'Thank you for your support, sir,' said Erika. 'We'll get to work on the *Crimewatch* reconstruction.'

'It's a big opportunity, a television reconstruction. Don't blow it.'

'No, sir.'

'Erika. I'm fifty–fifty about whether this is a female killer, but, as I say, it's your call.'

'I have a good track record, sir. You know I'm rarely wrong about these things. I always deliver.'

'I know.'

'So, speaking of my track record, any more news on the promotion?'

'Catch this crazy bitch, and then we'll talk promotions,' said Marsh. 'Now, I have to go. Keep me in the loop.'

He left Erika standing on the stairs, looking out over the city through the tall glass window.

It's funny how much we have in common, the killer and me, thought Erika. *We're both being doubted for our abilities as women.*

CHAPTER 41

A few days later, Erika and Moss were in Laurel Road, watching as the *Crimewatch* television reconstruction was being filmed. The heatwave had broken that morning, and the rain was torrential, hammering with a roar on top of two large BBC Television vans, which were parked at the top of the street.

Erika and Moss sheltered in front of one of the vans under a giant umbrella, and watched as an actor who had been cast to play Gregory Munro rehearsed walking along the street and going into 14 Laurel Road. A cameraman followed behind him, swathed in a vast rain poncho of clear plastic, a Steadicam strapped to his body with a black metal harness. The rest of the television crew were bunched together under umbrellas on a wall opposite, and the neighbours who weren't at work watched curiously from under their porches, sheltered from the rain.

At the bottom of the street, a row of crash barriers had been erected, lined with journalists and members of the public watching the proceedings.

They had been told by the producer and director that it takes a lot for rain to show up on camera, but as Moss and Erika watched the rehearsal, rainwater was surging down the road, spraying over the kerb and making the drains gurgle thirstily.

'This isn't exactly going to jog people's memories of a hot summer night,' said Erika, taking a drag of her cigarette. A runner, wearing another of the huge, clear rain ponchos, approached them holding a clipboard. With him was a small, dark-haired girl wearing black tracksuit bottoms and a black jumper. They were both huddled under a large umbrella.

'Hello, which one of you is DCI Foster?' asked the young guy.

'That's me,' said Erika, adding, 'This is Detective Inspector Moss.'

They all shook hands.

'I'm Tom, and this is Lottie Marie Harper, she's been cast as the murderer.'

The young girl was petite, with compact features and poker-straight hair. She had a small mouth which, when she smiled, showed a row of bottom teeth.

'This is rather odd,' said Lottie, speaking with a refined accent. She reached up and checked that her dark hair was still fixed in the topknot. 'I've never played a real killer before. What else can you tell me? My agent really wasn't all that specific…'

Erika looked over at the young runner.

'It's okay, we've had her sign the release and the confidentiality agreement,' he said.

Erika nodded. 'Okay. She's very methodical. We believe she prepares quite thoroughly, checking out the houses she's going to target days in advance. She's broken in to the houses on both occasions and lain in wait for the victims, waiting for them to drink or eat something she has laced with a sedative.'

'You're kidding!' said Lottie, putting a small, immaculately manicured hand up to her small mouth.

'Afraid not,' said Moss.

'I just can't imagine someone breaking into my flat, let alone someone doing it several times to learn things about me…'

Moss pulled out the plastic file from under her arm and found the picture of the killer under Jack Hart's bed. It had been digitally enhanced to show as much of a close-up as possible of the crouching figure. It was chilling. The bottom of her face was visible, but from her nose upwards her face vanished into shadow. The mouth was small and almost identical to that of the young actress.

'They've got the bottom half of the face right,' said Erika, holding up the picture beside Lottie. 'I take it you'll do some close-ups?'

'The director will do, yes,' said the young runner.

Lottie took the photo from Moss and looked at it in silence for a moment. There was a crackling sound as rain hit the umbrellas.

'And it all happened, for real, in that house,' she said, looking over her shoulder at number 14.

'Yes. And we're going to get her with your help today,' said Moss. 'Are you sure you're okay with this? You look far too sweet and kind to be a killer.'

'I trained at RADA, the Royal Academy of Dramatic Art,' said Lottie, a little sniffily, handing the photo back to Moss. There was an awkward pause, broken only when the director came over. He was a tall, ebullient-looking man with a red face.

'Okay, we're ready to start,' he said. 'We've got three hours, and then we'll be moving the unit over to Dulwich to shoot the second murder sequence.'

They went away, leaving Erika and Moss under their umbrella. The sound of the rain increased on the van behind.

'Does it worry you, that we think a tiny woman like that is our killer?' asked Moss. 'You've seen what they've been writing in the press.'

'I just find it odd that if we investigate a rape or a murder committed by a man, it's a given. Men rape women – they murder them, too – and people don't seem to think they need much of a "reason" to do it… But if a woman does the same, there's all this soul-searching from society, endless opinions as to the whys and the wherefores…'

Moss nodded. 'And this one fits the profile for a female serial killer. When women kill, it tends to be far more pre-meditated and well-planned. And poisoning is often a tool of the female multiple murderer.'

'Although this one couples it with violence, and she stalks her victims at night,' added Erika.

'The "Night Stalker"…That was in *the Sun* today.'

'I saw it,' said Erika, turning to look at Moss.

'It's good. I wish I'd thought it up,' grinned Moss.

'Yeah, well, I'll remind you of that in the future, when it comes back to haunt us,' said Erika.

They stared down the street as distant thunder began to rumble and Lottie rehearsed with the cameraman and the director. At the bottom of the road, behind a crash barrier, the banks of photographers snapped away, and members of the public gawked with their camera phones. Coupled with the lookalike actors, and the film crew, it all seemed farcical, reduced to pantomime.

'Does it worry you we might have it wrong?' asked Moss.

'Yes,' said Erika. 'But everything worries me. It's my instinct I have to listen to. My instinct is telling me that this could be our killer. And seeing herself on screen might prompt her to do something stupid and slip up.'

Her phone rang. She pulled it out of her bag and answered.

'Boss, it's Crane… You got a moment?' he asked.

'What is it?'

'Do you remember the rent boy who visited Gregory Munro, JordiLevi?'

'Yeah.'

'Well, I went ahead and contacted one of our covert Internet investigators, who set up a fake profile on Rentboiz. They've been messaging back and forth with him, pretending to be a punter. He wants to meet. Today.'

'Where?'

'The Railway pub in Forest Hill, at four o'clock this afternoon.'

'Great work, Crane. I'll meet you there at quarter to four,' said Erika. She came off the phone and relayed the info to Moss.

'I'll stay here and supervise our serial killer,' said Moss, looking over at Lottie, who was now waiting under an umbrella as a lady in a rain poncho applied make-up.

'Yeah, I bet you will,' grinned Erika, rolling her eyes.

CHAPTER 42

The Railway in Forest Hill was very close to where Gregory Munro's mother, Estelle, lived. The irony wasn't lost on Erika, as she pulled up in the car park. It was an old-fashioned public house, clad in porcelain tiles, polished brass lamps above every window and a swinging sign high above the car park.

A summer terrace extended into the car park, and she could see Crane sitting on his own at one of the tables, trying to look inconspicuous amongst the crowds enjoying a drink in the afternoon sun.

'He just went inside a couple of minutes ago,' said Crane, standing up when she approached the table.

'Good. Whose photo did they use? Who does he think he's meeting?' asked Erika, as they picked their way through the tables to the front entrance.

'DC Warren's… I thought it needed someone a bit better-looking than me!'

'Don't sell yourself short,' said Erika. 'As my husband used to say, every pan has its lid.'

'I'll take that as a compliment – I think.' Crane grinned.

The inside of the pub had all the original fittings, but the walls had been painted white, soft mood lighting had been added, and there was an expensive gastro-pub-style menu above the bar. There weren't many people inside and Erika saw the young lad straight away, sitting in a corner booth, nursing a half of lager and a shot.

'How do we do this?' murmured Crane.

'Softly, softly,' said Erika. 'I'm glad he picked a booth.'

They moved over to where the lad was sitting and stood at either side of the curved seat, so he couldn't run for it. He was wearing a shiny red and black tracksuit, and his hair was shoulder length and loosely parted in the middle.

They flashed their IDs. 'JordiLevi?' asked Erika. 'I'm DCI Foster, this is Sergeant Crane.'

'What? I'm having a drink? Nothing illegal about that…'

'And you're waiting for this guy, who you've arranged to meet up with,' said Crane, pulling out Warren's photo.

'You don't know that.'

'Yes, I do. I arranged it,' said Crane.

The boy pursed his lips and downed the shot. 'Well, nothing illegal about meeting someone in a pub,' he said, slamming the shot glass down on the table.

'No, there isn't,' said Erika. 'We just want to talk to you. What are you drinking?'

'Double vodka. And I'll have some Kettle Chips.'

Erika nodded at Crane and he went off to the bar. She took a seat.

'Jordi. Do you know why we want to talk to you?'

'I can take a wild guess,' he said, downing his pint and placing the glass back down.

'We're not from Vice. We're not interested about what you do for a living,' said Erika.

'What I do for a living! I'm not a bloody dental hygienist…'

'I'm investigating the murder of Gregory Munro, a local doctor. He was killed ten days ago.' Erika pulled a photo of Gregory Munro from her bag. 'This is him.'

'Well, I didn't bloody do it,' said Jordi, barely glancing at the photo.

'We don't think you did. But a neighbour saw you coming out of his house a few days before he died. Can you confirm you were there at the house?'

Jordi sat back and shrugged. 'I don't have a calendar, all days blur into one.'

'We just want to know what happened and if you saw anything. You'll be helping with our investigations. You are not a suspect. Please, look at the photo again. Do you recognise him?'

Jordi looked down at the photo and nodded, 'Yeah, I recognise him.'

Crane returned with the tray of drinks. He handed a double vodka and the crisps to Jordi, and gave Erika one of the two glasses of coke from the tray. Crane slid into the seat on the opposite side. Jordi tucked his hair behind his ears and opened the crisps. He had a whiff of body odour about him and his fingernails were grubby.

'Okay. We need to know if you were at Gregory Munro's house between Monday, the 20th and Monday, the 27th of June?' asked Erika.

He shrugged. 'I think so.'

Erika took a sip of her coke. 'In your opinion, was Gregory Munro gay?'

'He never said his real name, and yeah, he was gay,' said Jordi, through a mouthful of crisps.

'And you know that for sure?'

'Well, if he wasn't, I'm not sure what my cock was doing up his arse.'

Crane's eyebrows shot up.

Erika went on, 'How did you arrange to meet him?'

'Craigslist. I put an ad on there.'

'What kind of ad?'

'The kind of ad where I meet up with guys, and they can give me donations. Giving donations isn't illegal.'

'And did Gregory Munro give you a donation?'

'Yeah.'

'How much?'

'Hundred quid.'

'And did you stay the night?'

'Yeah.'

'What did you talk about, Jordi?'

'Not much. A lot of the time my mouth was full…' He smirked.

Erika pulled one of the crime scene photos out of her bag and placed it on the polished wood of the table in front of Jordi.

'Do you think this is funny? Look. Here Gregory is lying in bed, with his hands bound and a plastic bag tied over his head.'

Jordi gulped when he saw the photo, and what little colour he had in his face drained away.

'Now, please. This is very important. Tell me what you know about Gregory Munro,' said Erika.

Jordi took a gulp of vodka. 'He was just like all the other guilty married men. Gagging for a good hard shag and then got all guilty and teary afterwards. The second time I went he was really nervy. Kept asking me if I'd taken his key.'

'What key?'

'His front door key.'

'Why?'

'He thought I was a thieving whore… Lots of them think you're gonna steal, but then he asked me if I had been inside his house while he was out.'

Erika looked at Crane. 'Had you been in his house when he was out?'

Jordi shook his head. 'He said stuff had been moved around.'

'What stuff?'

'Underwear all laid out on his bed… He was really freaked out by it.'

'He was getting divorced,' said Erika, excitement rising in her. 'Do you think it could have been his wife?'

'He said it couldn't be her. He'd just had the locks all changed. No one else had a key. He called this woman out to check everything, from some security company.'

A look passed between Erika and Crane again.

'Did you see this woman?'

'No.'

'Did he say what she looked like?'

'No.'

'Okay, can you remember if he mentioned *when* this woman came to the house?'

Jordi pursed his lips as he thought. 'Dunno. Hang on; it was the second time I went over. She'd just been there. He seemed relieved that she'd checked everything.'

'Can you remember if it was a Monday? If so, that would make it the 21st June.'

Jordi grimaced at the photo again and bit his lip.

'Um, yeah… Yeah, I'm pretty sure it was a Monday.'

Erika rummaged in her bag, pulled out three twenty-pound notes and held them out to Jordi.

'What's this?' he asked, looking at the money.

'A donation,' said Erika.

'I agreed a hundred.'

'You're not in a position to negotiate.'

Jordi took the money, grabbed a small rucksack from under the table and squeezed past her.

'We're so bloody close,' said Crane, a few minutes after Jordi had gone. 'Do you think she staged a break-in, and then went back posing as someone from GuardHouse Alarms on Monday, 21st June?'

'Yeah. Dammit! If only Jordi had seen her, we could have gone into the *Crimewatch* reconstruction with an e-fit,' said Erika. The door to the bar opened and she suddenly sat up in her seat. Gary Wilmslow had come in with a tall, dark-haired man in jeans wearing a Millwall shirt. A small boy accompanied them, and Erika realised it was Peter, Gregory Munro's son.

'Jeez. This is just what we need,' said Crane. They went to the bar, then Gary noticed them. He said something to the dark-haired man and came over with Peter.

'Afternoon, coppers,' he sneered.

'Hello,' said Erika. 'Hi, Peter, how are you?'

The little boy stared up at Erika, his face pale and drawn. 'My dad's dead… Yesterday they dug a hole in the ground and they put him in it,' he said, tonelessly.

'I'm sorry,' said Erika.

'This your boyfriend?' asked Gary, tilting his head towards Crane.

'No, I'm Sergeant Crane,' said Crane, flashing his ID.

'Whoa, what's with the ID?' said Gary.

'You just asked who he was,' explained Erika.

The situation felt tense. Gary looked between the two of them. 'So, what are you two coppers doing here? You just having a drink in my local?'

'There's a lot of locals around here, Gary,' said Crane.

'Who's your friend?' asked Erika, as the man at the bar was paying for a round of drinks.

'Business associate… Now, I'm gonna get back.'

'Are you okay, Peter? Is everything okay?' blurted Erika, looking at the listless little boy.

'His dad's just died. What a stupid fucking question,' said Gary.

'Hey, easy,' said Crane.

'I am going easy,' said Gary. 'Now, I'm going.'

He walked off, pulling Peter with him. Erika wanted to grab the little boy and take him out of there, but she knew it would be crazy. How could she explain taking him, without blowing a major undercover investigation?

Erika and Crane left the bar and came out into the sunshine. The tables on the terrace were now full. Erika recognised a tall, skinny, dark-haired man sitting with a thin woman who was hunched over her phone, texting. She was wearing a sleeveless T-shirt with thin straps. She had a prominent nose and fair hair scraped back into a ponytail. The man was pale, with an acne-scarred face, and his shoulder-length greasy black hair was combed back from his high forehead. He was wearing a plain T-shirt and beige shorts.

As they picked their way through the tables, Erika stayed ahead of Crane and made a beeline for them.

'DCI Sparks?' she said, when they approached the table.

'DCI Foster,' he said, looking surprised. The woman with him sat up and her eyes darted over to the pub window.

'Day off? Having a drink?' asked Erika, following the woman's gaze.

'Um, sort of,' said Sparks. Crane caught up with Erika.

'All right, Sparks, long time no see… Where are you based now?' he asked.

'Erm, I'm heading my own Murder Investigation Team, based out in North London,' he said, looking between Erika and Crane. 'This is DI Powell,' he added. They all exchanged pleasantries.

'Crane, would it be okay if I met you at the car?' asked Erika.

'Okay,' said Crane. He gave Erika an odd look and then went off.

'So, you're both here, on a weekday, having a drink in South London, trying to look inconspicuous. Has it got anything to do with Gary Wilmslow?' said Erika when Crane was out of earshot.

'Excuse me, who are you?' asked the woman.

'DCI Erika Foster, an ex-colleague of Sparks here,' said Erika, in a low voice. 'You've got a couple of guys who are heavily involved with the production of child sex abuse videos in that pub, unsupervised with a small boy.'

'We know…' started the woman.

Sparks leaned over the table. 'You need to turn around and walk away, Foster. This is covert surveillance.'

'Operation Hemslow, yeah?' said Erika.

A look passed between Sparks and Powell.

'Yes. Erika. We've been drafted in for extra manpower,' said Sparks, eyeing the pub windows. 'Now you need to leave, before you blow our cover.'

'Yeah, well, you two stick out like a sore thumb. Have you any idea how vulnerable that little boy is right now? Peter, his name is.'

'We know. And if you don't leave immediately, you'll not only blow our cover, but I'll make sure to speak to your senior officer,' said Sparks.

Erika gave them a long look and then went off to the car.

'What was all that about, boss?' asked Crane, as she got in.

'Nothing,' said Erika. She was still shaking.

'I haven't seen Sparks since you got him chucked off the Andrea Douglas-Brown murder case… Not the best copper in the world, is he? Not what you'd call a details man.'

'No, he isn't,' said Erika.

'Was that his girlfriend?'

'I don't think so.'

'That figures. She's a bit out of his league, although most women are,' said Crane. 'Anyway, we've got another positive ID on a woman at Gregory Munro's place. I call that a result!'

'Yeah,' said Erika.

As they drove away, she thought of little Peter in there with Gary Wilmslow and his dark-haired 'business associate', and she felt powerless.

CHAPTER 43

The next evening, after a long week at work, Isaac Strong lay on his sofa with Stephen Linley. He had just cooked a meal for them both, to celebrate Stephen having finished his latest novel and submitted it to the publisher.

'Do you want some more champagne, Stevie?' asked Isaac.

'You mean from the champagne in the ice bucket, with the white cloth around its neck?' asked Stephen, looking up from where he lay on Isaac's chest.

'What's wrong with doing things properly?' Isaac murmured, planting a kiss on Stephen's forehead.

'I don't know anyone else who serves champagne at home as if they're having it in a restaurant,' laughed Stephen. He shifted over so Isaac could get up. 'And where did you get that?' asked Stephen, holding out his glass and pointing to the ice bucket, which was perched on a metal stand beside the sofa.

'The Lakeland catalogue,' said Isaac, lifting the bottle out with a clink of ice and topping up their glasses.

'And the stand?'

'That's from the mortuary. I normally keep the bone saw on it, and my scalpels... I thought it appropriately macabre to use it to celebrate your new book.'

'Mr Strait-laced stole from work! I'm honoured,' said Stephen, taking a sip of the crisp, cold champagne. Isaac came back and went to lie on the sofa. A timer went off in the kitchen and he got back up to turn it off.

'Not another course?' groaned Stephen.

'No, I set it because *Crimewatch* is on.'

'Bloody hell. Not your awful copper friend with the blunt manner... and the blunt bob.'

'Erika doesn't have a blunt manner. Or a blunt bob.'

'Well, that hair is certainly utilitarian. Is she a lesbian?'

Isaac sighed. 'No, she was married, I told you... She's a widow.'

'Topped himself, did he?'

'He was killed in the line of duty...'

'Oh yes,' said Stephen taking another gulp of champagne. 'I remember now, the drug raid. She was responsible for his death and for the deaths of four other members of her team... You know, that would make a good plot.'

'Stephen, you're being cruel. And I don't like it.'

'This is what you signed up for,' grinned Stephen. 'I'm a brutal bitch . . . Anyway, I'd change her name.'

'You are not putting that in a book... And we're watching *Crimewatch*. This is a case I worked on. I have a professional interest, as well as a personal one.'

Isaac grabbed the remote and turned on the television. The opening credits of *Crimewatch* began.

'So, it's a double murder, a serial killer. Yeah?'

'Yes.'

'That was a shocker. Jack Hart, wasn't it?' said Stephen.

'Shhh!' hissed Isaac. They watched in silence as the case was introduced by the *Crimewatch* presenter.

'The first victim was Dr Gregory Munro, a GP from Honor Oak Park in South London. He was last seen returning home from work around 7 p.m. on June the 27th...'

The actor playing Gregory on the screen walked up to the house in Laurel Road. It was still daylight, and a group of small children were playing jump with a skipping rope in the street.

'That's not accurate. Who lets their kids play out in the street these days?' started Stephen, sipping his champagne. 'They're all on lock-down. Parents keep them indoors where they sit on their computers and phones... And what's the number one way child abusers get to children? They groom them online, it's crazy...'

'Shush,' said Isaac.

On the screen, the young actress was dressed in black and walking along a stretch of darkened scrub path behind the house. The camera cut to a close-up of her face as it was lit by the train clattering past on the track behind.

'She's very pretty,' said Isaac.

'Quite elfin,' agreed Stephen. 'They really think it's a woman? She's no more than a slip of a girl...'

The screen cut to a view of the back of the house from where the girl stood on the path. Her hand reached up and pulled the branch of a tree down, and they saw the actor playing Gregory Munro moving around in his kitchen. The girl then pulled a black running hood over her face and ducked down, crawling through the fence and into the garden.

'How do they know all this?' asked Stephen.

'I can't discuss the case with you,' said Isaac. 'You know that.'

'We're watching it on BBC One with millions of other saddos on a Friday night. I think the cat's out of the bag,' said Stephen, rolling his eyes. 'Come on, let's stick on some porn and I'll let you fuck me. I'm slutty drunk...'

'Stephen, I need to see this!'

They watched as the woman moved across the lawn, broke into the house through a side window and stepped into the kitchen.

'It's a creepy thought,' said Stephen. 'Someone sneaking up on you, moving around your house without you knowing...'

CHAPTER 44

It had been a good day at work for Simone; she'd managed to spend some quality time with Mary. The doctor had been in, and had said that she was showing signs of improvement, going as far to suggest that she might even wake up. Thankfully, he hadn't said anything about the bruise on Mary's temple. He must have assumed that it happened before she was admitted to hospital. So it was good news all round. Mary was going to live, and Simone would be there for her when she was discharged. Simone had two spare rooms. She would paint both in lovely pastel colours, and Mary could choose between the two. Although she hoped that Mary wouldn't get better too fast. She still had a name left on her list, and she had preparations to make.

Before she went out, Simone decided to make her favourite food: tinned macaroni cheese, with the special topping – stale bread crumbled on top with a little grated cheese. She carried the steaming hot bowl on a tray into the living room, which was a mess of newspapers and magazines piled high around the sagging furniture. She sat on the sofa and turned on the television, looking for *Coronation Street*. She stopped and stared at the screen. For a long moment, she thought that the hallucinations were back.

But this was different.

The hallucinations were playing out on her television. She watched in morbid fascination as a woman with a likeness to her moved around inside Jack Hart's house.

She tilted her head to one side, confused.

The girl on the screen was petite, with small, attractive features. Simone, in comparison, was small but chunky. Her forehead was high and wide, furrowed even when resting, and her blue eyes were dull, unlike the girl's, which sparkled.

The pretty girl on the screen was now watching a man who looked like Jack Hart; watching him through the bathroom door as he showered. She then moved off into his bedroom. Her waist was defined, whereas Simone was straight up and down, with a slight curvature of her spine.

The *Crimewatch* music began to play and the screen cut to the television studio. The presenter began to speak.

'As I've said, we've left out the more distressing elements of the reconstruction. We're joined in the studio tonight by Detective Chief Inspector Erika Foster. Good evening…'

Simone leant forward as she got the first look at the police officer who was leading the investigation. *It was a woman.* She was pale and thin, with short blonde hair and soft brown eyes, and for a moment Simone thought this was good, that a woman might understand her, sympathise with what she had suffered. But as she listened to DCI Foster talk, Simone felt anger build inside her. Blood began to roar in her ears.

'We're asking anyone for information. If you've seen this woman, or if you were in the area on the night these murders happened, please get in touch. We believe she's small in stature but we advise the public not to approach her: she is a dangerous and deeply disturbed individual.'

Simone felt pain, and she looked down to see that her hands were clenching and unclenching in the bowl of boiling hot macaroni. The cheese sauce oozed between her fingers. She looked up again and saw the bitch on the screen, heard her repeat that they were looking for a disturbed woman who may have suffered psychiatric problems. She swept the bowl off the tray and it shattered against the wall.

'I'm the victim!' she shouted at the screen, getting to her feet. 'THE VICTIM, you fucking whore! You know NOTH-ING of the years of abuse! You don't know what he did to me!' She jabbed her finger up to the ceiling, towards her marital bed. 'You know NOTHING!' she screamed, and a spray of the thin, synthetic cheese sauce splattered over DCI Foster's face.

'So please, if you know anything at all, call or email. Your information will be treated as confidential. The details are there now, across the bottom of the screen,' finished the presenter.

Simone stood, shaking, and went to her computer in its nook under the stairs. She sat and dragged the keyboard towards her, not noticing her hands were a mess of sauce and scalded red skin.

She typed into Google: 'DCI ERIKA FOSTER' and began to read the results, her breathing slowing down as a plan began to form.

CHAPTER 45

It was late when the car from the television studio dropped Erika back at her flat in Forest Hill. When she came indoors, the sight of her living room was deeply depressing. She'd been on television before, and she'd made television appeals, but this had been different. It had been in a proper television studio, and she had been nervous. Moss had suggested that she should imagine she was talking to one family and visualise them sitting in their living room.

The only person she had been able to visualise was Mark: how he used to slouch on the sofa, and the way she fitted snugly under his arm. That's what she'd visualised during the live broadcast. And now she was home, she realised she'd found yet another way to miss him. She missed coming home to him sitting on the sofa, watching television. She missed having someone to talk to, someone to get her out of her own head. Here, she just had the four bare walls closing in on her.

Her phone rang and she fumbled in her bag to answer it. It was Mark's dad.

'You didn't tell me you were going to be on telly,' said Edward.

It had been a few weeks since they'd spoken, Erika realised guiltily. Her emotions caught in her throat for a split second. Edward sounded so much like Mark.

'It was all a bit last minute... I haven't seen it back yet. I didn't come across all schoolmarmish, did I?'

Edward chuckled. 'No, lass, you did well. Although it sounds like you've got another nutter on the loose. I hope you're going to be careful?'

'This one likes men,' said Erika. 'No – I don't mean to be flippant. So far, she's targeted men.'

'Yes. I saw the programme,' said Edward. 'Do you really think a woman's got it in her, to do all that?'

'You'd be horrified about the state of the human psyche if you came to work with me for a couple of days…'

'I bet I would. But as I always say, love. Be brave, but don't be stupid.'

'I'll try.'

'I've been meaning to give you a buzz, but seeing your mug on the telly jogged me into it. I wanted to ask for your sister Lenka's address.'

'Hang on, I've got it somewhere here,' said Erika, putting the phone under her chin, moving to the shelves and scrabbling about amongst the takeaway leaflets. She found her slim address book.

'How come you want Lenka's address?' she asked, flicking through pages.

'Isn't her little baby due soon?'

'Oh, yes, I almost forgot. She's due in a few weeks.'

'Doesn't time fly when you're hunting people on the run?' Edward said.

'Very funny! You should be a stand-up comedian,' Erika laughed.

'Her little boy and girl are lovely,' he said. 'I couldn't understand what they were jabbering on about, or your sister, but we got by!'

When Erika's sister had come to stay, Edward had travelled down on the train for the day and they'd all gone to the Tower of London. It had been an exhausting day. Lenka didn't speak a word of English and Erika had found herself having to be translator for her and the kids, Karolina and Jakub.

'Do you think they liked it, the Tower of London?' asked Edward.

'No, I think Lenka was a bit bored. All she really wanted to do was stock up on new clothes at Primark,' replied Erika, dryly.

'Weren't it expensive, though, the tower? I wonder what percentage the Queen is on?'

Erika smiled. She missed Edward and wished he lived closer.

'Ah, here it is,' she said, and she read out the address to him.

'Thanks, love. I was going to pop in some Euros, for the baby, if I can get to the big post office in Wakefield. Did you know they've shut the money exchange at our local post office.'

'It's the age of austerity,' said Erika.

There was silence. Edward cleared his throat. 'It's come round again, hasn't it?' he said, softly. He was referring to the anniversary of Mark's death.

'Yes, it has. Two years.'

'Do you want me to come down? I can stop with you for a few days. Your sofa's comfy.'

'No. Thank you. I've got so much work. Let's wait until I'm finished with this case and then do something properly. I'd love a few days up north… What are you going to do?'

'I've been asked to make up the team for indoor bowls. I think they know I need my mind taken off things.'

'Then you should do that,' said Erika. 'You take care.'

'You take care too, lass,' he said.

When he'd hung up, Erika flicked on the television just in time for the *Crimewatch* reconstruction recap show. She was quite horrified seeing herself in high definition: every line, bag and wrinkle. When the number flashed up at the end, her phone rang again. She answered it.

'DCI Foster?' came a muffled, high voice.

'Yes?'

'I saw you talking about me on the television… You know nothing about me,' the voice said, calmly.

Erika stiffened where she sat. Her mind started to whir. She jumped up, turned off the lights and went to her patio window. The garden was dark, the branches of the apple tree moved in the breeze.

'You can calm down. I'm nowhere near you,' the voice said.

'Okay. Then where are you?' asked Erika, her heart racing.

'Somewhere you won't find me,' said the voice. There was another pause and Erika tried to think what she could do. She looked at her phone, but had no idea how to record calls.

'It's not over,' said the voice.

'What do you mean?' said Erika.

'Come on, DCI Foster. I just looked you up. You were a rising star in the force. You have a degree in criminal psychology. You have a commendation. And lastly, you have something in common with me.'

'What's that?'

'My husband died too – although, sadly, unlike you, I wasn't responsible for his death.'

Erika closed her eyes and gripped the receiver.

'You were responsible, weren't you?'

'Yes, I was,' said Erika.

'Thank you for being honest,' said the voice. 'My husband was a brutal, sadistic pig. He enjoyed torturing me. I have the scars to prove it.'

'What happened to your husband?'

'I'd planned to kill him. And if I'd had the opportunity, none of this would have followed. But he dropped dead, quite by chance. And then I became the merry widow.'

'What do you mean when you say it's not over?'

'What I mean is there will be more men who will die.'

'This won't end well, I'm telling you,' Erika said. 'You are going to slip up. We've got witnesses who've seen you. We are so close to finding out what you look like...'

'I think that's enough for now, Erika. All I ask is that you leave me alone,' said the voice.

There was a click and the line went dead.

Erika quickly dialled 1471, but the recorded voice told her that the number was not available. She checked the sliding glass door was locked and took the key out, pushing it into her pocket. She then went to the front door and checked the deadbolt was on. She moved through the flat, shutting and locking the remaining windows.

It quickly began to warm up inside, with all the windows closed. She was starting to sweat when she called the number for Lewisham Row station.

Woolf answered. 'Oh, it's the new face of the Met Police. You did well on the telly,' he said.

'Woolf, have there been any phone calls for me?' asked Erika.

'Yes, we've had *Playboy* on the line; they want you to do a centrefold. I told them only if they do a good job. I don't want your naughty bits getting lost where they crease the paper...'

'Woolf, I'm serious!'

'Sorry, boss, I was only kidding. Hang on...' She heard him turning through the call log.

'There was only that producer, the one from *Crimewatch*. Did she get your handbag back to you?'

'I've got my bag,' Erika said, seeing where she'd dumped it on the coffee table.

'She rang saying that you'd left your bag in the studio, and asked if she could have your number... So, you didn't leave your bag?'

'No, I didn't. And you're going to tell me that the call was a withheld number?'

'Uh, yes, it was…' started Woolf. 'If it wasn't the producer, then who was it?'

'I just had a call from the Night Stalker,' said Erika.

CHAPTER 46

When Simone arrived back home, after her phone call to Erika Foster, a nasty smell hit her nose. She saw the macaroni cheese sauce smeared over the mirror in the hallway, over her computer in the hall. She went through to the living room and it was splattered everywhere: up the wall, over the TV.

As she cleaned, she turned things over in her mind. How did the police know it was her? How did they know it was a woman?

She'd been so clever, so careful.

She'd been nothing more than a shadow.

She was scrubbing at the living room carpet when she saw movement in the corner of her eye. She stopped scrubbing. There was a pat, pat, pattering coming from behind her. She gripped the wooden brush and turned.

Stan stood in the living room doorway, naked, the water running off his pasty skin, raining down on her clean carpet. His mouth fell open, showing a row of black teeth. Simone was surprised that she didn't feel scared. She slowly stood up, her knees cracking.

'*Duhu…kah,*' came a sound from Stan's mouth. It wasn't exactly a voice, more of a sigh. An exhale. '*Duhu…kah, Duhu… kah.*' His arm flopped down by his side and his mouth pulled up at both sides into a grin. It was the grin she remembered: hungry, looming close to her face, coupled with pain. He started to walk towards her, the water pouring off him and soaking the carpet. Now she felt fear.

'NO!' she screamed. 'NO!' She hurled the heavy wooden scrubbing brush at him. He vanished, and there was a crash as the brush hit the mirror in the hall. It burst into shards and they scattered down onto the floor.

Stan was gone. The carpet was dry, and she realised what he'd said.

Duke. He'd said *Duke*.

She hurried to her computer in the hallway under the stairs and logged on.

NIGHT OWL: Duke?

Moments later, Duke logged on.

DUKE: Night Owl, hi! Rough night?
NIGHT OWL: Why do you say that?
DUKE: I know u. Better than you know yourself.

Simone paused with her hands above the keyboard.

NIGHT OWL: Do you, though? Do you really KNOW me?

This time there was a long pause. Simone stared at the cursor, as it blinked. She wondered if Duke was sitting there with his fingers poised, trying to think what to type. Had he put things together?

For the first time, she wondered where Duke lived. She was used to thinking of him living here in her computer. She'd talked to him for the past few years about her plans, what she fantasised about, the pain she would inflict on her doctor, on the TV man, the others to come. Duke had always been the one to encourage her. And he'd spoken about his own fears – his fear of the dark, his failed suicide attempts. She remembered the harrowing description of how he'd attempted suffocation with a suicide bag without gas. He had placed it on his head, tightened the string around his neck and then, as he'd begun to asphyxiate, he'd panicked and clawed at the bag, eventually ripping it off his head – but the cord had caught his left eye, ripping the eyelid and tearing open his eyeball.

He'd said he would die without her, and she believed him.

Simone blinked. The cursor was moving again across the screen.

DUKE: Of course I know you, Night Owl. I know you better than all the rest of them. I love you. And I promise, your secrets will die with me.

CHAPTER 47

Erika was with Crane in one of the cramped technical suites leading off from the incident room.

'Okay, so here's your new phone,' said Crane. 'Keep the old one on you, charge it regularly, but only use it if she calls again. The number is now being monitored. If she calls, the trace equipment will kick in automatically. No delay. Just don't forget that – I've known officers who've been caught out accidentally making private calls, which have been recorded.'

'Don't worry. I won't forget. Although my private life is very boring,' said Erika, taking the phones. 'Hang on, this is a touch screen,' she added, seeing the new handset he'd given her. 'Is there nothing with buttons?'

'Well, technically it's an upgrade from that old handset, boss,' replied Crane.

There was a knock at the door and Moss stuck her head around. 'Boss, you got a moment?' she asked.

'Yeah.'

'I'll see if I can rustle you up an old Nokia,' said Crane.

'Thanks,' Erika said. She followed Moss out into the busy incident room, over to the huge map of Greater London pinned up on the wall. It was six-foot square and a maze of streets. Blotches of green indicated the many parks around the capital, but most prominent was the River Thames, a curving line of blue, carving through the centre.

'She used a payphone to call you,' said Moss. 'We traced it to Ritherdon Road, a residential street in Balham. It's about four miles from your flat in Forest Hill. The phone box in question gets no action. It was the first call made from there in three months. Because of this, British Telecom is planning to remove it at the end of the month.'

'Why a payphone? Are we thinking she hasn't got a phone?' asked Peterson, pushing a red pin into Ritherdon Road towards the bottom of the map.

'No, I think she's clever,' said Erika. 'She knows we can trace a mobile phone. Even if she were using a prepaid phone, we'd be able to trace the call to the nearest mobile phone mast and get her IMEI number and all the handset info. This way she remains anonymous. Dare I ask about CCTV?'

'Okay, so this is the phone box,' said Moss, pointing to the red pin in the map, 'and the first CCTV cameras are a quarter of a mile away.' She ran her finger further down to where Ritherdon Road met Balham High Road. 'There's a Tesco Metro on the corner of Balham High Road, also known as the A24, and there are CCTV cameras at intervals in both directions. We've got DC Warren over there on the blower, working on getting the footage from the Tesco car park security cameras, and the cameras along the A24 in both directions . . .'

'But look where the phone box is on the map. She could have gone in the opposite direction and made her way to any number of places through this web of residential streets, which aren't covered by CCTV,' finished Erika. 'Have you got anything else?'

'Well, the phone box was the good news,' said Moss, moving over to where Singh stood by the bank of printers. 'We finally got the data through from three of the websites who sell these suicide bags in the UK.'

'And?'

'And, as you can see, there's plenty to work through. Three thousand names,' said Singh. 'They were really reluctant to give us these names. And I can see from quite a few that they've paid with PayPal, which could make people more difficult to trace.'

'Shit,' said Erika. 'Okay, well, I say we start by discounting people outside Greater London. We should work on the theory that she saw me on *Crimewatch*. It made her angry and she went to a phone box and called me.'

'Okay, boss,' said Singh.

'What have we had back from the TV appeal?'

'Not a great deal,' said Peterson. 'We're working through the phone calls which came in, but I think the broadcast spooked a lot of people. A man in North London called during the show to say he scared a burglar trying to gain entry to a ground-floor window, another woman in Beckenham thinks she saw a small figure walking through her garden shortly after the broadcast... An old lady who lives close to Laurel Road woke up and scared an intruder in her bedroom, who climbed out of the window... Oh, and there are now three neighbours in Laurel Road who think they saw a small woman, matching the one in the reconstruction, delivering vegetable boxes in the area,' said Peterson. 'It's going to take us time to work through all of these.'

'Have we got a copy of the *Crimewatch* video?' asked Erika. 'I'd like to watch it back. Perhaps something I said made her seek me out, find out my number and call me. Get hold of Tim Aiken for me. You never know, he might have something useful to say for once.'

She looked back at the large map of London, stretching out across the wall.

Reading her thoughts, Moss said, 'So many places to hide in the darkness.'

CHAPTER 48

Erika, Peterson, Moss, Marsh and Tim Aiken were huddled around a television monitor in one of the viewing suites at the station. They were watching back Erika's appearance on *Crimewatch*.

Erika hated seeing herself on screen: her voice seemed higher, screechier. She was pleased, however, that the Met hadn't upgraded their televisions to high definition. These thoughts, though, were just fleeting, at the back of her mind. What she really wanted to know was why the killer had responded to the broadcast in the way she had, assuming she'd seen it.

They came to the end of the part where Erika was interviewed in the studio. '*We believe she's small in stature but we advise the public not to approach her. She is a dangerous and deeply disturbed individual,*' said Erika on the screen.

The presenter then started to read out the email address and phone number to contact, which flashed up on the bottom of the screen.

'So?' asked Erika, turning to Tim Aiken.

'There are many variables,' said Tim, rubbing at his stubbled chin, the multicoloured woven bracelets on his wrist shifting as he raised his arm.

'If the killer was watching, how might she have reacted to seeing her crimes recreated on screen?'

'It could have stoked her ego. Serial killers can be ego-driven, vain individuals,' said Tim.

'So the fact we got a nice, hot young woman to play her in the reconstruction could have been flattering to her?' asked Moss.

'It depends what you define as *hot*, or attractive,' said Tim.

'Well, *I* wouldn't kick her out of bed. Peterson? Sir?' said Moss.

Peterson went to open his mouth but was cut off by Marsh.

'I'm not getting into a debate about the attractiveness of the actor in the reconstruction,' he said, irritably.

Tim went on, 'Or she may be physically unattractive, and she could have objected to how she was portrayed. In the same way that she could be someone who is physically much stronger. She could have objected to an elfin girl such as this playing her in the reconstruction... We have to remember this isn't about her, it's about what she does, and why she does it. She targets and kills men. Both victims were tall and strong, with athletic physiques. She could have been abused by a man or men – a spouse, her father...'

'Can you give us a profile?' asked Marsh.

'I've already submitted a profile based upon this being a predatory gay male...'

'We've ruled that out, obviously,' said Marsh.

'It's extremely rare to come into contact with a female serial killer. Profiling them is very difficult. We have very little data.'

'Well, we're paying you enough. Try,' said Marsh.

'Tim, is there anything else you got from the video?' asked Erika.

'It could be that she has measured herself, her sense of self-worth, in relation to you, DCI Foster. By appearing on the show, you have presented yourself as the person who is going to catch her, regardless of the team you have working for you. She may see this as a fight for supremacy. You also called her out as being a "dangerous and deeply disturbed individual".'

'And she could feel like she's a victim,' finished Erika.

'Yes. And you called her out live on television. That would certainly rankle with her. It would certainly make her seek you out.'

When they had finished, Marsh asked Erika to stay back and have a word.

'I don't like this,' said Marsh. 'I've already had words with Woolf about giving out private numbers.'

'He didn't know.'

'If you'd like, I could have a car stationed outside your flat. Discreet. I can spare a couple of officers.'

'No, sir. She got lucky phishing for my number, and I don't want a car outside my flat. I'll keep my eyes peeled.'

'Erika,' said Marsh, looking frustrated.

'Sir. Thank you, but no. Now I have to go. I will keep you posted.' Erika left the viewing suite.

Marsh stood for a moment, looking at the blank TV screens, feeling uneasy.

CHAPTER 49

Simone had followed the man at a distance for most of the afternoon. Their journey had taken them from outside his flat on the Bowery Lane Estate, near Old Street in Central London. He'd left just after lunch and walked through the financial district to London's Liverpool Street Station. Simone had been confused at first, wondering where he was going with no bag, just wearing a fashionable pair of denim shorts and a sleeveless T-shirt. She had followed twenty yards behind. The throngs of people had been thick, as they surged towards the vast row of ticket gates, almost taking her with them, but he had gone off in the other direction, and for a moment she'd lost him.

Her eyes had darted to the bank of escalators on the far wall, which led up to the mezzanine with the shops, and high above it the vast glass roof of the station. She'd stood on her tiptoes, trying to see above the crowds, and then she'd seen him, heading down a set of double escalators to the public toilets. She went to the large WH Smith beside the escalators and joined several other people browsing at the rack of magazines, watching the toilets all the while.

She'd waited and perused the newspapers, many of them offering opinion pieces and shock articles about the identity of the 'Night Stalker'. She had squealed with pride when a journalist at *the Independent* called her 'a genius of subterfuge'. The woman next to her had glanced over and given her a funny look, so she'd glared at the woman until she put her magazine back on the shelf and hurried away with her suitcase.

Ten minutes had passed, and then twenty… Simone looked at the escalators going down to the public toilets. Was he ill? Had she missed him? Her eyes had been on those escalators every other second – well, apart from when that stupid woman had looked at her. It was only when she noticed the proportion of single men disappearing on the down escalator, and how long they seemed to stay down there, that she realised he was cruising. He had gone down to the toilets specifically for sex.

Many things disgusted Simone about men: their petulance, their sexual deviance, the way they resorted to violence when they wanted to control or didn't get their own way. This didn't surprise her – just another thing to add to the list – and it steeled her resolve. Simone always played the long game with the men she watched. She was prepared to wait weeks, to sit back and build a picture of each target on her list. Gregory and Jack had been ticked off in the same way.

She'd looked down at the copy of *The Independent* in her hand and read the description again: *genius of subterfuge*. She had to buy the paper, she thought. It was the first nice thing she'd heard about herself in years.

She was about to go to the till when he emerged up the escalator –

slightly red in the face, looking glassy-eyed and relaxed. Simone replaced the newspaper, let him get ahead of her, then started to follow. He moved to the back of the station and into a Starbucks.

She held back for a few minutes and then joined the end of the queue. She kept him in her peripheral vision and looked at the cakes and pastries through the glass. This was the closest she had been to him so far – just three people separated them.

Yes, he was young, and he worked out. He could be strong. Although he was thin – vainly so.

She watched as he reached the head of the queue and flirted with the handsome young black barista, leaning over and putting his hand on the young man's arm, spelling out his name, making sure it was written correctly on the cup.

Soon that cock-sucking mouth will breathe its last breath, she thought. Then she smiled at the barista and ordered a nice piece of fruitcake and a cappuccino.

'What's the name, love?' asked the Barista.

'It's Mary,' said Simone. 'It must be quite boring, compared to the exotic names you hear.'

'I like the name Mary,' said the barista.

'I got it from my mother. She's called Mary, too. She's in hospital right now. She's very ill. I'm all she's got.'

'Sorry to hear that,' said the barista. 'Is there anything else I can get you?'

'I'll just take a copy of *the Independent*. I'm planning on reading to her later. She loves hearing all about things going on in the world.'

Simone took her paper, coffee and cake, and moved over to a seat.

All the time watching her future victim.

CHAPTER 50

The break in the weather was short-lived. Over the next few days the sun began to beat down relentlessly again and progress on the case seemed to grind to a halt.

The *Crimewatch* reconstruction had remained on BBC iPlayer for a week and as people watched it on catch-up there were more phone calls and emails to work through.

As the remaining residents of Laurel Road returned from their holidays, word spread that their street had been featured in a nationwide TV reconstruction. Several of them now remembered seeing a young, dark-haired woman going door-to-door delivering leaflets, and others recalled a young girl delivering fruit and vegetable boxes, and a young girl in a plumber's van fixing a drain close to Gregory Munro's house.

This outburst of sightings spread the resources of Erika's team even thinner. They went as far as tracking down the plumber, who turned out to be a fresh-faced young man, and a dark-haired woman who delivered the 'Nature's Finest' seasonal weekly vegetable boxes around the local area. They both came in voluntarily, answered questions and even provided DNA samples. After a nail-biting twelve hours of waiting, the results came back negative. Their DNA didn't match the samples taken from Jack Hart's back door and the suicide bag.

Two of the residents from Laurel Road and one of Jack Hart's neighbours came to Lewisham Row and worked with an officer on e-fits of the woman they had seen delivering leaflets. Erika had high hopes that this would lead to a breakthrough, but the images all came back looking like Lottie, the actress who had appeared in the *Crimewatch* episode.

However, the most depressing job had been tracking down the London-based people who had bought suicide bags through the three websites. So many of the phone calls had been with grieving parents and spouses, who had informed the police that yes, one of the bags had been purchased, and that the suicide attempt had been successful.

On the afternoon of the 15th of July, the atmosphere in the incident room was subdued. The previous day, six members of Erika's team had been reassigned to a drug-trafficking case, and she had just finished a call with an angry man with three children whose wife had killed herself, and whose small daughter had been the one to find her body with the plastic bag over her head.

It was a Friday, and Erika could tell that the rest of her team was itching to get home and enjoy the weekend. She couldn't blame them; they had been working flat out. They had little to show for all their hard work, and the newspapers were full of pictures of people crowding to the beach and local parks.

Moss and Peterson sat at their desks, along with Crane and Singh. Erika looked over at the whiteboards for what seemed the thousandth time, at the pictures of Gregory Munro and Jack Hart. There was now also an image taken from one of the suicide websites, of a tanned, bald shop mannequin lying in a dingy bedroom with a suicide bag rigged up with a pipe and gas canister. Its eyelids were shaded with purple and long eyelashes were painted on.

'Boss, I've got Marsh on the phone,' said Moss, covering the handset.

'Can you tell him I'm out?' Erika replied. She figured that more of her team was about to be reassigned and she couldn't face another heated meeting.

'He'd like to see you in his office. Says it's important.'

'Maybe he's going to tell you we're getting decent air-con,' grinned Peterson.

'I live in hope,' said Erika. She tucked in her blouse, pulled on her jacket and left the incident room, climbing the four flights of stairs up to Marsh's office.

She knocked and he shouted for her to enter. She was surprised to see that he'd tidied the office: gone was the mess of discarded files and clothes, and the dismantled coat stand. There was a bottle of eighteen-year-old Chivas Regal on the table.

'Can I get you a drink?' he asked.

'Okay. Seeing as it's Friday.'

Marsh went to the corner of the office, and Erika saw that where the pile of coats and paperwork had been, there was now a small fridge. Marsh opened the fridge and retrieved an ice cube tray from the freezer compartment. She watched as he added ice to two plastic cups, and then poured a generous measure of whisky into both.

'You do take ice?' he said.

'Yes, thank you.'

He put the cork back in the bottle, placed it down on the desk, then handed her one of the cups.

'I know tomorrow is the second anniversary,' he said quietly. 'I just wanted to have drink with you. To let you know I hadn't forgotten. To toast Mark.'

He raised his cup and she bumped hers against it. They both took a sip.

'Do sit down, please.'

They both sat, and Erika looked down at the amber liquid clinging to the rapidly melting ice. She was touched, but determined not to cry.

'He was a good man, Erika.'

'I can't believe it's been two years,' she said. 'For the first year, I'd wake up most mornings and I'd often forget that he was gone. But now I've got used to him not being here, to a certain extent, which is almost worse.'

'Marcie asked me to send her regards too.'

'Thanks…' Erika wiped her eyes with her sleeve and changed the subject. 'We had the e-fits back. They've all given us a reproduction of the actress from *Crimewatch*.'

Marsh nodded. 'Yes, I saw.'

She went on, 'I fear our only breakthrough will be when she kills again. We're going to stay on it, though. Next week I'm going to get the team to revisit all the evidence. We'll start from scratch. There's always something, however small…'

Marsh sat back in his chair. He looked pained.

'You know how this works, Erika. She could strike again in the next few weeks, or days… Or it could be months. I worked on Operation Minstead. At one point, the attacker stopped for seven years.'

'Is this you letting me down softly?'

'No, I'm happy to give you more time, but I have to remind you that resources are not infinite.'

'So what's the whisky for?'

'It's a genuine gesture. Nothing to do with work.'

Erika sipped at hers and they sat in silence for a moment. She looked out at the view behind Marsh: the blue sky, the houses receding in the distance, giving way to patches of green on the horizon.

'What are you doing tomorrow? Will anyone be with you?' asked Marsh.

'Mark's dad did offer to come down to London, but I thought, with the case…' She trailed off.

'Take the day off, Erika. You've been on for three weeks without a break.'

'Yes, sir.'

She drank the last of the whisky and placed the plastic cup back on the table.

'I think she's planning her next murder, sir. She's not going into hibernation. I don't think it will be seven weeks, let alone seven years.'

CHAPTER 51

Simone followed the man on three more occasions. He liked to spend his afternoons in a gay sauna in Waterloo, tucked away behind the train station. Twice, she'd tailed him there, discreetly waiting in an Internet cafe further down the street. His visits had lasted several hours. On another morning, he'd taken the tube from the Barbican. She'd sat further down the carriage, tucked in amongst a row of commuters, pretending to read the *Metro* as the train trundled and lurched around the Circle line until it reached Gloucester Road underground station.

She'd felt uneasy shadowing him in West London. It was alien to her. It reeked of money, with its mix of smart Georgian houses and exotic people drinking at pavement cafes. He had called in at a smart office on a residential street and vanished inside without looking back.

She'd returned that day to watch the building where he lived. The Bowery Lane Estate was a large and rather bleak U-shaped six-storey block of flats, with an oblong of grass in the centre. It was a concrete brutalist design, built as council flats after the Second World War, when much of London had been a bomb site. Now, sixty years later, the flats had been hailed as a site of architectural importance. The concrete structure was a listed building, and each flat sold for half a million or more – the newer, moneyed residents rubbing shoulders uncomfortably with the remaining council tenants.

The main entrance and main stairway had once been accessible from the street, but an armed raid in the late eighties had led to this being boxed in with reinforced glass, and the large plate-glass door could only be accessed via a secure video entry system.

Observing from another Internet cafe on the opposite side of the road, Simone had tried to work out how to get inside. The obvious way would be to wait for someone who lived there to go in or out. This rarely worked for other people: on two separate occasions, she'd seen deliverymen being blocked from entering by elderly residents on their way inside. The residents had used a plastic key fob to open the door, pressing it onto a square contact pad under the grid of doorbells, releasing the lock.

This had worried Simone. She was good with locks, but it would be hard to get one of the plastic key fobs without questions being asked. Or without a mess to clear up.

Then, at 2 p.m., she'd observed a gaggle of old ladies emerging through the large glass doors, each holding a rolled-up bath towel. They'd waddled off across the grass courtyard and through a door at the back of the U-shaped building. An hour later, they'd returned with wet hair, chatting and ambling across the sunlit grass, pressing their key fobs to open the main door.

Simone had Googled 'Bowery Lane Estate' and had seen that there was a small council-run swimming pool on the ground floor. Four days a week it held an 'over-sixties' swim.

With this in mind, Simone waited until the timings worked. She followed the man to one of his regular sauna sessions in Waterloo and then doubled back to the Bowery Lane Estate in time for the old ladies to emerge for their swim.

Simone found that the simple things worked the best, so, dressed in her nurses uniform, with a short, dark wig liberated from the locker of a recently deceased cancer patient, she approached the glass front door as the ladies emerged.

All it took was a smile, an apology for losing her key, and the ladies let her pass. Sometimes it helped to be plain and unremarkable.

His flat was number thirty-seven, on the second floor. Each floor was a long concrete corridor, open to the air, with doors dotted along it. Simone moved confidently, passing the front window of each flat, realising that each of these windows looked on to the kitchen. In one, an old lady stood washing up; in another, she glimpsed a view of the living room through a hatch in the kitchen, where two small children sat on the carpet playing with toys.

She reached the door of number thirty-seven – the third flat before the end – with a key ready in her hand. She'd gambled on the front door having a pin tumbler lock. This was the most common type of lock, using a thin key. Duke had told her all about lock bumping. It was possible to force a pin tumbler lock with a special-shaped key with a jagged edge. The only problem was that it could be noisy. Once in the lock, they key had to be pulled out very slightly, then tapped sharply with a hammer or a blunt object. This forced up the five small pins that made up the mechanism of the lock, tricking it into thinking it was the correct key.

Duke had ordered her a bump key online, along with the suicide bags. Simone had practised with the key on her back door, but her heart was lurching as she approached the man's door. She was pleased to see that it did have a pin tumbler lock, and she inserted the key. In her other hand was a small, smooth stone and she tapped the key sharply –

once, twice – and turned the handle.

Triumph flooded through her when the door opened. If there had been a deadbolt, this would have been near-impossible, but the door opened and she slipped silently inside. She checked for an alarm and was glad to see there was none. It seemed that the video entry-phone system had lulled this man into thinking he didn't need extra security.

She stood for a moment with her back to the door, slowing down her breathing.

She quickly moved through the flat. The first door on the left led to the kitchen – it was tiny but modern. The hallway opened out straight ahead onto a large living room. Through a large glass window, she could see the high-rise tower of the Lloyd's building dwarfing several other tower blocks. Inside the room there was a flat-screen television, and a large L-shaped sofa. Above the sofa, a giant photo of a naked man stared at her malevolently. An entire wall was lined with books, and the bottom shelf was devoted exclusively to alcohol: fifty bottles, perhaps more.

It was far too many bottles. Would she need to resort to using a syringe?

In the back corner was a metal spiral staircase that vanished into the ceiling. Simone climbed the staircase and saw that the layout upstairs was also small: challenging.

Her heart began to beat with excitement and anticipation. She was more excited by this than she had been with the others. She checked the location of the electricity box and phone lines, and when she was satisfied, she came back to the front door. On the wall beside the door there hung a vast array of coats: long, short, thick and thin. A small plaque was screwed to the wall, and several keys hung from it. She lifted them off one by one, trying them in the front door until she came to one that opened it.

Sometimes things are just meant to be, she thought, leaving the flat and locking the door behind her.

CHAPTER 52

For the anniversary of Mark's death, Moss had invited Erika over for a barbecue at her house, saying she would invite Peterson too. Erika was grateful for their concern but said she wanted to spend the day alone.

What surprised her was that she heard nothing from Isaac. He'd been fairly quiet for the last week or so, and she realised she had last seen him at the post-mortem for Jack Hart. Maybe her objection to Stephen had cooled his friendship with her.

Erika woke early, and one of the first things she did was to take down her kitchen clock and the clock in her bedroom. She kept her TV, laptop and mobile phone switched off. Four-thirty in the afternoon was burned on her brain. This was the time, two years ago, when she had given the order to raid the house of Jerome Goodman.

It was another hot day, but she went for a run, pushing herself in the humidity as she pounded the streets, then circumnavigating Hilly Fields park amongst the dog walkers, the people playing tennis on the free courts and the children playing. It was the children playing who got to her. She stopped after two circuits and came home.

Once she was home, she started drinking, working her way through the bottle of Glenmorangie she'd opened for Peterson.

She sat on the sofa, the heat circulating through the house, the drone of a lawnmower in the background. Despite everything she had told herself about moving on, about moving forward, she felt herself being pulled back to that baking hot day on that run-down street in Rochdale…

She could feel the protective police gear sticking to her skin through her blouse. The stiff, sharp edges of the Kevlar bulletproof vest as it rode up, meeting her chin as she crouched against the low wall of the terraced house.

There were six officers on her team and they also crouched against the wall, three each side with the gatepost between them. Next to her was DI Tom Bradbury, known as Brad – an officer she'd worked with since she'd joined the Greater Manchester Police as a new recruit. He was chewing gum, breathing slowly. The sweat poured down his face and he shifted anxiously.

Next to Brad was Jim Black, or Beamer. He had a serious face, which could be transformed by an enormous smile, hence the nickname. It always made Erika laugh that he could be so fierce and stern in his police work, yet crack a wide dazzling grin. She and Mark had become close friends with Beamer and his wife Michelle, who was a civilian support officer at their nick.

On the other side of the front gate was Tim James, a rising star and new to her team. He was a brilliant officer. He was tall, slim and utterly gorgeous. He arrested rough-looking guys during the day, then went round the bars looking to hook up with them at night. Tim James had earned the nickname TJ when he'd joined her team, and when his fellow officers had heard he was into guys, he'd become BJ – but it was an affectionate nickname and he was sensible enough to realise that.

Next to BJ was Sal, whose full name was Salman Dhumal: a fiercely intelligent British Indian man with jet-black hair and eyes. His family went back four generations in Bradford, but he still had to suffer the taunts of 'go back where you came from' doled out by scumbags on the beat. His wife, Meera, looked after their three children, as well as being one of the top Ann Summers reps in the north-west.

And, finally, on the end was Mark. He was always just Mark. Not that he was boring, or uninteresting. He was everyone's friend, so easy-going and fiercely loyal. Mark had time for everyone, and Erika knew he was the reason she had so many friends – he took the edge off her abrasive personality. He softened her hardness, and in turn she had taught him not to just let everything wash over him.

So there they all were, at 4.25 p.m. on July 25th, sweating in a row outside the house of the drug dealer Jerome Goodman. He'd been on their radar for several years, and in the past eighteen months he had been involved in the bloody slaying of a major drug dealer in a pub in Moss Side. In the resulting power vacuum, Jerome had taken over the supply and manufacture of crystal meth and Ecstasy. And on this baking hot day on a run-down street in Rochdale, they were waiting to storm this large terraced house – one of his strongholds.

A vast support network at the nick had backed up Erika and her team. The house had been under surveillance for weeks, and images of it were burned into her brain. Bare concrete out front, overflowing wheelie bins. A gas and electric meter on the wall, with its cover ripped off.

An undercover officer had sought plans of the interior. They had planned their point of entry: straight through the front door, up the stairs. A door to the left of the landing led through to a back bedroom, and that's where they believed they were cooking the meth.

In the past few days, covert surveillance had seen a woman going in and out with a little boy. It was a risk. They had to anticipate that Jerome could use the kid as a shield, a bargaining tool, or, at his worst, threaten to end the little boy's life – but they were *prepared. Erika had drilled the routine over and over to her team. They worked well together.*

Fear rolled over her as her watch reached 4.30 p.m. She looked up and gave the order. She watched as her colleagues moved past the gateposts and surged towards the front door. She brought up the rear, moving stealthily past the gateposts. Something bright caught her eye, dazzling her. She realised it was the sunlight glinting off the disc in the electricity meter as it spun. It glinted again, and again, almost matching the thunk of the battering ram. On the third attempt, the wood splintered and the front door burst inwards with a clatter.

It was quickly apparent that Jerome had been tipped off. Within a few life-changing minutes, Brad, Beamer and Sal lay dead. Erika took a bullet to her vest, which knocked her back, and then a bullet passed through her neck, missing all the major arteries. Mark was close by as she clutched at her neck, the blood pouring between her fingers.

He looked at her, horror in his eyes at the realisation of what was happening – and then he seemed to stop.

It was then that Erika saw that the back of his head had been blown open.

Erika and DI Tim James were airlifted from the scene, badly injured. She left her officers – her friends and her husband – dead.

In reality, it had all been over within minutes, but since 4.30 p.m. on that fateful day, life had slowed down for Erika. From then on, she felt that she was walking through a nightmare from which she would never wake up.

CHAPTER 53

Simone stood back, looking at Mary lying awkwardly in the bed, half inside a patterned nightgown. She was out of breath and angry.

She'd seen the nightgown in a charity shop in Beckenham and had decided to buy it for Mary. It was a good place to pick up bargains; the people who tended to donate to charity shops in Beckenham were much better off than they were in her area and you could pick up some nice stuff.

The nightie had set her back twelve pounds. She'd hesitated before spending so much, but she loved the pattern of cherries against the white background, and she'd thought it would really suit Mary.

The problem was that it didn't fit. Mary's shoulders were too broad and Simone had spent fifteen minutes trying to wrestle her limp form into it, only for it to get stuck. The old lady was now lying with the garment over her head, pinching her shoulders together, which in turn lifted her arms so they jutted out limply in front.

Simone paced the small room. It was only minutes until protected mealtimes, when nurses would come round and feed the patients. Mary wasn't eating, but someone was bound to open the door.

'Why didn't you tell me you were bigger than a size twelve?' said Simone. 'You're not eating. I spent a lot of money on this!'

She grabbed at the collar of the nightgown and pulled. Mary's head flopped forward and then back, unsupported as her torso was lifted off the mattress. Simone wrestled with the nightie until it suddenly came free with a tearing sound and Mary flopped to one side, her head hitting the safety bar with a thud.

'Now look what you've done,' said Simone, holding up the torn nightdress. 'I can't even take it back to the shop!' She shook the old woman, feeling her limp body, small and frail, in her grip. She let go. 'Why is it that people always disappoint me?'

She roughly pulled Mary into her backless hospital gown and shoved her back under the blankets.

'I won't be talking to you for a while,' announced Simone, folding the nightgown and shoving it back into her bag. 'You've disappointed me. You're nothing but a fat old woman, and ungrateful too. I spend my hard-earned money on nice new clothes for you and you don't even have the decency to fit into them!'

Simone pulled her bag onto her shoulder and opened the door. The sounds of moaning echoed down the hallway outside.

She turned to Mary. 'No wonder George left you… I've got someone else I'm going to visit.'

CHAPTER 54

Erika opened her eyes. The living room was dim and gloomy. It was dark outside, and a breeze was rushing in through the open patio door. She got up and felt pain throbbing through her head: the beginning of a hangover from all the whisky she'd drunk.

A small pile of leaves had blown through the patio door and now flapped on the carpet in the breeze. She leant down and picked them up. They were long and waxy in her hand and she recognised them as eucalyptus. She put them to her nose and inhaled the honey-mint smell, fresh and warm. She felt warmth inside her chest as the memory of Mark came back. Eucalyptus had been his favourite smell. She used to buy him small bottles of eucalyptus oil to put in his bathwater. She held the leaves to her nose and stepped through the open patio door into the dark garden. Cool gusts of wind ruffled her hair, and she could see the dark outline of the huge eucalyptus tree out on the road behind the houses.

There was a crack of thunder, and a large raindrop hit her leg. Moments later there was another and another and then, with a roar, it began to pour down. She stood for a moment, turning her face up to the rain, enjoying the feeling of the cold water pounding down on her. Thunder crackled and rumbled as the rain moved up a gear, crashing down in sheets, soaking her to the skin and washing away the tears and sweat of the day.

And then she realised. The patio door had been closed when she'd sat down on the sofa and fallen asleep. She turned and looked back at the open patio door, gaping black. She couldn't see indoors. She moved to the edge of the garden, grabbing a large rock from the thin flowerbed running along the fence, and hefting it in her hand, she went back inside the flat.

She flicked on the light. The living room was empty. She moved through the hall, turning on the light, holding the rock up, ready to hit with it when she turned on the bathroom light. Nothing. She reached the bedroom door and turned on the light. It, too, was empty. She crouched down and checked under the bed, and then she saw it.

A thick cream envelope lay on her pillow. Written on it, in blue ink, was: DCI ERIKA FOSTER.

Erika stared at the letter, her heart pounding. She braced herself with the rock and moved through to the living room. She slammed the patio door, locking it. It was pitch black outside and the rain thudded onto the glass. She went to her bag and found a spare pair of latex gloves. It took several attempts to pull them onto her trembling hands. She returned to the bedroom and approached the note cautiously, lifting it off her pillow.

She'd been inside… inside her home. It was the Night Stalker, Erika was sure. She brought the note back through to the kitchen and placed it on the counter. The rain continued to hammer on the windows. She gently slit the envelope open with a knife and pulled out a card. It showed the image of a sunset above the sea. The sun was like a vast, bloody egg yolk, bursting on the horizon. She took a deep breath and carefully opened the envelope. Inside, in neat blue handwriting, was written:

Do not stand at my grave and weep.
I am not there; I do not sleep.

I am a thousand winds that blow,
I am the diamond glints on snow,
I am the sun on ripened grain,
I am the gentle autumn rain.
When you awaken in the morning's hush
I am the swift uplifting rush
Of quiet birds in circled flight.
I am the soft stars that shine at night.
Do not stand at my grave and cry,
I am not there; I did not die.

Beneath the poem was written:

You must learn to let him go, Erika . . .
From one widow to another. THE NIGHT STALKER

Erika dropped the card on the kitchen counter and took a step back, pulling the latex gloves off her shaking hands. She moved around the flat again, checking the windows and doors were locked. The Night Stalker had been inside the flat; she had been inside as Erika slept. How long had she been there? Had she watched Erika sleeping?

Erika looked around the living room and shivered. Not only had she been inside her home, it felt as if she were now inside her head. The poem was beautiful. It spoke to her, spoke to her feelings of loss and bereavement. How could someone so sick and twisted connect with her so deeply?

CHAPTER 55

Simone was running fast through the back streets, of which there were few in Central London. It was pouring with rain and she could feel blood running down the side of her neck; her mouth was numb and her top lip felt painfully engorged with blood. It hadn't gone to plan. She'd fucked up.

It started out smoothly. She gained access again to the Bowery Lane Estate flats in her nurse's uniform. The second floor hallway was empty and she moved stealthily, passing the open kitchen windows. Through one window a man lay sleeping in front of a flickering television. Simone stopped and stared at him for a moment. His feet splayed out in front, an arm across his chest, rising and falling in the flickering light...

She forced herself to move on through the shadows until she reached number 37, Stephen Linley's front door. She pressed her ear to the red paint and heard nothing. She slid the key in the lock and the door opened with a soft click.

Stephen Linley came home an hour later. She lay in wait for him, downstairs in the shadows, listening as he moved about in the kitchen. Through the glass hatch in the living room she watched him pour a large glass of the juice she had laced with the date rape drug. He drank it rapidly, then poured another and took it with him upstairs.

He passed so close to where Simone waited, behind the thick folds of the curtain in front of the large glass window. She felt the air shift as he moved past, and she smelled him: a sweet, overpowering scent of cologne, dank sweat and sex. It focused her hatred of him.

She listened as he went into the bathroom and she followed in the darkness, making no sound on the soft carpet. The bathroom door was pulled to and she heard the clink as he unhitched his belt and started to pee.

Hold onto it, it's the last time you'll get to use it, thought Simone. She moved through to the bedroom and softly opened the money belt she kept around her waist, pulling out the neatly folded plastic bag.

She moved to the bed and lay down on the carpet, sliding underneath. Simone enjoyed this part, the lying in wait. It reinforced all those childhood nightmares of the bogey man under the bed, of monsters crouching in a darkened cupboard. She was a monster, she knew that, and she revelled in it.

She listened to the muffled sounds of Stephen in the bathroom. The sound of the water being turned on, the rustle as he pulled the shower curtain across.

He finally emerged minutes later, and she watched as his feet appeared in her line of vision, as he unsteadily made his way around the bed. His phone began to ring, and he cursed, fumbling in his trouser pockets. There was a click as he cancelled the call, and then the phone dropped to the carpet beside her. Its screen glowed. Then he lost balance and crashed down onto the bed. Simone shrank back further under the bed and into the shadows. The mattress shifted above her.

'Jeez, how much did I drink?' she heard him murmur. Simone waited another minute before moving to where the phone lay on the carpet. She reached out and pulled it towards her, then switched it off. Slowly, softly, she slid out from under the bed. She could see he was lying on his side with his back to her; his hand was moving shakily over his face. She stood for a moment and watched him, listening to his groans, and then moved quietly from the bedroom and back down the stairs. The electricity box was in a small cupboard under the spiral staircase. She opened it and flicked off the power.

Her eyes had adjusted to the light. She looked across at the books he had written, which lined the shelves: *Descent into Darkness*, *From My Cold Dead Hands*, *The Girl in the Cellar*. It was Stephen Linley's mind she hated and feared the most. Her husband had enjoyed his books, had enjoyed the horror and the torture. She thought of how Stan had held her down and poured boiling water over her naked body… how he had lifted this particular torture out of *From My Cold Dead Hands*.

She stood for a minute and drank in the silence, interrupted by the murmurings from Stephen upstairs.

'I'm coming to get you. I'm coming to get you, you evil bastard,' whispered Simone. She moved quickly, back up the stairs and into the bedroom.

The bed squeaked and shifted as Simone climbed in beside him. There was a soft crackle of plastic as she reached across and slipped the bag over his head.

Stephen panicked and lashed out, catching Simone on the side of her head with his fist. She tried to ignore the pain and the burst of stars in her vision and jerked at the string, pulling it tight around his neck. He fought harder and lashed out again, punching her in the mouth. The strength of his blow surprised her; she thought, by now, he would have been very subdued and weakened by the drug pumping through his veins. She yanked the cord roughly and it tightened further, biting into the skin of his neck. He started to thrash around on the mattress, trying to move away from her across the bed. She thought he was trying to escape, only realising what he was doing when his arm came up and something very hard and heavy crashed down onto the back of her head. He didn't have the strength to land a serious blow, though, and the large object glanced off her head and rolled onto the mattress.

The bag was now tight on his head, the plastic starting to form a vacuum over his face and his groaning mouth. Simone held onto the bag with one hand and searched with her free hand for what had hit her. Stephen's elbow landed a painful blow to her temple and her hand closed around a large heavy marble ashtray. He was scrabbling madly at the plastic over his face, choking and retching. He placed his feet on the mattress and pushed up with his legs. Simone felt his head pull away from her. She lifted the ashtray high in the air and, with all her strength, brought it down on his head. There was a sickening thud as the front of his skull caved in. She lifted the ashtray and brought it down again, and again. On the third blow, the plastic bag burst and blood and bone mottled the wall.

She sat there on the mattress, shaking. She'd done it. She'd done it. But she'd screwed up badly. It was then that she ran out of the bedroom, falling down half the flight of stairs, and kept running, out of the flat. She didn't stop until she was safely away, shrouded by the darkness and the pouring rain.

CHAPTER 56

Erika jumped as her landline began to ring, cutting through the sound of the pounding rain. She didn't know how long she'd been staring at the neat handwriting in the card. She grabbed the phone off the floor beside her front door and answered.

'Erika, help me, he's dead!' came a voice she barely recognised.

'Isaac, is that you?'

'Yes! Erika, you have to help me. It's Stephen... I just came to his flat, and found him... Oh God... There's blood, there's blood everywhere...'

'Have you called the police?' asked Erika.

'No, I didn't know who else to call... He's lying on the bed, he's naked...'

'Isaac, listen, you have to call 999.'

'Erika... He's dead and he has a plastic bag over his head...'

The rain was torrential when Erika arrived at the Bowery Lane Estate. As her windscreen wipers worked to clear the deluge, the blue lights from the police cars crowding the entrance seemed to mix with the water in streaks. She parked behind one of the large support vans and climbed out into the lashing rain.

'Ma'am, move your car, you cannot park there!' shouted a uniformed officer running towards her. She pulled out her ID.

'I'm DCI Foster, I'm responding to the call-out,' she lied.

'Are you the Senior Investigating Officer on this?' asked the officer, putting a hand up to shield his eyes from the rain. It crackled as it landed on the waterproof covering on his helmet.

'I'll know more when I see the scene,' she said. He waved her past him. She walked towards the police cordon. Police cars were parked up on the pavement, and an ambulance had pulled into the courtyard on the grass, its lights adding to the symphony of blue and red that played across the block of flats.

Erika looked up and noted that lights were coming on in the windows. A uniformed officer was yelling for people to go back inside, and Erika saw a group of young girls in their pyjamas being herded in by their mother.

She showed her ID at the police tape.

'You're not on the list,' the uniformed officer shouted above the noise of rain and police sirens.

'I'm in the first response team. DCI Foster,' she shouted, brandishing her ID again. He nodded, she signed his clipboard and he lifted the tape for her.

A large glass door was propped open and she went through to a stark stairwell. The concrete was grey and mottled with years of stains. When she reached Stephen Linley's flat, it was crowded. She flashed her ID and was given a suit, mask and shoe covers, which she quickly pulled on in the corridor. When she went inside, every available space in the small flat was being dusted for prints, and photographed. The crime scene officers worked silently and paid her no attention as she climbed the spiral staircase with a sense of dread. She could hear soft murmurings coming from above, and the click and squeal of the crime scene photographer's camera.

The bedroom was worse than she'd imagined. A naked man lay on a white mattress, which was saturated with blood. His body was fairly unmarked but his head was unrecognisable inside a plastic bag. The white wall behind was streaked in red. The room was filled with officers –

one in particular stood out to Erika because of his tall frame. Beside him was a much shorter, fatter officer who had one of the drawers open in a large dresser and was pulling out a selection of dildos, leather harnesses and what looked like fetish hoods. He held one of the black PVC hoods up.

'Looks like a fetish breath control device,' he said.

'Jesus, no wonder he came a cropper,' said the tall officer. Erika's heart sank when she realised who the voice belonged to.

'DCI Foster, what are you doing here?' said DCI Sparks.

The large man beside him placed the hood in an evidence bag with his gloved hands, then turned. His eyebrows were long and bristly above craggy eyes.

'I… I received a call,' she said.

'From who? The first response were City of London Police. They called my team in,' said Sparks. 'This is Superintendent Nickson.'

Both Sparks and Nickson stared at her from behind their masks. The camera fired off two blinding flashes.

'You're a long way from home, don't you think?' added Nickson. He had a gruff, no-nonsense voice.

'I'm… er…. I got a call from the forensic pathologist, Isaac Strong,' Erika said, shakily.

'I'm the forensic pathologist, Duncan Masters,' said a small man with intense eyes, working in the corner. 'Dr Strong is being interviewed by uniformed officers. He's not here in a professional capacity.'

'Hello, Dr Masters,' said Erika. 'I've been working on the double murder asphyxiation of Jack Hart and Gregory Munro. I'm here also in a professional capacity. I believe that this murder could have been committed by the same person.'

'And what makes you think that? You've just barged into my crime scene,' said Dr Masters.

'This man was bludgeoned to death with a marble ashtray and he has an arse full of semen,' said Sparks. 'It looks like one of ours. We'll take it from here.' He beckoned to an officer. 'Can you take this woman out to one of the support vehicles? She needs to be questioned about her apparent tip-off about the crime scene.'

'It's DCI Foster and—' started Erika, before she felt a hand grip her tightly on the arm. 'Okay, okay. You don't need to man-handle me. I can see the door. I'm coming out.'

The officer clad in blue crime scene overalls walked her out. Even though just her eyes were on show, Erika knew everyone could see she felt deeply humiliated.

CHAPTER 57

Much as when high-level doctors are forced to become patients, DCI Foster didn't take kindly to being questioned by uniformed officers in one of the police support vans. The rain continued hammering down outside, hitting the metal roof of the van with a roar.

Two male officers, DI Wilkinson and DI Roberts, sat across from her at a table, whilst a female uniformed officer with chestnut brown hair scraped back off her youthful face watched from the open door.

'So what made Isaac Strong call you before he had even placed a call to 999?' asked DI Wilkinson. He had a thin, ratty face and teeth to match.

'He was frightened. He was in shock,' replied Erika.

'So you're close? Are you in a relationship with Isaac Strong?' asked DI Roberts. He was blond and handsome in comparison to his colleague.

'No, he's just a friend,' said Erika.

'Just good friends?' said DI Roberts, raising an eyebrow. 'Nothing more?'

'Is this the extent of your detective work, sussing out who's shagging who?'

'Answer the question, Ms Foster,' demanded DI Wilkinson.

'I've told you twice already, it's DCI Foster,' she said, pulling out her ID and slapping it on the table in front of them. 'I've been investigating a double murder where an intruder broke in and asphyxiated both victims by placing a plastic bag over their heads. Both victims were male. You've probably heard about it: the victims were Dr Gregory Munro and Jack Hart. I am the SIO on the case and Dr Isaac Strong is the forensic pathologist. I also know Dr Strong outside work. We occasionally socialise, as friends, and I know him to be gay. Now, it seems, our personal and professional lives have intertwined in that Isaac's partner, Stephen Linley, is the man lying upstairs with his head caved in. Dr Strong was understandably distressed when he found him and he phoned me. When you listen back to the transcript of that call, you will hear me clearly state that he must call 999. I then ended the call and came to the scene. I can tell you that the bag used in the previous murders is a very specific item, and I believe this same bag was used to kill Stephen Linley. Now, you'd better start listening to me, and being more respectful, because in a few hours, if you're still on this case, you'll be taking orders from me.'

She sat back and eyeballed the two officers. An uneasy look passed between them.

'Very good, ma'am,' said Wilkinson, who looked embarrassed.

'Now, do you have any more questions you would like to ask me?'

'I think that's all good for now,' said Roberts.

'Thank you. I'd like to talk to Dr Strong, please. Where is he?' asked Erika.

The officer on the door looked up from speaking into her radio.

'That was Control,' she said. 'I've just been told DCI Sparks has left Superintendent Nickson at the scene and has taken Dr Isaac Strong to Charing Cross nick.'

'Taken him?' asked Erika. 'Has he been arrested? Or did he go voluntarily?'

The officer repeated the question into her radio, and there was a pause, some clicks and beeps, then the voice came back confirming that Isaac had been arrested for the suspected murder of Stephen Linley.

CHAPTER 58

Erika hesitated before she reached out and banged the large brass door knocker. She stood back and looked up at the dark house. The rain had been replaced by a cold wind, and even though she was still soaking wet, the chill was a welcome change after the heatwave. She pulled her denim jacket closed and was about to knock again when the small window by the front door lit up.

'Who is it?' asked Marsh, brusquely.

'Boss, it's Erika, DCI Foster.'

'What the bloody hell?' she heard him mutter as several bolts shot home, two locks were turned and he finally pulled the front door open. He was wearing nothing but boxer shorts.

'I have a very good reason for this,' she said, putting up her hands.

Twenty minutes later, Erika's denim jacket was steaming lightly by the Aga and she was sitting with Marsh at the long, scrubbed-oak kitchen table. He'd pulled on a tracksuit, and his wife, Marcie, with her long dark hair on end and no make-up, was spooning tea leaves into a pot as the kettle boiled.

'Jesus,' said Marsh, after Erika had told him about Stephen Linley.

'I'm sorry to have intruded on you both, but I'm just concerned about making calls to you from my mobile,' said Erika.

'Don't you have a private mobile phone?' asked Marsh.

'No.'

'What do you do when you want to make a private call?'

'I don't make many,' said Erika. This hung in the air for a moment. The kettle came to the boil and Marcie poured water into the pot. 'My point is,' Erika continued, 'that my phone call with Isaac will be evidence in our case, now he's a suspect. But sir, he didn't do this. I saw the crime scene. It was the Night Stalker, I'm sure of it.'

'You said Stephen Linley had been bludgeoned over the head with an ashtray?'

'It was the same type of plastic bag, a suicide bag; he was naked in bed. Something could have gone wrong, the killer could have panicked. He most likely fought back at her.'

'You really think this is a woman?' asked Marcie, incredulously.

'Yes, we do,' said Erika. Marcie came over and placed cups of tea down in front of them. Marsh's phone rang on the table.

'It's Superintendent Nickson,' said Marsh, looking at the screen before he answered.

'He was at the scene with DCI Sparks,' said Erika.

'Hello? John, it's Paul Marsh...' He left the kitchen and closed the door behind him. Erika listened as his voice receded down the hallway. Marcie came and sat down opposite.

'Would you like one?' she asked, opening a tin of biscuits and placing it between them. 'You look a bit pale.'

'Thanks,' said Erika. They each took one and chewed in silence.

'I know what today is – the anniversary,' said Marcie. 'And I'm sorry. You know I'm sorry. It can't be easy.'

'Thanks,' said Erika, taking another biscuit. 'But I think tonight I sort of accepted it. Do you know what I mean? I still think about him all the time, but I sort of accepted that he's never coming back.'

Marcie nodded. Erika thought how pretty she was without all the make-up she usually wore. It softened her.

'Are you thinking of staying down south?' asked Marcie, taking another biscuit and daintily dipping it in her tea.

'I don't know. The past two years have been like the first two years of my life again. First it was a day since Mark died, then it was a week, a month, a year…'

'Planning anything is impossible,' finished Marcie.

'Yeah.'

'Have you still got the house up north, in Ruskin Road?'

'Yeah.'

'That's such a nice house, so cosy.'

'I've never been back, since. I had a load of professional packers go in and put everything in storage. It's rented out now,' said Erika, ruefully taking another bite out of her biscuit.

'You should sell up, Erika. You remember our house in Mountview Terrace? I saw online that it's just been sold for five hundred thousand pounds! I knew the prices had gone up in Manchester, but that's crazy. We sold it for three hundred thousand six years ago, when we moved down here. You could buy something in London. There are some lovely houses around Hilly Fields… And I saw a beautiful fixer-upper in Forest Hill…'

Erika strained to hear what Marsh was saying in the corridor.

'Marcie, I didn't come to talk about the price of houses,' said Erika.

Marcie noticeably stiffened. 'But you did come banging on our door at three o'clock in the morning. The least you can do is act politely.'

'It's been a long, horrible day, Marcie.'

'Is every day a long day for you, Erika?' Marcie said, standing and flinging the rest of her tea into the sink. It splattered up the tiles.

'I'm sorry.'

'No one else from Paul's department thinks it's okay to come round and make inappropriate house calls in the middle of the night.'

'This isn't…'

'What's so special about you?'

'Nothing. We've known each other a long time, and I didn't want to discuss it over the phone,' said Erika.

Marsh came back through the kitchen door. He looked at the tableau in front of him: Marcie standing over Erika with her finger pointing, about to say something.

'Marcie, could you excuse us?'

'Of course. Anything for one of *your* officers. I'll see you in the morning,' she snapped.

A look passed over Marsh's face. *Are they sleeping in separate bedrooms?* thought Erika.

Marsh closed the door and quickly recovered his composure. 'They're holding Isaac overnight. They're waiting for the DNA results.'

'Of what?'

'It seems that Stephen Linley is quite… promiscuous. He had a lot of leather and bondage gear, and some rather extreme pornography they found in the flat.'

'What kind?'

'Nothing illegal, but fetish stuff, some of it to do with suffocation… They've listened to the messages on Linley's phone, and it sounds like he and Isaac were going through a rough patch. Isaac left several messages saying he wanted to, and I quote, "fucking kill" him.'

'I've left messages like that, sir.'

'Erika…'

'No, you know the drill. If you try hard enough, anyone's private correspondence becomes incriminating. Isaac didn't do it.'

'And what do you want me to say, Erika? Okay, let's interrupt procedure because you think he's innocent?'

'We both know how stuff like this sticks! Has he got a lawyer?'

'I believe so, yes.'

'Could you get me access? If anyone is going to question him, I would like it to be me.'

'We both know that's not going to happen…'

Erika reached into her bag and took out the card.

'You should see this,' she said and pushed it, flattened open inside its plastic bag, across the table. Marsh went and grabbed his reading glasses from the kitchen counter, came back to the table and stared at it for a long moment. He turned it over, reading what was written inside.

'Where did you get this?'

'I fell asleep late this afternoon. When I woke up the door was open onto the patio and I found this on my pillow.'

'Your pillow! Why didn't you tell me?'

'I'm telling you now! I woke up, found the note – I haven't touched it, I wore latex gloves to handle it – then I got the call from Isaac. I drove straight over to Stephen Linley's flat and after that I came here.'

'This is all getting out of hand,' Marsh said. 'Call a briefing for first thing in the morning. I'll make a call, we need forensics to go over your flat.'

'That's fine.'

'Do you want to sleep on the sofa?'

'No, sir. It's coming up to four in the morning. I'll get a hotel, grab a few hours' sleep.'

'Okay. I'll see you at the station at 9 a.m. sharp.'

CHAPTER 59

It was pouring with rain again when Erika dashed from her car to the main entrance of Lewisham Row station. Woolf was on duty and the reception area was filled with a group of sullen-faced young women sitting on a row of plastic chairs. Two of them were rocking crying babies in pushchairs. Three toddlers stood on the chairs at the end: two boys and a girl. They stamped their little bare feet on the green plastic chairs, laughing and drawing shapes in the condensation on the window. Above their heads, out of reach, someone had written with the ghost of a greasy finger: **ALL PIGS SHUD DIE**. The children were scruffy and rowdy, but it touched Erika that behind them, on the concrete floor, were three little pairs of flip-flops, lined up neatly.

'Morning. Marsh has asked for everyone to meet in the incident room,' said Woolf, looking up at her from behind the front desk.

'Did he say why? I'm supposed to be briefing everyone at nine.'

Woolf leaned forward and said in a low voice, 'It's to do with them arresting Dr Strong for killing his boyfriend with an ashtray… I didn't even know he smoked, let alone took it up the arse!'

'Have you got nothing better to do, sergeant, than gossip? And are you ever off duty?' said Erika, giving him a hard stare. She swiped open the door, slamming it behind her.

Woolf watched her on the closed circuit TV screen as she marched down the corridor.

'Oi! How much longer do I have to wait?' shouted one of the women.

'You'll be reunited with the love of your life very soon,' said Woolf. 'And the rest of you, too. They're just being fingerprinted and charged with GBH.'

The women scowled at him and turned back to their conversation.

'No one seems to have a sense of humour this morning,' muttered Woolf, opening his newspaper and biting into a Danish pastry.

When Erika arrived in the incident room, everyone was present, sitting in silence. Marsh was waiting at the front, drinking a cup of coffee.

'Ah, Erika, please take a seat.'

'I thought I was briefing the team this morning, sir?'

'So did I, but things have changed. Please, sit down.'

Erika perched on the long row of tables at the back, where the row of printers was unusually silent.

Marsh began, 'Last night, Dr Isaac Strong, who has worked on this and several other investigations with us as our forensic pathologist, was charged with the murder of his partner, the author Stephen Linley.'

Marsh paused as the officers absorbed this.

'This has put us in rather a complicated situation. Much of the forensic evidence from our investigation into the deaths of Gregory Munro and Jack Hart has been processed by Dr Strong, and in two cases, his findings helped us to profile the killer. The way that Stephen Linley was murdered shares many of the same traits as the murders of Gregory Munro and Jack Hart. Stephen Linley was found with high levels of flunitrazepam in his blood. He was also suffocated using the same type of "suicide" bag, but in this instance he appears to have fought with his attacker. The post-mortem and toxicology have shown that Linley was a regular user of recreational drugs – benzodiazepines and Rohypnol, the brand name for flunitrazepam – and had a higher tolerance of such substances. The only forensic DNA evidence found at the scene is male.'

Marsh paused again to let the officers in the incident room take this in, then he went on. 'Stephen appears to have enjoyed many sexual partners, and last night he'd been to a gay sauna. CCTV shows he was at the Chariots gay sauna in Waterloo from 6 p.m. until leaving at 10 p.m. In addition to this evidence, the murder of Stephen Linley was on the Bowery Lane Estate, EC1, which puts this firmly in the jurisdiction of the City of London Police. So, not only was it not on our patch but it is outside the jurisdiction of the Met.'

'Sir, surely they don't think that Isaac Strong is the serial killer?' asked Erika.

'Can I finish, please?'

'I would have appreciated you briefing me beforehand, sir. I am the SIO on this case and now I'm hearing all of this information for the first time.'

The officers in the incident room shifted uncomfortably in their seats.

'Erika, I have only been briefed about this by the Assistant Commissioner in the past twenty minutes,' said Marsh. 'May I please continue?'

'Yes, sir,' said Erika.

'Dr Strong was found at the scene. He was initially held for routine questioning – he says he discovered Stephen's body.

Then results started coming back from the crime scene. There were a large number of photos on Stephen Linley's laptop, and a positive identification was found for a JordiLevi.'

'He was the rent boy we interviewed. He was at Gregory Munro's house a few days before the murder,' said Crane.

'Yes, several of the photos on the laptop showed JordiLevi with Stephen Linley and Isaac Strong: photos of them having sex. Police searched Dr Strong's house, and they found a small quantity of Ecstasy, marijuana and flunitrazepam, the drug used in all three murders. They also discovered several items of fetish gear: hoods and bags, the type of stuff used in erotic asphyxiation or breath control play – the semi-suffocation of yourself or your partner for sexual pleasure…'

Erika sat at the back of the room and her blood ran cold. Her mind began to race, thinking through the times she'd been to Isaac's house. Could it be true?

'Now, as always,' continued Marsh, 'a person is innocent until proven guilty, and there is added sensitivity in this case in that Dr Strong is one of our own, a fine forensic pathologist with an unblemished record. But the evidence against him has stacked up quite alarmingly, and so City Police had no choice but to arrest him for the murder of Stephen Linley. Isaac Strong is also now being looked at as a suspect for the murders of Gregory Munro and Jack Hart.'

'So where does that leave us, the team?' asked Erika.

Marsh paused. 'As you all know, we need to maintain transparency. You have all done fine work on this case, and thank you to every one of you. DCI Foster, you have also been working alongside Dr Strong, and we must now look into his reports and see if he could have influenced the investigation. Dr Strong also phoned you from the crime scene, before he alerted the police…'

All eyes in the incident room turned to Erika.

'I know Isaac – Dr Strong – socially,' said Erika. 'He'd just walked in on his boyfriend who had been murdered.'

'I'm not accusing you of anything, Erika. But he crossed a line when he called you. We can't have the SIO of a murder case receiving phone calls from the murder suspect at the scene of the crime. One of our former colleagues, DCI Sparks, attended the murder scene last night, and this coupled with the fact he now heads an experienced Murder Investigation Team means he will be taking over this case as SIO.'

Several officers in the incident room turned to look at Erika, and she tried to remain composed.

Marsh carried on speaking. 'I'm here to thank you all for your hard work, but I will need you to conduct a handover this morning as quickly as possible. DCI Sparks may retain some of you to join his team.'

Erika got up. 'Sir, can I speak to you, please?'

'Erika…'

'I'd like to speak to you in your office, sir. Now.'

CHAPTER 60

'Erika, I'm sorry,' said Marsh.

She was standing opposite him in his office. 'I can't believe that you told me in front of *my* team, without giving me the heads-up first.'

'As I said, I had Oakley on the phone first thing. It was a done deal. I was merely informed of the decision.'

'Oakley. That figures…'

'It wasn't personal. You heard me, down in the incident room.'

'Do you think he did it, Isaac?' she said, taking the seat opposite Marsh's desk.

Marsh moved to his chair and sat down as well. 'Don't ask me. I barely knew him. He's a fine forensic pathologist. You've been cosying up with him – what are your thoughts?'

'I've not been *cosying up*. I've been for dinner with him a few times.' Erika realised she was playing down their friendship and the realisation brought her up short. *Am I that much of a ruthless bitch?* she thought. *He's one of my closest friends.* But she had to admit, the evidence she'd just heard against him had shocked her.

'What about the boyfriend? What did you think when you saw them together?' asked Marsh.

'I knew that Isaac had a volatile relationship with Stephen Linley. Although he didn't go into great detail, I knew that Stephen had cheated on him and they'd split up. And then out of the blue I went over for dinner and Stephen was there again. I don't think Stephen liked me. Then again, I seem to be an acquired taste lately.'

'Lately?' grinned Marsh. Despite the situation, Erika grinned back.

'Have you ever read any of Stephen Linley's books?' asked Marsh.

'No,' said Erika.

'Marcie downloaded one of them, *Night Descending*, to read on our last holiday… She couldn't get past the first four chapters.'

'Why?'

'He seems to enjoy torturing women.'

'They *are* crime thrillers, sir.'

'That's what I said. I told her she should stick to romantic comedies . . . Anyway. I've had to arrange for everything pertaining to the Gregory Munro and Jack Hart murders to be transferred to DCI Sparks and his team. They're going to have a new forensic pathologist go over everything.'

Erika got up and stared out at Lewisham, glowering under a dark bank of cloud. 'How did that bastard Sparks end up taking over my case? That feels like the biggest kick in the teeth!'

'This is the problem when you create enemies, Erika. They go off and plot, and often flourish in the shade. Sparks is doing very well.'

'How well?' Erika asked. 'Cos he's certainly been going the extra mile… He's running his own team, he's been called in to lend a hand with covert surveillance on Operation Hemslow.'

Marsh paused.

'Sir, don't tell me he's in the running for the superintendent job too?'

'There are plenty of other officers in the running. It's not just the two of you.'

'So where does that leave me?'

'Off the case. And the only reason you are off it, in my eyes, is that you have a conflict of interest. You've socialised with the forensic pathologist who is now a suspect.'

'If I'm off the case, use me somewhere else. I'd be happy to go and work on Operation Hemslow. Sparks is now off it. They could use another DCI rank.'

'Superintendent Nickson wasn't too impressed with you barging into the crime scene last night… Or with the way you dealt with his officers.' Marsh saw the look on Erika's face. 'Yes, I did hear about that. So did Oakley.'

'Sir, I'm sorry but, believe me, all I ever do is try and be the best police officer I can. I don't set out to piss anyone off, but…'

'You're an acquired taste,' finished Marsh. 'Look. You've got three weeks' holiday you haven't taken. I suggest you get some sun. Sometimes it's good to make yourself scarce.'

'Sir, I'm not one for sunning myself by the beach.'

'Well, try. Buy yourself some factor 50 and bugger off somewhere nice. You've dodged a bullet with this Night Stalker case, I promise.'

'Yes, sir.'

'Oh, and Erika, if I hear you've been poking your nose in, it will be the quickest way to end your dream of that superintendent promotion.'

'It's not a dream…'

'Well, either way. Take a holiday.'

'Very good, sir.' Erika gave Marsh a nod and left his office.

The incident room was empty. The fluorescent lights had been left on. Erika stood for a moment in the silence, looking over the whiteboards where all the evidence from the past three hectic weeks was pinned up. The hard work of her team.

A woman knocked and entered. It was one of the police support officers, Erika didn't know her name. 'Sorry, ma'am, are we okay to start processing the handover of evidence?' the woman asked, looking around at the empty desks.

Erika nodded and left the room. She ran into Woolf coming towards her in the corridor.

'Sorry about earlier, boss… Did you know Dr Strong well?' he asked.

'Yes, but now I think, no…'

'Ah, well. It'll all come out in the wash,' Woolf grinned.

'What does that mean, that saying?'

'Blowed if I know. My mum always used to say it, God rest her soul. The miserable old bag. Anyway, I managed to get hold of this for you.' He handed her an old Nokia handset. 'It still works, no probs.'

'You remembered,' she said, taking it from him.

'It was the first thing you ever said to me when you joined Lewisham Row. "Get me a phone with buttons, you fat bastard!"'

'I never said "fat bastard"!' grinned Erika.

'Yeah, I made that up,' he said. They looked through the glass partition at the support officers pulling down the crime scene photos from the whiteboard.

'Where did everyone go?' asked Erika.

'Loads of them have been told to go home and wait to hear about being reassigned, and it's a Sunday. I think they wanted to take advantage of an unexpected day off before another busy week begins.'

Erika felt disappointed, and a little bit abandoned. She shook these feelings off, realising how stupid she was being. This was work.

'So what are you doing now, boss?'

'I'm on holiday for the next three weeks.'

'Oh, lovely. I would kill for three weeks off right now. Have fun!' Woolf patted her on the shoulder and moved off towards reception.

Fun… Erika couldn't remember the last time she'd had fun. She looked back at the whiteboards through the glass; they were now almost empty. She hitched her bag over her shoulder and left the station, unsure of what to do next.

CHAPTER 61

Erika spent the rest of the morning driving around aimlessly, feeling powerless and frustrated. She drove past Isaac's house in Blackheath and saw that it was being searched. There was an officer stationed outside the front door and police tape over the entrance. It felt strange seeing his smart house, with the two yucca plants outside the shiny black front door, and the sash windows gleaming in the sun, yet knowing that he was being held in custody.

She then drove over to Shirley, past Penny Munro's house. The road was quiet and in several of the houses the curtains were drawn against the heat. Penny's house stood out with its lush, green front lawn. It looked as if Gary was still flouting the hosepipe ban. Erika wanted to know what else he was doing and was about to slow the car down when common sense took over. She turned the car round and drove back to Forest Hill.

It started to rain again when she arrived home. She crashed about, searching for something to drink, but the fridge was empty and so were most of the cupboards.

She stalked around her flat, feeling like a caged animal, then switched her computer on and left it on the counter top as she poured herself the last of the whisky. She stared around at the room, hating her life, hating her career, hating everything. It was now raining harder. She opened the patio door and sheltered in the door frame, lighting up a cigarette. From behind her was a squidgy plopping sound – her Skype had popped up. It started to ring, and she rushed back inside, thinking it might perhaps be the Night Stalker.

It was her sister Lenka, calling from Slovakia.

'I'm going mad,' muttered Erika, when she realised she was disappointed. 'I'd rather get a call from a serial killer than my own sister.' She took a deep breath and answered the call.

'Ahoj zlatko!' chirruped her sister. Lenka was sitting in her living room on a large leather sofa, covered in a sheepskin rug. The wall behind was a startling shade of orange and there were several photos of her kids, Karolina and Jakub, dotted about. Her long blonde hair was scraped up into a knot on the top of her head, and despite having a huge pregnancy bump she wore a hot pink strappy top.

'Hi, Lenka,' Erika smiled, speaking in Slovak. 'You look like you're about to pop!'

'Yeah. Not long now,' said her sister. 'I had to phone you. I had my last scan and I've got news. It's another boy!'

'That's great, congratulations,' said Erika.

'Marek is thrilled. He just took me to the jeweller in town – you remember, the posh one on the high street – and bought me an ankle bracelet.'

Marek was Lenka's husband, and he had recently been jailed for receiving stolen goods.

'How did Marek manage that?' asked Erika.

'He's working again.'

'Working? I thought he was in jail?'

'He got parole a month ago.'

'How did he get parole all of a sudden? He was sent down for four years.'

'Erika, I knew you'd be like this…He remembered something that the police found useful, so they let him go… I'm also phoning to say you don't need to send me any more money. Thank you.'

'Lenka…'

'No, I'm fine, Erika. Now Marek is back, things are good.'

'Why don't you start up another bank account? I'll keep sending you the money and you put it to one side, keep it to yourself.'

'You don't need to look after me, Erika.'

'I do. You know that people who work for the mafia always end up either being killed or banged up for life. Do you want to be a single mother with two kids – three, now you're having another one with him?'

'He's worked hard at being good, and he got parole,' said Lenka, putting her hands up angrily, as if this now gave him the edge on other fathers. 'Life is different here, Erika.'

'That doesn't mean it's right.'

'You don't understand. Can't you at least be pleased? Marek looks after us. The kids have nice clothes, they've got iPhones. This little boy won't want for anything. We'll be able to get them into nice schools…'

'God forbid they have to spend all those tedious hours studying, when Marek can go and threaten to kneecap their teacher!'

'Erika, I don't want to talk about this any more. I didn't call to row with you,' said Lenka, adjusting the knot on top of her head with an air of finality. 'Anyway. Are you okay? I've been trying to ring your Skype. I phoned four times on Mark's anniversary.'

'I'm fine.'

'You should put up some pictures,' Lenka said, peering through the camera. 'Looks like a prison cell.'

'I'm keeping it like this for when you and Marek visit. So he feels at home.'

Despite this, they both began to laugh.

'This kids say hi,' said Lenka, when they'd calmed down. 'They're out at the lido with their friends.'

'Give them a kiss from me,' said Erika. 'And let me know when you go into labour, okay?'

'Okay… I'll let you know. Love you.' Lenka put her fingers to her lips and blew a kiss. Erika returned it and then the screen went black.

After the Skype call, the silence was deafening in the flat. Erika's eyes moved around the bare walls and then came to rest on the bookshelf, piled high with assorted junk. Next to the copy of *Fifty Shades of Grey* was the signed book Stephen Linley had given her. She got up and pulled out the copy of *From My Cold Dead Hands* and started to read.

CHAPTER 62

Moss had taken advantage of her unexpected free Sunday and was glad to be home for her son Jacob's bath and bedtime. She had just finished reading him a story and saw that he was asleep. She kissed his sleeping face and wound up his night light so it would continue to play its twinkly lullaby for a little while longer.

When she came outside onto the landing, her wife, Celia, was holding the phone.

'It's Erika Foster,' said Celia. Moss took the phone and went along the landing to the small bedroom they used as an office. She closed the door.

'Sorry to call you at home, Moss,' said Erika.

'That's okay, boss. What's up?'

'Everyone kind of scarpered today.'

There was an awkward pause from Moss. 'We did. Sorry about that. I thought you would be busy with Marsh?'

'Oh, I was. Did you have a good day off?'

'Yeah, we've been to St James's Park. It was lovely.'

'Can you talk?'

'Yes. I've just finished reading *The Hungry Caterpillar* to Jacob and I'm now craving salad – which I think is a first.'

'I've been reading one of the DCI Bartholomew books, the ones Stephen Linley writes, wrote…'

'And you want to start a book club?' said Moss.

'Very funny. No, I started reading *From My Cold Dead Hands* and I'm finding it pretty disturbing…'

'In what way?'

'I'm fine with gore, but this is deep, dark stuff. There's this serial killer who abducts women at night and then he keeps them in his basement and tortures them.'

'Like *The Silence of the Lambs*?'

'No, *The Silence of the Lambs* has an elegance and restraint in its description of violence. This is just torture porn. I've just forced myself through pages and pages of a long, drawn-out series of graphic rapes, and in between the killer pours boiling water on their naked bodies.'

'Jeez.'

'It's almost as if he's getting off on writing this… This is a long shot, but what if the Night Stalker killed Stephen because of his attitude to women?'

'I thought the new line of investigation was that Isaac Strong killed Stephen? And I thought you were off the case?'

'Do you believe that Isaac could have done it, Moss?'

'No. But then again, I didn't know him that well.'

'I was at the crime scene, Moss. Everything about it points to this being the same killer. I've just Googled Stephen Linley and he sells a shedload of books, but he's often run into a lot of controversy at literary events. He's had quite a few people come and question his treatment of violence towards women; there's something about a boycott of his work. What if that's the link? What if his book inspired someone to be violent towards the Night Stalker? During the phone call I had with her, she told me that her husband had tortured her, but he had dropped dead before she could kill him.'

'It's a good theory, boss. Or are you trying to work out who-dunnit from a whodunnit?' asked Moss.

'I just think that we haven't looked into the motive clearly. We wasted time thinking that it was a spurned gay lover with Gregory Munro, and the whole thing with Jack Hart being in the public eye sort of skewed it too.'

'There's only one problem, boss. *We're off the case.* I've been temporarily reassigned to a CCTV steering group,' said Moss.

'What about Peterson?'

'I don't know. I heard he's been reassigned too, but I'm not sure where.'

'Well, I'm on holiday,' said Erika, ironically.

'Then you know what people normally do when they're on holiday? They go and visit friends… Maybe you should go and see Isaac. If you can't be a policewoman right now, be a friend.'

CHAPTER 63

Erika lined up for visiting at the Belmarsh Prison visitors' centre, waiting to go through security. It was a long, low, dank concrete building and space was cramped for the forty people waiting to go through the metal detectors. It was raining outside, and the high, thin windows were all steamed up. The smells of damp skin, body odour and perfume mixed in with the stink of industrial floor cleaner. There were a few men and women there on their own. Some looked in shock at having to visit a friend or a loved one for the first time. A rowdy group of prisoners' wives with their screaming kids were holding things up ahead at the metal detectors. A woman had objected to the guard asking to see what was inside her baby's nappy.

When everyone was through security, there was a further wait in a long reception room before they were shown through to what looked like a huge gymnasium, with row after row of plastic chairs and tables. The prisoners were all sitting still as Erika entered. They were wearing yellow sashes, so that they couldn't blend in with the visitors and walk out at the end of visiting.

She found Isaac at a table on the end of the third row. She was shocked by his appearance: his eyes were bloodshot, with dark circles around them. His usually sleek hair was a mess and there were shaving cuts on his face.

'It's so good to see you,' he said.

'I'm so sorry about Stephen,' said Erika.

Isaac searched her eyes. 'Thank you. Why are you here?'

'I'm here as your friend,' she said, reaching out and taking his hand. It was cold and clammy and he was shaking. 'I'm sorry. I should have come sooner.'

'It's like a living nightmare, this place. The filth, the screaming, the constant threat of violence and menace,' Isaac murmured. 'I didn't do it. Please believe me, I didn't do it... You do believe me, don't you?'

Erika hesitated. 'Yes, I do.'

'I found out he was going to a gay sauna in Waterloo. He was screwing guys, bareback – you know, without using protection. I'd suspected it, and confronted him, and he'd told me he was just at the gym. Then the stupid idiot took my iPod and left it in a locker at the sauna, and they got in contact with me... I take it you've heard about the phone call where I say I'm going to fucking kill him?'

'Yes.'

'I didn't, though. I didn't kill him. I showed up at his flat for an argument, let myself in with my key and...' Isaac gulped and his eyes filled up. Tears fell on the table top with a soft patter. He wiped them with his sleeve.

'Hang on, you let yourself in with a key?'

'Yeah, we'd got to that point. He'd committed to me and given me a key. I was so pathetically grateful.'

'His flat is on the second floor, no balcony?'

Isaac nodded.

'Then it wasn't a break-in, if it was locked when you arrived. He either let the person in, or they got in with their own key.'

'Is that why you're here? About the case?'

Erika quickly told him what had happened, about being taken off the case.

'So you're investigating this, alone? You think you can help me?'

'I don't know if I can do anything, Isaac.'

'Please. I can't… deal with this.'

Erika saw she had already used up ten minutes of their precious half-hour.

'Isaac, I have to ask: why Stephen? You have such a sorted life: respected job, home, friends. What attracted you to him? He was a regular drug user, he hired prostitutes.'

'He excited me, Erika. He was a bad boy. I was the good boy who grew up with braces, and glasses, and no coordination and stick-thin legs in PE class. I was a virgin until I graduated from medical school at twenty-three. I'd always done the right thing and worked hard, but Stephen was sexy and dangerous, and unpredictable. He had this sort of abrasive funniness about him….' Isaac shrugged. 'He was incredible in bed. I knew he wasn't right, and he didn't fit into my life… But I let him back in and it pushed you away… I'm sorry, Erika. You needed me, didn't you? I even forgot about Mark, the anniversary. I'm sorry.'

Erika leant across and grabbed his hand.

'It's okay. Isaac, it's okay. I'm here, and you are my friend,' she said.

He looked up at her and smiled weakly.

'Look, I have to ask more,' said Erika. 'I've read two of Stephen's books, *From My Cold Dead Hands* and *The Girl in the Cellar*…'

'I know,' said Isaac, almost reading her mind. 'He wrote shocking stuff.'

'There's so much torture of women – and then there's DCI Bartholomew. He's meant to be the hero of the books and he's also a wife beater?'

'An anti-hero,' said Isaac, shrugging. 'It was his work, that's what Stephen used to say. It got all the bad stuff out of his system. Think of all the horror writers out there – they don't necessarily act out on what they write. And think of what we do – well, what I do? I cut people up for a living. I dissect their bodies. I dig into their brains. What I do is just as invasive.'

'But what you do is different, Isaac. You help catch the bad guys. Stephen was creating them, albeit fictionally,' said Erika.

'To his fans, his characters were just as real as you and me.'

'Did Stephen have any crazy fans? Do you know of any disturbing fan mail that he might have had?'

Isaac wiped his nose with his sleeve. 'I don't know. He didn't get mail exactly. I know a lot of his fans would write through his Facebook page.'

'Would his agent get any fan mail, on his behalf?'

'Yes. Probably. They're based in West London…I had a life, Erika… Do you think I'll be able to go back to it? I know how this system works. I'm tainted. I hold a position of trust and that has now been called into doubt.' He began to cry.

'Isaac, stop, don't do this here,' said Erika, noticing some of the other prisoners glancing over at him. 'I'm going to do everything I can to get you out of here,' she said. 'I promise.'

He looked up at her. 'Thank you. If anyone can do it, you can,' he said.

CHAPTER 64

The phone box was on the outskirts of London, on Barnes Common. Simone had remembered it. It was part of a long-ago happy memory, when her mother had taken her to Kew Gardens. She'd had to hide in her mother's coat until they had been past the ticket kiosk, but once they'd got inside she'd loved the flowers and the trees. Her mother had been desperate to go into the tropical house. It was like a giant greenhouse, very warm, and stuffed with plants from all over the world. 'Rare Flora and Fauna', Simone remembered the sign had read.

Of course, her mother had only come to Kew Gardens to meet her dealer. They'd gone off into the bushes to do adult stuff. But the young Simone had enjoyed a couple of hours free to wander. And she'd known that if her mother was happy, she would be happy.

On the bus back home, she'd pressed her face against the window and had seen the phone box shining red against the expanse of green on Barnes Common. It looked much the same, all these years later. The drought had turned it from green to yellow, and the red paint was peeling off the phone box, but there wasn't a soul in sight.

Erika Foster answered the phone after several rings.

'Did you get my card, DCI Foster?'

There was a pause.

'Yes. Thank you. Although most people would have used the letterbox,' said Erika.

'I'm not most people, DCI Foster,' said Simone. She gripped the receiver and looked through the grimy glass across the empty common.

'Do you think you're special?' asked Erika. 'Have you been sent here with a higher purpose?'

'No, far from it. I'm unremarkable. I'm not pretty, or clever, but I'm full of anger and grief... Grief in particular gives you so much energy, doesn't it?'

'Yes, it does,' said Erika.

'I decided to use that energy to take revenge... I've been reading about you. About how you tried to do your job, tried to catch that drug dealer and it all went terribly wrong. Not only did you lose your friends and your husband, but the very people who you served turned on you. Blamed you.'

'What if I said that you could get help, if you stopped?' interrupted Erika.

'What if I said that you could get help if *you* stopped?' replied Simone.

'What do you mean?'

'I saw where you live. The pathetic flat. Your worldly goods that amount to nothing. What have you got to show from devoting your life to the force? Wouldn't life be easier if you stopped trying to save the world?'

There was a pause again, and then Erika replied with a trembling voice, 'I'm going to find you. And when I do, I'm going to look you in the eye and I'll see how smart you think you are.'

'Catch me if you can. I'm not finished yet,' said Simone.

There was a click, and Simone heard the dialling tone.

She winced, not from fear but from pain. It hurt to smile where she had been struck by the ashtray.

CHAPTER 65

Moss reached up with her free hand and knocked on the door. In the other hand she held a pizza box. Moments later, it opened. Erika stood in the open doorway with her hair on end.

'I thought you might like some pizza,' said Moss, holding it up. 'Pepperoni?'

'Thank you, come in,' said Erika, standing to one side and letting her in. The rain had cleared and through the patio window there was a beautiful dusk as the sun slowly sank down with shades of soft blue and orange.

'I just dropped Celia and Jacob for swimming in Ladywell. Thought I'd pop over and see how you are enjoying your holiday...'

'Just find a spot and put the box down,' said Erika, pulling out plates from the cupboard.

Moss looked around and saw that every available space, and parts of the floor, were strewn with paperwork from the Night Stalker case.

'They let you take all this with you?'

'No. I downloaded it to my laptop.'

'So the holiday's going well?' said Moss, moving a couple of grey folders and perching the pizza box on the end of the coffee table.

'I got another call.'

'From the Night Stalker?'

'Yeah.'

'What did she say?'

'She phoned to screw with me. She told me she wasn't finished yet.'

'Did they get a trace?'

'Yes, Crane called me. He's been reassigned to the case, at Sparks' request. They traced it to a phone box in West London. Again, no CCTV... He couldn't tell me much more... How is she not slipping up? How? I've been printing everything off from the case. It helps, having hard copies. I've been going back through everything.'

Erika handed Moss a plate and a napkin. She opened the box and steam rose from the thin crust pizza, which was cooked to perfection. As they began to eat, Erika relayed what had happened when she visited Isaac and detailed how she was revisiting all the evidence after the phone call.

'I just feel we never had a real crack at working her out, the Night Stalker. Like the card she sent me.' Erika handed Moss a printout of the scanned card. 'Why did she choose that poem?'

'She's a vicious serial-killing bitch. Why should she be any more imaginative than the rest of us?' said Moss. 'As a poem, "Do Not Stand At My Grave And Weep" is not hard to seek out. It's the go-to poem for funerals. It's like books: we all scan the bestseller lists, we see what reviewers are telling us to read and we buy them to make ourselves feel clever. I was one of the many millions who read half of *The Goldfinch*.'

'That's what the Night Stalker said on the phone.'

'That she only read half of *The Goldfinch*?'

Erika shot Moss a glare.

'Sorry, boss, just trying to lighten the mood...'

'She said on the phone that she wasn't clever,' said Erika.

'But she is clever. Or bloody lucky. Three bodies so far and virtually no evidence. She slips in and out unseen,' replied Moss, taking a bite of pizza.

Erika shook her head. 'Why go to all the effort of finding my flat, breaking in and leaving a card? *And* she signed it "The Night Stalker".'

'Maybe she thinks she has a new friend or ally in you, boss.'

'Then why not sign it with her real name, if she's that confident? Serial killers often hate the names they're given in the press. They think it erodes how they are seen by people. They think what they're doing is serious: a noble deed, or series of deeds; a service to society.'

'Maybe she just wants to screw with your head,' said Moss.

'I've also gone back over the victims, trying to see if they had anything in common, but they're vastly different people. The only thing they have in common is that they are male, and that they were killed in exactly the same way – except that Stephen had his head smashed in as well. I also looked back over the names of people who bought these suicide bags online.'

'I've been through the names, too. So many of the London-based women who bought them are now dead,' said Moss.

'There's something that Isaac said when I saw him this morning. When he discovered Stephen's body, he'd let himself into the flat with a key. The door was closed and locked. No forced entry. The flat is on the second floor, with no balcony or other doors.'

'So the Night Stalker had a key?' asked Moss.

'Yes. I got the report from the crime scene. The lock had been bumped. It was damaged inside from someone using a bump key.'

'They're pretty common in burglaries, and you can buy them online for nothing these days,' said Moss.

'Exactly. And there's one person on the list of people who bought suicide bags online who also bought a bump key online,' said Erika.

'Really?'

'Yeah, when we followed up on the names, we went as far as accessing bank accounts and financial transactions. This person bought a suicide bag three years ago, and then in the last three months has bought five more. Who needs five? They also bought the bump key online three months ago.'

'Bloody hell! Why didn't we follow it up?' asked Moss.

'It must have been overlooked – we weren't looking for a bump key, and we were focusing on women. This person is a thirty-five-year-old male. He's been wheelchair-bound since childhood. He lives in Worthing, on the south coast, not far from London.'

'Have you told Marsh?'

'Not yet.'

'So what are you going to do? Have a day out by the sea?' asked Moss.

'Would you be interested, in a day out by the sea?' replied Erika.

Moss paused. 'Sorry, I'm due at a CCTV steering group tomorrow. I can't... No, I can't risk it.'

'No worries,' grinned Erika.

'But I have your back. Anything I can do on the sly, to help.'

'Thanks.'

'Just be careful, boss, yeah? You've pissed off enough people already.'

'Often you have to piss people off to get to the truth, but I'm not doing this for my ego,' said Erika. 'You should have seen Isaac yesterday. He didn't do it. And I'm going to prove it.'

CHAPTER 66

Simone had lain low since fleeing the scene of Stephen Linley's murder. Where the ashtray had struck her, she'd been left with a huge swollen lip and a nasty bruise on the side of her head. She'd also lost a tooth: her left incisor was broken off, close to the gum. She didn't know if she had swallowed it, or if it had skittered off into a dark corner of Stephen Linley's flat. The exposed nerves had left her in terrible pain, but she was too scared to go to see her dentist. He might X-ray her teeth and then her dental records would be on file.

She'd tried to remember if she'd had her teeth X-rayed in the past. She had a vague memory of being left alone in a large room with insulated walls, of being told to lie very still whilst her mother waited outside. Had that been an X-ray? She didn't know. She knew she had never been fingerprinted, nor had her DNA been taken.

At first, she had been convinced that it was all over. She'd screwed up; it hadn't gone to plan. She had cancelled going into work at the hospital, telling them she was sick. As the days and nights had passed, sleep had evaded her completely. No amount of medication helped.

On the third sleepless night, she was lying in bed just after midnight when she heard a soft *pat, pat, pat* sound coming from outside her bedroom door. Like water running onto the carpet. It was coupled with the sound of laboured breathing, as if through a blocked nose.

Simone jumped up off the bed and wedged the chair from her dressing table under the door. The noise had continued: *pat, pat, pat, pat, pat... Inhale, exhale.*

She put her hands to her aching, throbbing temples. *It wasn't real.* But still, the noise continued.

Pat, pat. Inhale, exhale. A loose, phlegmy cough.

'You're not real!' she called out. 'Stan, leave this place!'

Pat, pat, pat, pat, pat... Inhale, exhale.

She lifted the chair away and turned the door handle, opening the door. Her throat constricted when she saw it wasn't Stan standing there, dripping with water. It was Stephen Linley.

He was dressed in trainers, blue jeans, a white T-shirt and a thin black jacket. The plastic bag was tied tight around his neck and half-filled with gunk and blood, which was dripping from under the cord around his neck, down his clothes and onto the pale carpet.

Pat, pat, pat...

His forehead was caved in, where Simone had hit him with the ashtray, and his face was almost unrecognisable. Inside, against the plastic, the mouth was moving. The ruined face was trying to breathe.

'NO!' screamed Simone. 'YOU. ARE. DEAD!' With each word, she advanced on the gruesome corpse, prodding it. It took faltering steps backwards, towards the top of the stairs, arms flailing.

'YOU DESERVED TO DIE!' she cried. They reached the top of the stairs. Simone gave the body a shove and it fell backwards, rolling down the stairs with bumps and crashes, landing in a limp heap at the bottom.

She closed her eyes and counted to ten and then opened them. It was gone. Everything was back to normal. She was alone. Shakily, she went down the stairs and checked the living room and kitchen. There was nothing. She went to her computer and switched it on. When it had booted up, she started to type.

NIGHT OWL: You there?

For a while, nothing happened. She was about to go and make herself a drink when Duke came online.

DUKE: Hey Night Owl, what's cooking?
NIGHT OWL: I've missed you.
DUKE: I've missed you too.
NIGHT OWL: I'm scared. I'm seeing things again.
DUKE: You got new meds?
NIGHT OWL: No, I've stopped taking them.
DUKE: I was worried something had happened to you.
NIGHT OWL: I'm OK.
DUKE: Did it work out?
NIGHT OWL: Yes, and no. I got bashed up. My lips are all puffy.
DUKE: You're lying. You've had your lips done for when we go on our trip together! Collagen. LOL.
NIGHT OWL: It's just the bottom lip.
DUKE: Very sensible. So you're saving up for the top lip.

Simone giggled and touched her hands to her face. It still felt tender. She'd missed talking to Duke. There was a beep and she saw text moving across the screen.

DUKE: So, Night Owl. Are we going?
NIGHT OWL: Going where?
DUKE: On our trip. We've talked about it so much. Let's make it happen!

DUKE: You do still want to go, don't you?

DUKE: Night Owl?

NIGHT OWL: I'm here.

DUKE: So?

NIGHT OWL: I have one more name on my list.

DUKE: I've waited through three of those names. One more will be okay. But I want to know when.

NIGHT OWL: A day.

DUKE: A day!

NIGHT OWL: No, a week, a month. A year... I don't know! Don't rush me, Duke, do you hear?

DUKE: I'm sorry. I just need to know...

DUKE: ... but it will be quicker than a year?

NIGHT OWL: Yes.

DUKE: Phew! *** Wipes sweaty brow***

NIGHT OWL: I'll let you know soon. I promise. And then we can go and be together.

DUKE: OK. I love you.

Simone stared at the screen for a long time. In all the years they had talked, Duke had told her many things – his deepest, darkest secrets – and she had reciprocated. But this was the first time he'd said he loved her. It made her feel powerful.

She logged off the chat room and went up to bed. She felt much better. She'd go back to work. Then she'd start to make preparations for number four. The fourth, and final.

CHAPTER 67

'All right, boss, so where are we going, exactly?' asked Peterson when he climbed into the passenger seat. He was dressed casually in jeans and a T-shirt, and carrying a small backpack. It was almost 9 a.m. and Erika had picked him up outside his flat, a smart, squat building on a quiet leafy street in Beckenham. A sign on the neat lawn out front announced that the building was called Tavistock House.

'Worthing,' said Erika, handing him a folded-up map. A curtain twitched in the front ground-floor window and a slight, pretty, blonde girl peered round, showing just her face and a bare shoulder. She waved at Peterson whilst giving Erika the once-over. He gave her a small wave in return and pulled a sunglasses case from his backpack.

'Is that your girlfriend?' asked Erika, as Peterson polished a pair of Ray Bans with a small grey square of cloth and slipped them on. The girl was still watching.

He shrugged. 'Go on, boss. Let's go,' he said, looking uncomfortable. They pulled away, driving in silence for a minute, the reflection from the canopy of leaves above playing across the windscreen.

'We need the M23, then the A23,' said Erika, realising that Peterson didn't want to elaborate on his house guest.

'Why did you ask me today?' he said, unfolding the map and peering at her over the top of his shades.

'Moss has been reassigned, and when I called you, you said you were free... Why did you say yes?'

'You've intrigued me,' he grinned.

She grinned back.

'I've been reassigned, too,' he said.

'Where?'

'Operation Hemslow.'

Erika turned to face him and the car swerved towards the right lane. Peterson leaned over and straightened the wheel.

'Don't get excited. I've just been working in Control. It's pretty dull stuff, mostly watching Penny Munro and Peter.'

'And?'

'They're safe... The kid goes to school, comes home, goes swimming once a week, likes to feed the ducks...' Peterson blew his cheeks out. 'They're very close to nailing Gary Wilmslow. The focus is now on a lock-up in Crystal Palace. They just need to get Wilmslow inside the lock-up. Simple as that, but very complicated. He's managing to place at least three people between him and the production of the videos, the procuring of kids... It's a case of how long we can wait it out before we move in and shut it down.'

'You *have* to get Wilmslow,' said Erika.

'No one wants to see him brought down more than me... You know I shouldn't be telling you any of this, boss.'

'I know. Thanks.'

'Did you know Sparks is close to charging Isaac with the deaths of Gregory Munro and Jack Hart, in addition to Stephen Linley?'

'Shit.'

'Why haven't you told them about this? What we're doing today?' asked Peterson.

'Because I just need to look into this. They've made their minds up, obviously. It's easier to charge Isaac… Ends it all neatly, case solved.'

'You don't think he did it?'

Erika looked at Peterson. 'No, I don't. I just need to check this out myself. It's a long shot, but if I phone it in, it'll get shoved to the bottom of the pile and it might be too late before anyone gets to it. You okay with this?'

He shrugged and grinned. 'As you said on the phone, boss. It's just a day out by the sea.'

'Thanks.'

Erika thought how things had changed. She was now on the outside. She started to fill Peterson in on what she had discovered and how she'd like to proceed.

Ninety minutes later they came off the dual carriageway and approached Worthing via a complex and unattractive one-way system. When they arrived in the town, though, it looked picturesque. It was an old seaside town, which in the height of the summer looked more sumptuous than crumbling. Erika followed the road along the promenade. The beach was crowded with people sunbathing and sitting on old-style deckchairs. It was lined with terraced houses, flats and an eclectic selection of shops. She parked on the seafront and they stepped out onto the busy promenade, where people sauntered along, eating ice creams and enjoying the sun.

'How should we play this?' asked Peterson, joining her at the parking meter by the kerb.

'We have no authority to be here, but he doesn't know that,' said Erika, feeding coins into the machine. 'I'm hoping the element of surprise will work in our favour.'

She took the ticket from the machine and they locked up the car. The address they were looking for was further down the seafront, where the souvenir shops and tearooms thinned out. The terraced houses here were much more run-down and had been turned into flats and bedsits.

'Here, this is it,' said Erika, as they came to a large five-storey house with a small concreted-over front garden which contained five black wheelie bins with flat numbers painted in white on the lids. The windows were all open and music blared out from the top floor.

'I can smell weed,' said Peterson, stopping to sniff the air.

'We're not here about weed,' said Erika. 'Just remember that.'

They went up the steps and Erika rang the bell for the ground-floor flat. They waited as the music ceased for a second, then Nirvana's 'Smells Like Teen Spirit' began to play.

The lights were all blazing in the downstairs window, which looked out over the bins and was half-obscured by hanging clothes. Erika rang the bell again and through the frosted glass in the door she saw a large, dark bulk move from the shadows. The door opened an inch, then stopped. Moments later there was a whirring noise and the door was slowly pulled open.

The dark bulk she had seen was an enormous motorised wheel-chair, which had heavy-duty wheels and oxygen tanks strapped to the back. A concertina mechanism whirred and elevated the seat, in which a tiny man sat. He had small, plump features, thick glasses and wisps of mousy hair clinging to his bald head. He wore an oxygen tube under his nose. His body was compact – they could see he suffered from dwarfism – and his even tinier pair of emaciated legs, which just reached the edge of the seat, contrasted his small body. One of his arms was tucked into the side of the seat and the other was holding the piece of string he had used to open the front door. He let the string go, grabbed the remote control beside his chair and moved forward, blocking the threshold.

'Are you Keith Hardy?' asked Erika.

'Yes,' he said, his eyes darting between them. He spoke with a higher-pitched voice.

Erika and Peterson held out their IDs.

'I'm DCI Erika Foster and this is my colleague, DI Peterson. Could we have a word?'

'About what?'

Erika looked at Peterson. 'We'd prefer to discuss this inside.'

'Well, you're not coming in.'

'We won't take up much of your time, Mr Hardy,' said Erika.

'You won't take up any.'

'Mr Hardy...' started Peterson.

'You got a warrant?'

'No.'

'Then go away and get one,' the man said. He reached out and grabbed for the string attached to the inside lock. Erika leaned over and plucked it from his grasp.

'Mr Hardy, we're investigating a triple murder. The killer used suicide bags... We've accessed your bank accounts and we see you've bought five of these, and yet you're still alive. It's just a case of clearing up any misunderstanding.'

Keith wrinkled his nose and pushed his glasses up, then backed up the wheelchair and let them in.

CHAPTER 68

Keith Hardy's flat was carpeted throughout with a dated pattern of lime green, yellow and red hexagons. Erika and Peterson followed him down the corridor, the wispy top of his head just visible over the high back of his whirring wheelchair. Through the first door to the left was his bedroom; on the back wall, opposite the large bay window, Erika saw a large hydraulic hospital bed on wheels. Next to the bed was an old polished wood dresser with a three-panelled fold-out mirror. The dresser was crowded with an array of medication: large tubs of medical creams, preparations and a bale of wispy cotton wool. Clothes hung off the curtain rail, and the bay window looked out over the seafront promenade, where people moved past and seagulls could be heard cawing faintly. A ceiling light burned brightly, along with two small lamps on the bedside and the dresser.

They passed another tiny room, which was packed with junk, including an old manual wheelchair, piles of books and another electric wheelchair with the back panel off, its wires and innards spilling out. Another door on the right-hand side of the corridor led to a large, specially equipped bathroom.

Keith reached a frosted glass door at the end of the hallway, manoeuvred his chair through, and they followed him into a poky kitchen-living room with views of a tiny courtyard backing onto a tall brick building. The kitchen was old and grubby, with specially adapted low counters. There was a whiff of drains, mixed with fried food.

In the other half of the room, three of the walls were filled with floor-to-ceiling shelves containing hundreds of books, video cassettes and DVDs. A small gas fire sat against a chimney breast, and above it were more shelves, loaded with more books, paperwork and a mismatched selection of table lamps – which were all switched on, so that the space, although small and cramped, was brightly lit. Nestled in one corner was a PC on an old metal stand. A series of coloured balls bounced around its screen.

'I don't get a lot of visitors,' Keith said, indicating a small armchair on the opposite side of the gas fire, which was covered in piles of magazines and newspapers. 'There are a couple of stacking chairs in the gap beside the fridge,' he added. Peterson went and pulled them out.

Keith moved to the computer in the corner and, using the joystick, swivelled his chair round to face them. He pushed his glasses up his nose and peered at them through the greasy lenses, his large eyes shifting from side to side. Erika imagined that if a fly buzzed past, his tongue might shoot out and catch it.

'You can't arrest me,' Keith blurted. 'I never leave this flat… I haven't done anything.'

Erika pulled some paperwork from her bag and unfolded it, smoothing out the pages. 'I have here details of your bank account with Santander. Can you confirm this is your account number and sort code?' She passed the paper to him. Keith looked at it briefly and passed it back.

'Yes.'

'It shows that in the past three months you have ordered five items from a website called Allantoin.co.uk. Five suicide bag kits. I've highlighted the transactions on your bank statement…' Erika leaned forward to hand it to Keith.

'I don't need to see it,' he said.

'So you acknowledge this is your bank statement and these transactions are correct?'

'Yes,' he said, biting his lip.

'You also ordered what is called a bump key. That's also highlighted on your bank statement...'

'I got it from eBay, and it's not illegal,' Keith said, sitting back and folding his short arms across his chest.

'No, it's not,' said Erika. 'But we have a real problem here. I have three murders committed in and around London by someone who has used a) a suicide bag to asphyxiate the victims and b) a bump key to gain entry to one of the properties.'

Erika reached into her bag and pulled out a crime scene photo of Stephen Linley. She held it up to Keith, who winced.

'As you can see, the suicide bag on this occasion burst... The intruder used a bump key to gain entry.'

Erika put the photo away and pulled out photos of Gregory Munro and Jack Hart lying dead with the bags over their heads. 'On these occasions, the bags remained intact, but still did the job...'

Keith gulped and looked away from the photos. 'I can't be the only person to have bought these items,' he said.

'We've been given a list of people who have purchased suicide bags in the past three months. Many of them bought them for the purposes of ending their lives and, tragically, are not here to speak to us. You are one of the few who has bought multiple bags and is still here to tell the tale.'

'I've been suicidal,' said Keith.

'I'm sorry to hear that. Have you attempted to take your own life?'

'Yes.'

'Do you have the five bags here? If you can show them to us, we can tick you off our list.'

'I threw them out.'

'Why?' asked Peterson.

'Dunno.'

'And the bump key?'

Keith wiped his sweaty forehead. 'I got it in case I get locked out.'

'You just told us you never leave your flat?' said Peterson.

'I have a carer who comes over three times a week. I bought it for her.'

'Why not give her a normal key?' fired back Peterson. 'Or get another key cut? Why go to the trouble of ordering a skeleton key online?'

Keith gulped and licked sweat from his upper lip. His eyes, large behind his glasses, slid between them both.

'What is this country coming to? I've done nothing illegal,' he said, suddenly regaining his composure. 'I never leave this flat, and you can't prove anything. Now you are being bullying and inappropriate and I'd like you both to leave before I call your superiors.'

Erika looked at Peterson and they both stood.

'Very well,' she said, collecting up the photos and bank statements and pushing them into her bag. Peterson folded up the two chairs and tucked them back beside the fridge. Keith started forward in his chair. As it whirred towards them, they were forced out of the room, past the frosted glass doorway and back out into the hall.

'I can make a complaint. I'll say you've been harassing me!' said Keith.

'As you can see, we're just going,' said Erika. She stopped at the large disabled bathroom and pushed open the door, stepping inside. Peterson followed.

'What now?' asked Keith, stopping outside the door. There was a large white bath with a motorised bath lift platform, a low sink and mirror, and a disabled toilet with a huge metal safety bar on one side which was on a hinge at the wall, enabling it to be swung up and out of the way.

'Who answers if you pull this alarm?' asked Erika, touching a red cord hanging down from the ceiling beside the toilet.

'The police, and social services. It links to a control centre,' said Keith. Erika came out of the bathroom and looked at the small junk room opposite.

'What's this?' she asked.

'That's my storage room,' replied Keith.

'You mean, a second bedroom?'

'It's a store room,' said Keith, gritting his teeth.

'No, that's a second bedroom, Keith,' said Erika.

'It's a store room,' insisted Keith.

'No, I'd definitely call that a second bedroom,' said Peterson, emerging from the bathroom to join them. Keith was now gripping the arms of his chair, looking agitated.

'You could fit a big bed in there… definitely a second bedroom,' said Erika.

'Yup, second bedroom,' agreed Peterson.

'That's NOT a bedroom! You know nothing!' shouted Keith.

'Oh, we know a lot!' said Erika, moving close to Keith. 'We didn't just come all this way for you to piss us around! We know that the government has cut your disability benefits because you have a second bedroom… We also know you haven't been able to rent it out, and you can't afford to live here much longer. When they evict you, which they will, where are you going to go? I presume the only other place you can afford on your disability is out on one of the estates, miles from the shops, banks and doctors. You'll be reliant on piss-stinking lifts and murky walkways filled with drug dealers.'

'And life on one of those estates is tough for anyone, let alone someone like you,' said Peterson.

'Or you could go to jail for obstructing the course of justice, aiding and abetting a murderer. I doubt being banged up would be a picnic for you either,' said Erika. She let it hang in the air for a moment. 'Of course, if you help us with our investigation instead of lying, then, perhaps, we can help you.'

'All right!' Keith shouted. 'All right!' He was now in tears and anxiously pulling at his remaining wisps of hair.

'All right, what?' asked Erika.

'I'll tell you. I'll tell you what I know… I think I've been talking to her online. The killer…'

'What's her name?' asked Erika.

'I don't… I don't know her real name, and she doesn't know mine. She only knows me as Duke.'

CHAPTER 69

'I met Night Owl online a few years ago,' said Keith. They were sitting back in his cramped, brightly lit living room.

'"Night Owl"?' asked Erika.

'Yes, that's her handle; the name she uses in the chat rooms. I don't sleep much, and I go and talk to like-minded people.'

He saw Peterson glance at Erika.

'I'm not a like-minded person like Night Owl... What I mean is, she's different with me. We've connected on a deep level. We can tell each other anything.'

'Has she told you her real name?' asked Erika.

'No, I only know her as Night Owl... But that doesn't mean we're not close. I love her.'

Erika realised they were dealing with something far darker than they had thought. Keith was in deep.

'What exactly did you talk to her about?' asked Peterson.

'Everything. We started off just chatting, for months really, about what we liked on telly, favourite foods... And then one night the chat room was busy, other users kept butting in, so I invited her to go and have a private chat, one that other people in the chat room couldn't see. And things got... heavy.'

'How do you mean, "heavy"? Cyber sex?' asked Peterson.

'Don't say "cyber sex" – it was more than that,' said Keith, shifting awkwardly.

'I understand,' said Erika. 'Did anything else happen that night?'

'She started talking about her husband and how he would rape her.'

'Rape her? Where?'

'At home, in bed, during the night… He'd just wake up and make her do it. She said lots of people don't think that's rape, but it is, isn't it?'

'Yes, it is,' said Erika.

Keith let that sink in for a moment.

'I just listened to – well, I read – what she said on the screen. She poured it all out. He was violent and abusive to her, and she felt trapped. What was worse was she couldn't sleep. She's an insomniac. Like me.'

'When was this?' asked Erika.

'Four years ago.'

'You've been talking to her for four years?' asked Peterson.

'There are times when she goes off the radar, and I have times too, but we hook up most nights. We're going to be together. She wants to run away with me…' Keith looked down for a moment, realising. 'Well, that was the plan.'

'What did you tell her about yourself?' asked Erika.

Keith opened and closed his mouth a few times, unsure of how to say it. 'She thinks I have my own business, a charity, for clean drinking water. She thinks I'm unhappy in my marriage too. That my wife doesn't understand me like she does.'

'And I take it you're not married? Divorced?' asked Peterson, looking around at the tiny living area.

'Neither,' replied Keith.

'How did you describe yourself, physically?' asked Peterson. Erika shot him a look; she didn't want Keith closing down on them. There was another awkward pause.

'It's okay. So you weren't entirely truthful with her. What happened next?' she asked.

'She said she fantasised about killing her husband... At the same time, I was going through a very dark patch in my life and I was looking at how to commit suicide. You see, with my condition I'm not expected to live beyond the next few years... I'm often in constant pain... I'd been on this forum where it explained how you could buy one of these suicide bags, and together with a gas canister you could use it to kill yourself. No pain, just drift away.'

A look passed between Erika and Peterson.

'And you gave her details of this bag, and how to kill her husband?'

Keith nodded.

'And did she ask you to buy one of these bags for her?'

'No. At this stage, I had one. I posted it to her.'

'You posted it?'

'Yes, well, I got my carer to put it in the post, to a PO Box address in Uxbridge, West London. She told me she'd set it up, the PO Box, so her husband wouldn't find out. He didn't, but before she could go through with it he died.'

'How?' asked Erika.

'He had a heart attack. I thought she'd be happy, but she felt like she'd been robbed of the opportunity to do it herself. She then got really obsessive and angry, looking at her life. She seemed confused. She started to talk about all the men she wished she could kill. Her doctor was one; she'd gone to him because her husband had started to be abusive in other ways. He'd held her down and poured boiling water over her.'

'Jesus. That's what happens in one of Stephen Linley's books,' said Erika to Peterson.

'That's why he was her third victim,' Keith said. 'She hated Stephen Linley. Her husband was obsessed with his books and he acted out a lot of the scenarios from them.'

'And didn't you think you should talk to someone, call the police?'

'You have to realise… I'm condensing years and years, hours upon hours of our chats here.'

'Keith, come on!'

'I love her!' he cried. 'You don't understand! We… we were going to run away. She was going to get me out of…of… THIS!'

Keith broke down, his head forward on his chest, sobbing. Erika went to him and put her arm around his shoulders.

'Keith, I'm so sorry. Are you still talking to her?'

He looked up from his sobbing and nodded. The lenses of his grimy glasses were wet with tears.

'And what? Were you about to leave together?'

Peterson pulled out a small pack of tissues and handed one to Keith.

'Thanks,' Keith said, through his sobs. 'We were going to take the train to France. The Eurostar has disabled access. I checked. And then we were going to make our way down slowly on trains, staying in French chateaus, heading to Spain to live by the sea.'

Erika noticed that pinned up above the computer stand were some pictures of Barcelona and a seaside town in Spain.

'When were you planning on going?' asked Peterson.

Keith shrugged. 'When she's done.'

'Done what?' asked Erika.

'Done… All the names on her list.'

'How many names are on her list?'

'She said there were four.'

'And has she given you any idea of who the fourth victim will be?' asked Erika.

'No, all I know is that when she's done, we'll be together.' Keith bit his lip and looked between Erika and Peterson. He started to cry again. 'It IS real. She loves me. She might not know what I am but we have a real connection!' He took some deep breaths and took off his glasses, beginning to clean them with the edge of his T-shirt.

'Keith, you do know that now you've spoken to us, there are implications? This woman is wanted for three murders.'

Keith put his glasses back on and his face crumpled.

Erika's voice softened. 'And you're sure at no point she gave you her real name, or a location where she lived – any kind of idea about who she is?'

Keith shook his head. 'She said London, once. And I checked, the PO Box is anonymous.'

'Have you ever tried to trace her using an IP address?' asked Peterson.

'I tried, but I couldn't trace her IP address. She's probably using Tor. I do.'

'What's Tor?'

'Encryption software, so no one can know what you do on-line.'

Erika put her hand to her temple. 'So you're saying it's going to be impossible to trace her whereabouts when she accesses the chat room.'

'Yeah,' nodded Keith. 'Impossible.'

CHAPTER 70

Erika and Peterson stepped outside Keith's flat for a moment and walked across the street to the promenade. The small waves down on the shore pulled softly over the shingle and there was a murmur of chatter and laughter from the beach.

'I know it's wrong, but I feel sorry for him,' said Peterson.

'I feel sorry that his life has ended up like that. But he's been protecting whoever this woman is, Night Owl,' said Erika.

'We shouldn't leave him too long,' said Peterson, looking back at the flat. 'Who knows what he's going to do?'

'He's not going to go anywhere fast,' said Erika. 'What do you think we should do?'

'What we *should* do is pass this information on to the SIO of the case, which is Sparks,' said Peterson.

'But Sparks is convinced it's Isaac Strong who killed Stephen, and he's convinced he can link Isaac to the two other murders,' said Erika. 'If I tell Sparks or Marsh about this, they could tell me to hand it over or not to pursue it, and then that would mean if I *do* pursue it, I would be going against a direct order.'

'So, right now we're...' started Peterson.

'Right now, we're still just visiting someone in Worthing,' said Erika.

'Our good friend Keith...' finished Peterson.

Erika looked over at the Pavilion Theatre, which loomed up like a giant curved jelly mould, the pier stretching out to sea behind it. A large flock of seagulls huddled together on the end, their heads buried in their feathers.

'What if we can engineer a meeting between Keith and "Night Owl"?' said Erika.

'Where? And how would we get him there? And if she saw him, wouldn't she just turn around and...'

'No, Peterson. Keith wouldn't be waiting for her. We would. Along with half the Met Police.'

CHAPTER 71

Later that day, Erika had managed to call in a favour from Lee Graham, an old colleague from the Met who was now with Sussex Police. He came over to Worthing to look at Keith's computer. He was a brilliant, young and slightly intense forensic computer analyst.

A couple of hours later, Lee, Erika, Peterson and Keith were all crammed into Keith's tiny living room.

'Okay, so you've now got his computer—' started Lee.

'My name is Keith,' said Keith, regarding Lee suspiciously.

'Yes, you've now got Keith's computer here networked in with these,' said Lee, handing two laptops to Erika. 'You'll be able to see what's happening in real time and you can also jump in at any time and type. Whoever is chatting with Keith online won't be any the wiser.'

'Thank you,' said Erika.

'I can also keep a log and I'll be able to monitor the chat room remotely from my office. I'll have a crack at tracing this Night Owl's whereabouts, but if she's using the Tor network it'll be virtually impossible.'

'So, how does this Tor network operate?' asked Peterson.

'Say you use the Internet normally, for example to send me an email. It goes from your computer via a server to my computer. Both of us can easily find out where the other person is via their IP address. An IP address is a unique string of numbers separated by full stops that identifies each computer using the Internet Protocol to communicate over a network. With the Tor software on your computer, it directs Internet traffic through a free, worldwide volunteer network of computers. There are more than seven thousand of these acting as relays to conceal a user's location and usage from anyone conducting network surveillance or traffic analysis.'

'They call it onion computing, because there are so many layers in the relay,' said Keith.

'That's right. Using Tor makes it more difficult for Internet activity to be traced back to the user. This includes visits to websites, online posts, instant messages and other forms of communication,' said Lee.

'And anyone can download this Tor program?' asked Erika.

'Yep. Free online software,' said Lee. 'Makes it a bloody nightmare for us.'

'If you can't trace Night Owl, then why do you want to spy on me talking to her?' asked Keith.

A look passed between Erika and Peterson.

'We want you to arrange a meeting with her,' said Erika.

'I can't meet her. I'm not ready. I wanted to be able to prepare!'

'You're not really going to meet her,' explained Erika.

'No, no, I can't... I'm sorry. No.'

'You will,' said Peterson, with an air of finality.

'London Waterloo train station,' said Erika.

'How am I going to suddenly think of a way to get her to meet?' cried Keith, panicking.

'You'll think of a way,' said Peterson.

'I saw that you've saved your entire chat room history with this Night Owl,' said Lee. 'I've copied it across to your laptops,' he told Erika and Peterson.

'But… those were private chats!' insisted Keith.

'We have a deal here. Remember?' said Erika.

Keith nodded, nervously.

When everything was set up, Erika and Peterson came out of the flat to say goodbye to Lee. The air was still and warm, and from far down on the beach they could hear the squeaky strains of a Punch and Judy show.

'I also got a copy of his hard drive. I'll check out if there's anything dodgy we need to know about,' said Lee, going to his car, which was parked by the kerb. He opened the boot and put his bag inside. 'I sometimes wish that the Internet had never been invented. Too many people with too much time to indulge their sick fantasies.'

'It seems every time I see you I'm giving you something nasty to look into,' said Erika. 'Thanks for doing this.'

'Maybe the next time we meet should be outside work,' he said with a grin.

Peterson looked between them, as Erika blushed red and was lost for words. 'Thanks again!' she said finally.

'No probs. I hope it helps you catch this nasty bitch. I'll be in touch online when you boot up your computer,' he said, then got into his car.

'I didn't know you knew him so well,' said Peterson, as they watched Lee's car drive off along the promenade.

'What's it to you?' asked Erika.

'Nothing,' he shrugged.

'Good, let's get back inside. I'm worried Keith is going to bottle out on us.'

CHAPTER 72

Simone was buzzing with excitement as she walked to work. She'd taken the bus to King's Cross and was walking through the back streets behind the station to the Queen Anne Hospital. She liked working nights, the feeling of going to work when so many were returning home. She was like a salmon, swimming against the tide. When she worked nights, she didn't have to stress about not sleeping, about being alone in her house and vulnerable.

She didn't have to stress about seeing things.

It was a warm, balmy evening and as she waited to cross the road she found that she was excited to see Mary again. The old lady was a fighter, and she'd still be there, Simone was sure. She'd brought presents for Mary: a picture frame for the photo with George and a new hairbrush. She was sure that Mary's hair would be tangled.

A nasty, warm smell of urine and disposable nappies hit Simone's nose as she walked the long corridor to Mary's ward. A few nurses nodded at her, and she nodded back and exchanged pleasantries. Many of the nurses looked surprised to see the big grin on her usually sullen face.

When Simone reached the door to Mary's room, she opened it without knocking and was shocked to see a smartly dressed elderly woman sitting in *her* chair, beside Mary's bed. The woman's hair was cut in a sleek silver bob. She wore crisp white slacks, black patent leather court shoes and a silk floral blouse. The bed was empty and Mary was sitting in a wheelchair beside the woman, dressed neatly in a pair of smart charcoal trousers and a houndstooth jacket. Her hair was neatly tied back with a red ribbon, and the woman was leaning down and helping put Mary's feet into a pair of new shoes.

'Who are you?' asked Simone, looking between them. The woman slipped on Mary's second shoe and stood. She was very tall.

'Hi there, nurse,' said the woman. She had a drawling American accent.

'What's going on?' asked Simone sharply. 'Does the doctor know you're here?'

'Yes, honey. I'm Dorothy Van Last, Mary's sister. I'm here to take her home.'

'Sister? I didn't know Mary had a sister. You're American!'

'I was born here, honey, but I've been away from England a long time.' Dorothy looked around the dingy hospital room. 'Seems things haven't changed much.'

'But Mary,' said Simone, 'you belong here with... with us...'

Mary cleared her throat. 'Who are you, dear?' she asked, searching Simone's face. Her voice was quavering and very frail.

'I'm Nurse Simone. I've been caring for you.'

'Have you? My sister heard from my neighbour that I was here. She flew all the way over from Boston. I don't know what I'd have done if she didn't come,' said Mary, her voice weak.

'But you're... my... I was going to...' started Simone, feeling her eyes start to water.

'The doctor says she's made *quite* the recovery,' interrupted Dorothy. 'I'm gonna stay with her until she's better.' She took the brake off Mary's wheelchair and manoeuvred her round the bed.

'But Mary...' said Simone.

Mary peered up at her from the chair. 'Who is this?' she asked her sister.

'She's a nurse, Mary. They all look the same after a while. No offence, honey.'

Dorothy pushed the chair past Simone, out of the room and away down the corridor. Simone moved to the door and watched Mary being wheeled away. Mary didn't even try to look round and see Simone. Then they rounded a corner and were gone.

Simone locked herself in one of the disabled toilets. She stood for a moment, shaking. She then opened her bag, pulled out the picture frame she'd bought for Mary and hit it repeatedly on the edge of the sink until it smashed. She stared at her reflection, anger growing inside her. She had been abandoned. Abandoned again.

CHAPTER 73

Erika booked two rooms in the aptly named Sea Breeze Hotel, which was cheap and cheerful and a few doors down from Keith's flat. The rooms were next to each other, rather small and poky, and overlooked the dustbin-filled courtyard behind. They grabbed some food from the restaurant downstairs, then came back up to Erika's room and prepared to wait.

To kill time until darkness fell, they started to look through the colossal amount of chat logs that Lee had downloaded from Keith's computer. There were four years' worth in total, and reading through the pages and pages of data would have been impossible. After dividing the chat logs into years, they imported each year into a Word document. They then spent time searching through a list of keywords which could take them directly to specific exchanges.

'This chat is disturbing,' said Peterson, who was sitting in a chair by the small window. 'I just put in the keyword "suicide" and I've got pages and pages where Keith is talking about killing himself, and exactly how he would do it. Listen to this: "I'd turn off the lights in my flat. It would be the one time I would let the darkness envelop me. I'd take a hit on the gas canister and pull the bag over my head, filling it with gas to stop me from panicking. I would then draw it tight and breathe, taking in great gulps until I passed out. I'd just slip away, painlessly, easily... like a dream which never ends."'

'When was this dated?' asked Erika.

'This was three years ago, early on in their correspondence,' said Peterson.

'I've put in a search for the words "wheelchair" and "disabled",' said Erika, working at her laptop. 'There are only fleeting mentions from Simone, one talking about seeing a disabled man in the street and how sorry she felt for him, and another minor mention. He's never told her.'

'She talks here about being scalded by her husband,' said Peterson, after a silence. 'It's dated around the same time. He tried to rape her and she ran and locked herself in the bathroom. He came after her with a pan of boiling water, punched her in the face and then put her in the bath, half-unconscious, stripped her and slowly poured the scalding water over her naked body. She says she was badly scarred, but didn't go to the doctor until a week later and only because the sores became infected.'

'Did she say who he was? Does she name the doctor?' asked Erika.

'No, but she says that the doctor didn't believe her when she said her husband had burned her.'

Erika looked up at Peterson in horror.

'She says the doctor thought that the medication she was taking, coupled with chronic lack of sleep, was making her hallucinate… She'd previously come to him with similar burns when she had accidentally filled a bath with scalding water and stepped into it. Her husband had, in the past, confided in the doctor about her psychotic episodes and she had previously been sectioned.'

'Jesus,' said Erika. 'He believed the husband over her…'

It was now dark outside and they could hear, through the open window, the faint sound of the waves dragging at the shingle.

'In the press they always describe people as monsters, and we use that term too,' said Erika. 'But surely monsters aren't born? A tiny baby is never a monster. Doesn't everyone come into this world good? Isn't it their lives and their circumstances which turn them bad?'

A beep came from the laptop Peterson was using.

'It's Keith,' he said. 'He's started talking online with Night Owl.'

CHAPTER 74

Keith sat at his computer stand in his tiny living room. The lights seemed to beat down on him and he was drenched in sweat. It dripped down from his wispy hair onto the black PVC of his seat. Erika and Peterson sat on the folding chairs behind him.

'I don't know what to say,' he said, turning to face them.

'You need to just talk normally for a bit. We don't want her to get suspicious,' said Erika.

He nodded, turned back and started to type.

DUKE: Hey, Night Owl. What's up?
NIGHT OWL: Hi.
DUKE: What's up?

A few moments passed. Erika opened another button of her blouse and fanned the material. She looked over at Peterson, who was sweltering too. 'Can we turn off any of these lights?' he asked, wiping his forehead with his shirtsleeve.

'No! No, I don't like the dark. The shadows,' said Keith. 'You can open a window, if you like.'

Peterson went to the small kitchen and opened the window above the sink. The smell of blocked drains floated across the garish carpet but at least it was cooler.

'She's not typing,' said Keith, turning to Erika and Peterson again.

'Is this normal?' asked Peterson, coming back to his folding chair.

'I dunno… I don't normally have an audience here when I talk to her. People breathing down my neck. What if she knows?'

'She doesn't know,' reassured Erika. They sat in silence for a few more minutes.

'I'm just going to use your bathroom,' said Erika. Keith nodded and turned back to the screen. She left the living room and came out into the hall. She could hear a dull drone of music from upstairs, and the bulbs glowed brightly. She came to the bathroom and closed the door.

She gingerly hovered over the grubby toilet and peed as quickly as she could. When she reached around to see where the toilet paper was, her shoulder bashed painfully against the large safety rail. She pushed it and watched as it swung upwards, almost like a bizarre guillotine in reverse. She quickly finished and washed her hands. The bathroom was deeply depressing, almost like a hospital. She had to crouch down to see her reflection in the mirror; she wished she hadn't bothered. She looked exhausted.

When she came back to the living room, it seemed even hotter under the blazing lights. Peterson was just browsing through the shelves of DVDs.

'Hang on, she's typing,' said Keith, leaning toward the computer screen. Erika and Peterson both moved over to join him.

NIGHT OWL: Sorry, I had some food on the stove.
DUKE: Ooh, what are we eating?
NIGHT OWL: Poached egg on toast.
DUKE: Yum. Is there one for me? Can mine have a dollop of brown sauce?
NIGHT OWL: Yes, I bought some for you especially.

'This is good,' said Erika, as she and Peterson peered over the back of Keith's chair. They stayed and watched the conversation unfold.

'This has to be a first for me, watching a serial killer talk about her crap day at work and explain how she likes her eggs poached,' murmured Peterson, as he sat watching the screen, resting his chin on the heel of his hand. 'What time is it?'

'Two-thirty,' said Erika, looking at her watch.

At five-thirty, as it started to get light, the conversation was still going. The courtyard outside the kitchen window began to brighten with a bluish tinge.

Erika nudged Peterson, who had managed to sleep in the folding chair, his head tipped back. He rubbed his eyes as he awoke.

'I think he's finally cutting to the chase,' whispered Erika. They watched the screen.

DUKE: So... I've wanted to tell you something for a while.
NIGHT OWL Uh-huh?
DUKE: I went to see the doctor the other day.
NIGHT OWL: Oh yeah?
DUKE: I know you hate doctors.
NIGHT OWL: Fucking loathe them.
DUKE: Mine's a woman. She's OK.
NIGHT OWL: You two-timing me?
DUKE: Course not. She said I have very high cholesterol. My job is high stress... I need to take it easy or I could...
NIGHT OWL: Could?
DUKE: I could get a heart attack. It's freaked me out, really. Made me put things in perspective.

NIGHT OWL: I thought you wanted to die. To end it all.

DUKE: It comes and it goes. But right now, the sun is coming up outside and life is short... And I love you.

DUKE: So, I wanted to ask, and I know it's a big ask, if you wanted to meet me. For real. As real people.

There was a long pause.

'I've done it. I've scared her off,' said Keith, his tired eyes beginning to show panic. 'I've tried. You've seen me, here all night, trying!'

'It's okay,' said Erika. 'Look.'

Keith turned back to the screen.

NIGHT OWL: OK, then. Let's meet.

'Jesus,' said Keith. He started typing.

DUKE: That's GREAT!!!

NIGHT OWL: But I don't want you to be disappointed.

DUKE: Never. Never. NEVER!

NIGHT OWL: Where?

NIGHT OWL: And when?

'Where? What should I write?' asked Keith.

'Tell her you want to meet at Waterloo Station, in London,' said Erika.

'No, ask her first, suggest it,' added Peterson. 'And then if she says yes, arrange it for 5 p.m. this evening, under the clock on the concourse.

Keith nodded and started to type again:

DUKE: How about London Waterloo train station?

NIGHT OWL: OK. When?

DUKE: Tomorrow. Well, that's today really. Under the clock at 5 p.m.

NIGHT OWL: OK.

DUKE: YESSSSS! I'm so happy!!! How will I know it's you?

NIGHT OWL: Don't worry.

NIGHT OWL: You'll know.

She logged off from the chat room. They sat in silence for a moment. Keith was grinning. His hair was dank and stood on end, and he stank of body odour.

'Five p.m. is rush hour at Waterloo Station,' said Peterson. 'We should have got him to say earlier.'

'It's going to make grabbing hold of her much tougher,' agreed Erika. 'But there's also less leeway.'

'Boss, you're going to have to tell Marsh. There's no other way to get a big surveillance op authorised… Let's hope he'll authorise it.'

'Yeah,' said Erika. She looked at her watch. It was quarter to six. 'Let's get something to eat, and give Marsh a chance to wake up before I tell him.'

'I've got to get back. I'm on duty in two hours,' said Peterson.

'Course you are,' said Erika. 'Sorry. You go. I don't want to get you into any trouble. And, er, you weren't here. Well, if the shit hits the fan, you weren't here. If it's a triumph, you were.'

CHAPTER 75

It was 6.30 a.m. when Erika said goodbye to Peterson outside Keith's house on the promenade. She was surprised at how sad she was to see him go. When his taxi drew up at the kerb, he surprised her by giving her a hug goodbye.

'Quick hug!' he grinned. 'I must stink!'

'No – well, a little. I must do too,' she grinned back.

He shook his head. 'Keep me posted, boss.'

'I will,' she said. He gave her the fingers crossed sign, as he climbed into the taxi. She watched as it drove away.

She crossed the road to the beach. It was the start of a beautiful day, and in the early morning sun the air was fresh and the sand empty apart from a couple of dog walkers and a young guy who was setting out deckchairs for hire. She went and sat on a bank of shingle, a few feet from where the waves were lightly breaking on the shore, took a deep breath and called Marsh. She tried his house phone first. Marcie answered – she didn't sound pleased to hear Erika's voice. She didn't exchange pleasantries, just dropped the phone on the table and yelled up the stairs for her husband. She heard him come thudding down the stairs and pick up the phone.

'Erika, I hope that you're calling me from somewhere hot and you want my address for a postcard?' he said.

'About that, sir . . .' said Erika. 'I'm not in London. I'm in Worthing.'

'Worthing? What the bloody hell are you doing there?'

Erika told him, quickly getting to the point that she had made a major breakthrough in the Night Stalker case and detailed the meeting that had been arranged later that day at London Waterloo.

'So you defied my orders, again?' said Marsh.

'Is that all you can say, sir? This is a HUGE breakthrough. I know that I should have told you, but you know I work on my instincts. Now, we need surveillance in place asap. In and around Waterloo station. I really do think that she's going to show up and we need to be there to bring her in. I have evidence of conversations between her and this man, Keith Hardy. He uses the chat room handle "Duke". She calls herself "Night Owl".'

'Where are Moss and Peterson?'

'They've been reassigned. I'm here on my own, sir.'

There was a long pause.

'Erika, you are so naive. You act as if there are no rules, as if there is no line of authority.'

'But, sir, I've made a breakthrough, a huge one! When I get back to the hotel room, I can send you everything – the details of the meet, chat logs. We've only touched the tip of the iceberg. This guy, Keith, he's been talking to her online for four years. We have a log of all those conversations. I also believe she was a patient of Gregory Munro. She was badly burnt. We can use this information to look back over medical records.'

'Okay, you are to send this over to me the second you get off the phone.'

'Absolutely.'

'And Erika, I am ordering you to take that holiday and really think about your position in the force. If I see you near the nick, or any other nick for that matter, you will be suspended, and don't think it will be easy to get your badge back for the fourth time! And if I see you near Waterloo station, I won't just take your badge. You'll be fired. Do you hear me?'

'So that means you're going to go ahead? Sir?'

'I will phone you,' he said, and then hung up.

Despite the telling off, Erika had heard the excitement in his voice.

'We're going to get you, Night Owl. We're going to get you,' said Erika. She sat back on the shingle, looking out at the vast expanse of horizon and adrenalin began coursing through her veins.

CHAPTER 76

'I don't see why this is necessary,' protested Keith. Erika was crouched under his computer stand, pulling out the leads and plugs, which all seemed to be feeding into one extension lead. The carpet, with its pattern of lime green, yellow and red hexagons was covered in a thick layer of dust, much of which was now floating around and sticking to her with static.

'You should be careful with all this stuff running off one socket,' said Erika, crawling out from under the computer stand.

Keith flicked the joystick on his wheelchair towards him and his chair backed away to the shelves behind, giving Erika room to get back up.

'It's fine,' he said.

A clock above his greasy cooker said it was 3 p.m. 'Is that clock right?' Erika asked, pulling out her phone.

'Yeah. What happens now?' he asked, staring up at her through his dirty glasses. He suddenly looked vulnerable.

'A police officer will be ready to meet Night Owl and take her into custody for questioning…'

Erika was being economical with the truth. On the strength of the chat logs that Erika had emailed over to Marsh, a major surveillance operation had been hastily arranged in Waterloo station to arrest Night Owl at 5 p.m. Erika looked around at the cramped and brightly lit room and tried to tell herself she was still part of this. It was important that she stayed with Keith, to make sure he didn't tip off the killer.

'I meant, what happens to me?' replied Keith.

'You'll be called as a witness. And it's most likely that you will be arrested for aiding and abetting and withholding evidence, but with your circumstances and the fact you are going to cooperate, I doubt the CPS will want to prosecute. As long as you cooperate fully. And we'll sort your housing problems. I want to at least make that right.'

'Thank you,' he said.

They sat in silence for a few minutes. The clock on the greasy cooker ticked.

'What must you think of me?' asked Keith.

'I don't think anything. I think about the victims. I think about catching her,' said Erika.

'One of the most important friendships in my life was with someone who is a mass murderer. I'm in love with her… What does that make me?'

Erika leaned over and took his small hand. 'Plenty of people have been duped by friends, by lovers and spouses. You met her online, where people pretend to be someone else. They often create another life for themselves. So they can be seen differently.'

'Online, I can be the person I want to be. I'm not constrained by… Keith adjusted the tube under his nose and looked down at his chair. 'Do you want to watch a DVD? I'll show you my favourite *Dr Who* episode, when Tom Baker regenerated.'

'Yes, okay,' said Erika. They still had two hours, which she knew were going to feel like an eternity.

CHAPTER 77

As the largest train station in the United Kingdom, London Waterloo is busy before first light and until late at night. The concourse is more than eight hundred feet long, contains over twenty platforms, with shops and a mezzanine with restaurants. More than a hundred million passengers pass through its doors every year.

Detective Chief Superintendent Marsh was stationed with DCI Sparks in the vast CCTV control room. It was a window-less concrete square, high above the station. A wall of twenty-eight CCTV monitors offered a portal to the station from every angle. Thirty-five officers had been drafted in – the majority in plain clothes – to watch the exits and to patrol up and down the concourse. Support vehicles were waiting at the north, south, east and west exits, each with three police cars. The transport police, some of whom were armed, were also doing their regular patrols of the station perimeter.

At 4.50 p.m. it looked as if every one of the hundred million people had converged on the station at once. The marble floor of the concourse vanished under the throngs of travellers. They surged up through escalators from the underground station, they poured in through the four main entrances and exits, they milled around under the giant electronic boards running the length of the twenty-two busy platforms and they congregated outside the shops or queued at the long ticket hall opposite the platforms.

'This is going to be a fucking nightmare, sir,' said Sparks, leaning against a bank of computer screens where the Transport for London employees were quietly monitoring the station. Sweat glistened on his acne-scarred face.

'There's nowhere else in London with more eyes. The moment she makes herself known, we have her,' said Marsh, scanning the wall of CCTV monitors.

'And you think DCI Foster's hunch is right, sir?'

'It's not a hunch, Sparks. You saw the material she sent through,' said Marsh.

'I did. But at no point is this woman named or described physically. Whatever happens, this is going to be bloody expensive.'

'Leave me to worry about that. You do your job,' said Marsh.

A young Asian guy approached and introduced himself. 'I'm Tanvir. I'm supervising the control room today. We've got these four screens, which will be covering your key area,' he said. On cue, a wide shot of the station clock flashed up. Below it stood Sergeant Crane, dressed in jeans and a light jacket, and clutching a cheap-looking bunch of roses.

'Are you reading me, Crane?' said Sparks, into his radio. 'Touch your ear to show you can hear me.'

From the wide shot Crane looked normal, but a close-up from another angle showed he had tilted his head to his jacket lapels and was touching his free hand to his left ear. 'You sure I don't stand out? I'm the only one here in a jacket – it's boiling hot!' he said, his voice coming through the radio.

'It's all good, Crane. This Keith fellow arranged to meet her under the clock in half an hour. It's romantic. It figures that he'd get dressed up,' said Marsh into his radio, adding, 'And it doesn't show that you're wired up. Now, no more chatting… we'll keep you posted via radio.'

'What time is it?' asked Crane.

'Jesus, he's under a fucking clock,' said Sparks. He grasped his radio. 'It's four-thirty. Look up next time you need to know.'

Marsh turned back to Tanvir. 'Which camera gives us a view of the side entrance leading away from under the clock?'

'Can you put camera seventeen up on these screens?' said Tanvir to a woman wearing a headset by a computer in the corner. Another view of Crane from behind came into view, although this time it was from above an escalator leading up behind the clock.

Marsh gripped his radio again. 'Okay, Crane, we've got all eyes on you. Just stay calm. We'll count you down. Don't get too close to her, if she approaches you earlier. You're covered from all sides. She makes a move and we're there in seconds.'

'What time is it?' asked Crane again, nervously.

'He's under the fucking clock,' muttered Sparks.

'Four thirty-three,' said Marsh. 'We'll be in constant contact.'

CHAPTER 78

Erika sat on the wall by the line of wheelie bins and lit up a cigarette. Keith had objected to her smoking inside and she'd said she wouldn't leave him on his own, so as a compromise he'd come as far as the front door.

'Would you like to just walk along the promenade – I mean *go* along? It's nice and sunny,' said Erika.

'I don't like it, leaving the flat,' said Keith, craning his head suspiciously up to the clear blue sky.

Erika carried on smoking and stared out at the water, which was still and glittering in the sunshine. A group of kids were making sandcastles by the shore, watched over by their parents on deckchairs. A pink-and-white themed tourist train trundled past, a bell ringing tinnily by the miserable-looking driver's head. Groups of kids eating ice-creams and candyfloss waved from behind the cloudy plastic windows in the carriages.

Keith waved back, which Erika found touching. She looked at her watch: it was coming up to 4.50 p.m. She checked her phone and saw that she had a strong signal and battery.

'It's like a watched pot,' said Keith. 'Never boils.'

Erika shook her head ruefully and lit another cigarette. She could have screamed with frustration at having to stay so far away from the action. She thought of DCI Sparks, who would be heading up the team, giving the orders and taking the glory.

As well as feeling frustrated, she felt robbed.

CHAPTER 79

It was now 5.20 p.m. and no one had approached Crane, who was still stationed underneath the clock in Waterloo station.

Marsh and Sparks watched from the control room, as the crowds in the concourse swelled even more. It had become difficult to keep Crane in their sights on the close-up CCTV screen, so they were now using a long shot from across the concourse, which had been blown up to a huge size on the centre screen in the control room.

'Crane, you okay? You need to stick to your spot. Dig your heels in,' said Sparks into his radio. They could see from the long shot that the surging crowds were jostling him.

'Yes, sir,' he murmured. He sounded panicky.

Marsh looked across the screens and spoke into his radio. 'We're still on you, Crane. You've got six plain-clothes officers stationed around, who can be with you in seconds. You've also got two armed transport police officers in the walkway behind you. Just stay calm… She's a woman, she's decided to be fashionably late,' he added, trying to ease the tension.

'She's not fucking showing up,' said Sparks. 'We should be concentrating on Isaac Strong, not pissing away resources on some blind date.' Marsh shot him a look. 'Sir,' he added.

Just then, on the large screen, the crowds around Crane shifted and a group of women approaching Crane were shoved forward. One fell, hitting the concourse floor, causing the crowd around her to bump and surge. Crane was pushed and the flowers he was holding were knocked from his grasp.

'What's going on here?' said Marsh. 'Crane, talk to me?'

'Hang on, sir,' said Crane, as he was jostled along.

'Look. It's a fight, a bloody fight,' said Sparks, pointing to the CCTV monitor, showing the escalator behind the clock. A group of young lads in baseball caps came into view, shouting and jeering and parting the crowd of commuters like the Red Sea. Two of the boys, one dark and one blond, were fighting, and they went down on the floor. The dark-haired boy landed a punch to the blond one, and his face was quickly a mess of blood. The crowd surged away in all directions and the British Transport Police waded in, clasping their guns, which caused even more screams and commotion.

Crane had managed to get himself into the doorway of a Marks & Spencer convenience store, and watched as his meeting place under the clock was overrun with police, as they restored order. The two boys were put in handcuffs and the police began the laborious task of booking them.

'Fucking hell!' shouted Marsh into his radio. 'Get them to bloody well move, this is screwing up our meeting place.'

'She isn't going to be crazy about meeting him there, even if she does show up!' said Sparks.

'Crane, can you hear me?' said Marsh, ignoring Sparks.

'Yes, sir. Things got a bit hairy there,' said Crane as he stepped out from the doorway of the Marks & Spencer.

'We've still got you on camera, Crane. All okay?'

'I've dropped the flowers,' he said.

'Don't worry. We're going to get the uniform crowd moved on, and then you move back,' said Marsh.

'What the fuck is this? Mrs Mop?' said Sparks, looking up at the view under the station clock. A wizened old cleaning lady had stopped her cart where blood had splattered from the blond-haired boy's nose, and she was dipping her grotty mop in a bucket of grey water with slow determination. One of the boys being interviewed started to heckle her, but she either didn't hear or paid no attention, and starting to mop the concourse floor at a glacial pace.

'Where is DC Warren?' asked Sparks. There was a beep and Warren came on the radio.

'Yes, sir.'

'What's your position?'

'I'm at the WH Smith on the concourse opposite.'

'Get that old dear out of the way, will you? And don't let her put one of those yellow signs up under the clock,' he started.

'Hang on, hang on, hang on,' said Marsh. He was looking back at the screen where Crane was waiting close to the clock. A small dark-haired woman wearing a smart black jacket was approaching him. Marsh grabbed his radio. 'Shit! All units, a dark-haired woman is approaching Sergeant Crane. I repeat, a dark-haired woman is approaching Sergeant Crane. Stand by.'

'All units standing by,' came a voice through the radio. Two of the large screens on the wall cut to a view of Crane from above and an angle on the other side. The woman was now talking to him, looking up at him enquiringly. They talked for another minute or so, then Crane said something back and she walked away.

'Crane, report, what the hell is going on?' asked Marsh.

'Sorry, boss, false alarm. She was asking if I wanted to buy car insurance.'

'Shit!' said Marsh, slamming his hand down on one of the desks. 'Shit! Sparks, I want that woman questioned anyway. Stop her, ID her and find out everything you know.'

'Something tells me she's not going to hit her sales target,' said Sparks as the woman was surrounded by three plain-clothes police officers.

CHAPTER 80

At 6.30 p.m. Erika was almost climbing the walls in Keith's tiny flat. Her phone beeped in her bag and she pulled it out. It was a text from Marsh:

WE'RE STANDING DOWN AT WATERLOO. SHE DIDN'T SHOW. WE NEED TO TALK. I WILL PHONE YOU LATER TONIGHT.

'What is it?' asked Keith, watching in dismay as Erika put her head in her hands.

'She was a no-show…' she said. 'You've had nothing there from her? Nothing in the chat room?'

Keith shook his head.

'Are you sure?'

'Yes. I'm sure, look, I'm logged in…'

Erika had a terrible sinking feeling, like a huge, heavy cannon ball was weighing her stomach down. She rubbed at her sweat-drenched face.

'Look, Keith, we need to turn some of these lights off. It's unbearable in here…'

'No! I'm sorry, no. I told you, I don't like the dark…'

Erika looked at the time. She felt completely devastated.

'What happens now?' asked Keith.

'I'm waiting for my senior officer to call back… Later tonight…'

'What happens to me?'

'Um, I don't know. But I stick by what I said to you.' Erika looked at Keith in the huge wheelchair. She had recently helped him to change his oxygen tank.

She made a decision. 'I need to step outside for an hour or so… Can I trust you here? Your computer is still being monitored. I take it you're not going to run away?'

'What do you think?' he said.

'Okay. Here is my mobile phone number,' she said, scribbling it on a piece of paper. 'I'm going to go for some air… Do you want some food? I don't know, do you eat chips?'

Keith's face lit up.

'Battered sausage, chips and mushy peas, please. The place opposite the pier is the best. My carer always gets them from there.'

Erika came out onto the cool promenade. The sun was sinking down into the sea and a light breeze was coming off the shore. She stared at the text from Marsh again and tried to call him. Her call was cancelled, it went straight to voicemail.

'Shit,' she muttered. She set off towards a bar she'd seen further down on the promenade. The front windows were folded back and it was crowded with lairy, red-faced old men and drunken women. The 'Macarena' blared out of the sound system. Erika fought her way to the bar and ordered a large glass of wine. The barmaid was run off her feet and served her quickly, slamming a glass down on the bar.

'Can I take this on the beach?' asked Erika. The girl didn't answer, just rolled her eyes, pulled down a plastic pint glass and tipped in the wine.

'And could I please have some ice?' said Erika.

She took her drink, bought some more cigarettes from the machine and came back down onto the beach. The tide had gone out quite far, and she sat back on the shingle, looking out at the expanse of wet sand. As she was lighting a cigarette, her phone rang. She pushed her pint of wine into the shingle and answered the call. Her eyes went wide as she listened to the voice on the other end.

CHAPTER 81

The sun had now sunk below the horizon and a cold breeze blew across the street. Simone moved quickly along the pavement beside the row of houses. She carried a small backpack, and she was dressed in her black running gear.

A few of the street lamps were broken. She moved faster when she hit an arc of orange sodium light, relaxing again when she was back in the shadows. She felt jumpy. It was early evening, and the row of terraced houses she moved past seemed to teem with life. Lights came on, music was being played. A row was kicking off in a top-floor window where the curtains were open and just a bare bulb hung from the ceiling.

Simone kept her head down when a man approached her from the other direction. He was tall and thin and moving quickly. Her heart began to beat fast and she felt her blood pressure increase. He was coming straight at her. Even her scar began to throb, as if it were engorged with blood. It wasn't until the man was almost upon her that she saw he was also dressed in running gear. He loped past without giving her a second glance, his headphones giving off a tinny sound of music. She realised she had to calm down, get a hold of herself.

Simone knew the house number she was looking for but didn't have to strain too hard in the darkness to find it on the brick walls. The numbers were painted gaudily on the wheelie bins which filled the small concrete front gardens.

She counted down the numbers, feeling none of the usual rush, none of the anger and excitement.

And then she arrived at the house. She approached the window, took a deep breath and placed her small hands on the sill. Looking around, she heaved herself up.

CHAPTER 82

'Erika! I had the baby, they got it wrong. It's a girl!' her sister cried, sounding breathless and exhausted. It took Erika a few seconds to realise it was Lenka.

'Oh, Lenka! That's wonderful! What happened? I thought you weren't due for a couple more weeks?'

'I know, but Marek took me for lunch and just after we ordered my waters broke. You know what he's like – he insisted on waiting for it to be packed up as takeaway – but it all happened so fast... The contractions started coming and then there wasn't even time for gas and air when we got to the hospital, she just popped out.'

'What's her name?'

'We're calling her Erika, after you. And after Mum, obviously,' said Lenka.

Erika felt herself welling up with emotion and wiped her face with the sandy back of her hand. 'Oh, Lenka. Oh, that's wonderful. Thank you,' she said. Tears and exhaustion washed over her.

'I wish Mum could be here, and you, of course,' her sister said, also getting teary.

'Yeah, well, things have all got out of hand here...'

There was a rustling noise, then Erika's brother-in-law, Marek, came on the phone. She chatted away to him for a few minutes. It felt so surreal, being sat on a dark beach whilst her family was hundreds of miles away, celebrating. Lenka came back on the phone and then said she had to go.

'I promise that when this case is over I'll come and see the baby,' said Erika.

'That's what you always say! Don't take too long,' said Lenka, wearily. There was a wail of the baby and then she was gone.

Erika sat for a long time, smoking and drinking a toast to her sister and niece. As the sky darkened, so did Erika's spirits. She was an aunt, and despite the fact she and her sister weren't close, she felt so happy for Lenka. Happy, yet dismayed at the way in which their lives had gone in such different directions.

It was only the cold breeze and the knowledge that Keith was waiting back in his flat that made her get up off the cold sand.

As she walked back along the beach, she saw the rows of houses and bed and breakfasts stretching away to where her hotel sat on the end of the prom. She came up off the beach via the steps and stopped in front of Keith's flat. The windows above were lit up, and the twang of a sitar and smell of weed wafted down, but Keith's windows were in darkness. She was about to knock on the door, when she pulled back her hand. Keith always left the lights on. He was scared of the dark.

Erika stepped off the small front path and into the square of concrete with the wheelie bins. She moved to the front bay window and saw that it was open. She peered into the darkness. A smell of damp and disinfectant wafted out.

She made a decision, hauled herself up onto the windowsill and climbed inside.

CHAPTER 83

Erika stood inside Keith's dark bedroom and listened. The air was thick with heat and dust. She tried to tune out the muffled music coming from the flat above, but couldn't hear anything beyond the bedroom door. She moved past the gloomy bulk of Keith's hospital bed and into the hallway. There was a pool of light cast through the glass in the front door, but as she crept down the hall she moved into the shadows. She passed the door to the second bedroom, which was ajar – she could just see the two wheelchairs, silent and empty. The two large wheelchairs loomed in the shadows.

The music ceased for a moment, and in the silence Erika strained to hear something. Then it started up again: a dull, tuneless throbbing. She kept moving, staying alert, past the wide-open bathroom door. The light pollution from the sea-front seeped through a tiny window above the sink, helping her eyes adjust to the murkiness.

Erika stopped and stiffened when she heard a snuffling and then a crackle over the throb of the music. She inched towards the frosted glass door at the end of the hallway and pulled out her phone. As she turned the corner into the living room, she activated the phone's light.

Erika almost cried out. Standing in the centre of the room was a woman. She was small, with ghostly pale skin, and an uneven bob of coarse black hair. Her eyes were pools of black that contracted rapidly to pinpricks when Erika trained the bright light on her from the camera phone. Beside the woman, she could see Keith slumped back in his chair, arms flopped apart. A plastic bag was tied tight over his head, so tight that the thick lenses of his glasses were mashed into his eye sockets.

'Who are you?'

'My name's Simone,' the woman sniffed, wiping a tear from her eye. 'I didn't want to kill him.'

'Jesus,' said Erika, her voice trembling. She moved the light from Keith's body and trained it directly in Simone's face, attempting to dazzle her, to give herself enough time to think, but Simone moved fast and Erika suddenly found herself slammed up against the back wall with a knife to her throat.

'Give me the phone,' Simone said in her calm, oddly high voice. Erika felt the cold steel prick the skin of her throat. 'You've seen what I can do. I'm not bluffing.'

Erika slowly handed over the phone. It took effort to keep her eyes open. Simone was small but stared up at her with a chilling intensity. Simone worked quickly with her free hand. The phone light blinked off and Erika heard the battery hit the carpet with a thud. In the gloom, Simone's pupils dilated like a crazed drug addict. She dropped the phone and Erika heard it crunch under her foot.

'Why did you have to come here, Erika Foster? I was going to do this and vanish off the face of the earth. You'd never have heard from me again.'

Erika glanced around the room.

'No, no, no – you keep your eyes on me,' said Simone. 'We're going over there,' she added, tilting her head towards Keith's still, seated form. She loosened her grip a little, but still held the knife to Erika's throat. They moved in a morbid dance, shuffling around until Erika was next to the wheelchair.

'Now I'm going to step back, but if you try anything I'll slash you. I'll go for your eyes, and your throat. You understand?'

'Yes,' gulped Erika. She was sweating and she could smell Keith next to her in the chair, a goaty mix of body odour and shit. Simone moved back to the doorway and flicked on the light. The room blazed bright. She came back, training the knifepoint on Erika.

'Take the bag off his head,' said Simone.

'What?'

'You heard me. Take it off.' She advanced on Erika, the blade glinting under the harsh lights.

'Okay, okay,' said Erika, putting up her hands. She slowly lifted Keith's head. His neck was still wet with sweat, and for a moment she thought he might still be alive – but his face was a bloated, bluish purple.

'Come on, quicker,' said Simone. Erika started to untie the cord from around his neck, unwinding it, panicking as it seemed to tangle. She loosened and worked the cord until it was free. Keith's head lifted up, and there was a sucking sound as Erika gently pulled at the plastic. His glasses came too, sliding up off his nose and over his forehead with the plastic bag. His head flopped back against the wheelchair. Simone suddenly came close, and Erika shrank back as she snatched the bag, holding it out.

'Take out his glasses, and put them back on him,' Simone said. Erika did so, gently placing them back on the bridge of Keith's nose, tucking the arms behind his ears.

'Why did you kill him?' asked Erika.

'He had to die because he'd figured me out. He told you.'

'He didn't tell me. I worked it out.'

'He wanted to meet. He'd never wanted to meet before... I'd tried to get him to in the past, but he'd chickened out. I fig-

ured you might have made the link. My paranoia was correct…
Paranoia doesn't work in a relationship,' she finished, looking
back at Keith.

'He loved you,' said Erika, looking between Keith's body
and Simone.

'Oh, then that's all I need, the love of a man,' said Simone,
her mouth curling up with sarcasm.

'What's wrong with being loved?' asked Erika, her mind
whirring. She was trying to work out what the woman was planning next, and until then she wanted to keep her talking.

'The right people never love you back!' spat Simone. 'Mothers should love you. Husbands. The people you trust. But they
let you down! And once one lets you down, it's like a domino
effect… You become vulnerable, people exploit you, they see a
chink in your armour.'

'I'm sorry,' said Erika, seeing Simone was getting danger-
ously wound up.

'No, you're not. But I bet you understand, don't you? How
did people change around you when your husband died? They
see your weakness. They leave you, or they stay and exploit you.'

'Simone… I understand.'

'Do you?'

'Yes.'

''So… You see why I did all this. Why I killed the doctor
who didn't believe me when I was in pain and terror; the writer,
whose sick creative mind found new and original ways to inspire
my torturer; the journalist who was responsible for me being
taken away from my mother when I was nine years old…'

'Jack Hart?'

'Jack Hart. The man has a name like Hart, but he doesn't
have one! I particularly enjoyed wiping him out. He'd made a
career feeding off the misery of others, making money on tears

and distress. He thought he was a hero, writing about my mother... exposing my childhood... But I knew how to survive with her, because deep down she loved me, *she loved me...* And when things got really bad I could connect with that love... I never saw her again, I ended up in a children's home! Do you know what happens to children when they go to those places?'

'I can imagine,' said Erika, shrinking back as Simone hysterically swiped at the air with the point of the knife.

'NO, you can't!'

Erika put her hands to her face. 'I'm sorry, no, I can't. Please, Simone. It's over, let me get you some help.'

'I need *help*, do I? There's nothing wrong with me! I just stopped taking all the shit that was being thrown at me! I wasn't born like this! I was innocent, but that innocence was torn from me!'

'Okay,' said Erika, putting her hands up to protect herself as Simone swiped the knife closer.

'Come on, be honest, Erika. Wouldn't you love the opportunity to wipe out all those men, the ones who've been the architects of your future? The men who've shaped your life for the worse? Jerome Goodman? The drug dealer who killed your husband and your friends? Look me in the eye and tell me that you wouldn't do to him what I've done. Take control and revenge!'

Erika gulped. She felt the sweat on her forehead run down into her eyes and it stung.

'Tell me! Tell me you'd do the same!'

'I'd do the same,' said Erika. As it came out of her mouth she knew she was saying it to stay alive, to keep Simone happy – but she also knew that a part of her understood Simone, and it shook her to the core. She looked around the room, trying to work out how she could get away.

'Don't you take your eyes off me!' shouted Simone.

'I'm sorry,' said Erika, frantically trying to think. She knew she was close to death. 'I know he burnt you, Simone. Your husband. And I'm trying to understand your pain and your anger. Help me to understand even more. Show me.'

Simone started to tremble and tears ran down her cheeks.

'He ruined me. He ruined my body,' she said. She grappled at her T-shirt and lifted it. Erika gulped when she saw the angry, swirling mass of scar tissue all across Simone's stomach and ribs. The skin was shiny and pinched where she'd lost her bellybutton.

'I'm so sorry, Simone,' said Erika. 'I understand. Look at you... Look at you: a brave, brave warrior.'

'I am, I'm brave...' sobbed Simone.

'You are, you're brave. And you proudly show the scars,' said Erika.

Simone pulled her T-shirt up higher to show more, and in the split second the fabric moved up to her face, Erika leaned back and kicked into the mass of red scar tissue. Simone doubled over, crying in pain. Erika managed to just get past her, but Simone recovered quickly and was on her. They crashed into the frosted glass door. Erika kicked and fought and managed to get half-up and run halfway along the corridor before Simone caught up with her again.

'You bitch!' she cried, launching herself on Erika. They crashed down hard on the concrete floor in the doorway of the bathroom. Erika rolled onto her back as Simone loomed above her and punched her in the face. Simone punched her again and Erika saw stars. She started to black out.

'You lying cunt,' hissed Simone. Erika felt herself being dragged across the cold bathroom floor and then she was pulled up into a sitting position with her back against the cold porcelain of the toilet. Simone's sharp little face was above her, and then Erika's vision was obscured as the plastic bag was slid over her head. The same bag Simone had used to kill Keith.

Erika heard the plastic crackle with her breathing, the blood roar in her ears, and then felt the cord tighten around her neck. Simone was sitting up on the lid of the toilet. Her legs were either side of Erika and she was pulling on the cord at the same time as her feet were pinning Erika's arms at her side, keeping her on the floor. Erika gasped and gagged as the bag began to form a vacuum over her head.

'You are going to die here, and I'm going to leave your body, all alone,' hissed Simone, her grip now tight.

Erika's arms flailed uselessly on the floor. Her hand brushed the walls behind the toilet. And then she felt a strip of thick fabric fluttering against the skirting board. It was connected to the huge swinging safety rail. Her fingers scrabbled against it and just managed to grip. Her vision was fading fast, and with a spurt of adrenalin she pulled herself forward. Simone was dragged off the toilet seat, and at the same time Erika yanked down the strip of fabric. The huge safety rail came thundering down with great force and struck Simone on the head.

Simone lost grip of Erika and went crashing to the floor. Erika grabbed at the cord around her neck and managed to loosen it, scrabbling frantically, finally getting the bag off her head. Sucking the glorious clean cold air into her lungs, she yanked on the red emergency cord beside the toilet and an alarm began to sound.

Simone lay on her front on the bathroom floor, starting to shift and moan. Erika yanked the red cord hard again, and it snapped off. She sat on Simone's legs, pinned her hands behind her back and started to wind the red cord tight around her wrists.

'I'm arresting you, Simone,' Erika said breathlessly, struggling to speak, 'for the murders of Gregory Munro, Jack Hart,

Stephen Linley and Keith Hardy... And the assault and attempted murder of a police officer. You do not have to say anything, but it may harm your defence if you do not mention,
when questioned, something which you later rely on in court.
Anything you do say may be given in evidence.'

She slumped back, sitting on Simone's legs and holding on
tight to her bound wrists. Her face was throbbing where she'd
been punched. As her breathing slowed down, she heard the
distant wail of sirens.

CHAPTER 84

It was raining lightly over the back garden, and the early morning sky hung grey. Moss and Peterson huddled with Erika in the doorway of her patio window, eating croissants and drinking coffee.

The newspapers were strewn on the floor around them.

'Now this is what I call a proper British summer: stuck indoors staring out at the rain and pretending to have fun,' said Moss. It was the first time she and Peterson had seen Erika since Simone had been arrested four days before. 'That last bit was a joke,' she added.

'Thanks for bringing all this over,' said Erika, lifting up her takeaway cup of coffee.

'We're just glad you're okay, boss,' said Peterson, bumping his cup against hers.

'I got punched. I've been through worse,' said Erika.

'You've got quite a shiner, though,' said Moss, looking at the large purple bruise decorating Erika's eye and cheek.

'I've never felt more disturbed or conflicted about a killer,' said Erika. 'When they took her off on the stretcher, she called for me... Her eyes were full of fear. She said she wanted me to go in the ambulance with her and hold my hand. And I nearly did. Crazy...'

They sipped their coffee.

'Well, I'm glad you didn't, boss,' said Moss. 'You remember what happened at the end of *The Silence of the Lambs*? Those people who got in the ambulance with Hannibal Lecter.'

Peterson gave her a look.

'What? I'm trying to lighten the mood here,' said Moss.

Erika smiled.

'It's like they're all competing for a name to give Simone Matthews,' said Peterson, grabbing one of the newspapers off the floor. 'The Angel of Death... The Night Stalker... The Night Owl'.

'What was angelic about her?' asked Moss, taking a gulp of coffee.

'*The Sun* has her pictured in her nurse's uniform,' replied Peterson, holding up a picture of Simone posing with a group of nurses in a staff kitchen. The nurses at the front were holding a giant cheque for three hundred pounds, money they had raised for Children in Need. Simone was to the left of the group, grinning and holding the cheque. 'The NHS Trust is now panicking that she's been bumping off patients, terrified of a lawsuit, I've no doubt.'

'I don't think she did bump any patients off. She was focused on who she wanted to kill,' said Erika. She picked up the *Daily Express* and looked at the article that had disturbed her most. It was Jack Hart's original account of Simone's mother, reproduced with details of Simone's murder spree.

Simone had been brought up in Catford, in a grotty top-floor flat. Her mother, also called Simone, had been a prostitute and drug addict. After several concerned phone calls from neighbours, police had broken in to find that Simone's mother had been keeping her daughter tied to the radiator in the bathroom. The young Jack Hart had been with the police when they'd broken in. The photo that broke Erika's heart was of a small, hollow-cheeked girl with bare feet, wearing what looked like a grubby pillowcase. One of her thin arms was tied to a grotty, yellowing radiator and she was looking up at the camera with large, confused eyes.

'She didn't have a chance, did she? She just wanted to be loved… To have someone to love.'

'Come on, boss, you'll start me off again,' said Moss, grabbing Erika's hand. Peterson reached into his pocket and pulled out a pack of tissues, handing her one.

'You always have tissues,' said Erika, wiping her eyes.

'He just does it so he can chat up tearful women,' said Moss. Peterson rolled his eyes and grinned.

'Anyway,' said Erika, recovering her composure, 'it's not all bad. You got Gary Wilmslow…'

'I didn't get him. I was in control when it happened,' said Peterson. 'Armed police swooped on the lock-up in Beckton. They arrested Wilmslow and six associates about to move the hard drives containing images and videos of level-four child pornography, and twelve thousand DVDs containing level-four child porn ready for distribution in Europe.'

'You think they can nail the bastards and make it stick?' asked Moss.

'I hope so,' said Peterson.

'How do you think Penny Munro is doing?' asked Erika.

'It can't be easy. First her husband and all this, and then her brother,' said Peterson.

'And what about little Peter? How could this screw him up for the future?' said Erika. They looked back at the photos of the young and old Simone.

Moss looked at her watch. 'Come on, we should get going. We don't want to be late for this briefing at the nick,' grinned Moss.

'Did Marsh give you any idea why we've all be called in?'

'No, I think it's going to be a final briefing on the results of the Simone Matthews case,' said Erika.

'I have a feeling it's going to be a bit more than that, boss,' said Peterson. 'I think you're about to get an almighty pat on the back!'

When they arrived at Lewisham Row station, they were told to go down to the incident room. It was crowded, and Erika, Moss and Peterson only managed to say a quick hello to some of the team and find a space at the back before Sparks and Marsh appeared at the front. Finally, Assistant Commissioner Oakley entered, with three officers carrying bottles of soft drinks and plastic cups.

'Can I have your attention, PLEASE!' shouted Oakley. He stood at the front, immaculate in his uniform, with his hair neat and his braided cap held against his chest. The vast row of whiteboards behind him was empty. The room fell silent. 'This has been quite a week for the Metropolitan Police. I'd like to thank you all for achieving the impossible. Yesterday morning, officers working on Operation Hemslow broke one of the UK's biggest underground paedophile networks. Over sixty-seven thousand images of abused children and twelve thousand DVDs have been seized, along with Gary Wilmslow and six associates who the Met have had under surveillance for over a year.'

There were whoops and clapping from the officers. Moss grinned and slapped Peterson on the back.

'And I haven't finished!' said Oakley. 'Thanks to the hard work from DCI Sparks' team in association with Detective Chief Superintendent Marsh's division, we have caught the Night Stalker! Simone Matthews has been arrested for the murders of Gregory Munro, Jack Hart, Stephen Linley and Keith Hardy.'

There was another round of applause from the officers in the incident room. Erika caught Marsh's eye. He leant over and said something to Oakley, who added, 'And of course we are very grateful to DCI Erika Foster, who was in the right place at the right time, or should that be the wrong place! We hope you continue to make a full recovery.' He looked vaguely in her direction. The officers in the incident room began to turn to Erika, but Oakley went on.

'And finally, I have the pleasure to announce that in the light of these admirable results there will be several promotions. Firstly, I would like to introduce you to our new commander, Commander Paul Marsh!'

Everyone applauded as Marsh made a show of being sheepish and muttered his thanks.

Then Oakley stepped forward again. 'I would also like to announce a further promotion. In light of his many achievements, both on this case and others, DCI Sparks will be promoted, and from now on known as Superintendent Sparks.'

Oakley led the applause and Sparks beamed and stepped forward, giving a grand, over-ironic bow. A plastic cup was shoved into Erika's hand. She looked around the room at Moss and Peterson, who looked dismayed.

'I propose a toast. To results,' said Oakley.

'To results,' repeated everyone in the room, raising their plastic cups.

'Now I encourage you all to eat, drink and be merry!' cried Oakley.

There were whistles and a round of applause, but Erika didn't join in. She was furious. She pushed her way through the crowds of officers to where Marsh stood at the front.

'Sir, a word please,' she snapped.

'Erika, can it wait?' asked Marsh.

'No, it can't,' she said loudly. Oakley and Sparks looked over from where they were talking. Sparks gave her a nasty smirk and raised his cup to her.

Marsh followed Erika outside the incident room and into one of the adjacent empty offices.

'What the hell was that?' she said.

'I beg your pardon?'

'I led you all to Simone Matthews. I did all the legwork on this case. And if you haven't forgotten, sir, DCI – sorry, *Superintendent* Sparks – was taken off the last major murder investigation case for incompetence! I solved this case!'

'I have no control over decisions made by Oakley.'

'But you did know a promotion was in the offing, didn't you? And you've kept me at arm's length. Kept me away, strung me along, made me do all the dirty work!'

Marsh then lost it. 'Do you know how frustrating it is to see how you operate, Erika?'

'Don't call me Erika, we are NOT friends! I am a police officer who—'

'You were a great officer, Erika, really great, once. But you continue to go against orders, against protocol… Now you're just…'

'I'm just what?'

Marsh looked at her for a long moment.

'You think you have this incredible instinct, but it's blind luck and stupidity. You're a vigilante. And you're on borrowed time. And because of that, you'll remain DCI Foster. In light of what happened, of you defying orders, refusing to take leave when I ordered you to, I couldn't recommend you for promotion.'

Erika gave Marsh a long, hard look. 'Well, I am not sticking around here to take orders from Superintendent Sparks. You'll have my letter putting in for a transfer first thing tomorrow morning.'

'Hang on… transfer? Erika!' said Marsh, but she turned and left the office, walking off down the corridors and out of Lewisham Row station.

EPILOGUE

It was a warm, sunny day. Erika stepped out of her car. She took off her sunglasses and looked at the small door within a door at the huge Victorian gates of Belmarsh Prison.

She leant on the roof of the car and saw that it was twelve minutes past eleven. He was late.

Moments later, the small door opened with a squeak. Isaac stepped out and looked around him, taking in the clear blue sky, the silence and Erika.

He had a brown paper bag in one hand and his suit jacket over the other arm. He walked towards her, through the gates and out onto the street. They hugged for a long time without saying anything.

'All charges dropped. I told you so,' said Erika with a grin.

'You didn't tell me so,' he answered wryly. 'And why did it take so long?'

'Forensics. You know what your lot is like. They take ages. Simone Matthews gave them a full confession, but they had to ensure it was her DNA at the Jack Hart murder scene. Moss and Peterson have been keeping me in the loop.'

'I keep thinking someone is going to come out and tell me it's a terrible mistake and I'm…' Isaac put a hand to his face.

'It's okay. You've been cleared. And you keep your licence to practise medicine.'

Isaac stood for a moment, breathing in the air. Then he opened the car door and got in. Erika went round to the driver's side and climbed in beside him.

'What did you mean, Moss and Peterson have been keeping you in the loop?' asked Isaac. 'I thought you solved the case?'

'I did. It's a long story. The short version is that I've put in for a transfer. And I'm taking a break.'

'A transfer. Where?'

'I don't know yet. Marsh is trying to talk me out of it. Hence the break... For the first time in years, I just want to take my foot off the gas. Work out what it's like to be a normal person,' said Erika.

'Let me know when you find out,' said Isaac, wryly.

They drove away and rode in silence. Isaac put his head back and closed his eyes. A short while later, he noticed they were driving along the high street in Shirley.

'Why have we come this way?' he asked.

Erika pulled into a space a little way up from Penny Munro's house. In the front garden, Penny was standing with a white face, watching little Peter as he held the hose, watering the lawn. He put his thumb on the end of the hose and laughed in delight as the water sprayed back over them both.

'He's such a nice kid. Do you think he'll be okay?' asked Erika as they watched.

'Honestly, who knows? You've got to have faith that good will win out,' said Isaac.

'He's so young to lose his father, and now the memory of his uncle is forever destroyed.'

Isaac put his hand on hers.

'You can't save the world, Erika.'

'But I could do a better job trying,' she said, wiping away a tear.

'You saved me. And for that I'll be forever grateful,' Isaac replied. They sat in silence for a few minutes, watching as Peter started to spray Penny with the hose, chasing her around the garden until she burst out laughing and grabbed him, showering him with kisses.

'What are you going to do?' asked Isaac.

'There's a new baby in my family. I have a new niece.'

'Congratulations. Your sister, in Slovakia, yeah?'

'Yes. She named her after our mother and me. I was planning to go and visit.'

'I've always wanted to visit Slovakia,' said Isaac.

'Would you want to come with me?' asked Erika. 'You could meet my crazy sister and her mafia husband, and then when we've had enough of them we could go visit the High Tatras, the hot springs, get drunk and forget about things for a bit.'

'That sounds heavenly,' grinned Isaac.

Erika put the car in gear and they pulled away, not thinking about the past or the future. For once, just enjoying the present.

A NOTE FROM ROB

First of all, I want to say a huge thank you to you for choosing to read *The Night Stalker*. If you did enjoy it, I would be very grateful if you could write a review. It needn't be long, just a few words, but it makes such a difference and helps new readers to discover one of my books for the first time.

I wrote in the back of the previous Erika Foster novel, *The Girl in the Ice*, that I would love to hear from you. Thank you for all the wonderful messages I've received. I've loved hearing from each and every one of you, and how much you loved the characters, and the story, and where you'd like to see this series go in the future. I particularly loved the very funny message from a lady who said she enjoyed the book immensely but wasn't keen on Erika's habit of smoking and stubbing out her dog ends in a tea cup! In this book I have tried to ensure that Erika, where possible, uses an ashtray. Keep the messages coming and thank you.

You can get in touch on my Facebook page, through Twitter, Goodreads or my website, which you'll find at www.robertbryndza.com. I read every message and will always reply.

There are lots more books to come, so I hope you'll stay with me for the ride!

Robert Bryndza

P.S. If you would like to get an email informing you when my next book will be released, you can sign up to my mailing list using the link below. Your email address will never be shared and you can unsubscribe at any time:

www.bookouture.com/robert-bryndza

@RobertBryndza
bryndzarobert
www.robertbryndza.com

ACKNOWLEDGEMENTS

Thank you to Oliver Rhodes and the wonderful team at Bookouture. You guys are all amazing, and I'm so happy to be working with you. Special thanks also to Claire Bord. Working with you is an absolute joy. You bring out the best in my work, and you've pushed me to be a better writer. And, as an added bonus, you always recommend great new TV shows to watch!

Thank you to Henry Steadman for another stunning cover, and to Gabrielle Chant for editing the manuscript with such care and a keen eye for detail. Thanks to Caroline Mitchell for answering my questions about police procedure, and to Kim Nash for your hard work promoting and spreading the word about our books at Bookouture.

Special thanks to former Chief Superintendent Graham Bartlett of South Downs Leadership and Management Services Ltd, who read the manuscript and gave me such valuable feedback on police procedure and helped me to tread the fine line between fact and fiction. Any liberties taken with fact are mine.

Thanks to my mother-in-law Vierka, who couldn't read what I wrote in my last dedication, so this is for her: Mojej svokre Vierke, ktorá má talent vystihnúť tie najdôležitejšie chvíle. Keď ide písanie ťažko a pracujem do neskorých nočných hodín, zjaví sa pri dverách s úžasným domácim jedlom a láskou, čo ma vždy dokonale povzbudí.

A massive thank you to my husband, Ján. I couldn't do any of this without his love and support. You are the best. Team Bryndza rules!

And lastly, thank you to all my wonderful readers, all the wonderful book groups, book bloggers and reviewers. I always say this, but it's true, word of mouth is such a powerful thing, and without all your hard work and passion, talking up and blogging about my books, I would have far less readers.